STINKY CECIL

IN TERRARIUM TERROR!

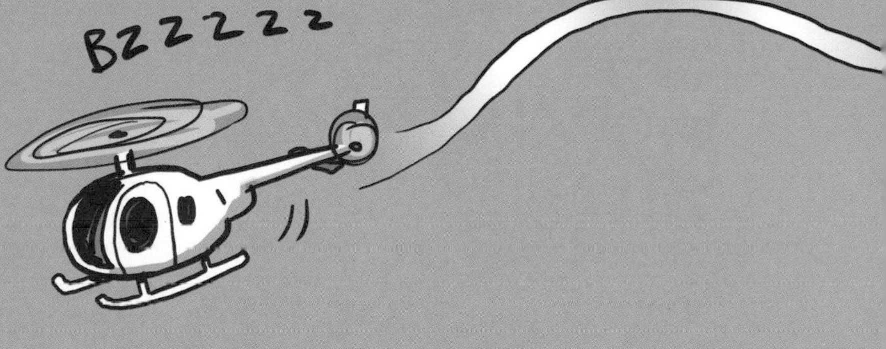

BZZZZZ

PAIGE BRADDOCK

Andrews McMeel
Publishing®

a division of Andrews McMeel Universal

STINKY CECIL

IN TERRARIUM TERROR!

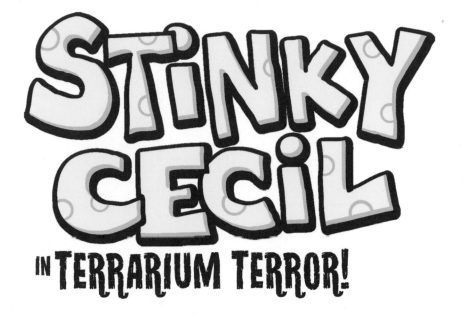

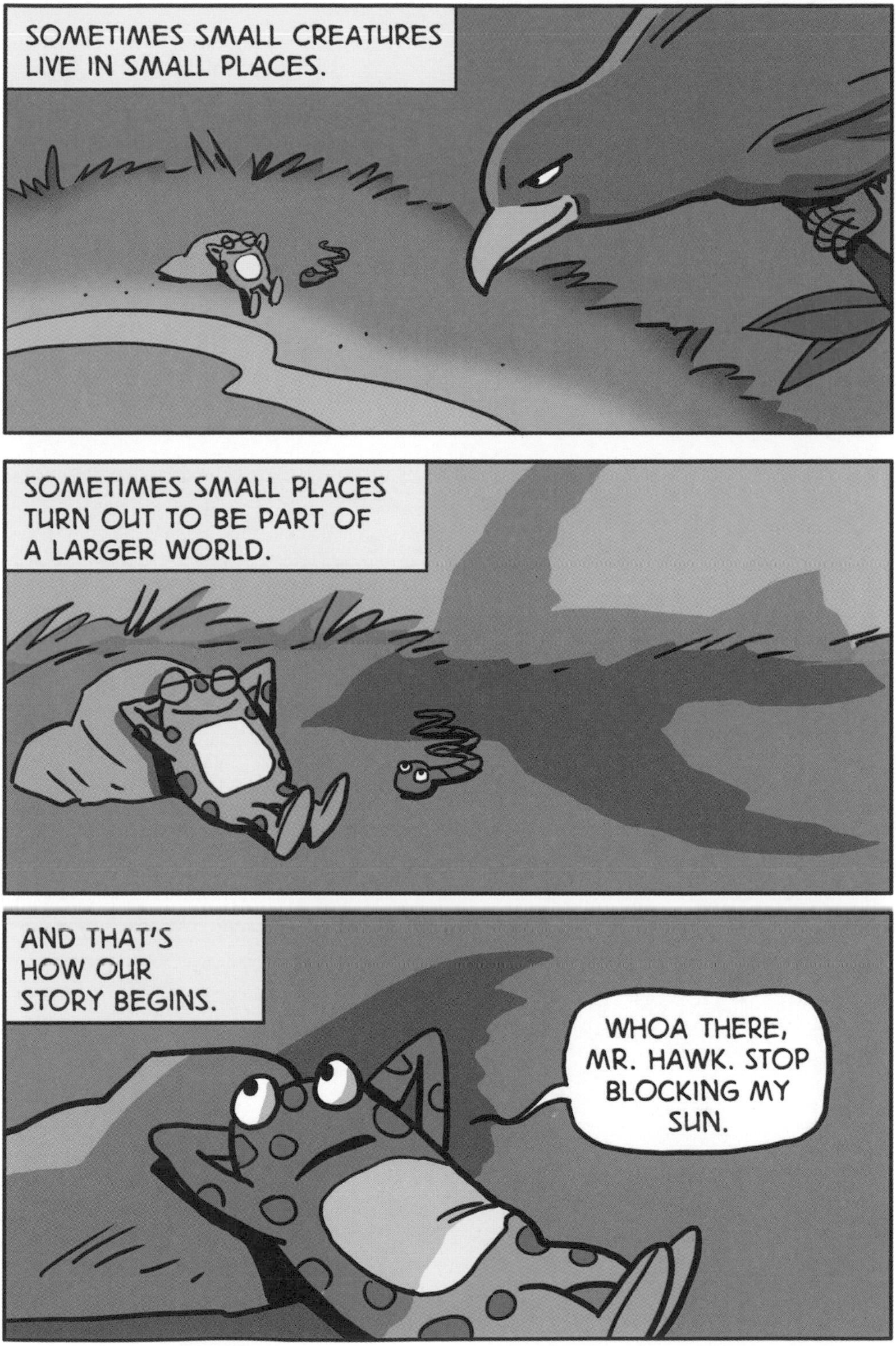
SOMETIMES SMALL CREATURES LIVE IN SMALL PLACES.
SOMETIMES SMALL PLACES TURN OUT TO BE PART OF A LARGER WORLD.
AND THAT'S HOW OUR STORY BEGINS.
WHOA THERE, MR. HAWK. STOP BLOCKING MY SUN.

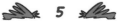

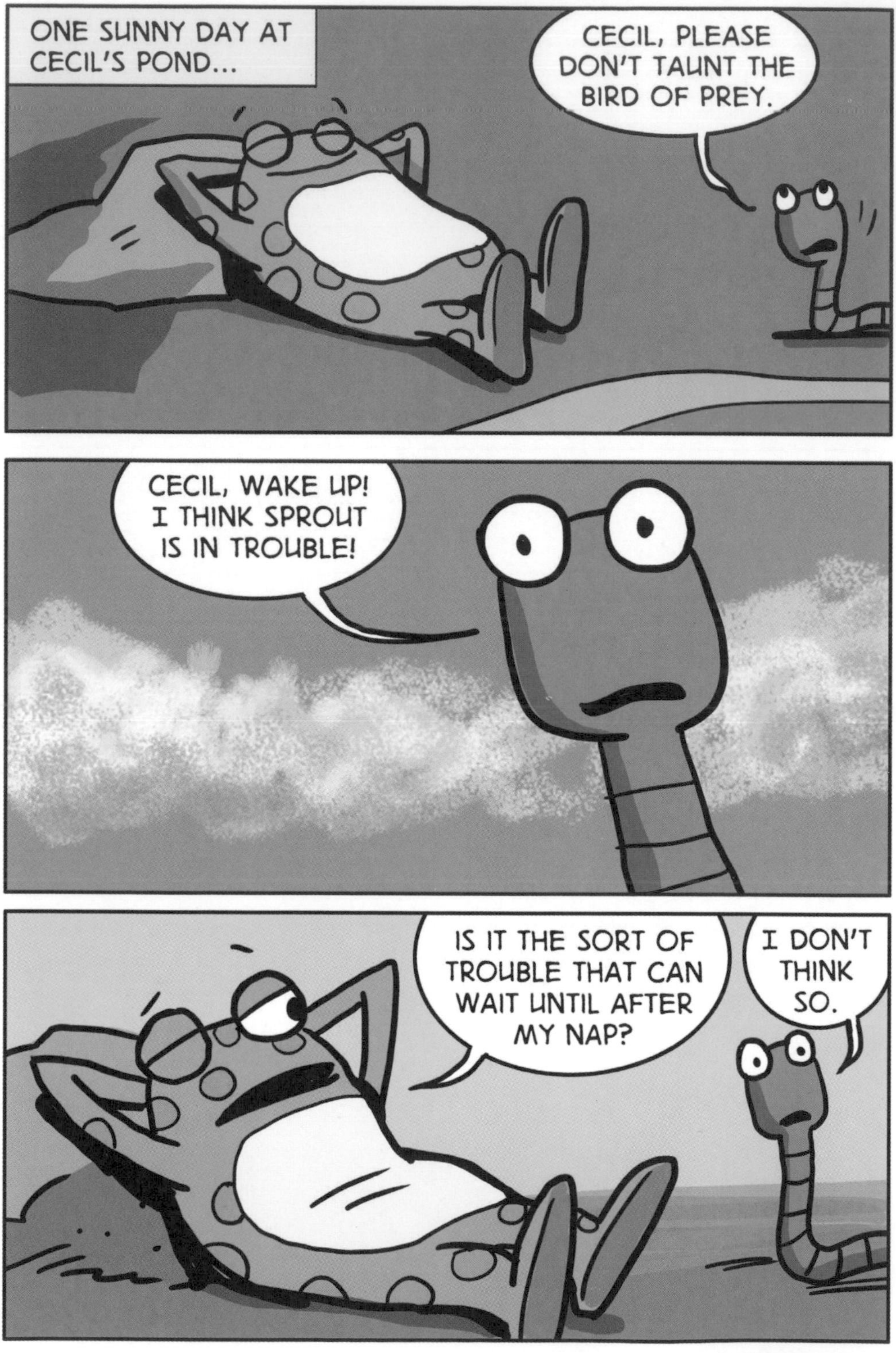
ONE SUNNY DAY AT CECIL'S POND...
CECIL, PLEASE DON'T TAUNT THE BIRD OF PREY.
CECIL, WAKE UP! I THINK SPROUT IS IN TROUBLE!
IS IT THE SORT OF TROUBLE THAT CAN WAIT UNTIL AFTER MY NAP?
I DON'T THINK SO.

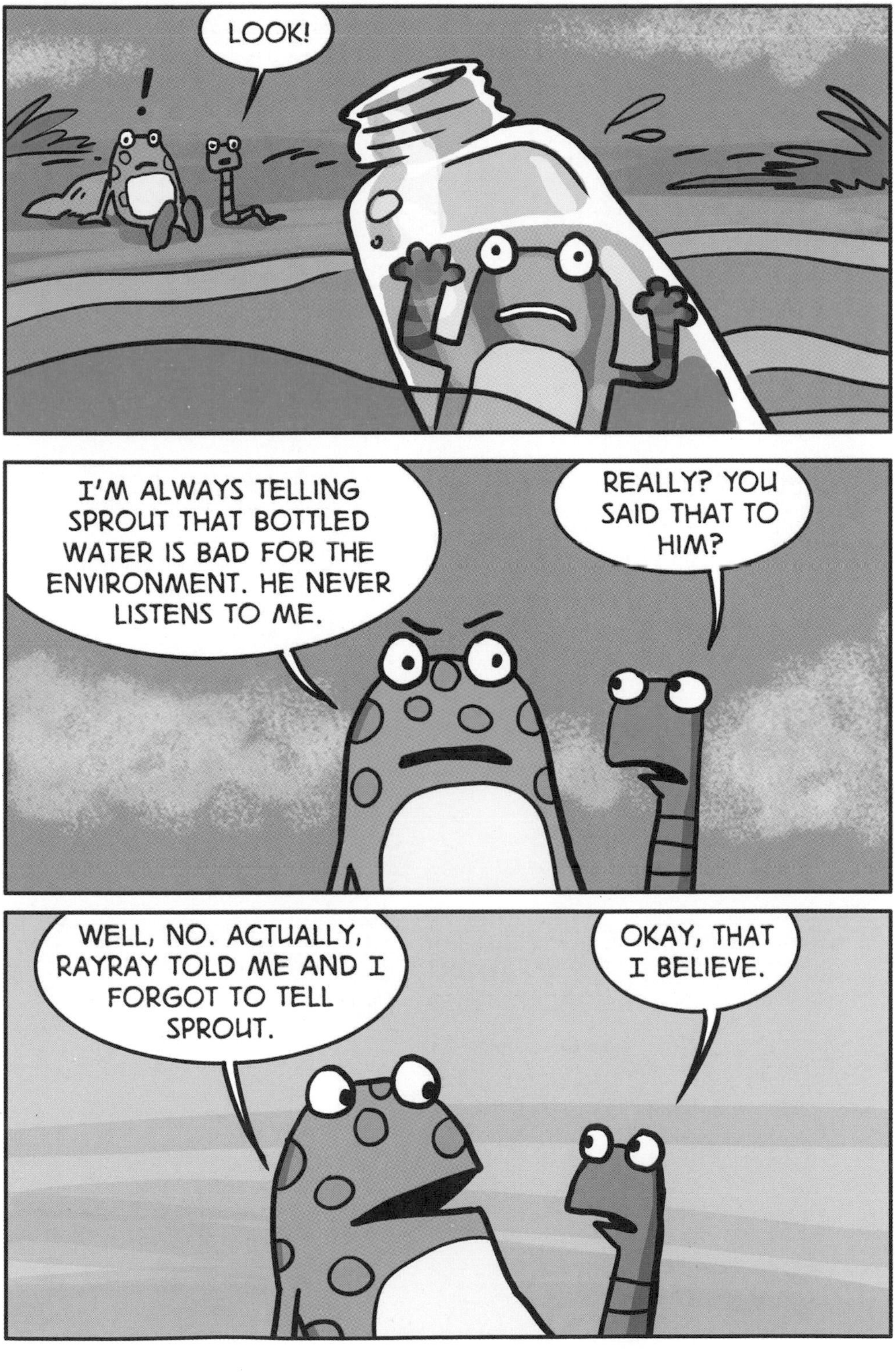
LOOK!
!
I'M ALWAYS TELLING SPROUT THAT BOTTLED WATER IS BAD FOR THE ENVIRONMENT. HE NEVER LISTENS TO ME.
REALLY? YOU SAID THAT TO HIM?
WELL, NO. ACTUALLY, RAYRAY TOLD ME AND I FORGOT TO TELL SPROUT.
OKAY, THAT I BELIEVE.

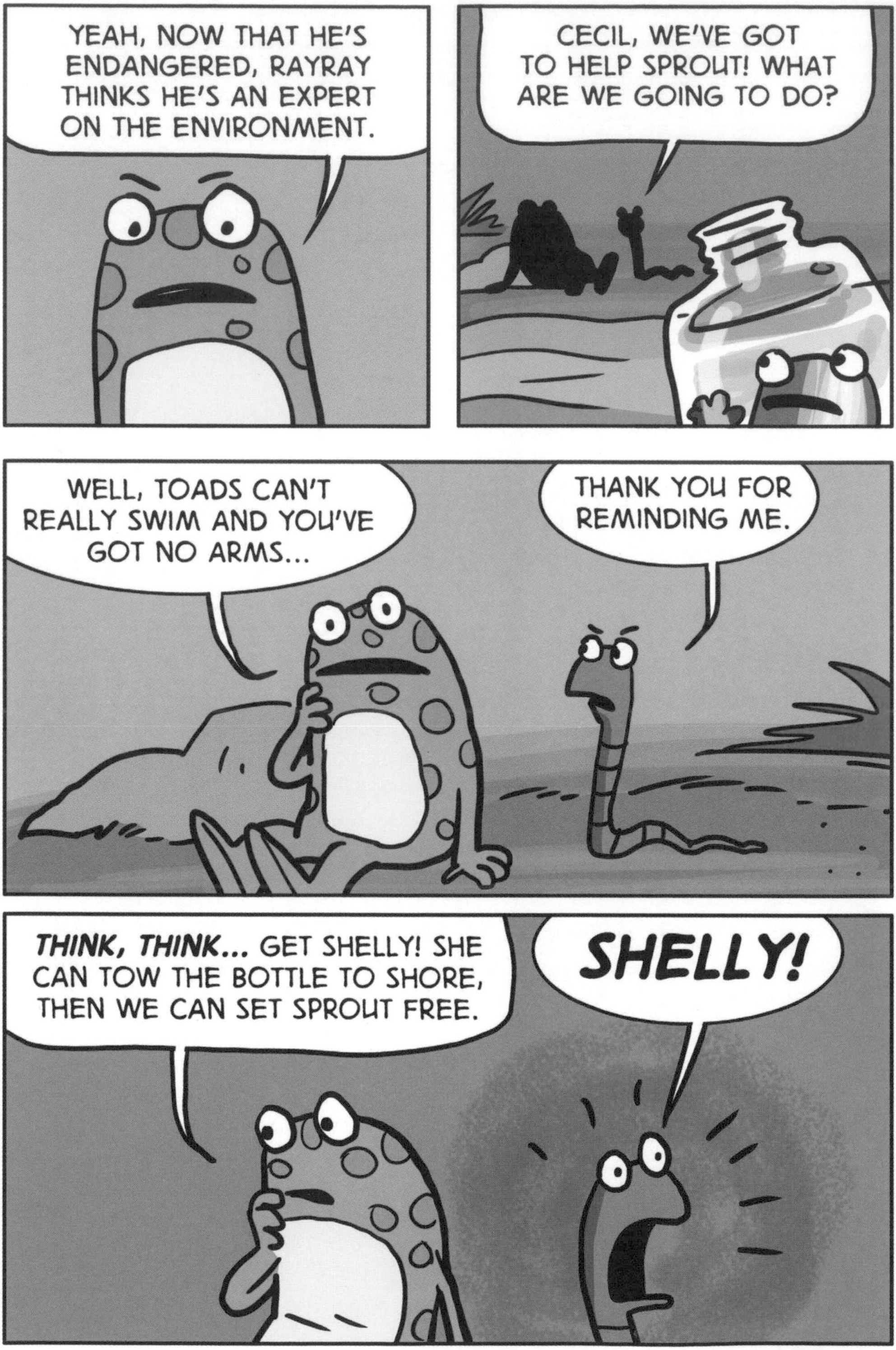
YEAH, NOW THAT HE'S ENDANGERED, RAYRAY THINKS HE'S AN EXPERT ON THE ENVIRONMENT.
CECIL, WE'VE GOT TO HELP SPROUT! WHAT ARE WE GOING TO DO?
WELL, TOADS CAN'T REALLY SWIM AND YOU'VE GOT NO ARMS...
THANK YOU FOR REMINDING ME.
THINK, THINK... GET SHELLY! SHE CAN TOW THE BOTTLE TO SHORE, THEN WE CAN SET SPROUT FREE.
SHELLY!

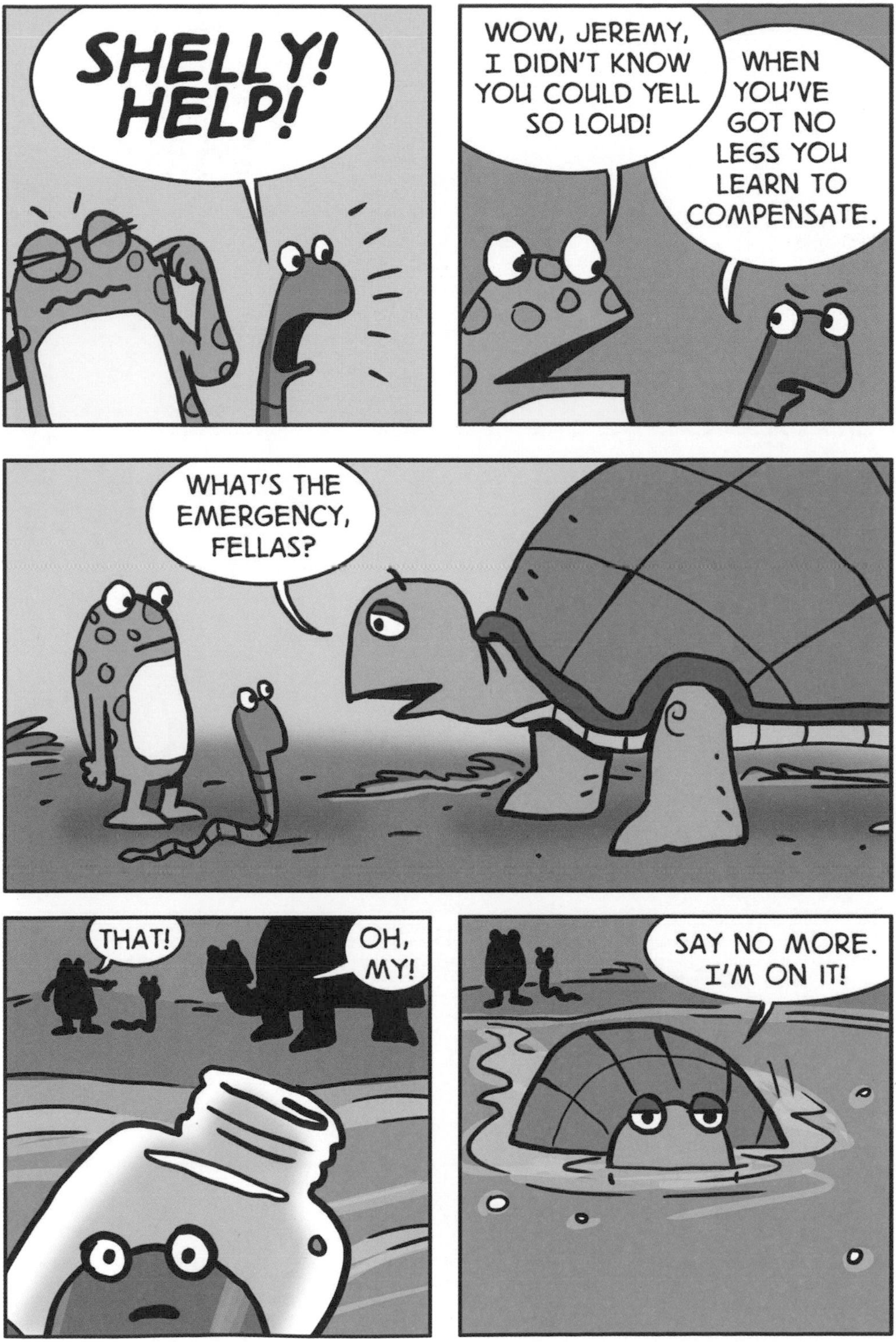
SHELLY! HELP!
WOW, JEREMY, I DIDN'T KNOW YOU COULD YELL SO LOUD!
WHEN YOU'VE GOT NO LEGS YOU LEARN TO COMPENSATE.
WHAT'S THE EMERGENCY, FELLAS?
THAT!
OH, MY!
SAY NO MORE. I'M ON IT!

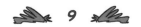

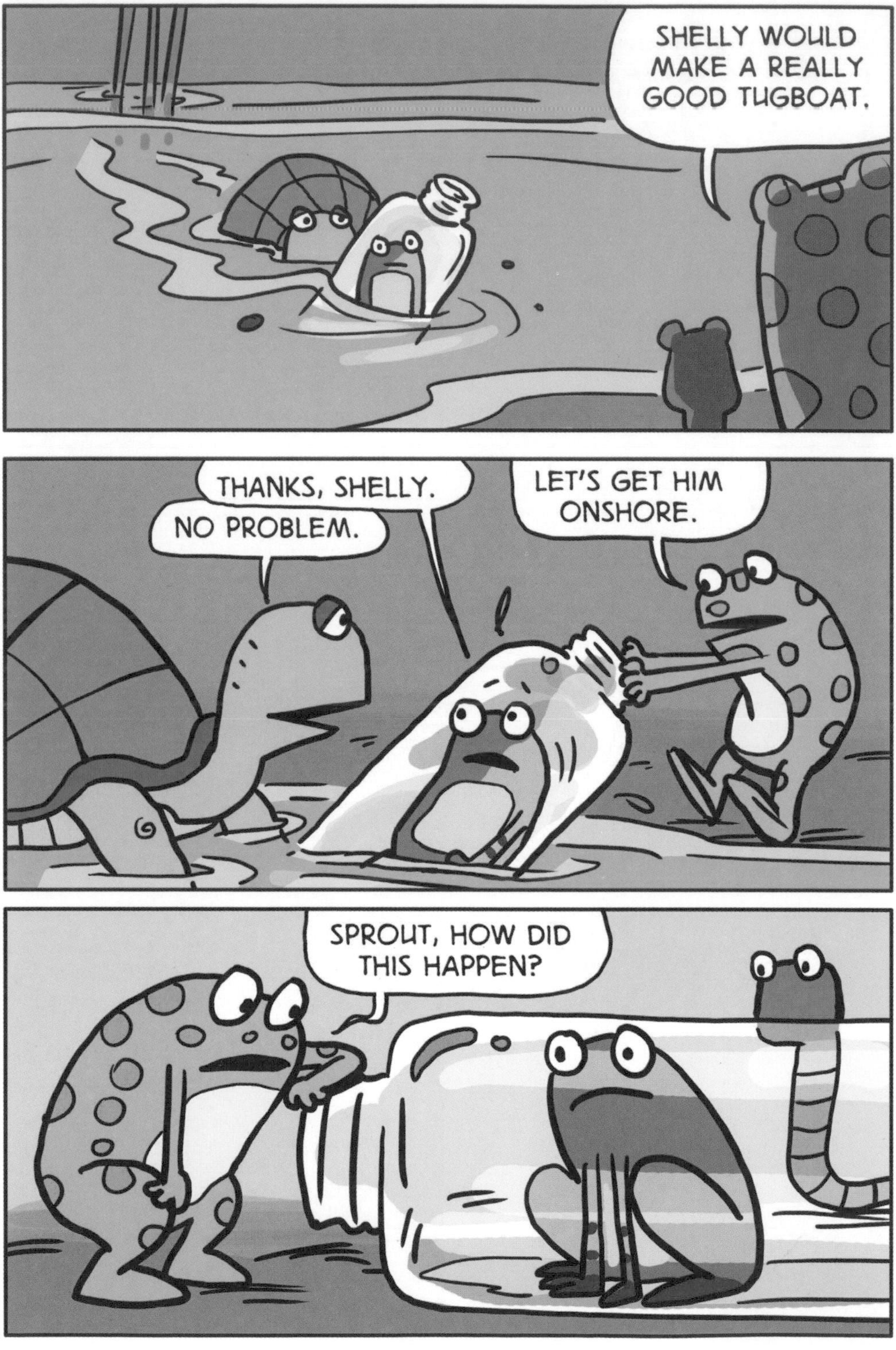
SHELLY WOULD MAKE A REALLY GOOD TUGBOAT.
THANKS, SHELLY.
NO PROBLEM.
LET'S GET HIM ONSHORE.
SPROUT, HOW DID THIS HAPPEN?

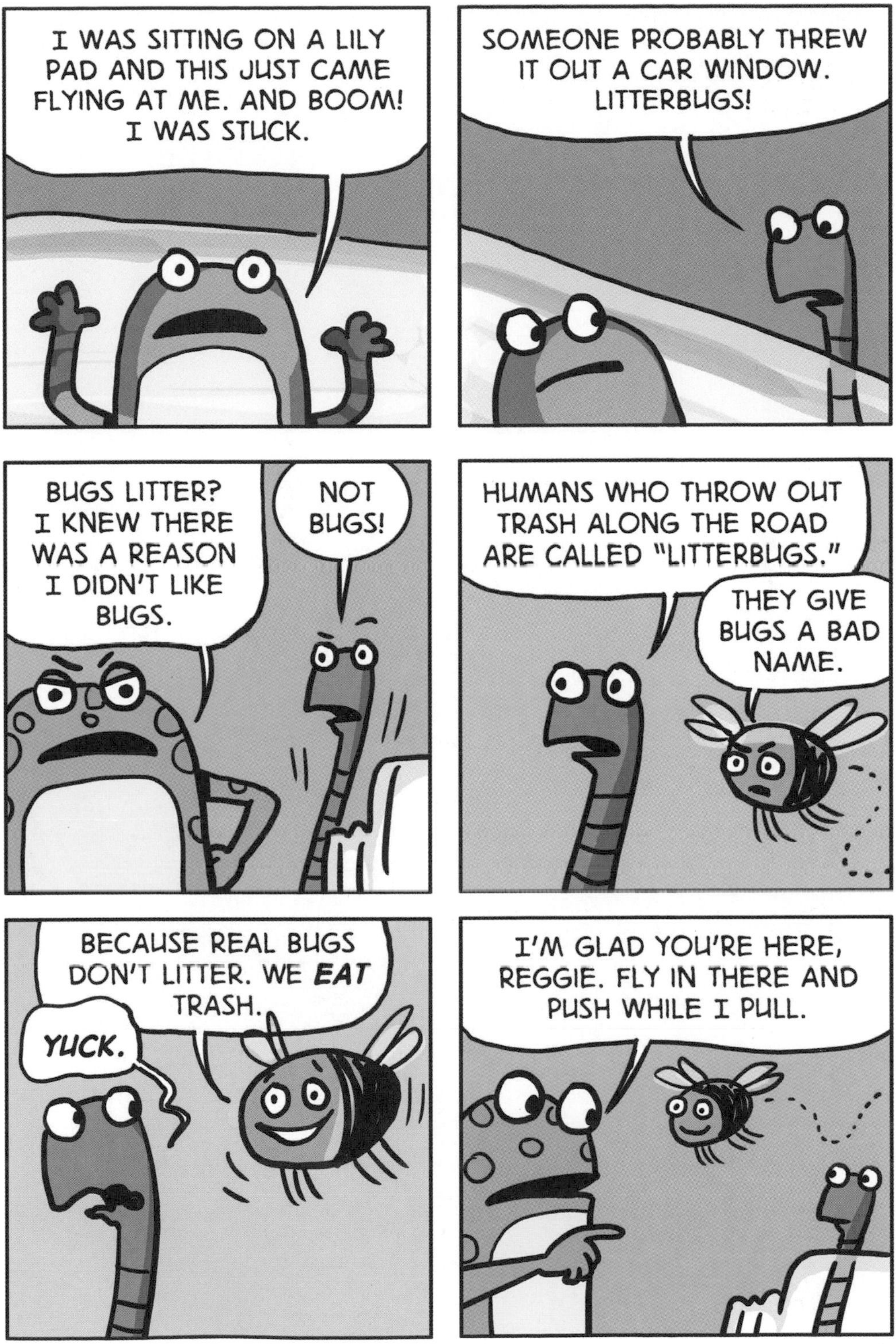
I WAS SITTING ON A LILY PAD AND THIS JUST CAME FLYING AT ME. AND BOOM! I WAS STUCK.
SOMEONE PROBABLY THREW IT OUT A CAR WINDOW. LITTERBUGS!
BUGS LITTER? I KNEW THERE WAS A REASON I DIDN'T LIKE BUGS.
NOT BUGS!
HUMANS WHO THROW OUT TRASH ALONG THE ROAD ARE CALLED "LITTERBUGS."
THEY GIVE BUGS A BAD NAME.
BECAUSE REAL BUGS DON'T LITTER. WE ***EAT*** TRASH.
YUCK.
I'M GLAD YOU'RE HERE, REGGIE. FLY IN THERE AND PUSH WHILE I PULL.

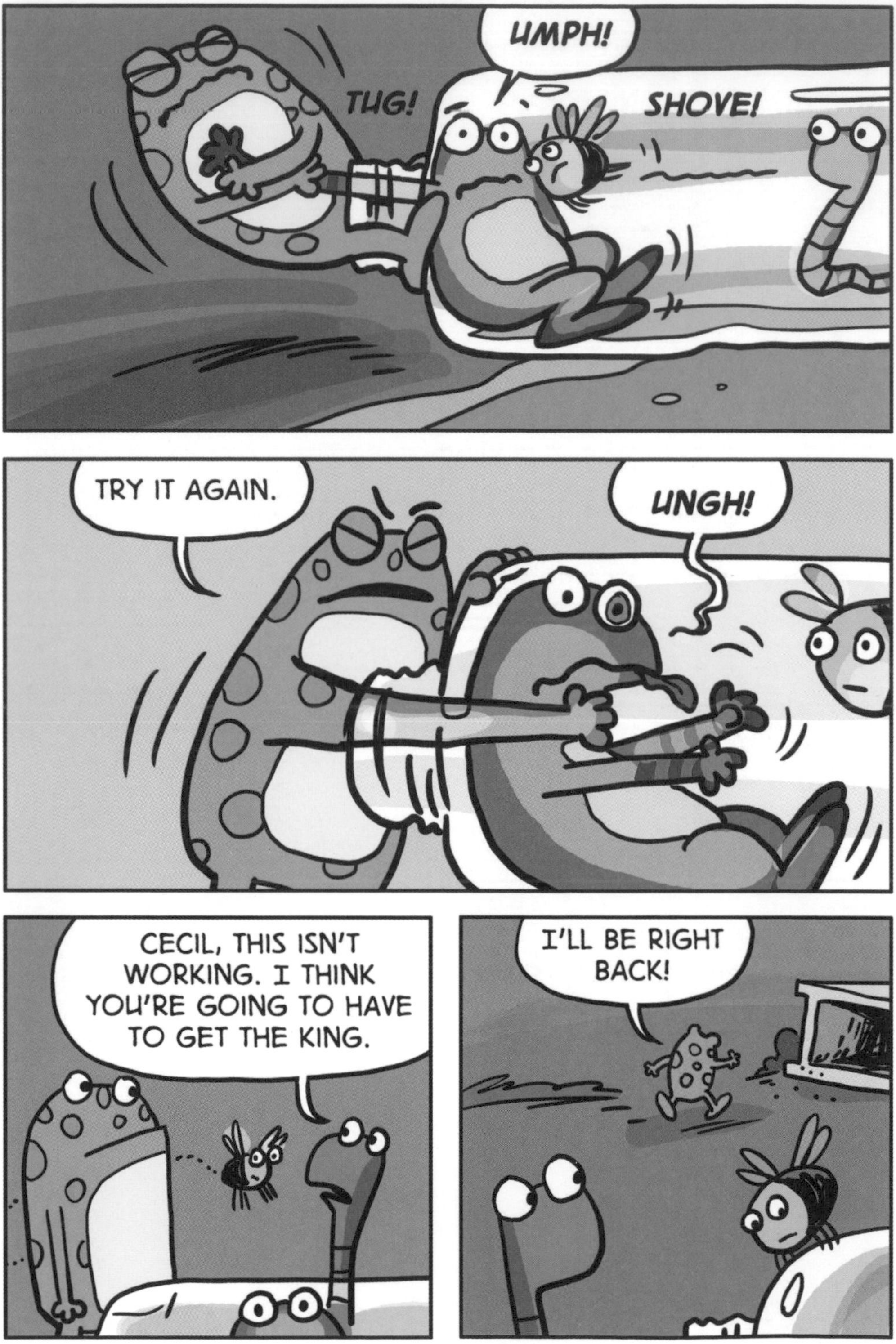
UMPH!
TUG!
SHOVE!
TRY IT AGAIN.
UNGH!
CECIL, THIS ISN'T WORKING. I THINK YOU'RE GOING TO HAVE TO GET THE KING.
I'LL BE RIGHT BACK!

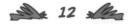

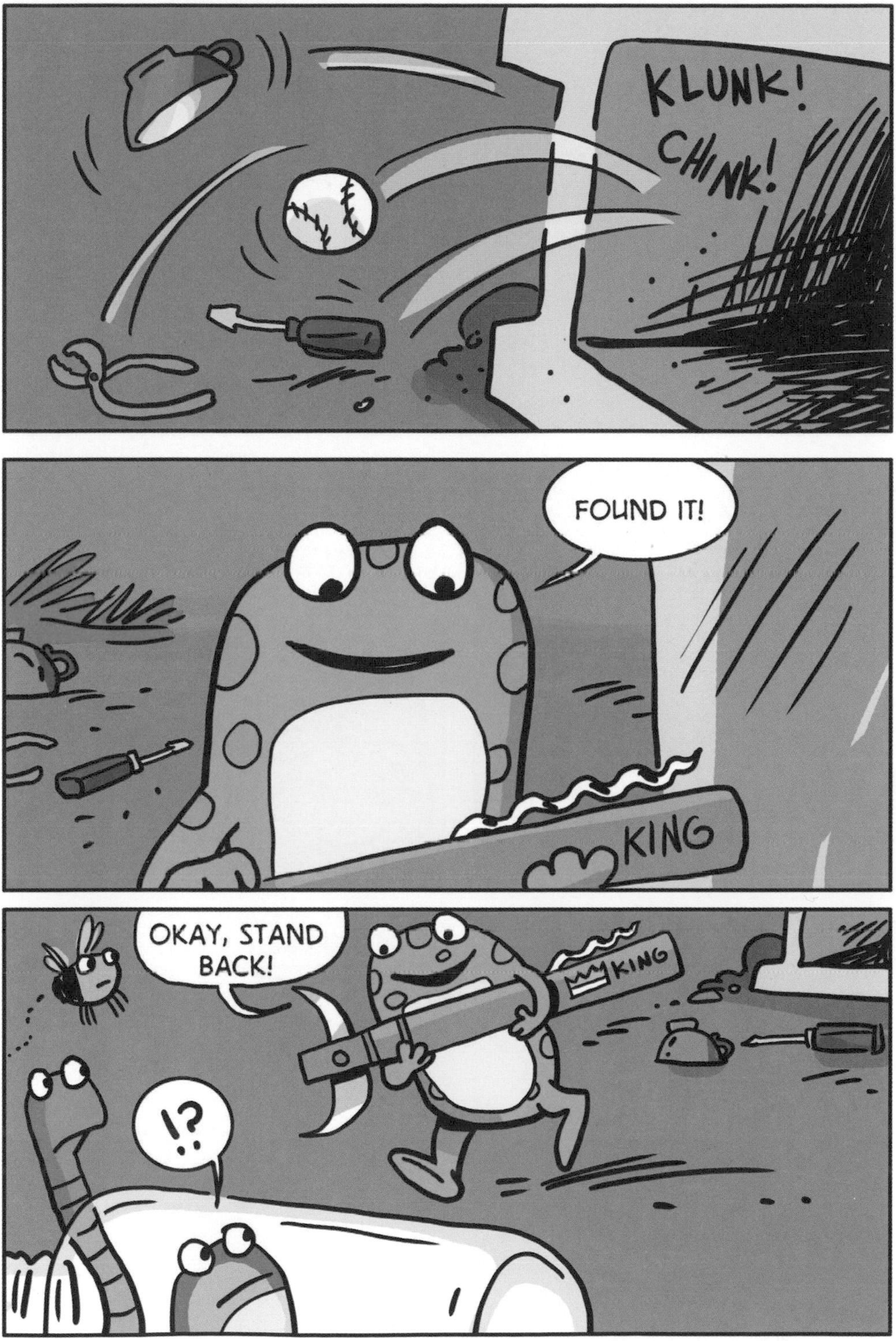
KLUNK!
CHINK!
FOUND IT!
KING
OKAY, STAND BACK!
KING
!?

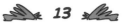

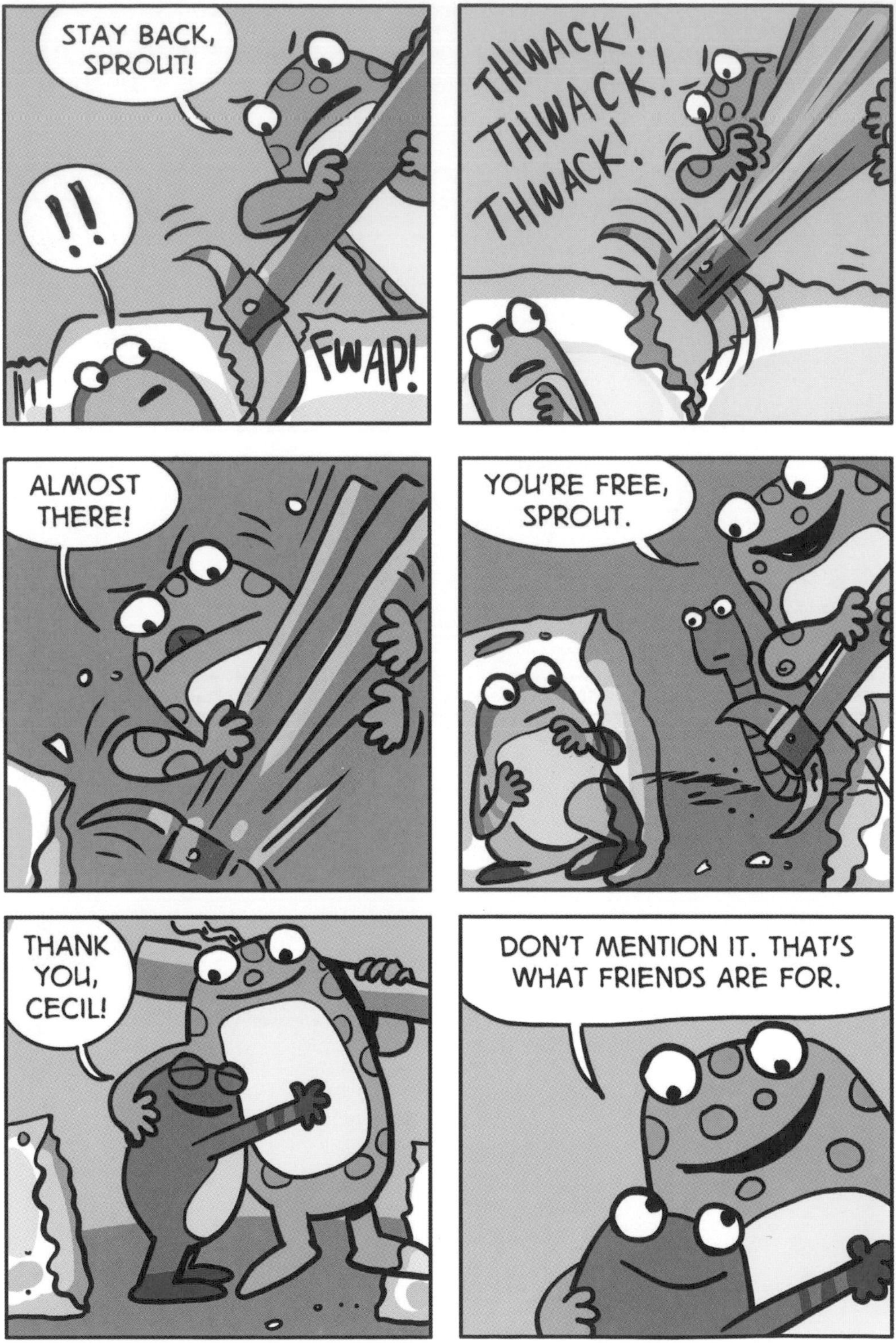
STAY BACK, SPROUT!
!!
FWAP!
THWACK! THWACK! THWACK!
ALMOST THERE!
YOU'RE FREE, SPROUT.
THANK YOU, CECIL!
DON'T MENTION IT. THAT'S WHAT FRIENDS ARE FOR.

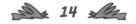

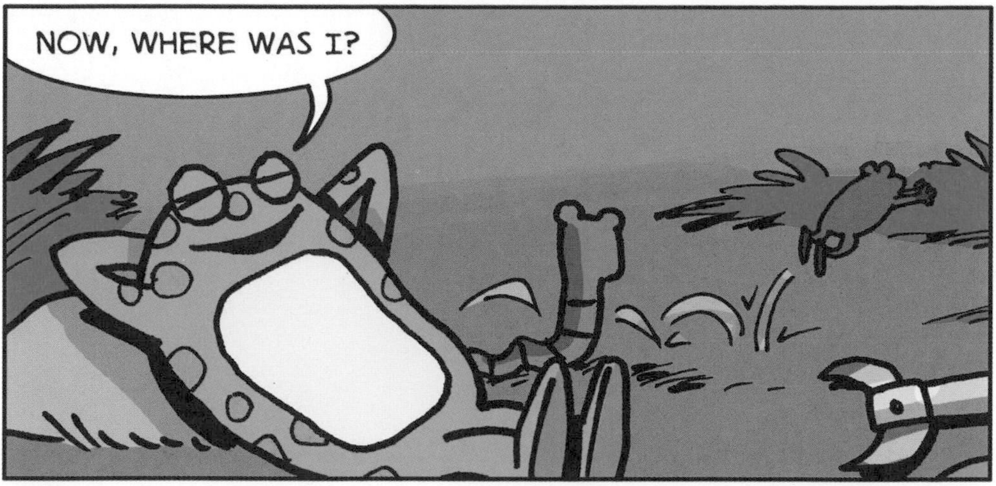
NOW, WHERE WAS I?

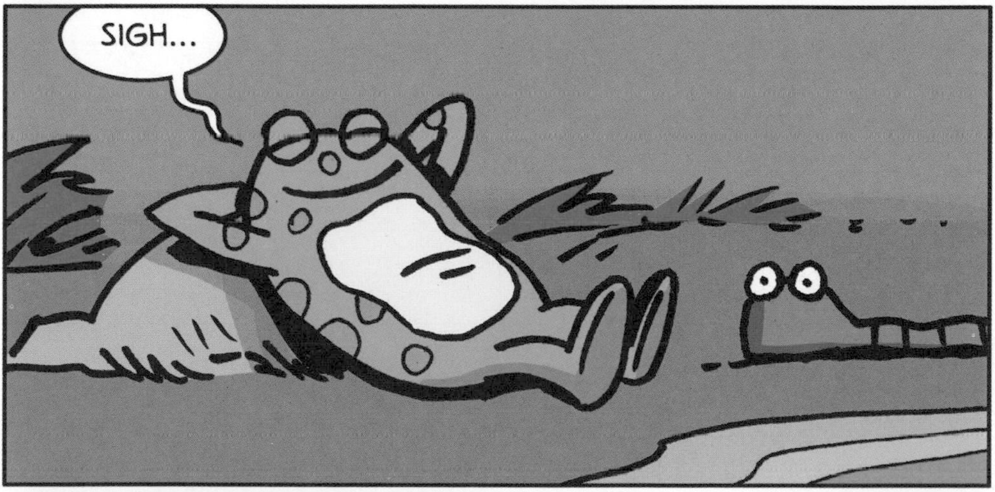
SIGH...

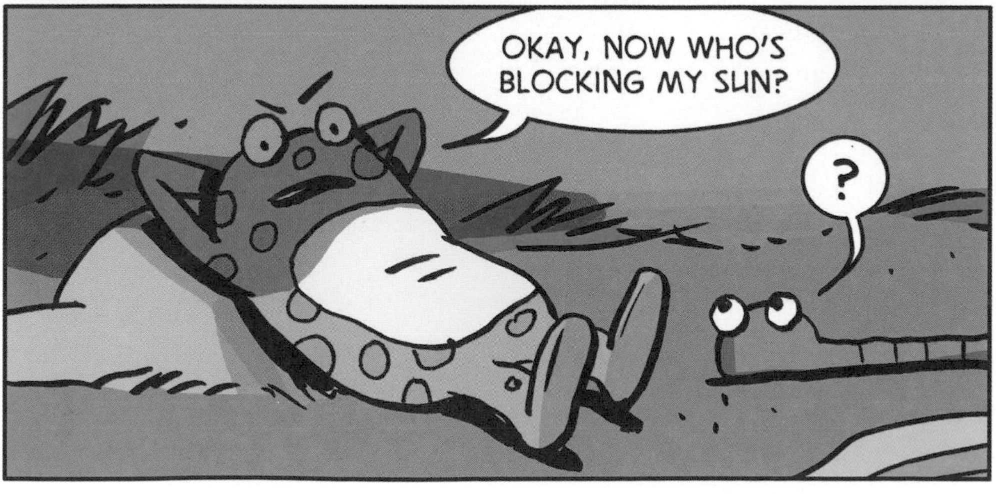
OKAY, NOW WHO'S BLOCKING MY SUN?
?

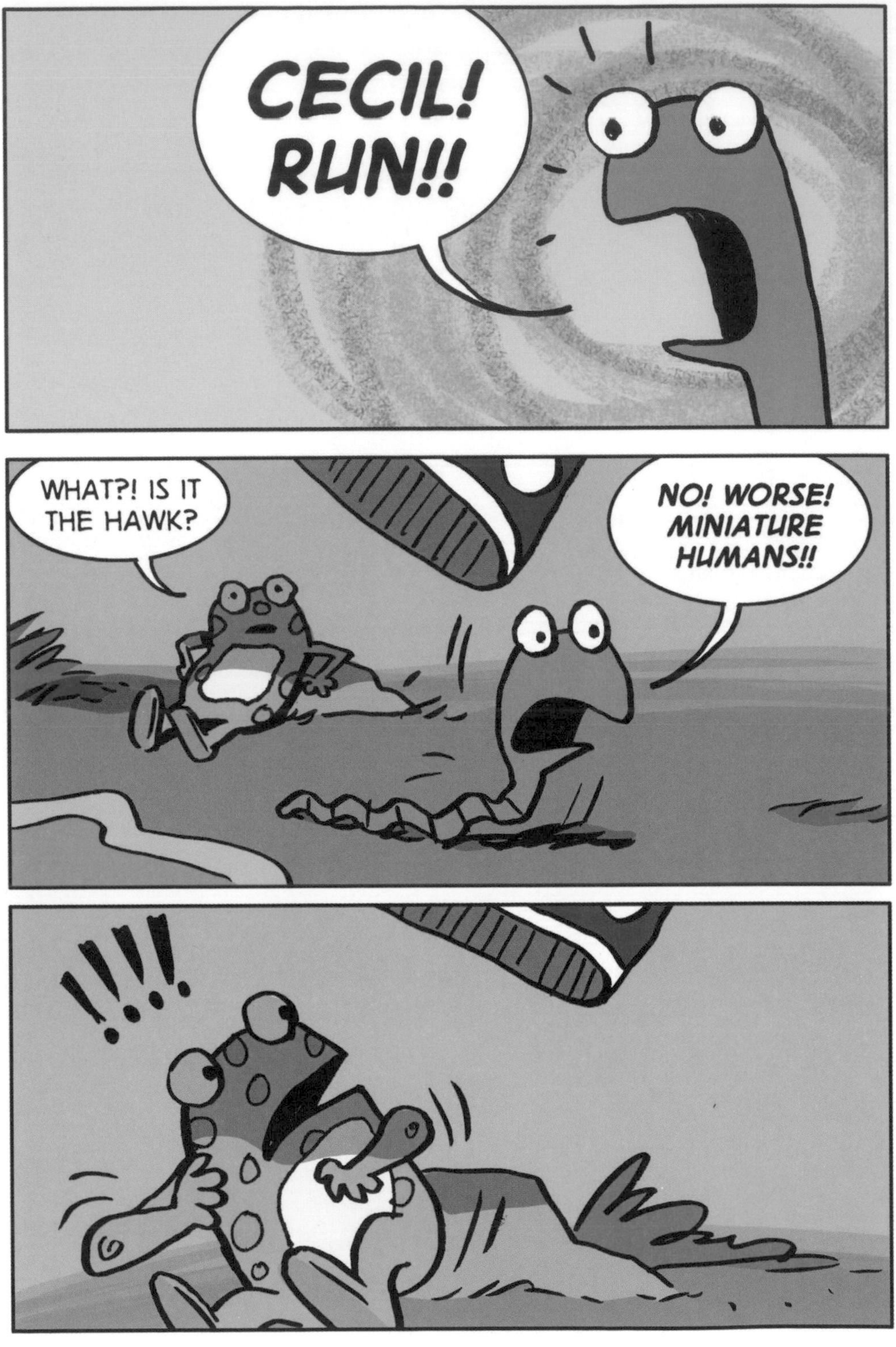
CECIL! RUN!!
WHAT?! IS IT THE HAWK?
NO! WORSE! MINIATURE HUMANS!!
!!!!

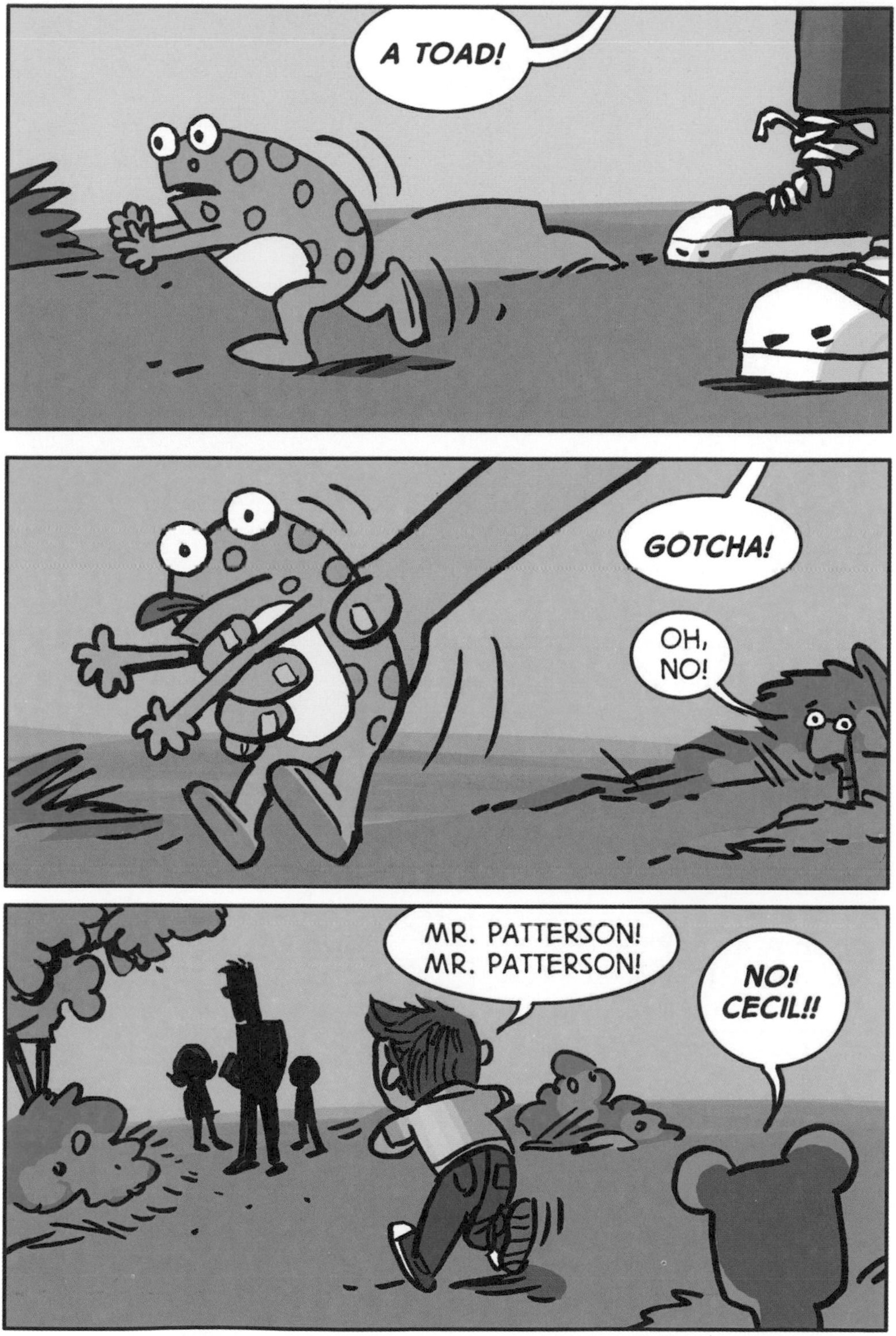
A TOAD!
GOTCHA!
OH, NO!
MR. PATTERSON! MR. PATTERSON!
NO! CECIL!!

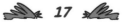

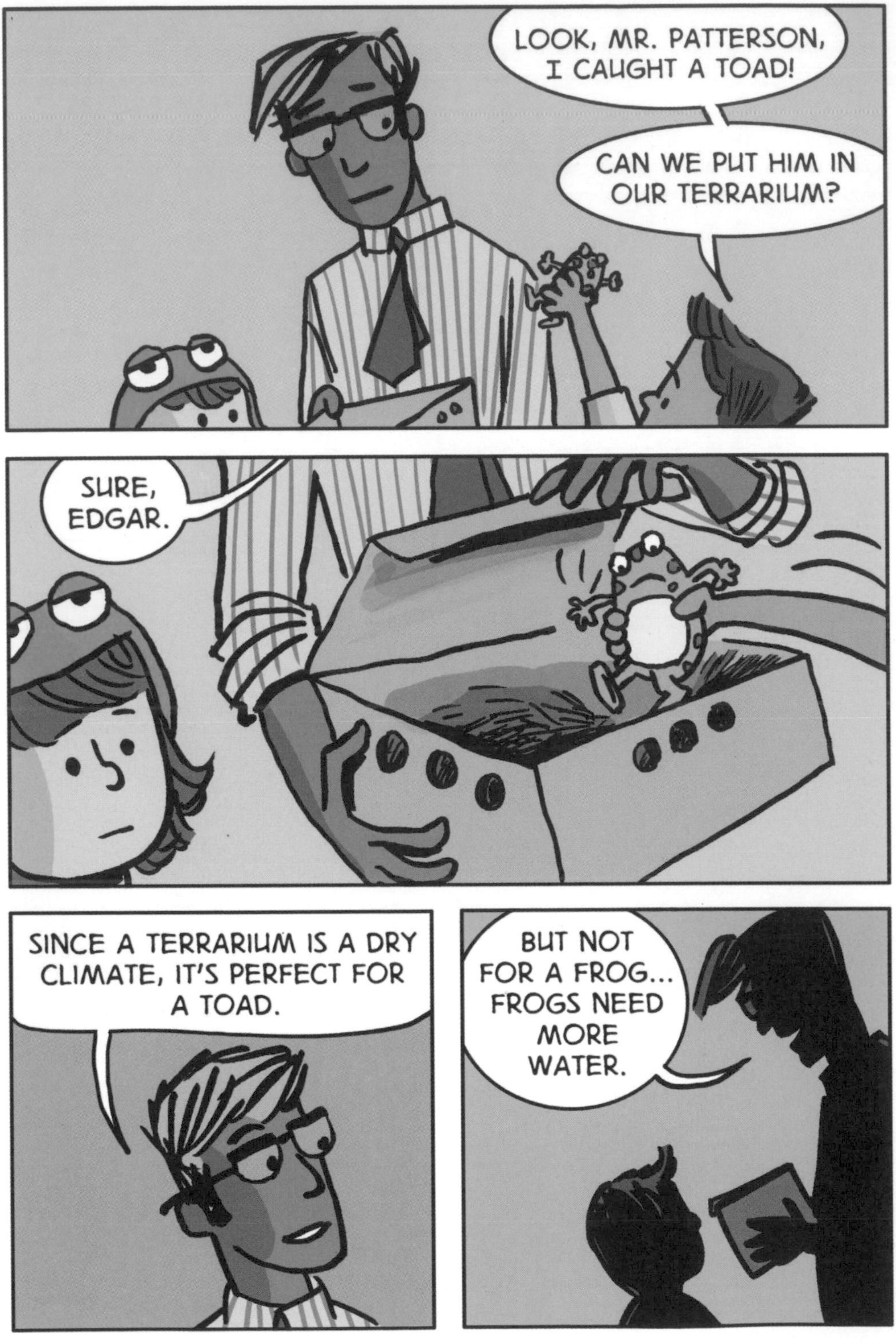
LOOK, MR. PATTERSON, I CAUGHT A TOAD!
CAN WE PUT HIM IN OUR TERRARIUM?
SURE, EDGAR.
SINCE A TERRARIUM IS A DRY CLIMATE, IT'S PERFECT FOR A TOAD.
BUT NOT FOR A FROG... FROGS NEED MORE WATER.

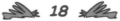

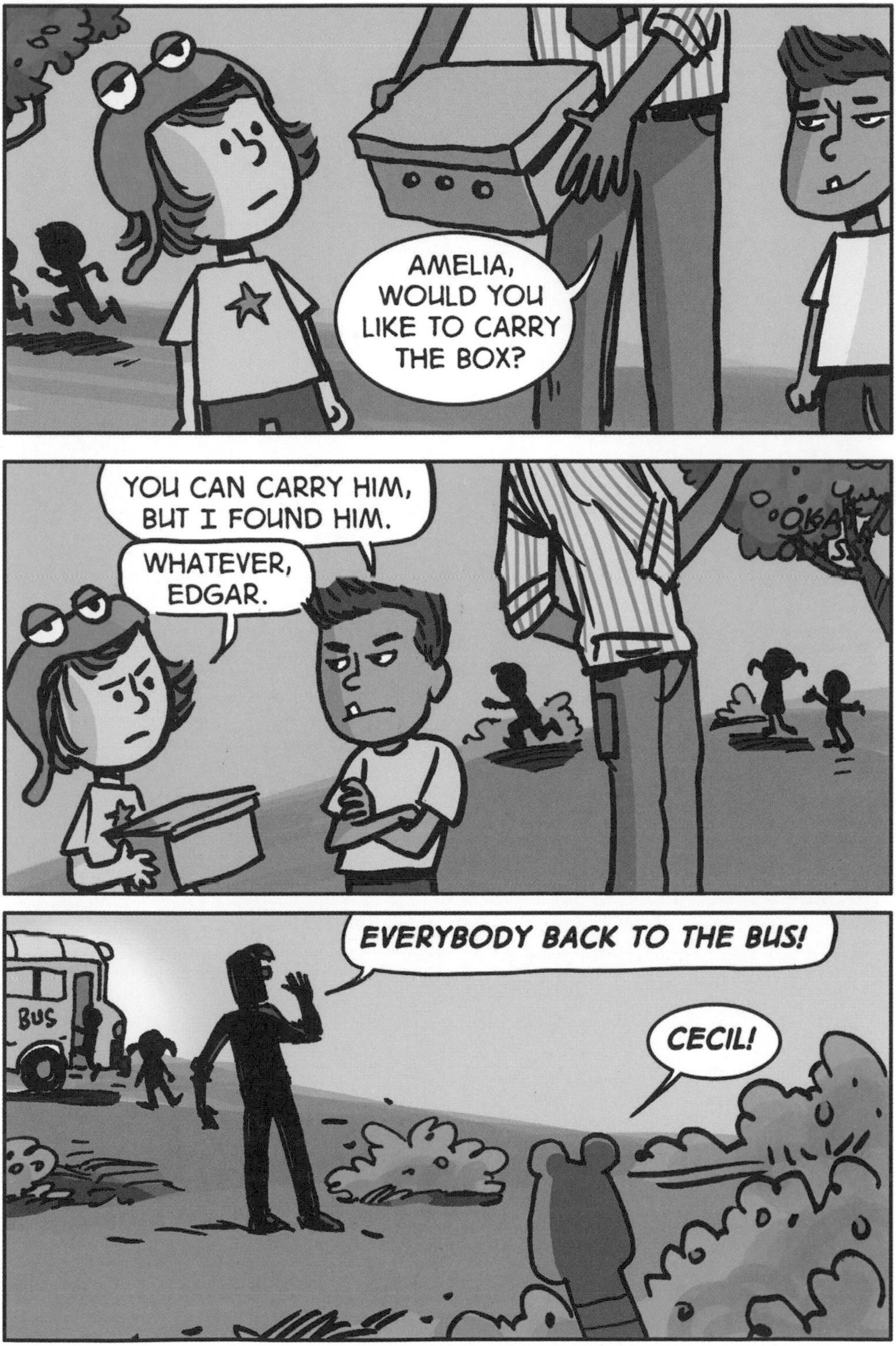
AMELIA, WOULD YOU LIKE TO CARRY THE BOX?
YOU CAN CARRY HIM, BUT I FOUND HIM.
WHATEVER, EDGAR.
BUS
EVERYBODY BACK TO THE BUS!
CECIL!

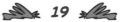

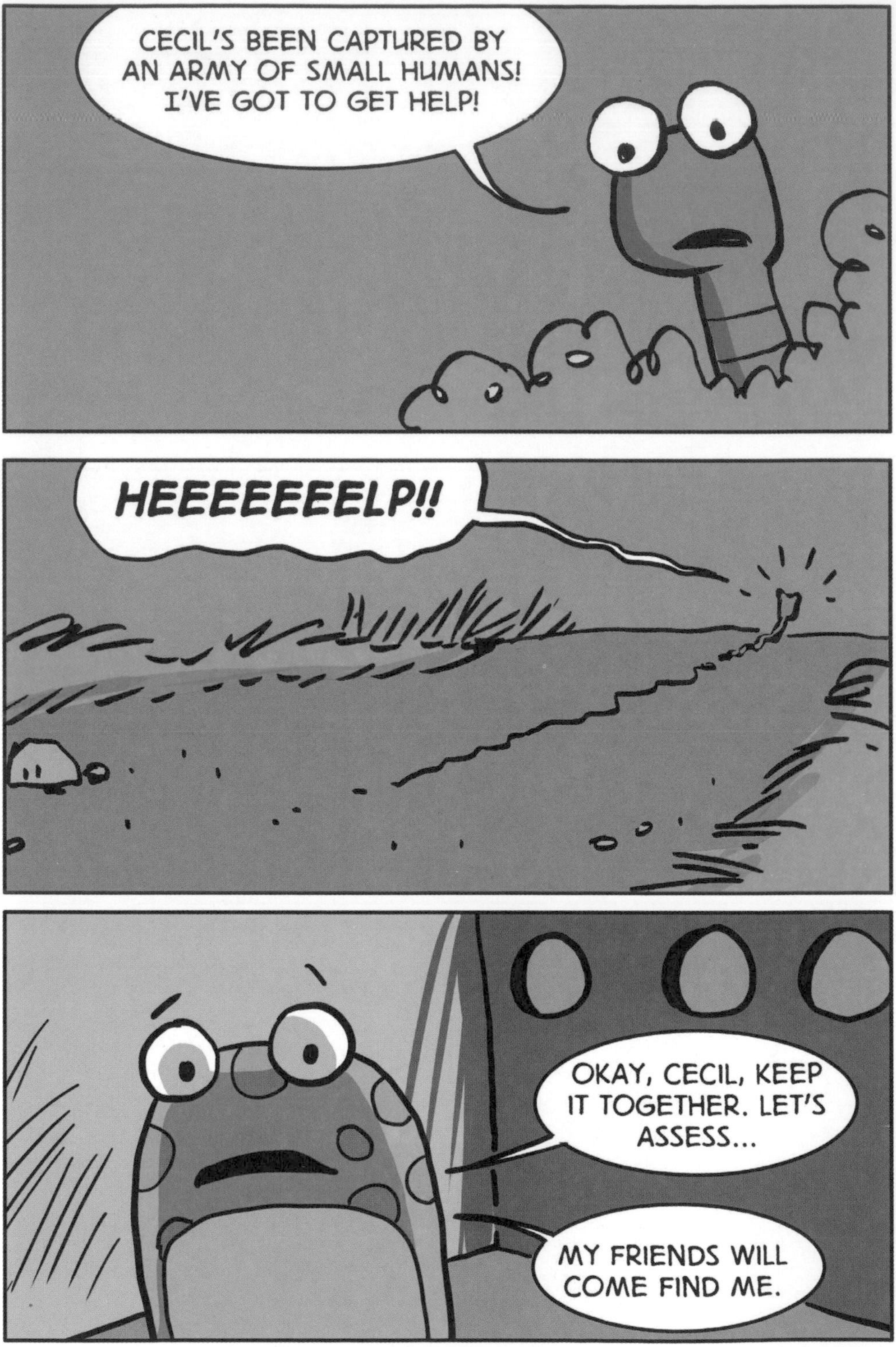
CECIL'S BEEN CAPTURED BY AN ARMY OF SMALL HUMANS! I'VE GOT TO GET HELP!
HEEEEEEEELP!!
OKAY, CECIL, KEEP IT TOGETHER. LET'S ASSESS...
MY FRIENDS WILL COME FIND ME.

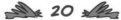

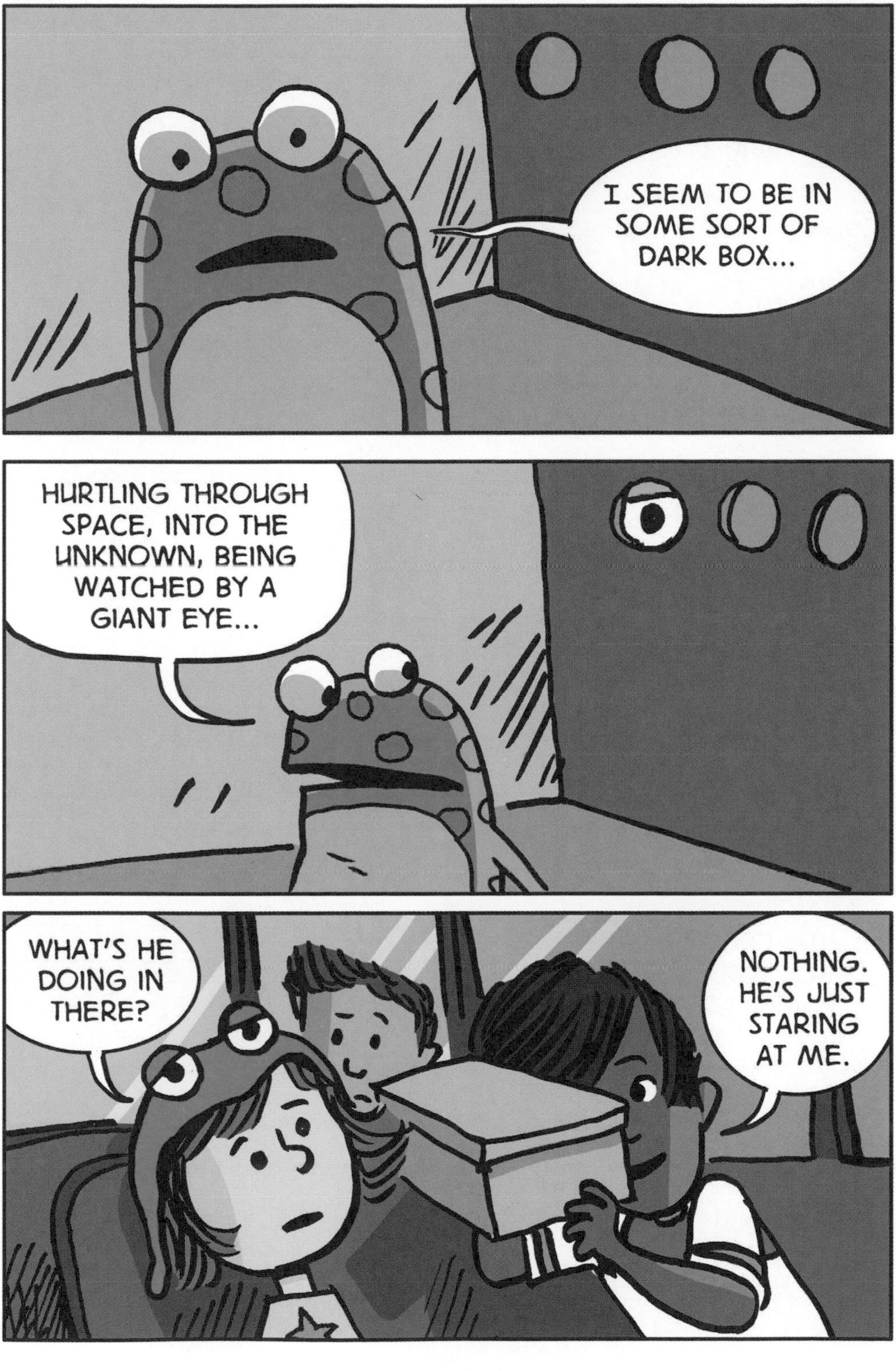
I SEEM TO BE IN SOME SORT OF DARK BOX...
HURTLING THROUGH SPACE, INTO THE UNKNOWN, BEING WATCHED BY A GIANT EYE...
WHAT'S HE DOING IN THERE?
NOTHING. HE'S JUST STARING AT ME.

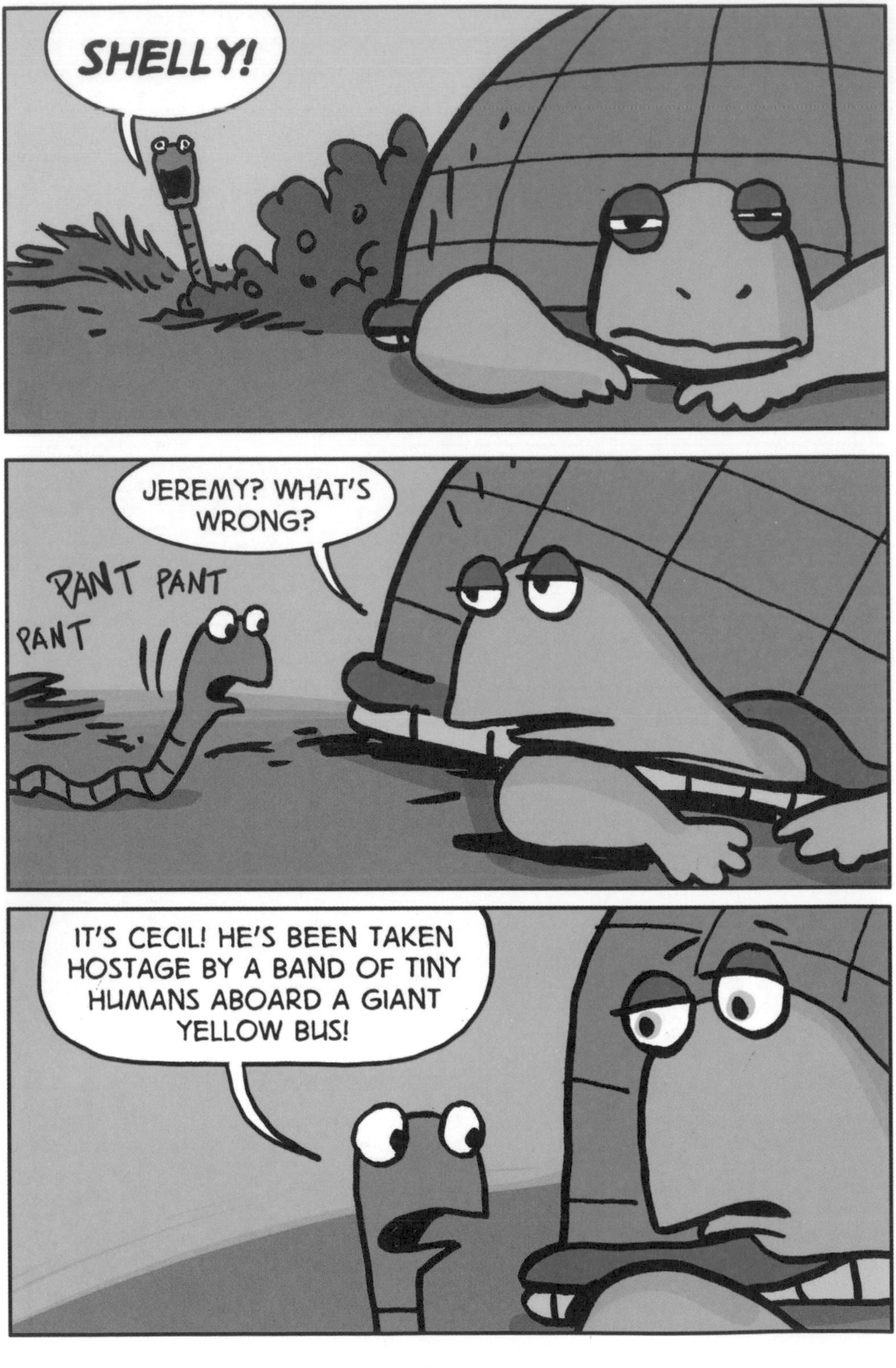
SHELLY!
JEREMY? WHAT'S WRONG?
PANT PANT
PANT
IT'S CECIL! HE'S BEEN TAKEN HOSTAGE BY A BAND OF TINY HUMANS ABOARD A GIANT YELLOW BUS!

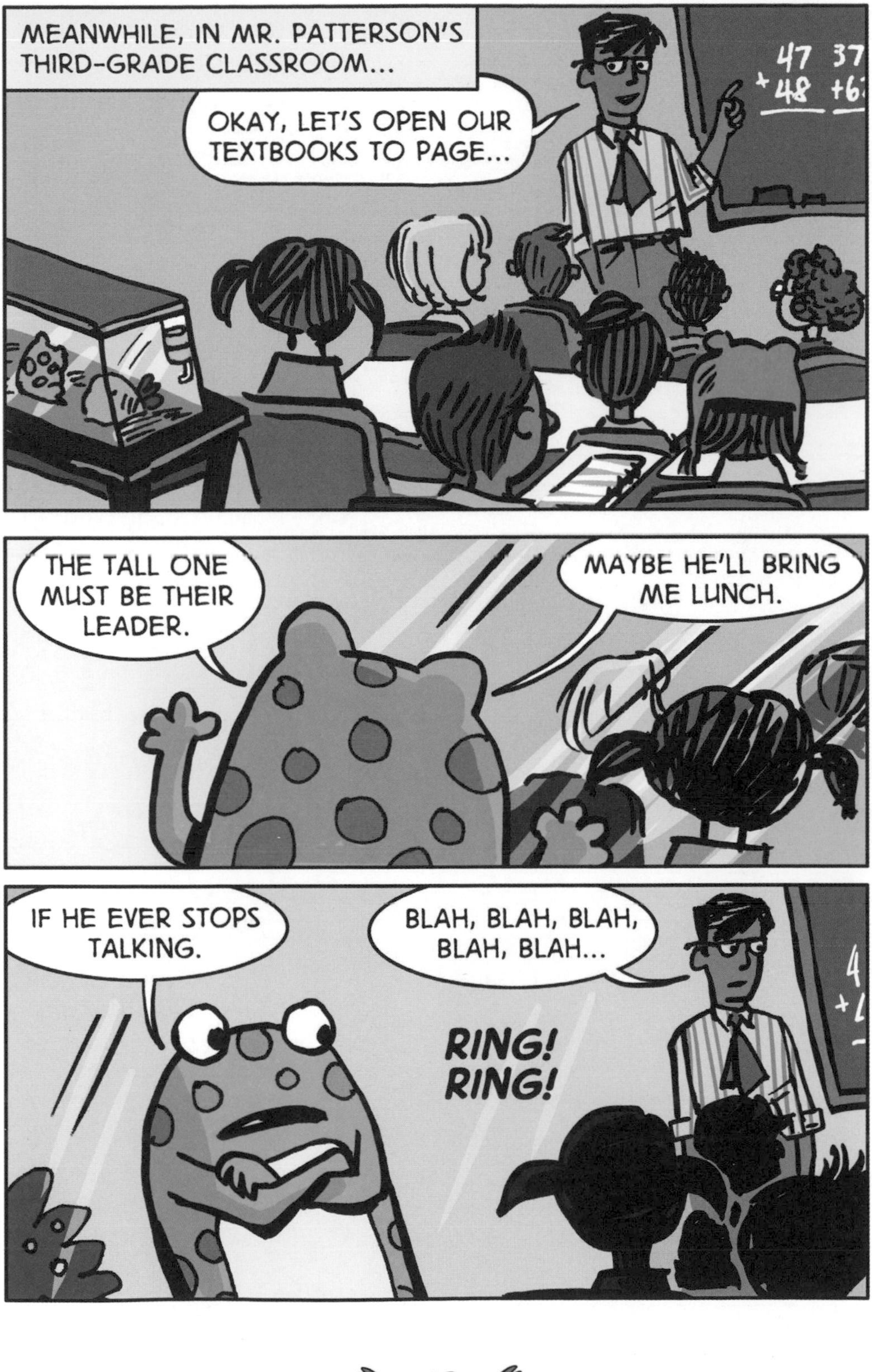
MEANWHILE, IN MR. PATTERSON'S THIRD-GRADE CLASSROOM...
OKAY, LET'S OPEN OUR TEXTBOOKS TO PAGE...
47 + 48
THE TALL ONE MUST BE THEIR LEADER.
MAYBE HE'LL BRING ME LUNCH.
IF HE EVER STOPS TALKING.
BLAH, BLAH, BLAH, BLAH, BLAH...
RING! RING!

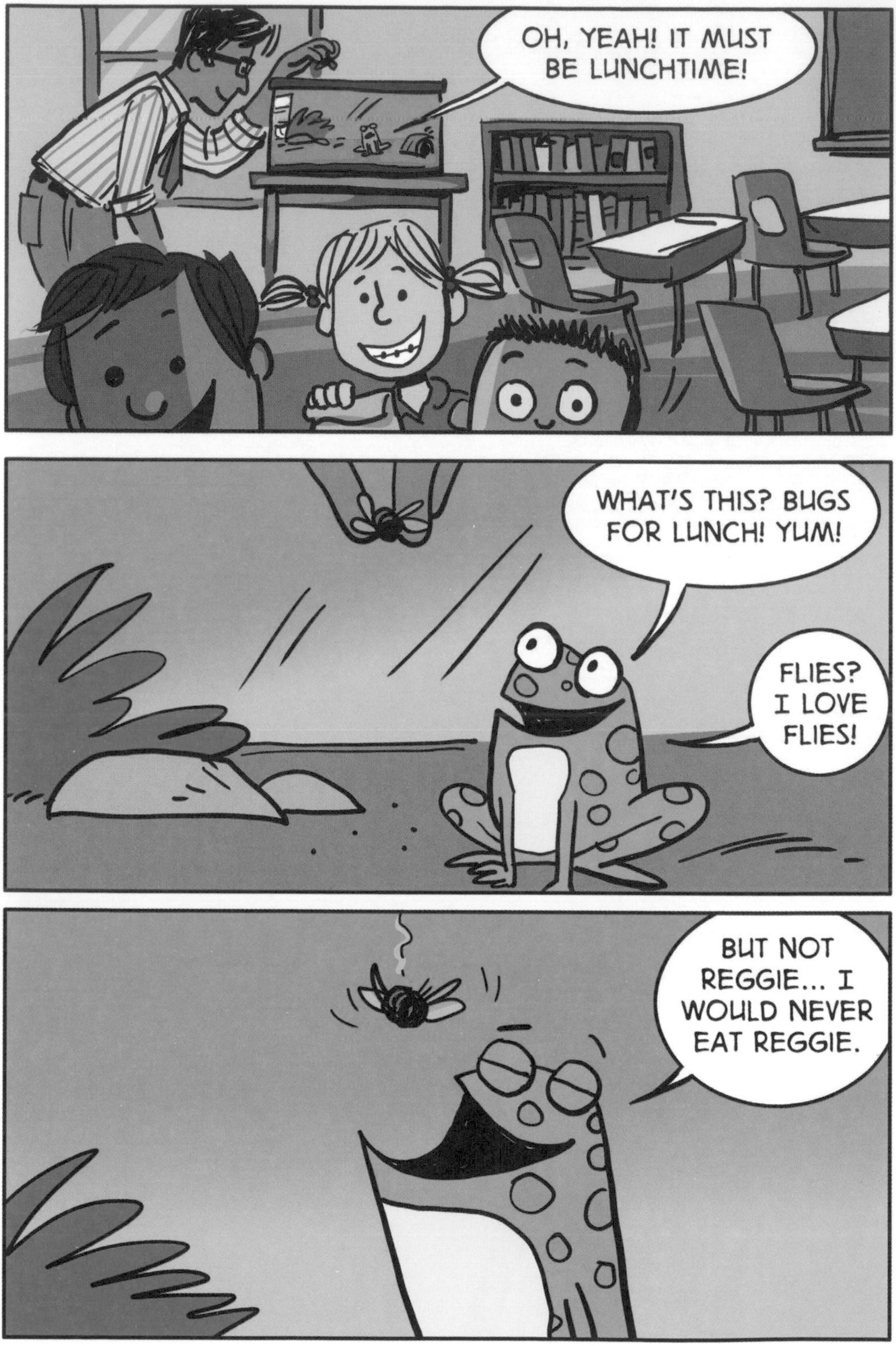
OH, YEAH! IT MUST BE LUNCHTIME!
WHAT'S THIS? BUGS FOR LUNCH! YUM!
FLIES? I LOVE FLIES!
BUT NOT REGGIE... I WOULD NEVER EAT REGGIE.

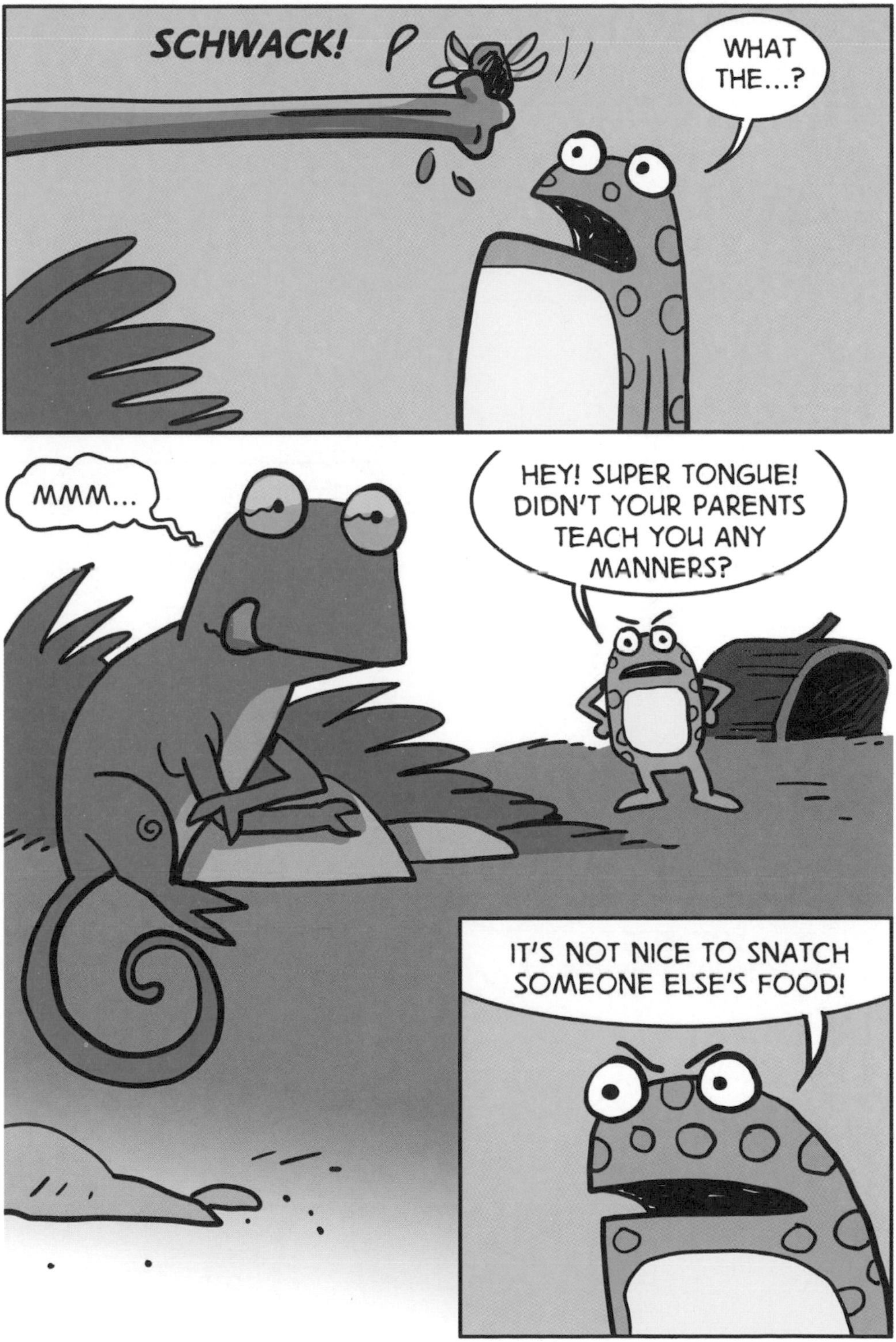
SCHWACK!
WHAT THE...?
MMM...
HEY! SUPER TONGUE! DIDN'T YOUR PARENTS TEACH YOU ANY MANNERS?
IT'S NOT NICE TO SNATCH SOMEONE ELSE'S FOOD!

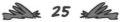

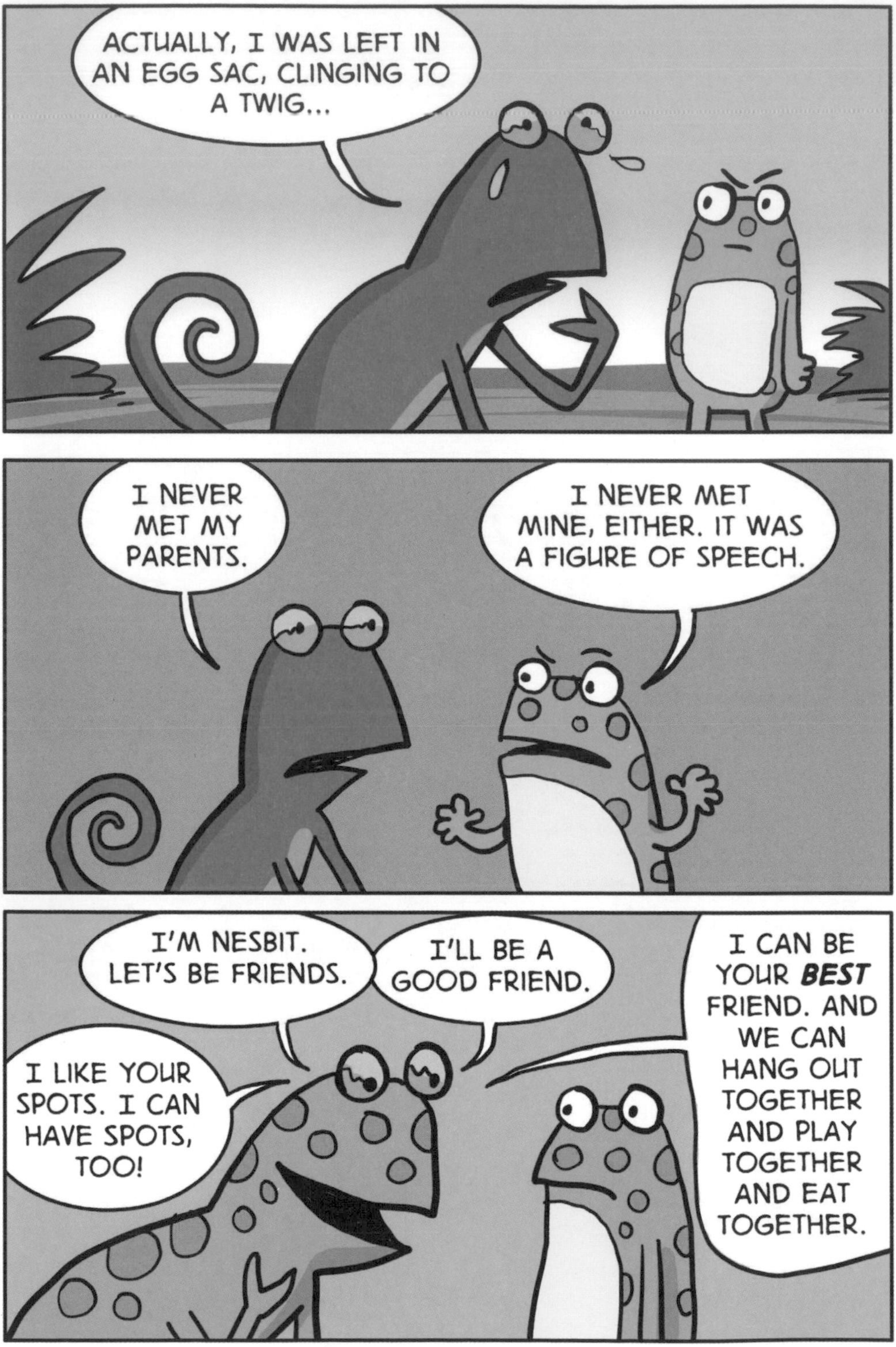
ACTUALLY, I WAS LEFT IN AN EGG SAC, CLINGING TO A TWIG...
I NEVER MET MY PARENTS.
I NEVER MET MINE, EITHER. IT WAS A FIGURE OF SPEECH.
I'M NESBIT. LET'S BE FRIENDS.
I'LL BE A GOOD FRIEND.
I LIKE YOUR SPOTS. I CAN HAVE SPOTS, TOO!
I CAN BE YOUR **BEST** FRIEND. AND WE CAN HANG OUT TOGETHER AND PLAY TOGETHER AND EAT TOGETHER.

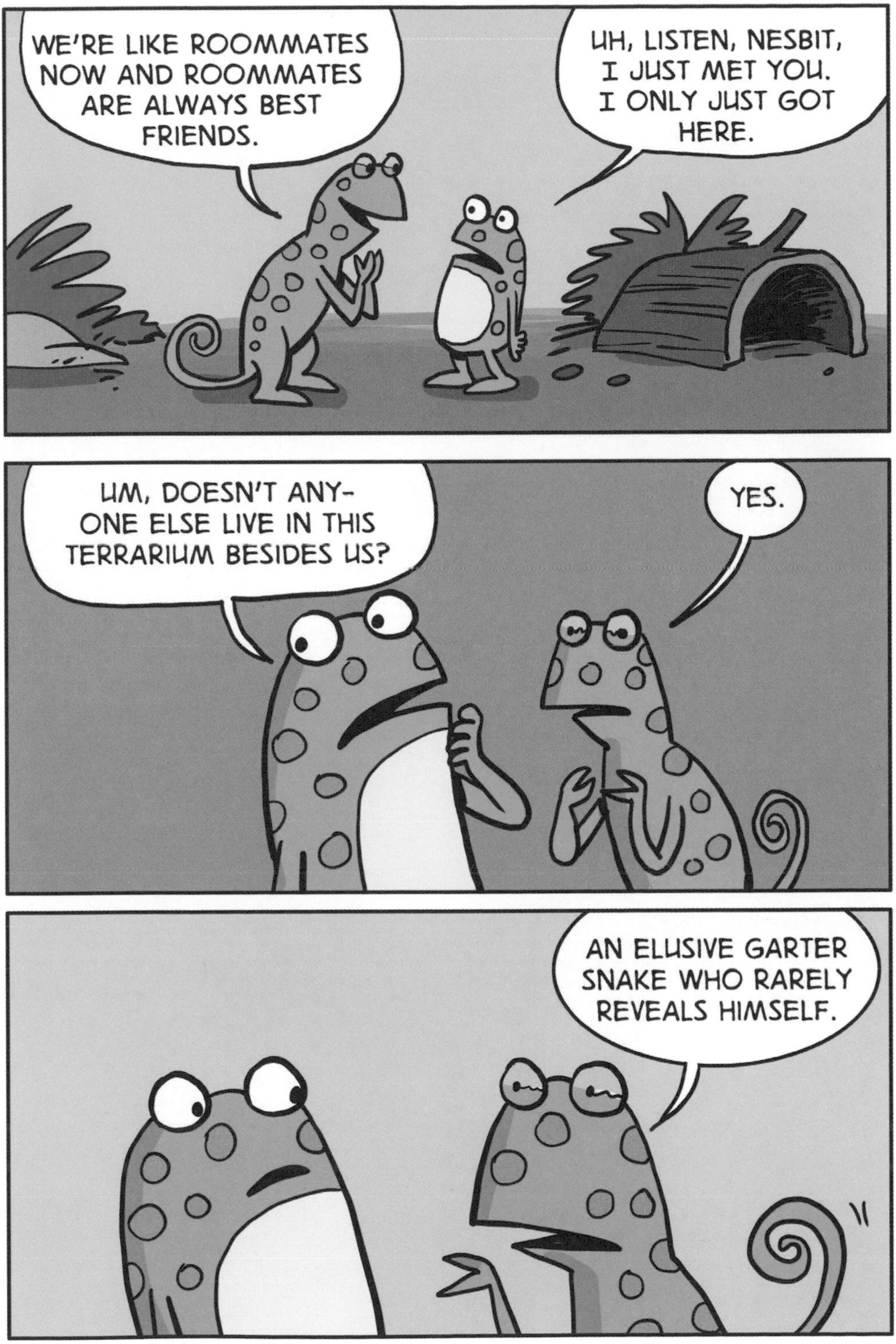
WE'RE LIKE ROOMMATES NOW AND ROOMMATES ARE ALWAYS BEST FRIENDS.
UH, LISTEN, NESBIT, I JUST MET YOU. I ONLY JUST GOT HERE.
UM, DOESN'T ANY-ONE ELSE LIVE IN THIS TERRARIUM BESIDES US?
YES.
AN ELUSIVE GARTER SNAKE WHO RARELY REVEALS HIMSELF.

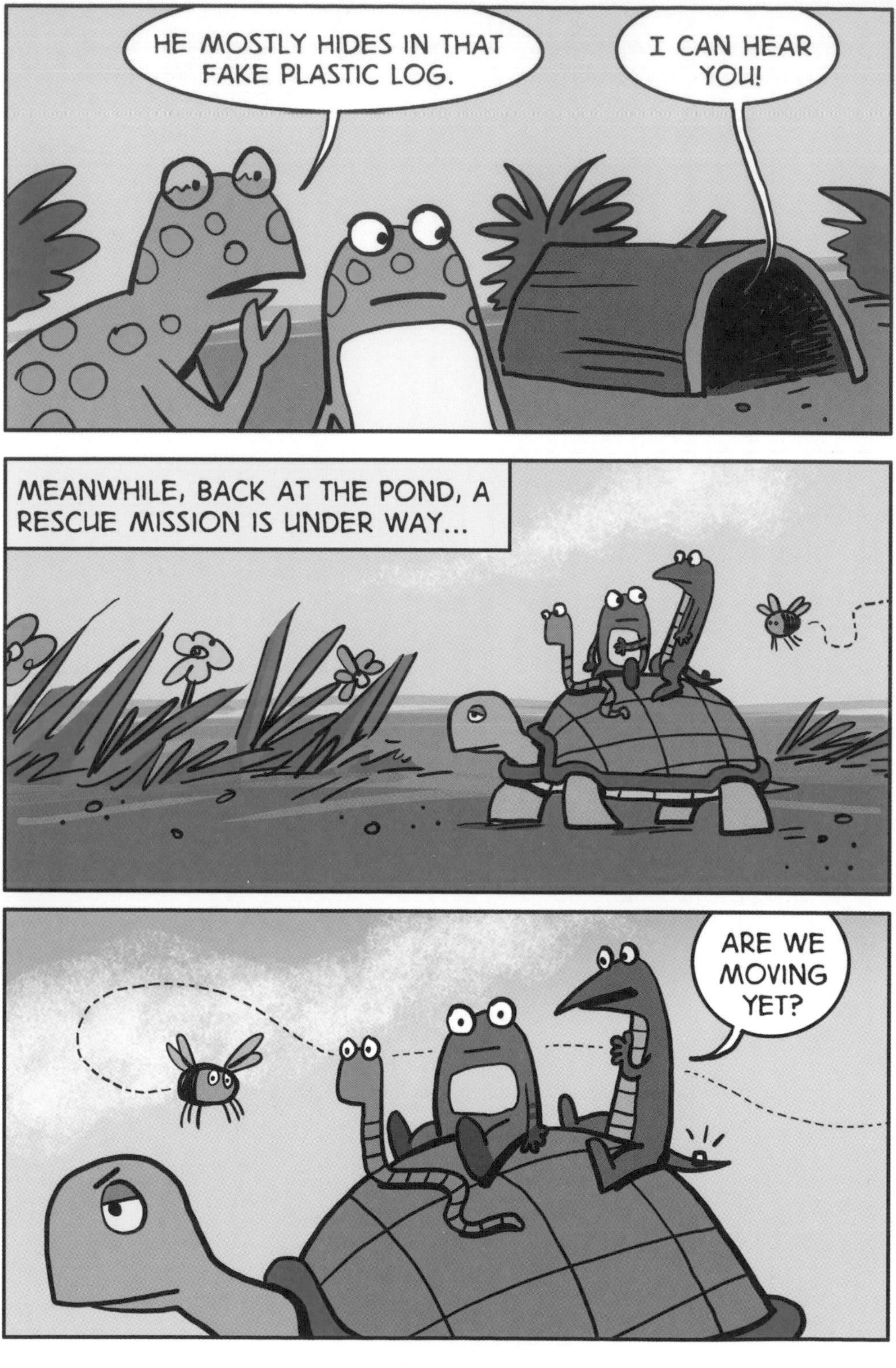
HE MOSTLY HIDES IN THAT FAKE PLASTIC LOG.
I CAN HEAR YOU!
MEANWHILE, BACK AT THE POND, A RESCUE MISSION IS UNDER WAY...
ARE WE MOVING YET?

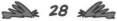

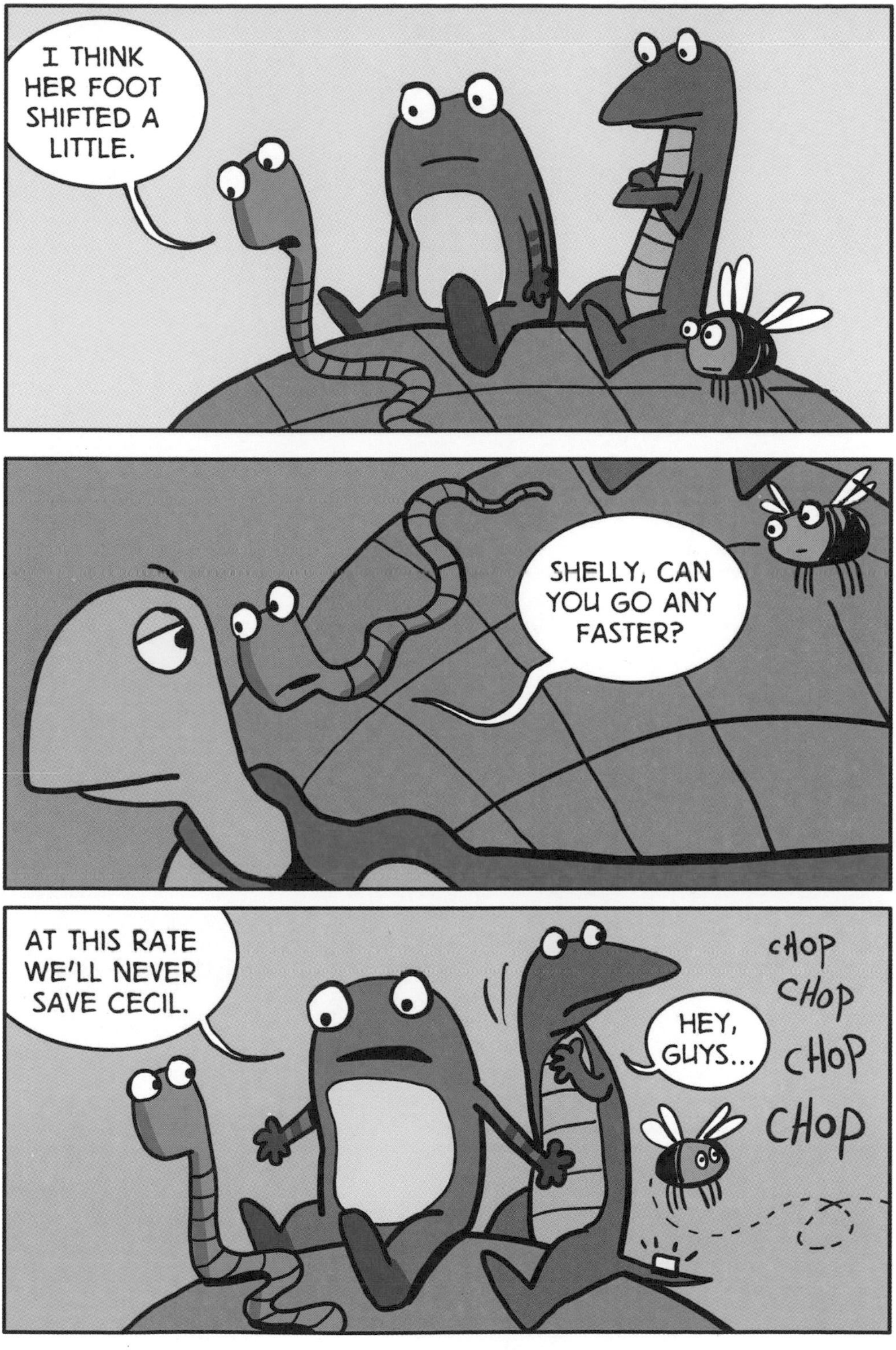
I THINK HER FOOT SHIFTED A LITTLE.
SHELLY, CAN YOU GO ANY FASTER?
AT THIS RATE WE'LL NEVER SAVE CECIL.
HEY, GUYS...
CHOP
CHOP
CHOP
CHOP

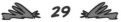

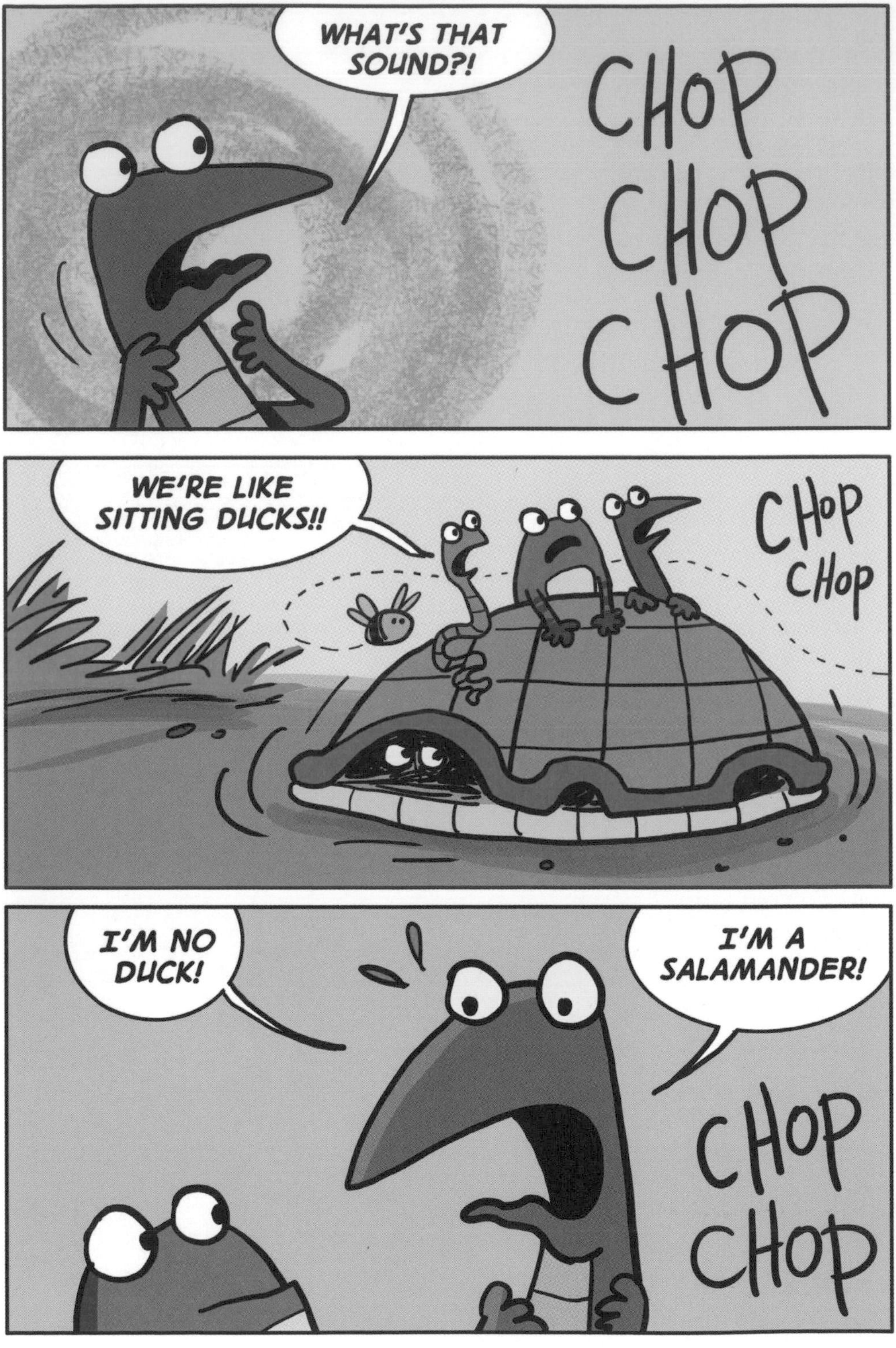
WHAT'S THAT SOUND?!
CHOP CHOP CHOP
WE'RE LIKE SITTING DUCKS!!
CHOP CHOP
I'M NO DUCK!
I'M A SALAMANDER!
CHOP CHOP

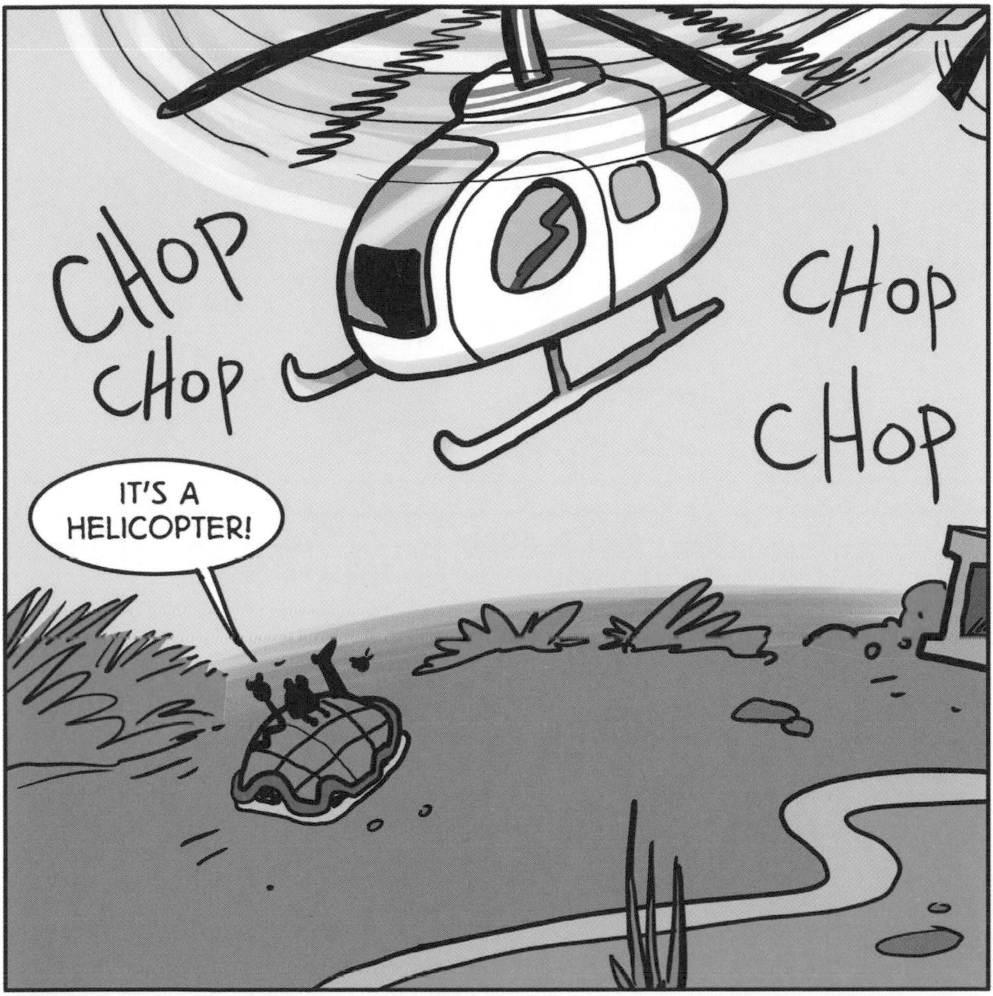
CHOP
CHOP
CHOP
CHOP
IT'S A HELICOPTER!

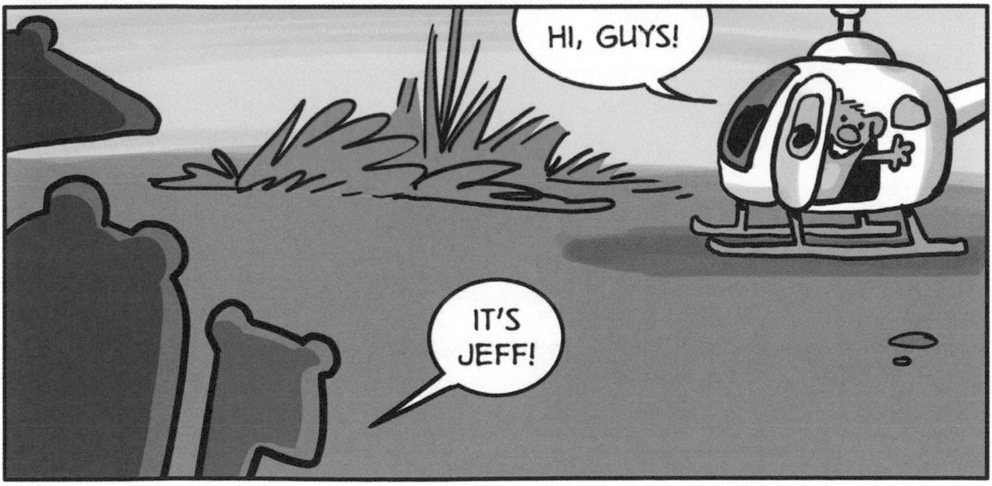
HI, GUYS!
IT'S JEFF!

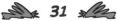

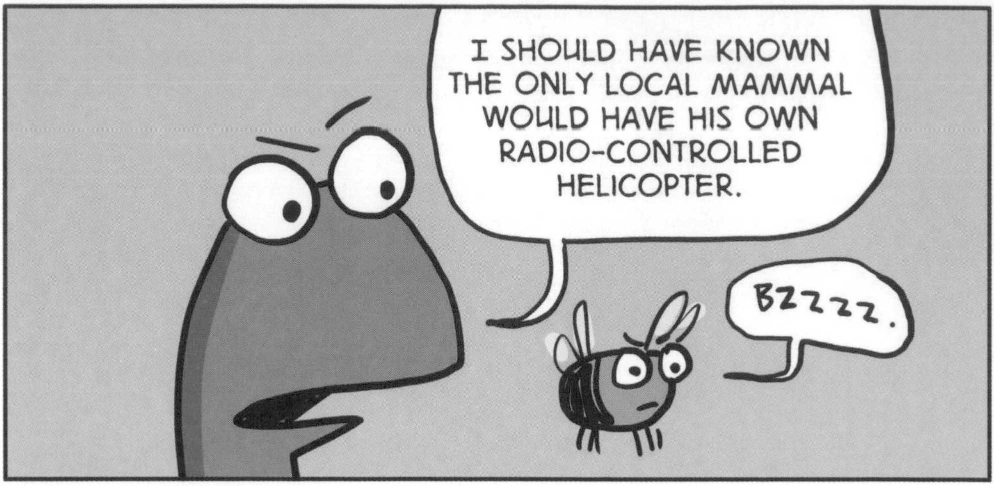
I SHOULD HAVE KNOWN THE ONLY LOCAL MAMMAL WOULD HAVE HIS OWN RADIO-CONTROLLED HELICOPTER.
BZZZZ.
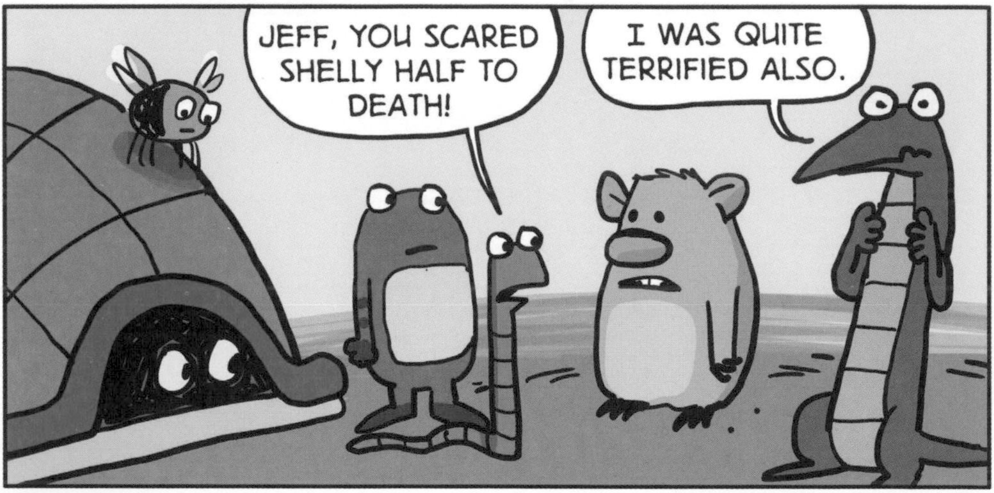
JEFF, YOU SCARED SHELLY HALF TO DEATH!
I WAS QUITE TERRIFIED ALSO.
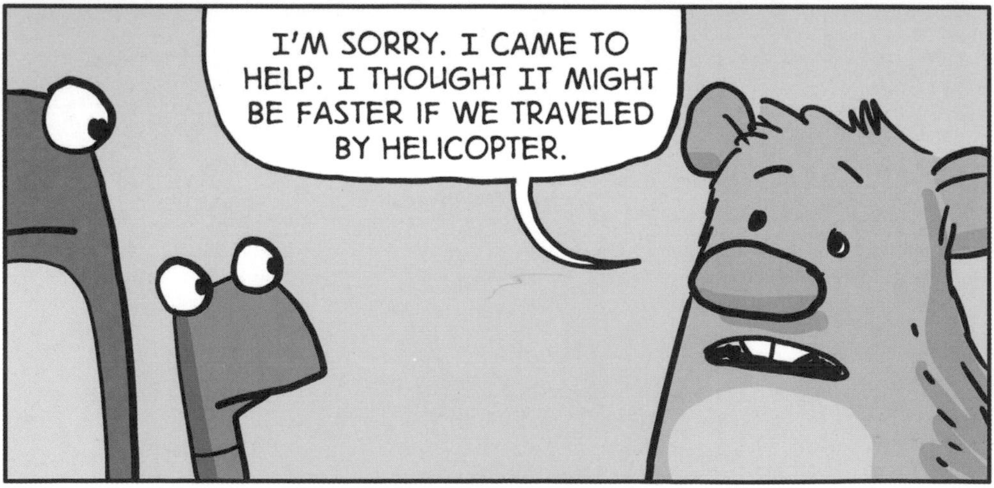
I'M SORRY. I CAME TO HELP. I THOUGHT IT MIGHT BE FASTER IF WE TRAVELED BY HELICOPTER.

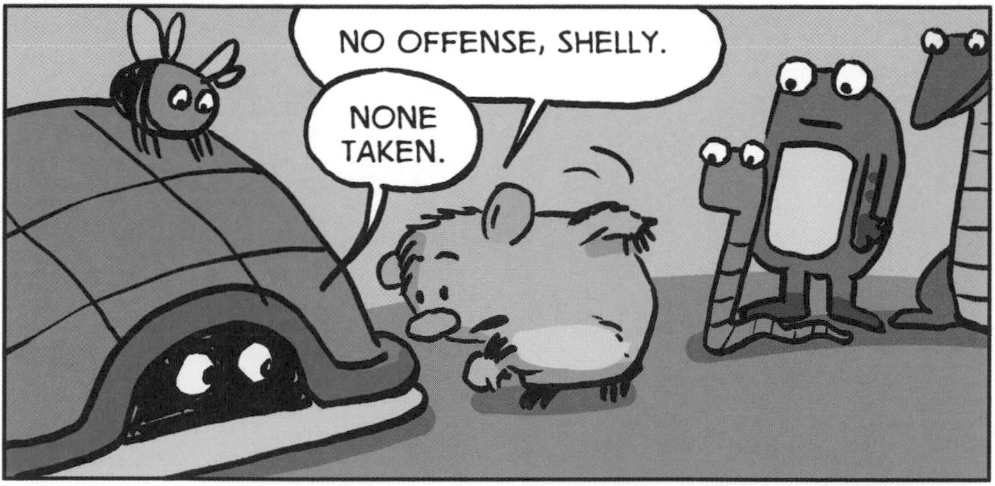
NO OFFENSE, SHELLY.
NONE TAKEN.

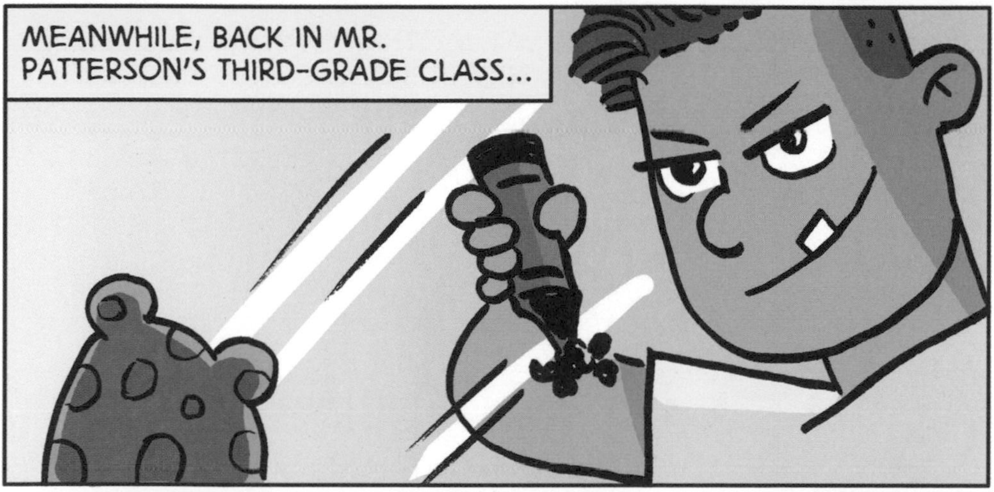
MEANWHILE, BACK IN MR. PATTERSON'S THIRD-GRADE CLASS...

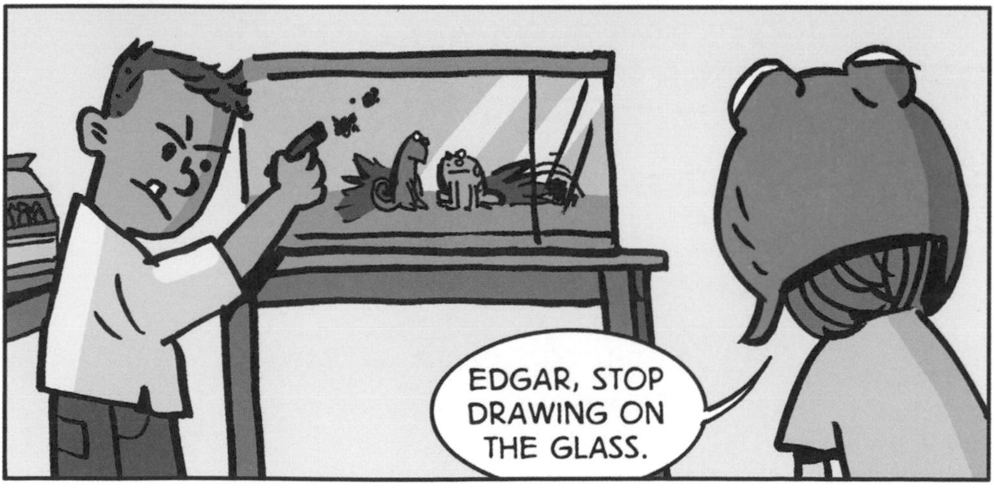
EDGAR, STOP DRAWING ON THE GLASS.

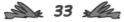

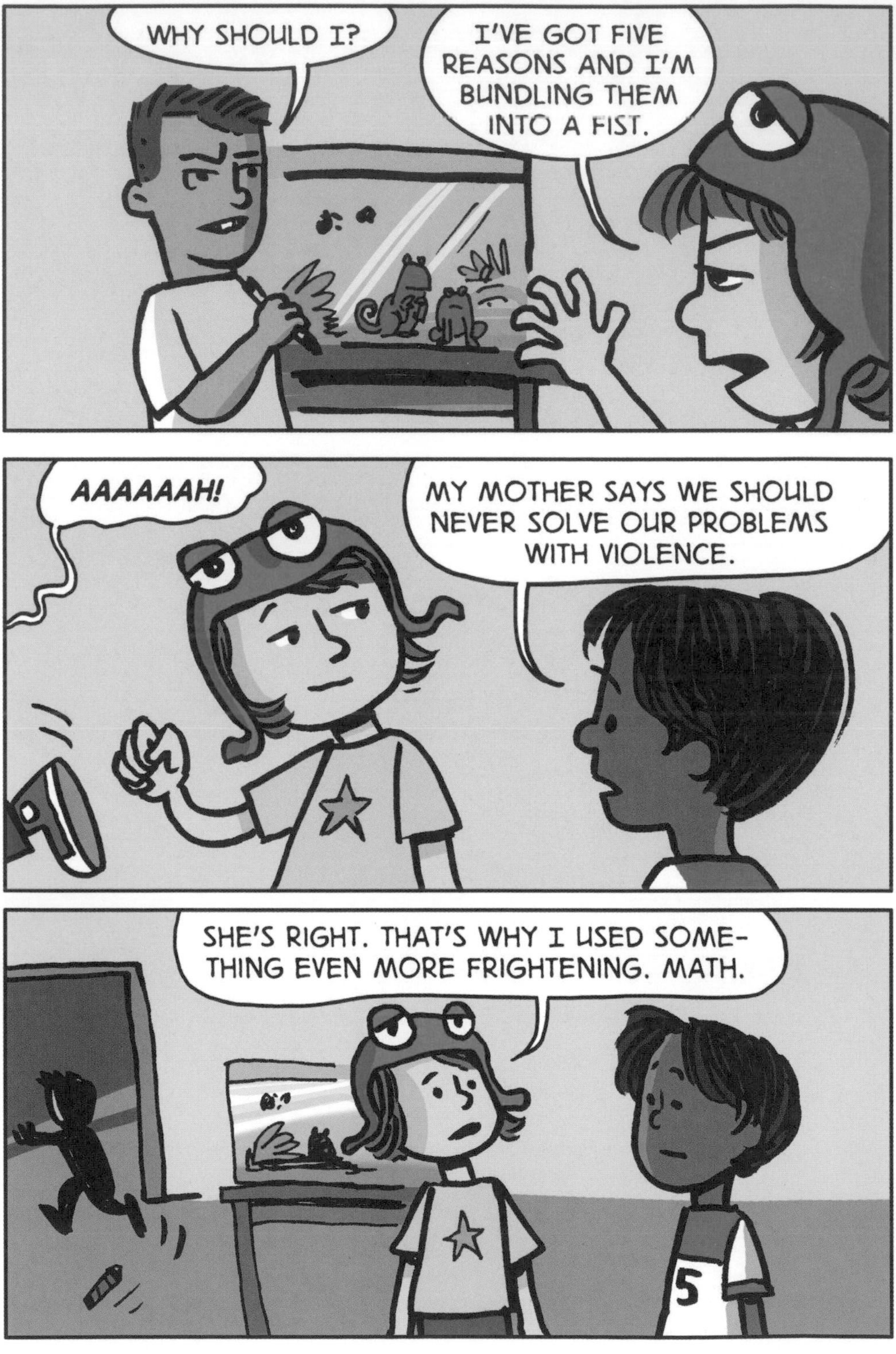
WHY SHOULD I?
I'VE GOT FIVE REASONS AND I'M BUNDLING THEM INTO A FIST.
AAAAAAH!
MY MOTHER SAYS WE SHOULD NEVER SOLVE OUR PROBLEMS WITH VIOLENCE.
SHE'S RIGHT. THAT'S WHY I USED SOME-THING EVEN MORE FRIGHTENING. MATH.
5

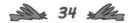

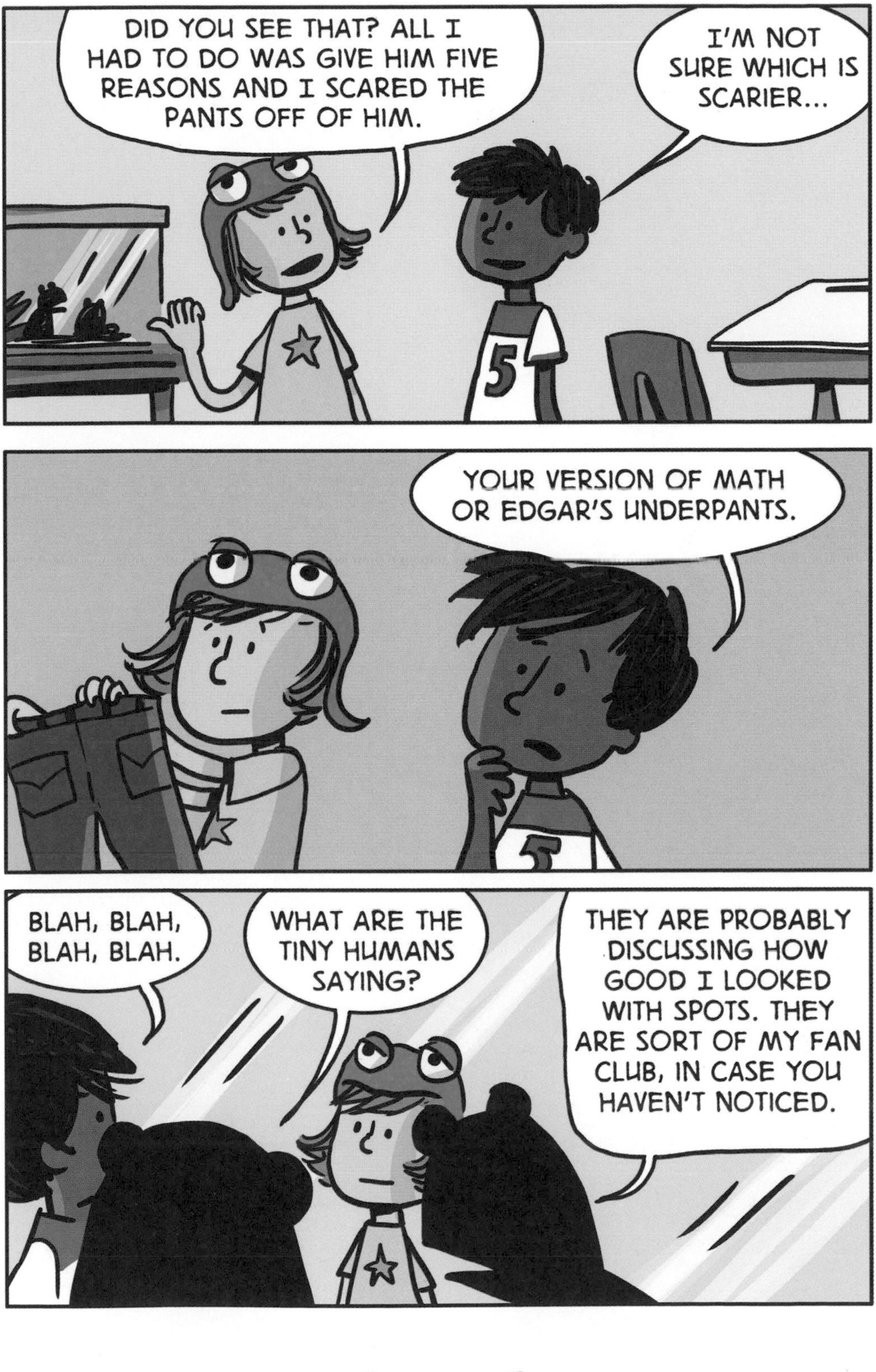
DID YOU SEE THAT? ALL I HAD TO DO WAS GIVE HIM FIVE REASONS AND I SCARED THE PANTS OFF OF HIM.
I'M NOT SURE WHICH IS SCARIER...
YOUR VERSION OF MATH OR EDGAR'S UNDERPANTS.
BLAH, BLAH, BLAH, BLAH.
WHAT ARE THE TINY HUMANS SAYING?
THEY ARE PROBABLY DISCUSSING HOW GOOD I LOOKED WITH SPOTS. THEY ARE SORT OF MY FAN CLUB, IN CASE YOU HAVEN'T NOTICED.

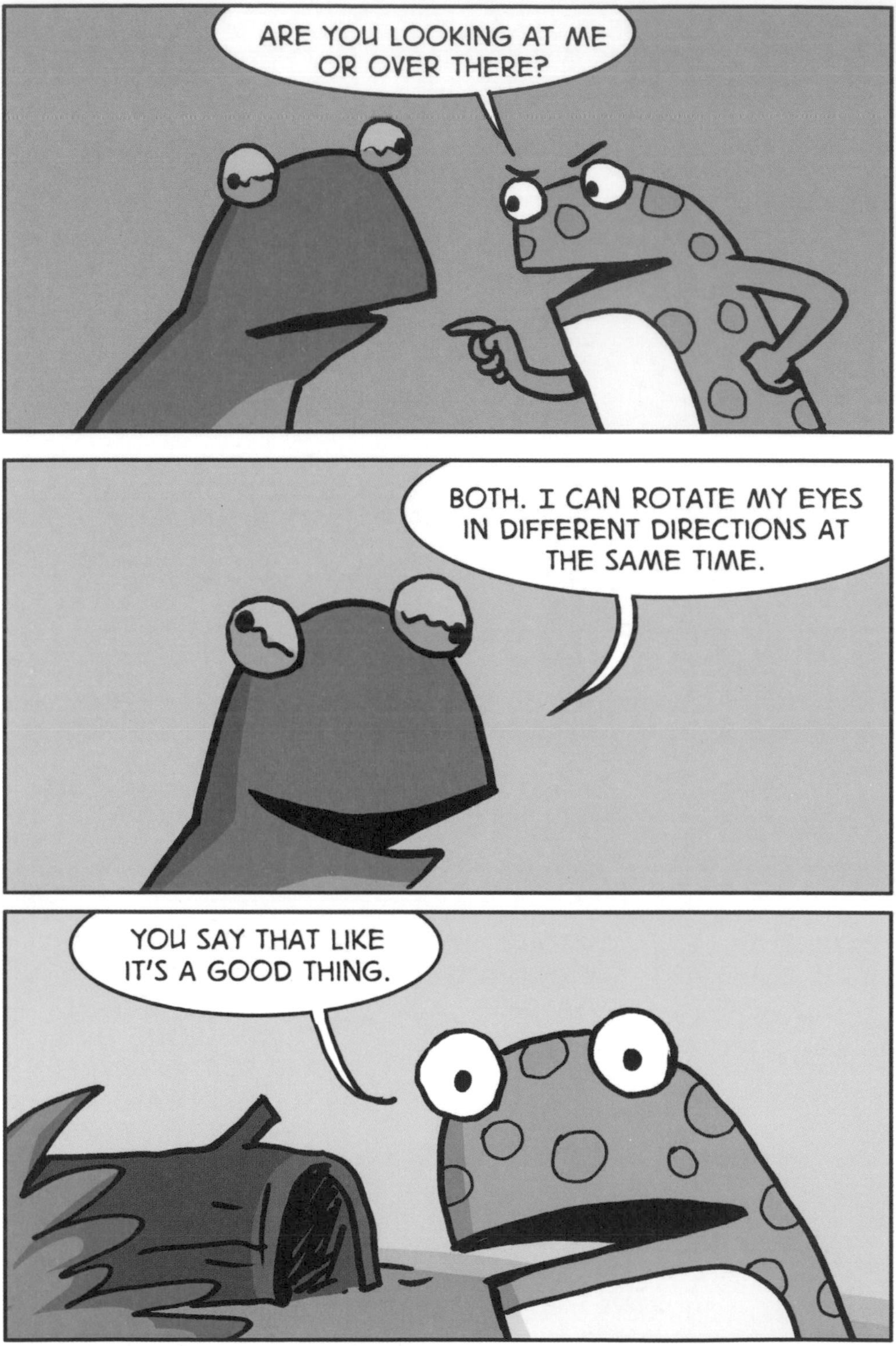
ARE YOU LOOKING AT ME OR OVER THERE?
BOTH. I CAN ROTATE MY EYES IN DIFFERENT DIRECTIONS AT THE SAME TIME.
YOU SAY THAT LIKE IT'S A GOOD THING.

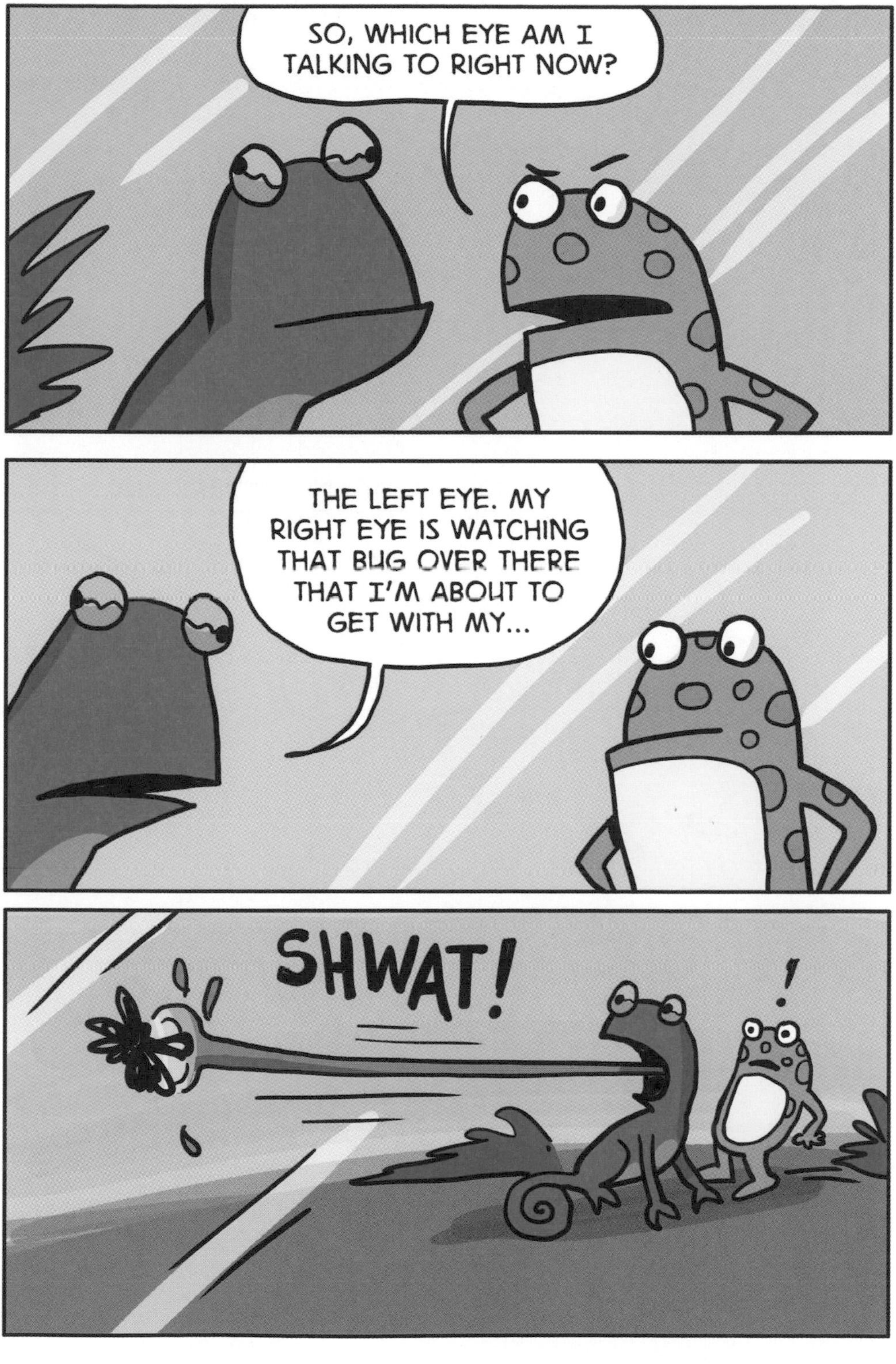
SO, WHICH EYE AM I TALKING TO RIGHT NOW?
THE LEFT EYE. MY RIGHT EYE IS WATCHING THAT BUG OVER THERE THAT I'M ABOUT TO GET WITH MY...
SHWAT!
!

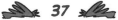

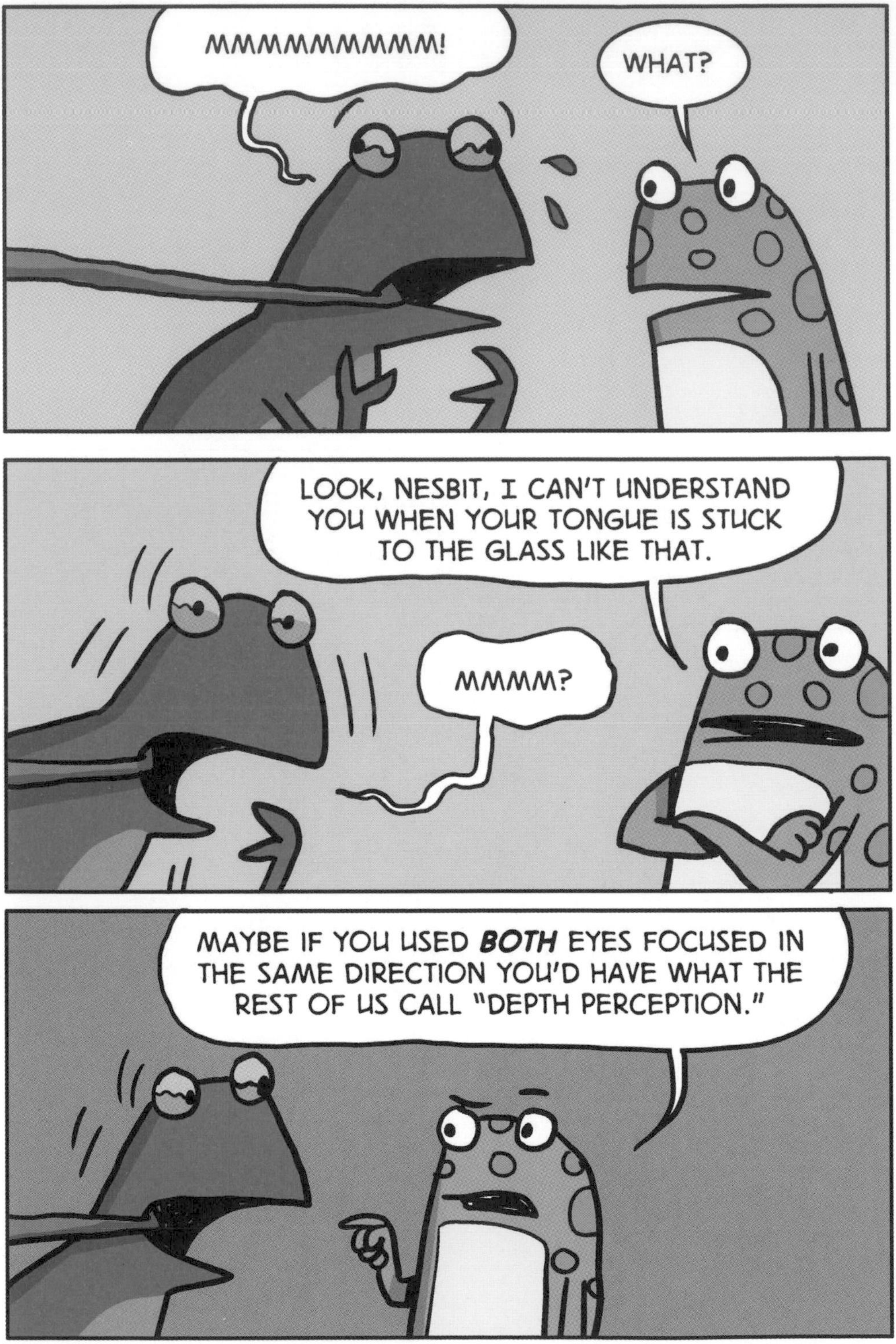
MMMMMMMMMM!
WHAT?
LOOK, NESBIT, I CAN'T UNDERSTAND YOU WHEN YOUR TONGUE IS STUCK TO THE GLASS LIKE THAT.
MMMM?
MAYBE IF YOU USED ***BOTH*** EYES FOCUSED IN THE SAME DIRECTION YOU'D HAVE WHAT THE REST OF US CALL "DEPTH PERCEPTION."

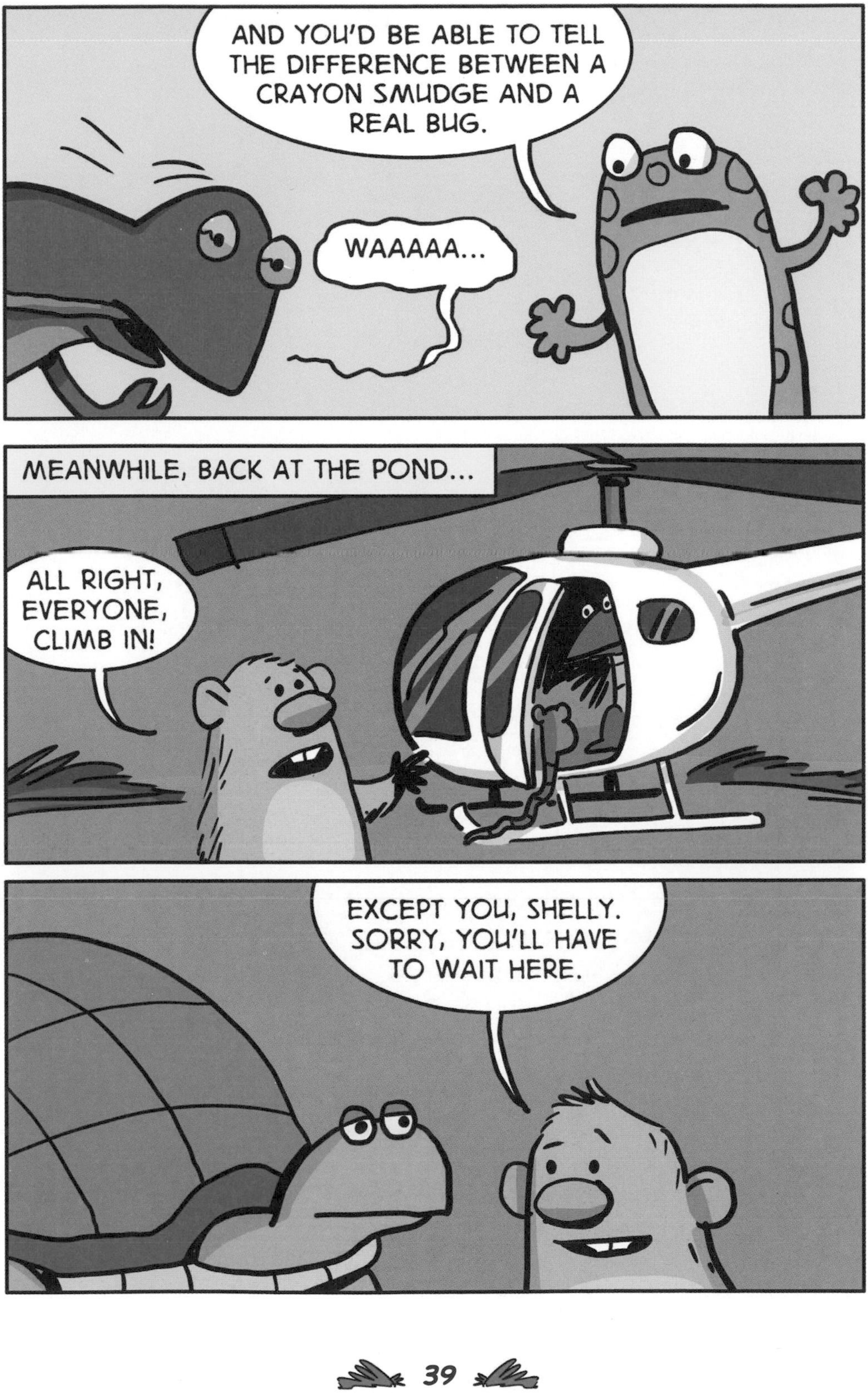
AND YOU'D BE ABLE TO TELL THE DIFFERENCE BETWEEN A CRAYON SMUDGE AND A REAL BUG.
WAAAAA...
MEANWHILE, BACK AT THE POND...
ALL RIGHT, EVERYONE, CLIMB IN!
EXCEPT YOU, SHELLY. SORRY, YOU'LL HAVE TO WAIT HERE.

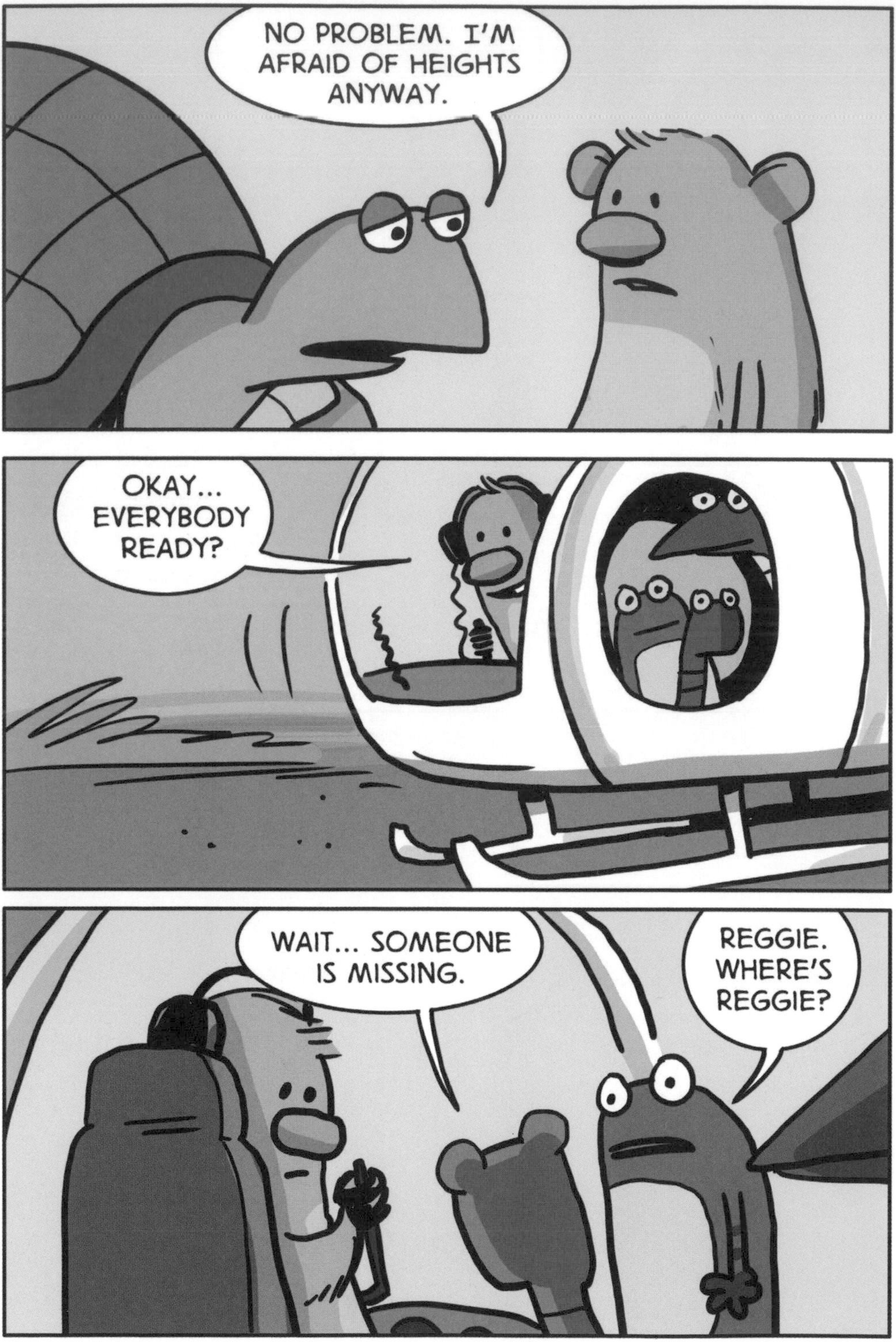
NO PROBLEM. I'M AFRAID OF HEIGHTS ANYWAY.
OKAY... EVERYBODY READY?
WAIT... SOMEONE IS MISSING.
REGGIE. WHERE'S REGGIE?

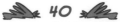

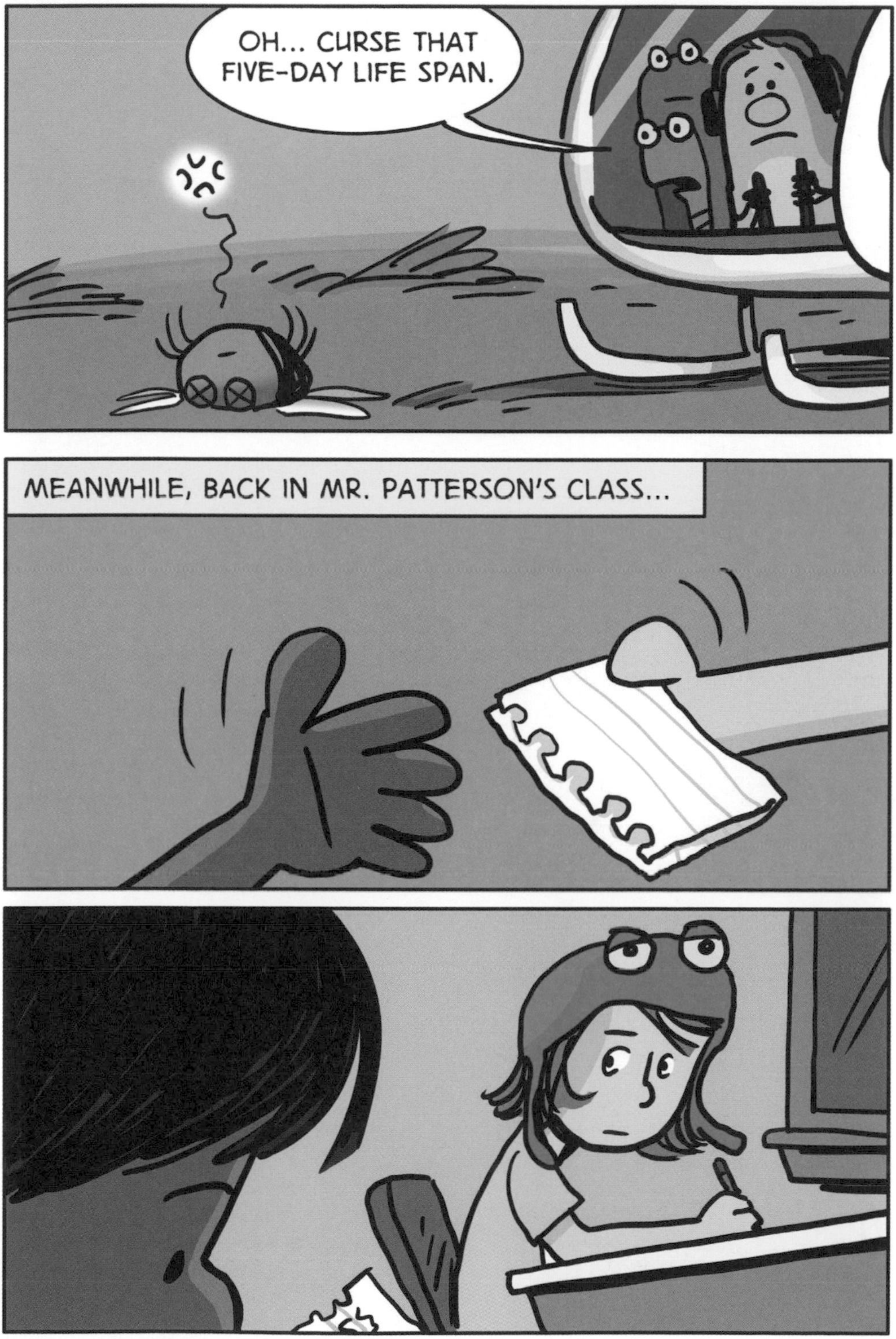

OH... CURSE THAT FIVE-DAY LIFE SPAN.
MEANWHILE, BACK IN MR. PATTERSON'S CLASS...

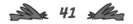

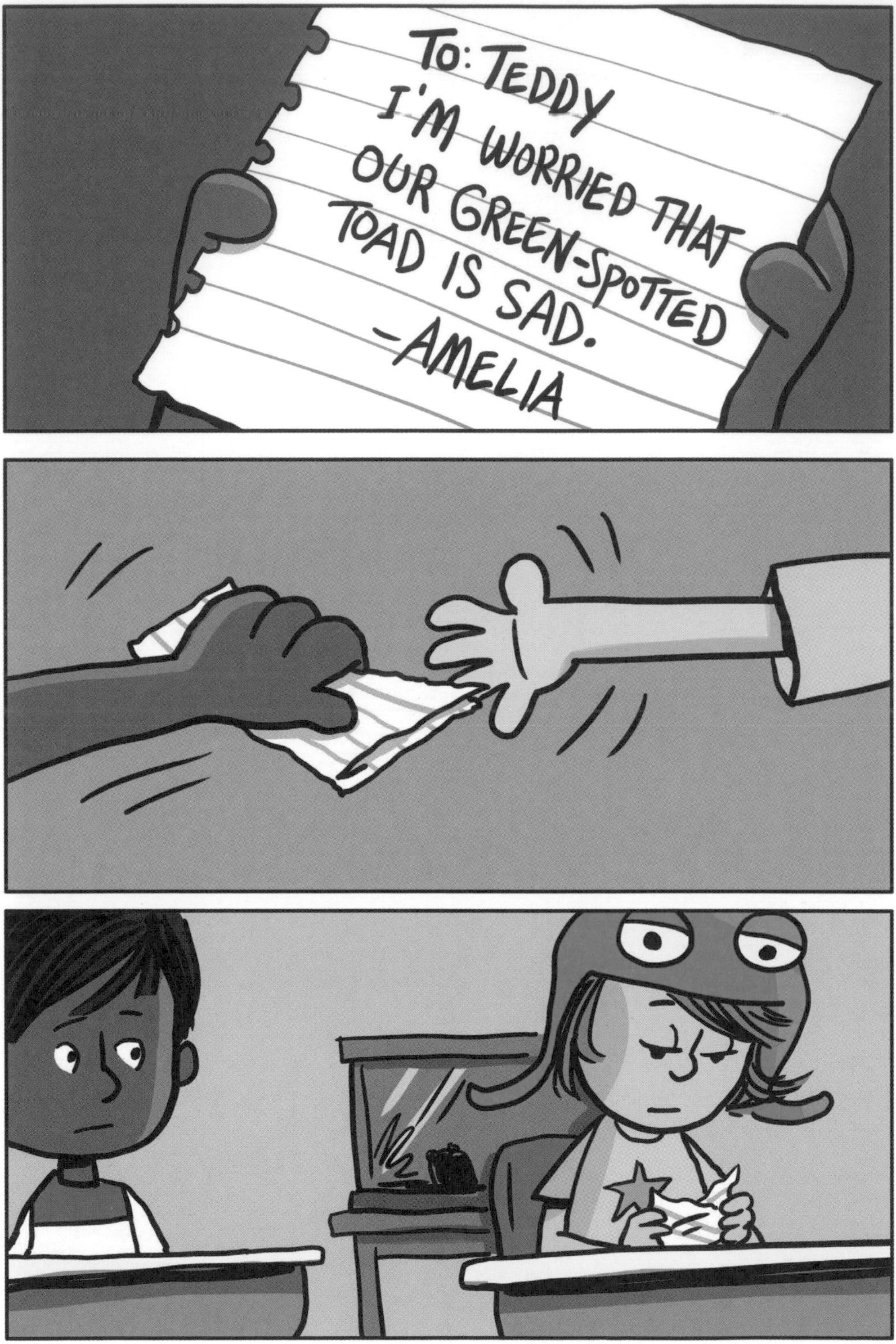
TO: TEDDY
I'M WORRIED THAT OUR GREEN-SPOTTED TOAD IS SAD.
-AMELIA

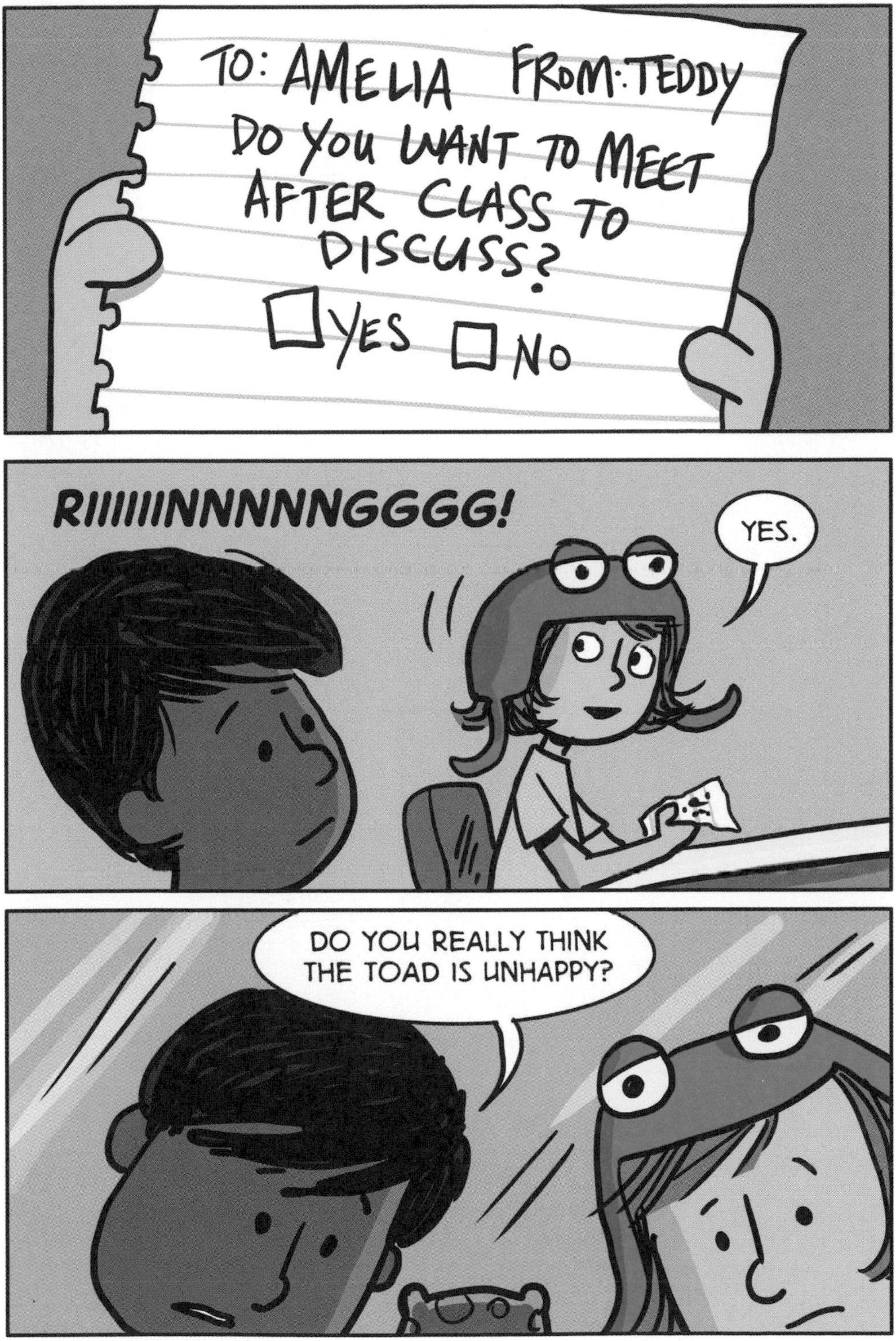
TO: AMELIA FROM: TEDDY
DO YOU WANT TO MEET AFTER CLASS TO DISCUSS?
YES
NO
RIIIIIINNNNNGGGG!
YES.
DO YOU REALLY THINK THE TOAD IS UNHAPPY?

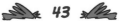

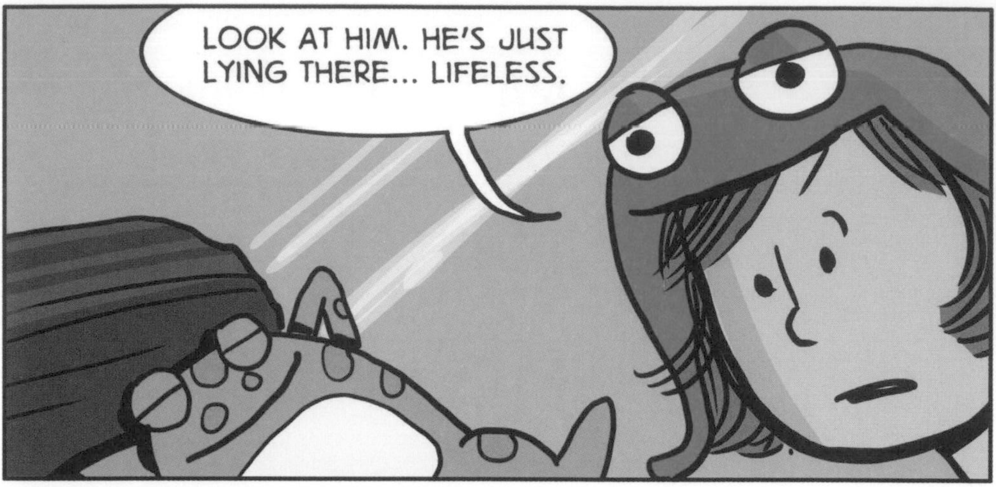
LOOK AT HIM. HE'S JUST LYING THERE... LIFELESS.

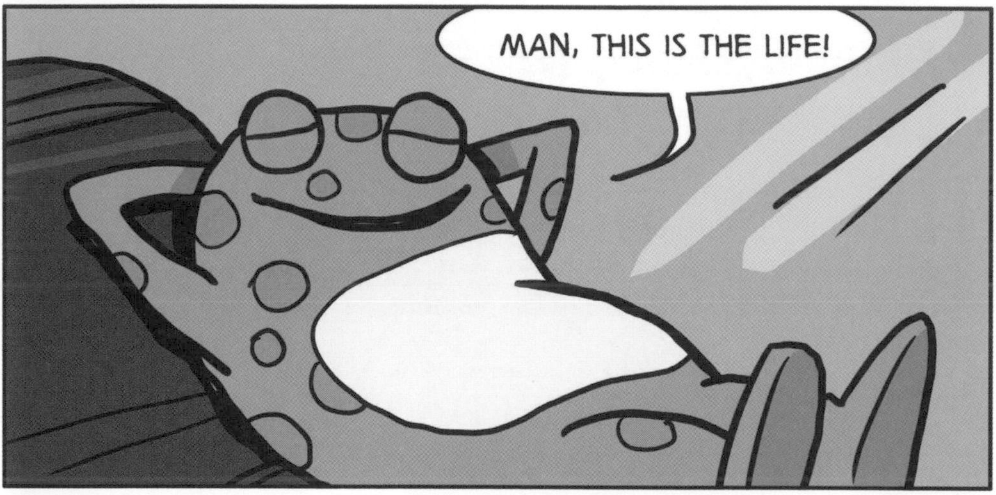
MAN, THIS IS THE LIFE!

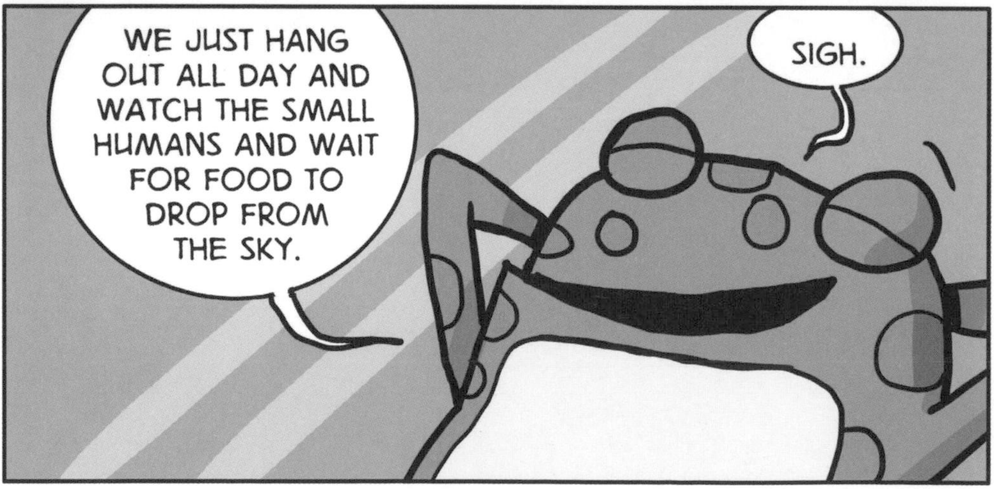
WE JUST HANG OUT ALL DAY AND WATCH THE SMALL HUMANS AND WAIT FOR FOOD TO DROP FROM THE SKY.
SIGH.

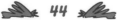

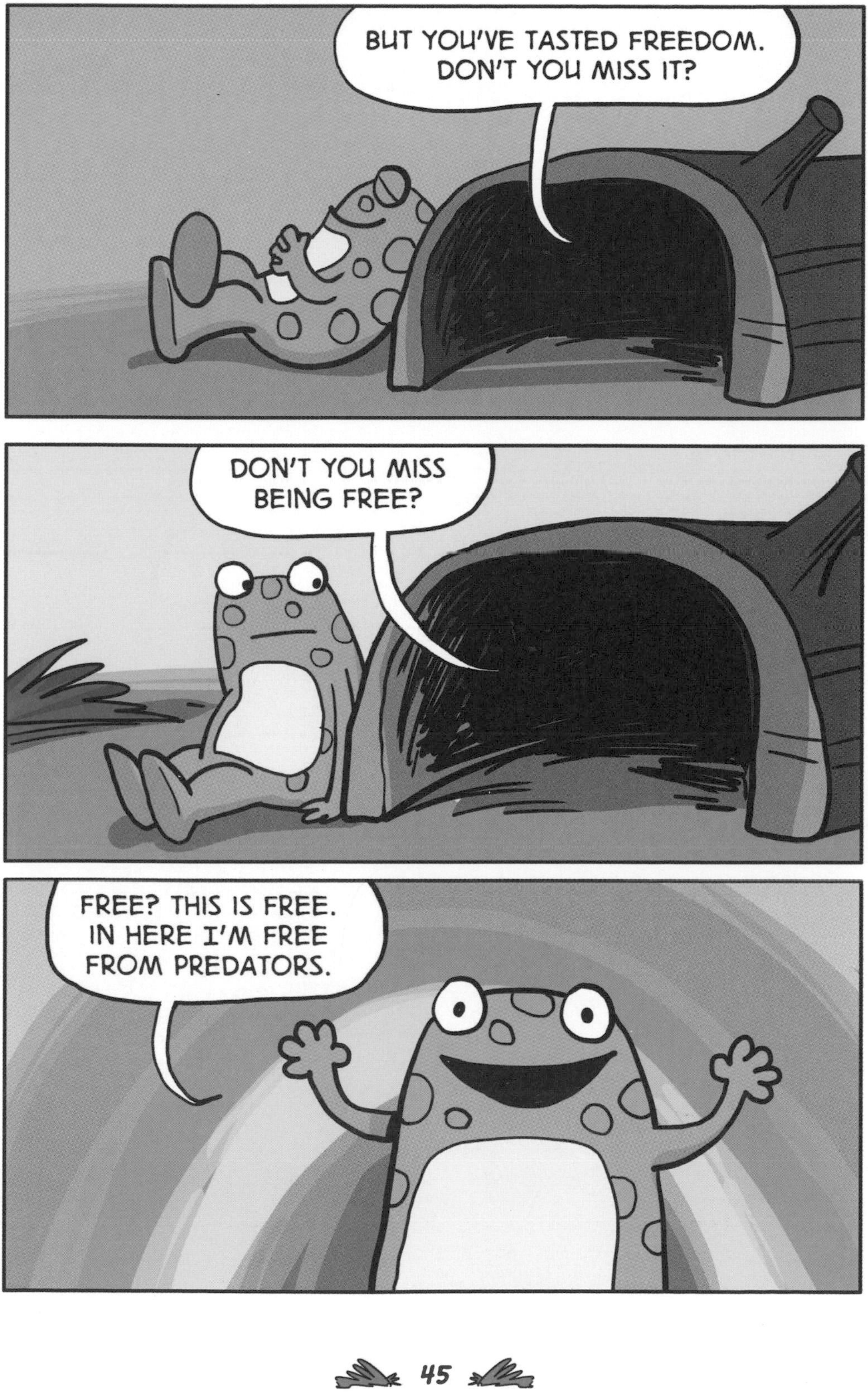
BUT YOU'VE TASTED FREEDOM. DON'T YOU MISS IT?
DON'T YOU MISS BEING FREE?
FREE? THIS IS FREE. IN HERE I'M FREE FROM PREDATORS.

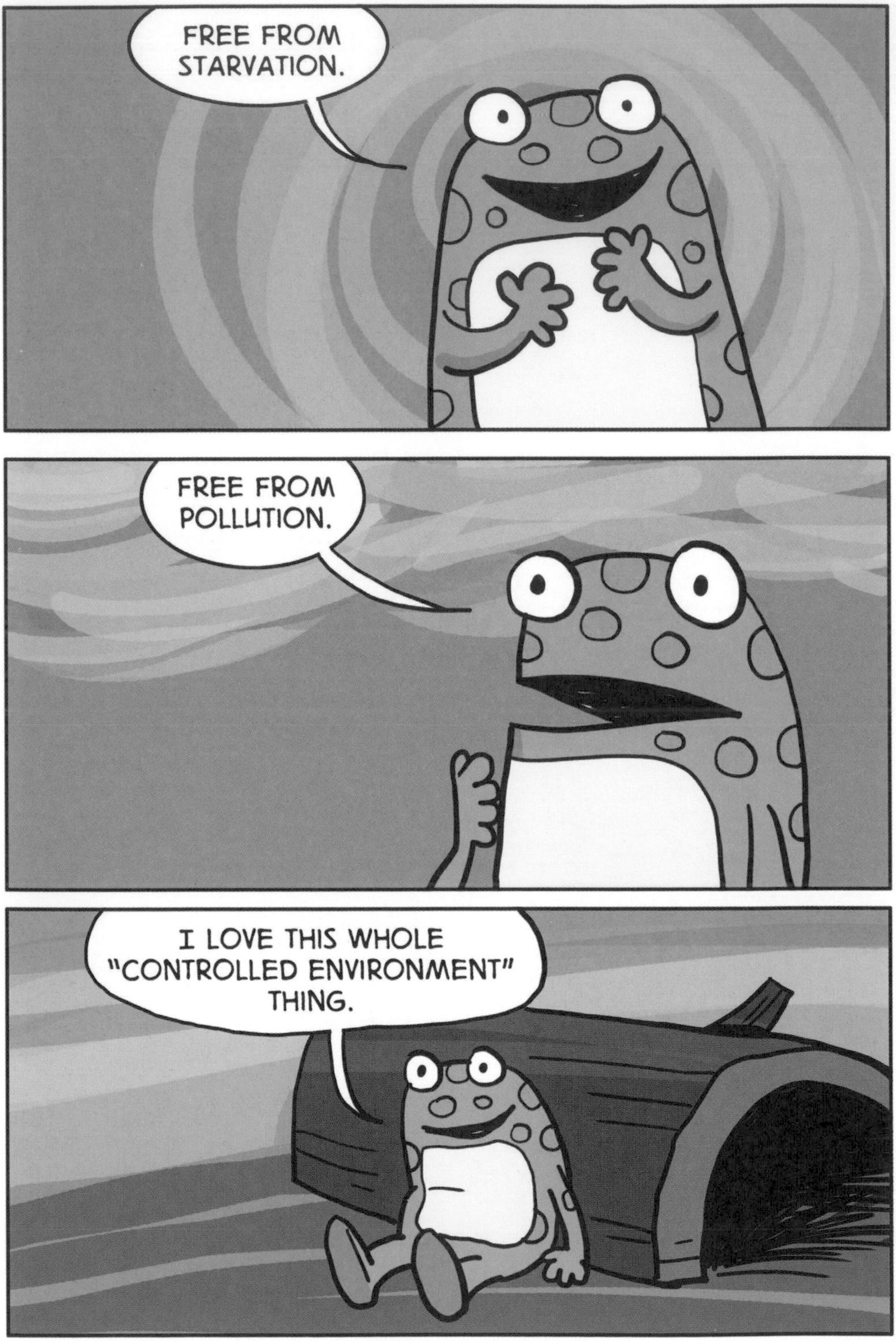
FREE FROM STARVATION.
FREE FROM POLLUTION.
I LOVE THIS WHOLE "CONTROLLED ENVIRONMENT" THING.

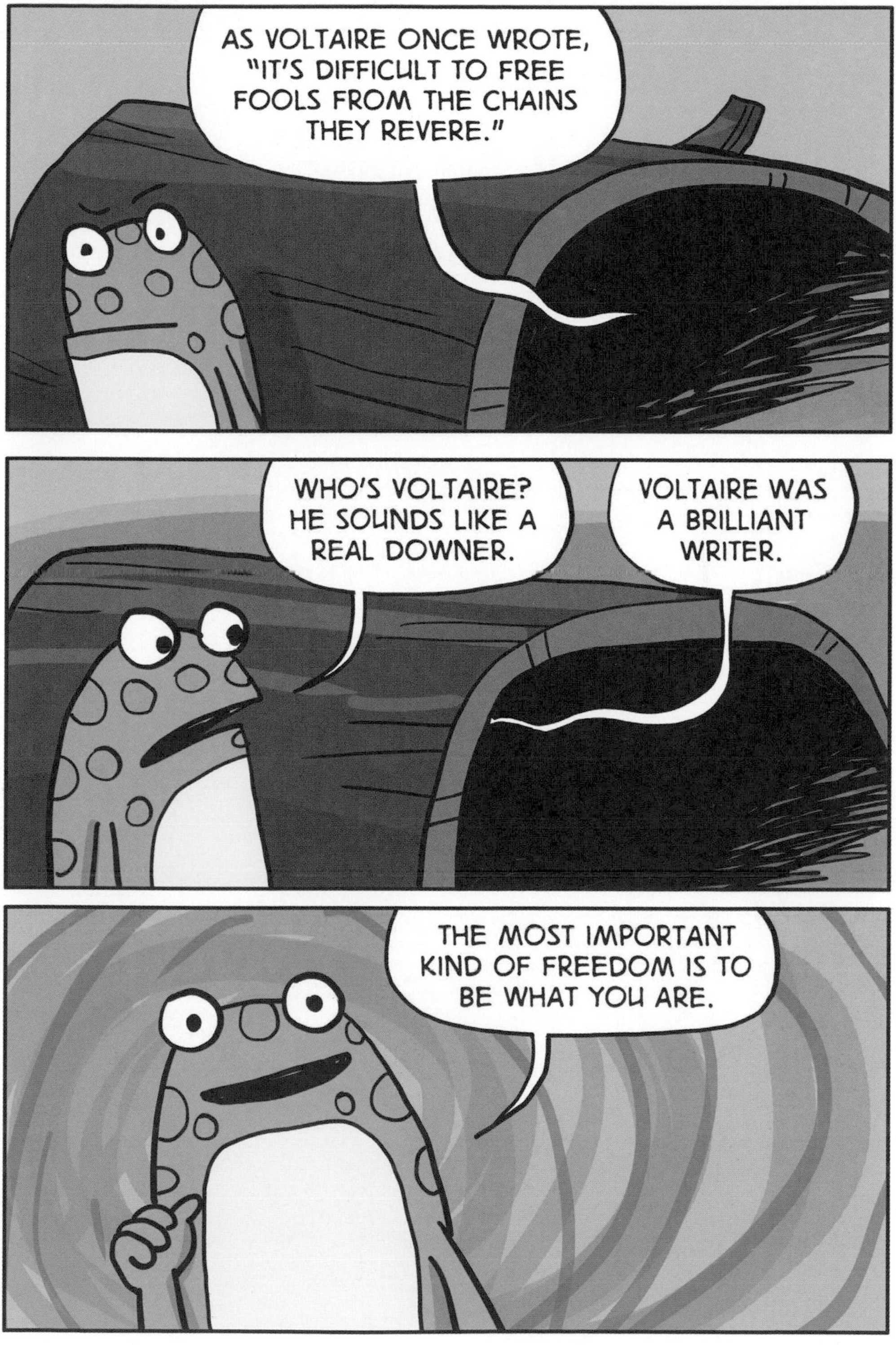
AS VOLTAIRE ONCE WROTE, "IT'S DIFFICULT TO FREE FOOLS FROM THE CHAINS THEY REVERE."
WHO'S VOLTAIRE? HE SOUNDS LIKE A REAL DOWNER.
VOLTAIRE WAS A BRILLIANT WRITER.
THE MOST IMPORTANT KIND OF FREEDOM IS TO BE WHAT YOU ARE.

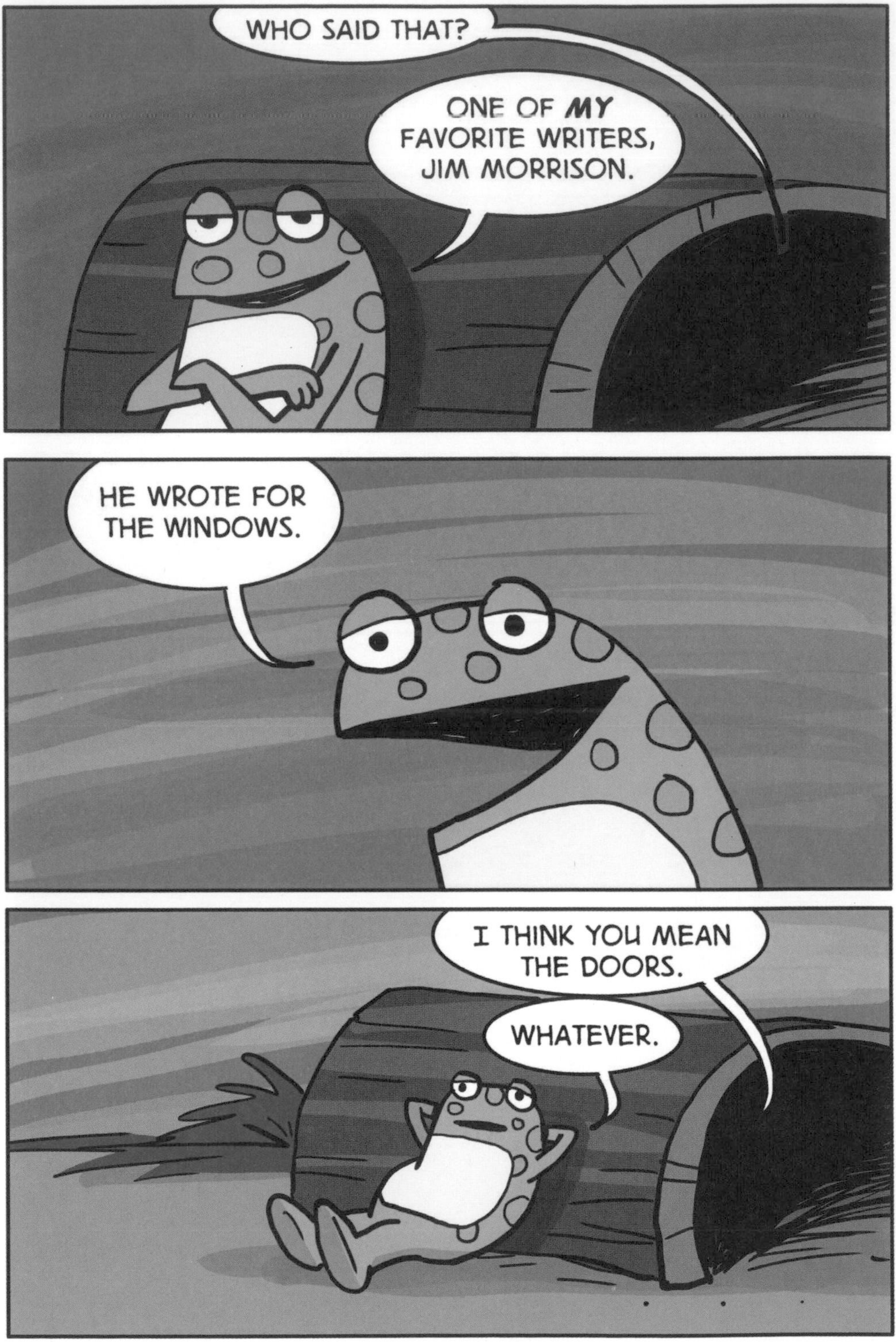
WHO SAID THAT?
ONE OF MY FAVORITE WRITERS, JIM MORRISON.
HE WROTE FOR THE WINDOWS.
I THINK YOU MEAN THE DOORS.
WHATEVER.

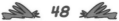

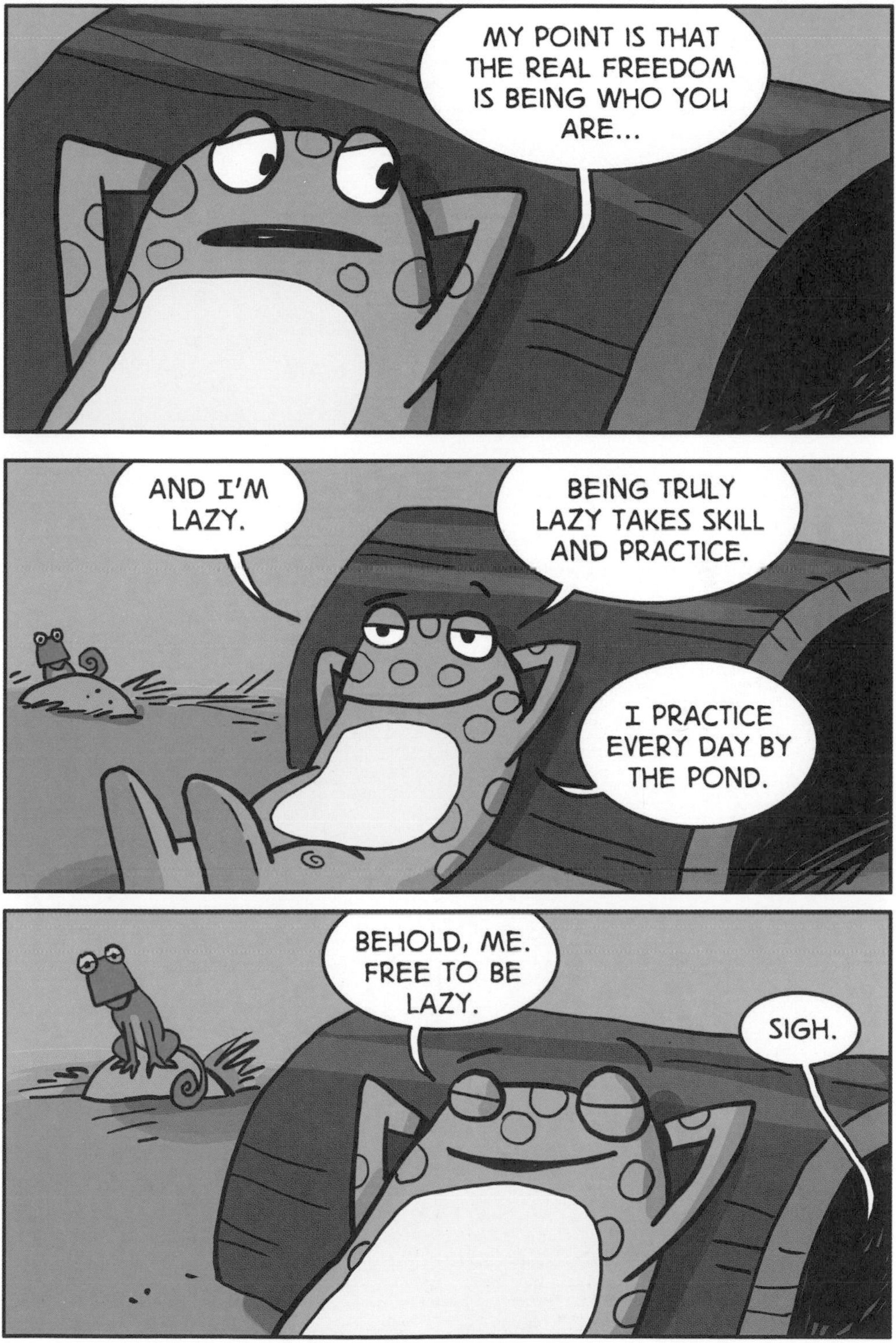
MY POINT IS THAT THE REAL FREEDOM IS BEING WHO YOU ARE...
AND I'M LAZY.
BEING TRULY LAZY TAKES SKILL AND PRACTICE.
I PRACTICE EVERY DAY BY THE POND.
BEHOLD, ME. FREE TO BE LAZY.
SIGH.

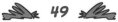

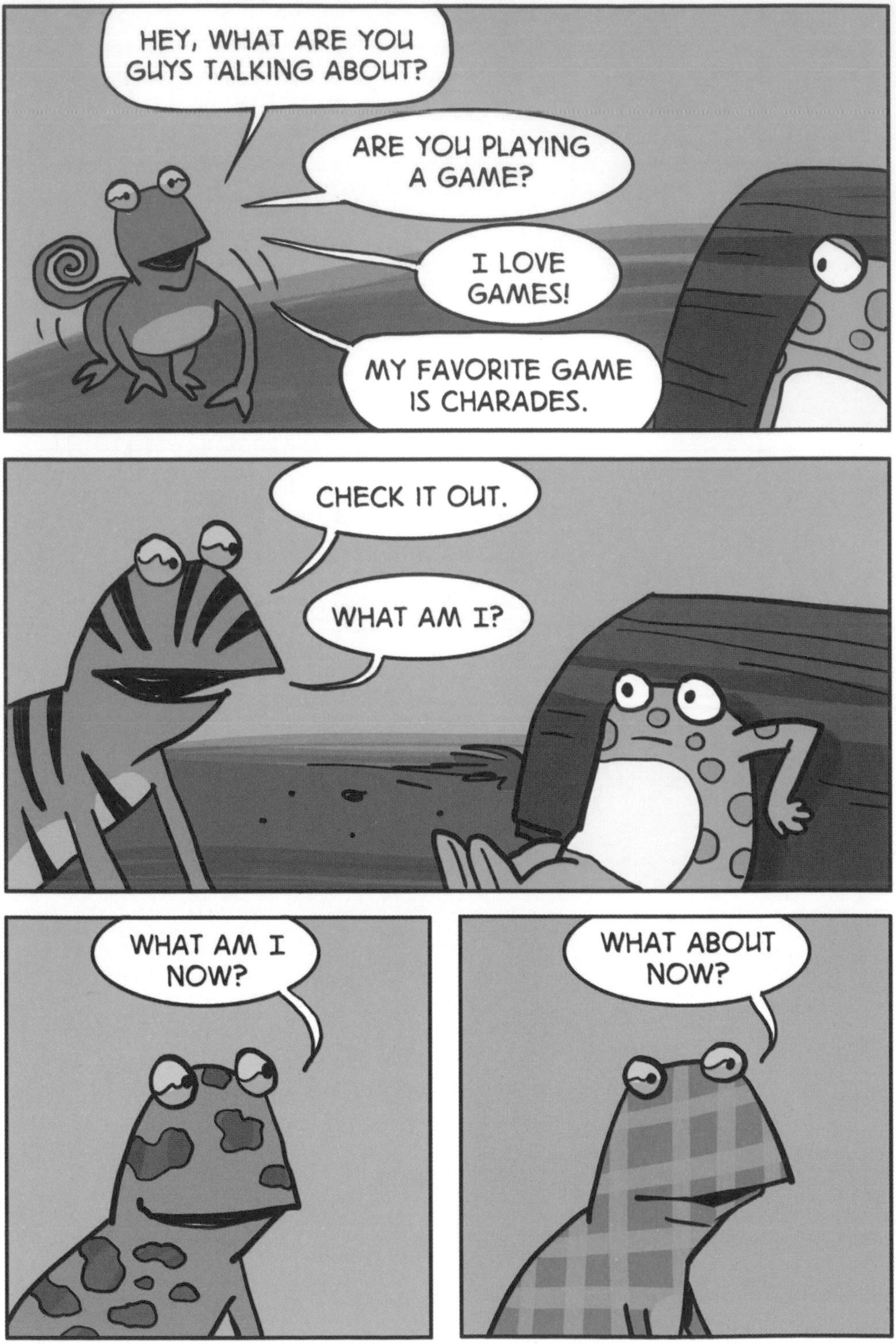
HEY, WHAT ARE YOU GUYS TALKING ABOUT?
ARE YOU PLAYING A GAME?
I LOVE GAMES!
MY FAVORITE GAME IS CHARADES.
CHECK IT OUT.
WHAT AM I?
WHAT AM I NOW?
WHAT ABOUT NOW?

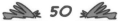

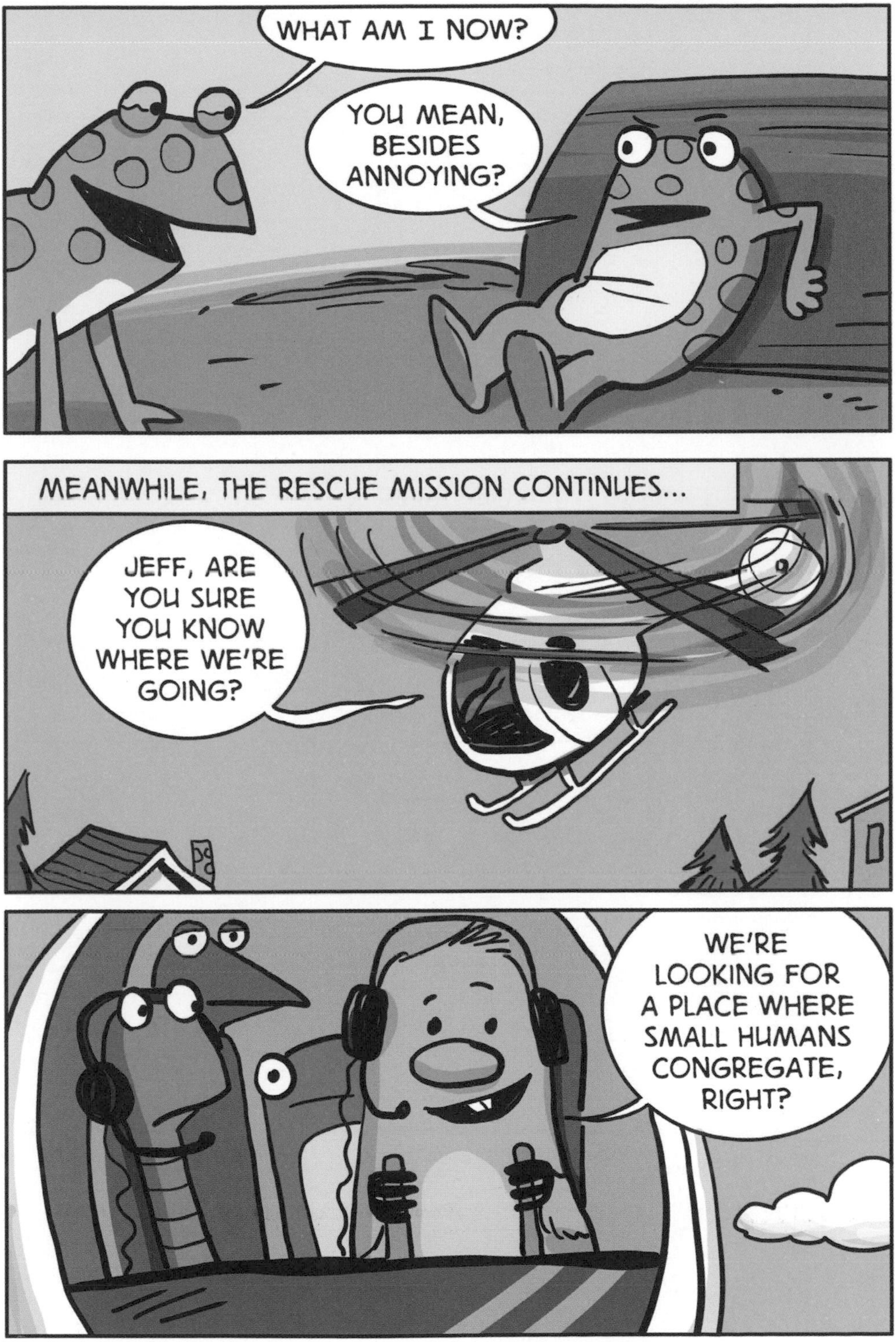
WHAT AM I NOW?
YOU MEAN, BESIDES ANNOYING?
MEANWHILE, THE RESCUE MISSION CONTINUES...
JEFF, ARE YOU SURE YOU KNOW WHERE WE'RE GOING?
WE'RE LOOKING FOR A PLACE WHERE SMALL HUMANS CONGREGATE, RIGHT?

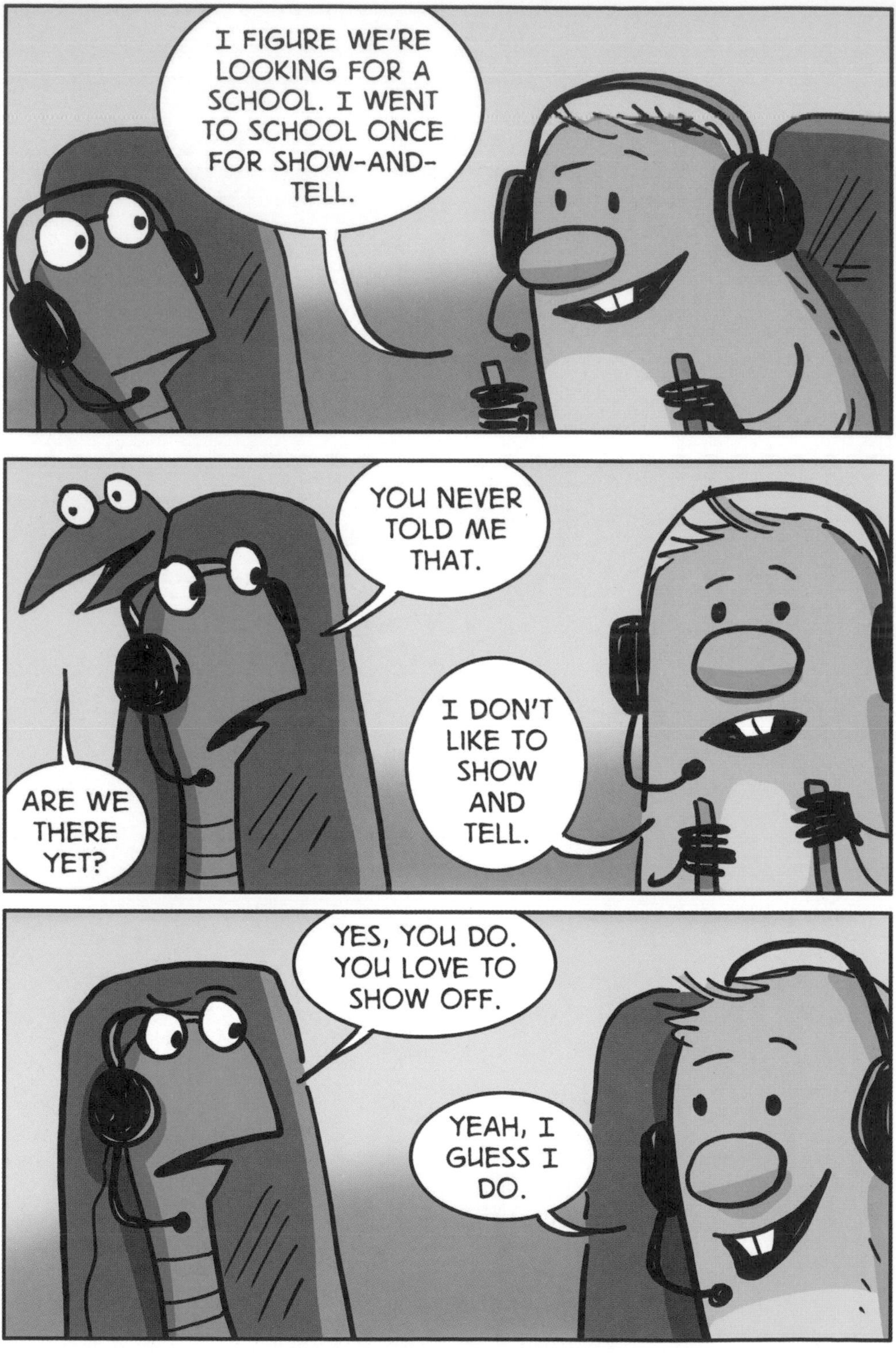
I FIGURE WE'RE LOOKING FOR A SCHOOL. I WENT TO SCHOOL ONCE FOR SHOW-AND-TELL.
YOU NEVER TOLD ME THAT.
ARE WE THERE YET?
I DON'T LIKE TO SHOW AND TELL.
YES, YOU DO. YOU LOVE TO SHOW OFF.
YEAH, I GUESS I DO.

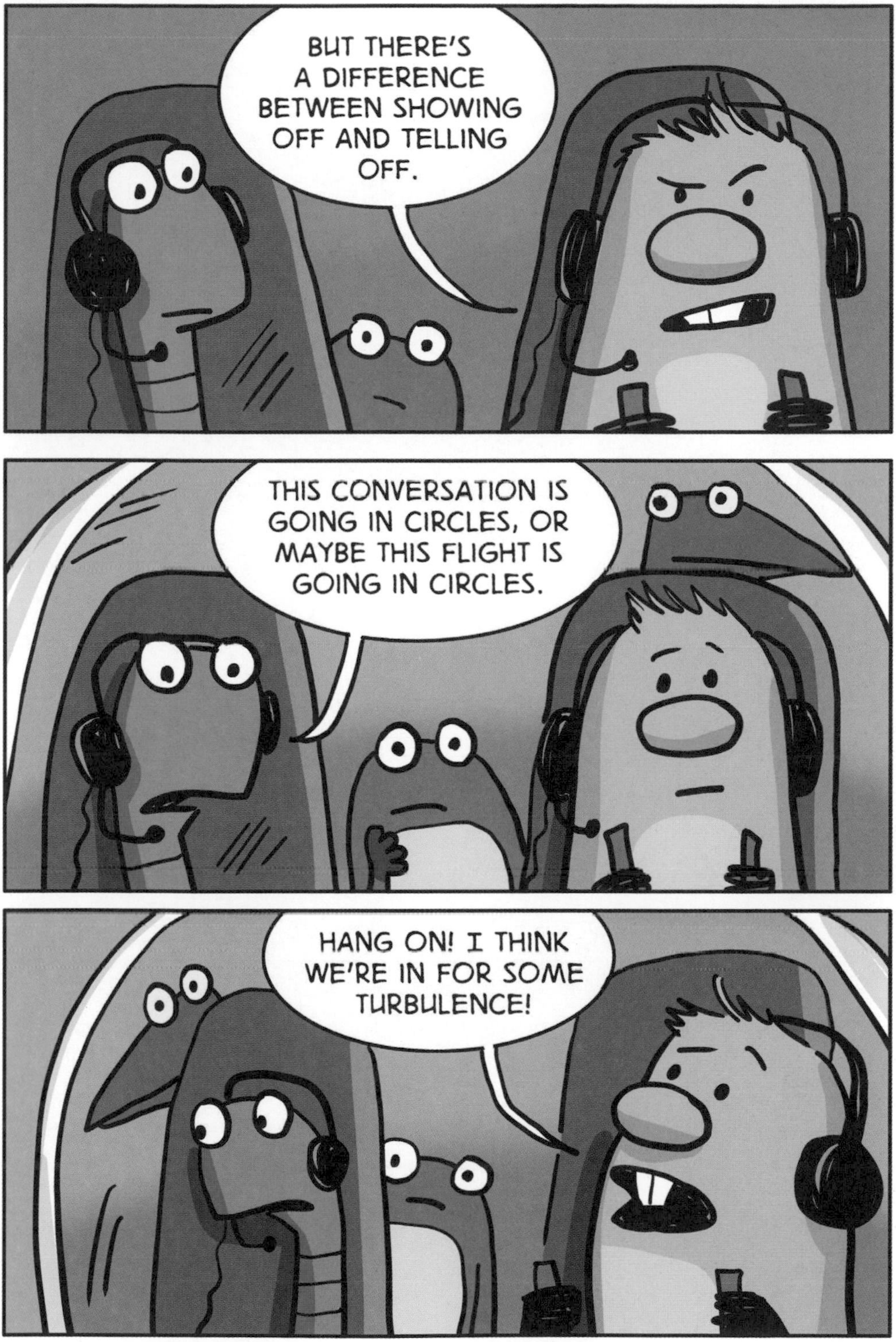
BUT THERE'S A DIFFERENCE BETWEEN SHOWING OFF AND TELLING OFF.
THIS CONVERSATION IS GOING IN CIRCLES, OR MAYBE THIS FLIGHT IS GOING IN CIRCLES.
HANG ON! I THINK WE'RE IN FOR SOME TURBULENCE!

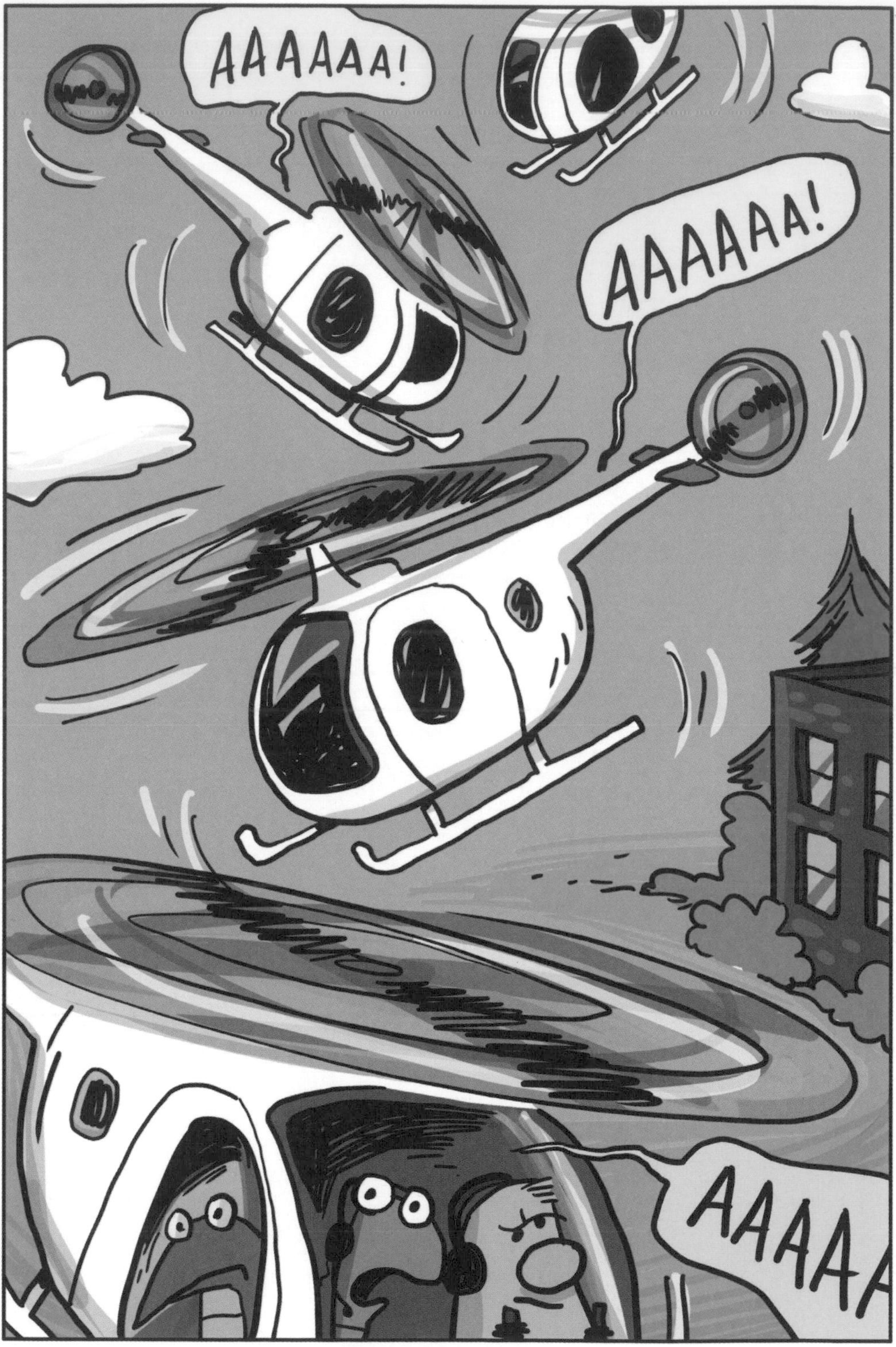
AAAAAA!
AAAAAA!
AAAAA

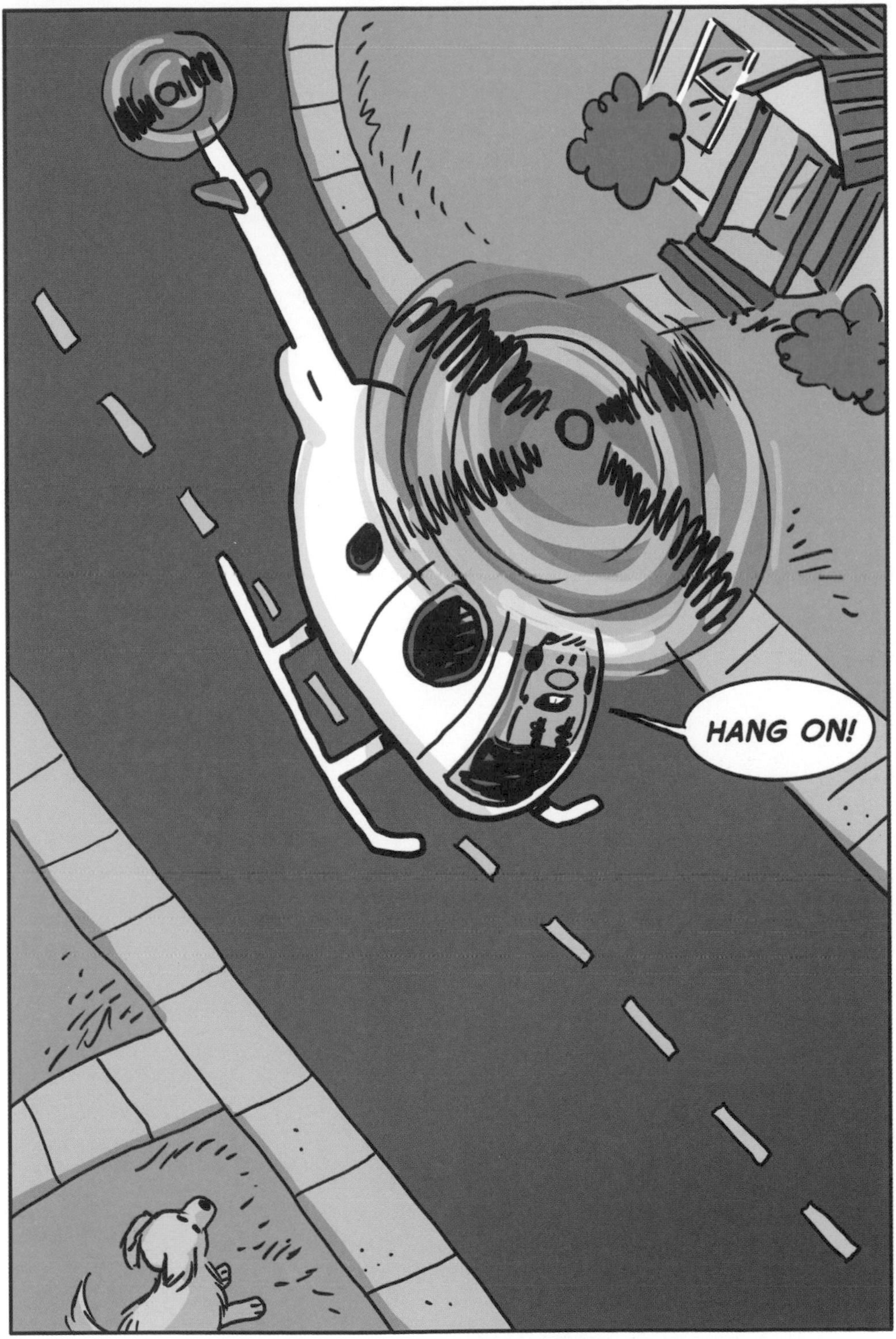
HANG ON!

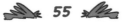

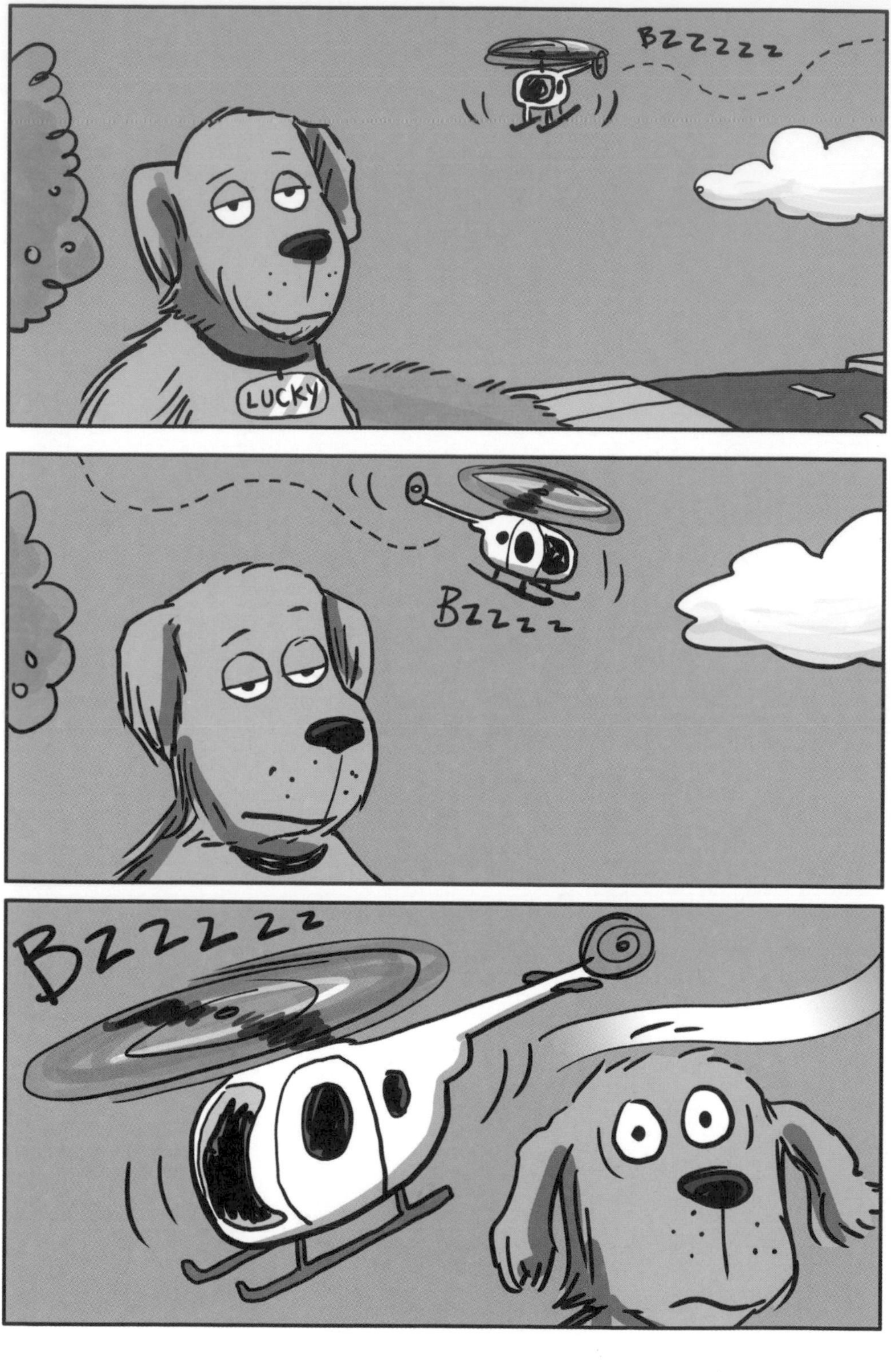
BZZZZZZ
LUCKY
BZZZZZ
BZZZZZZ

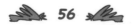

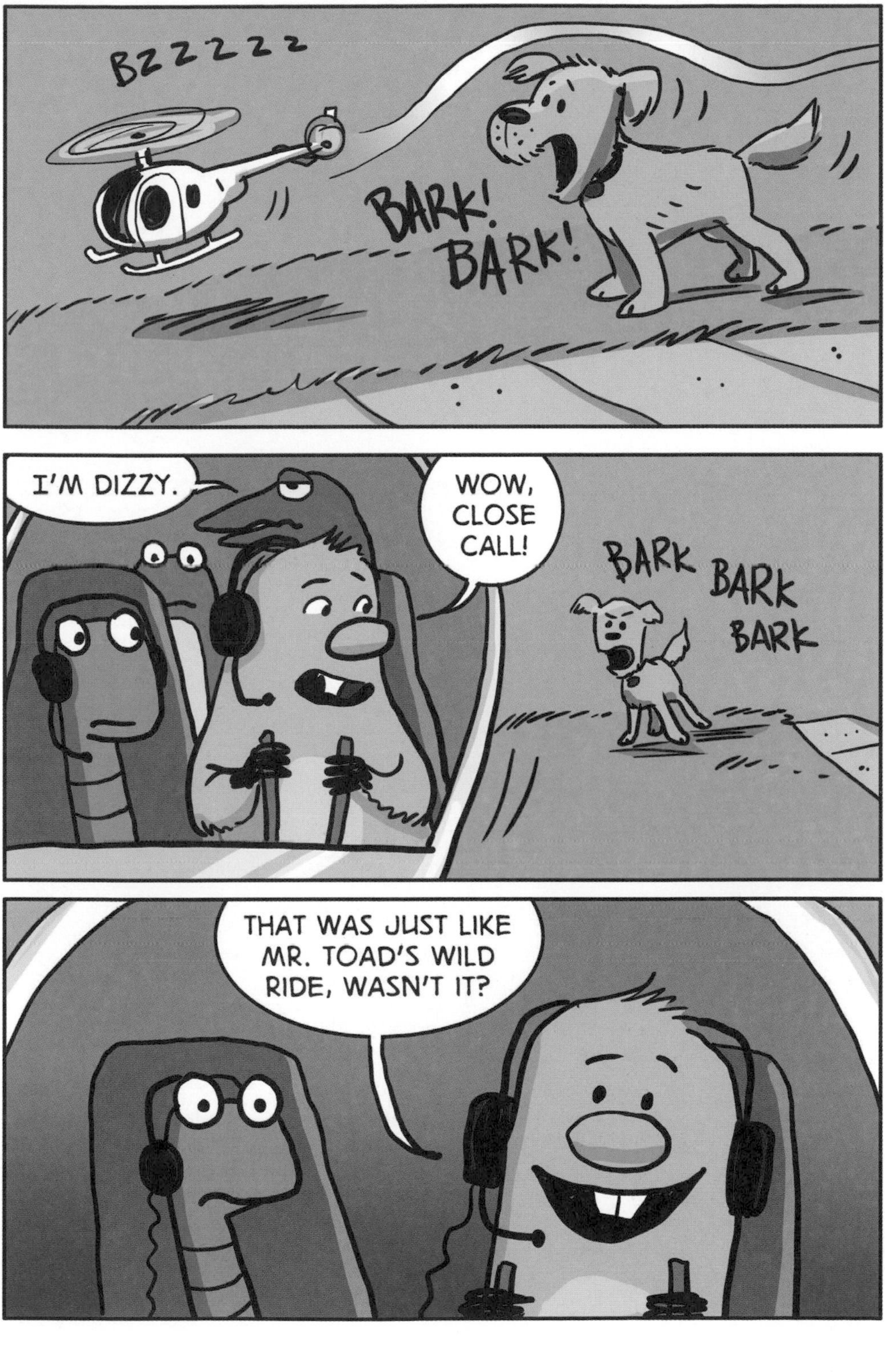
BZZZZZZ
BARK! BARK!
I'M DIZZY.
WOW, CLOSE CALL!
BARK BARK BARK
THAT WAS JUST LIKE MR. TOAD'S WILD RIDE, WASN'T IT?

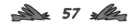

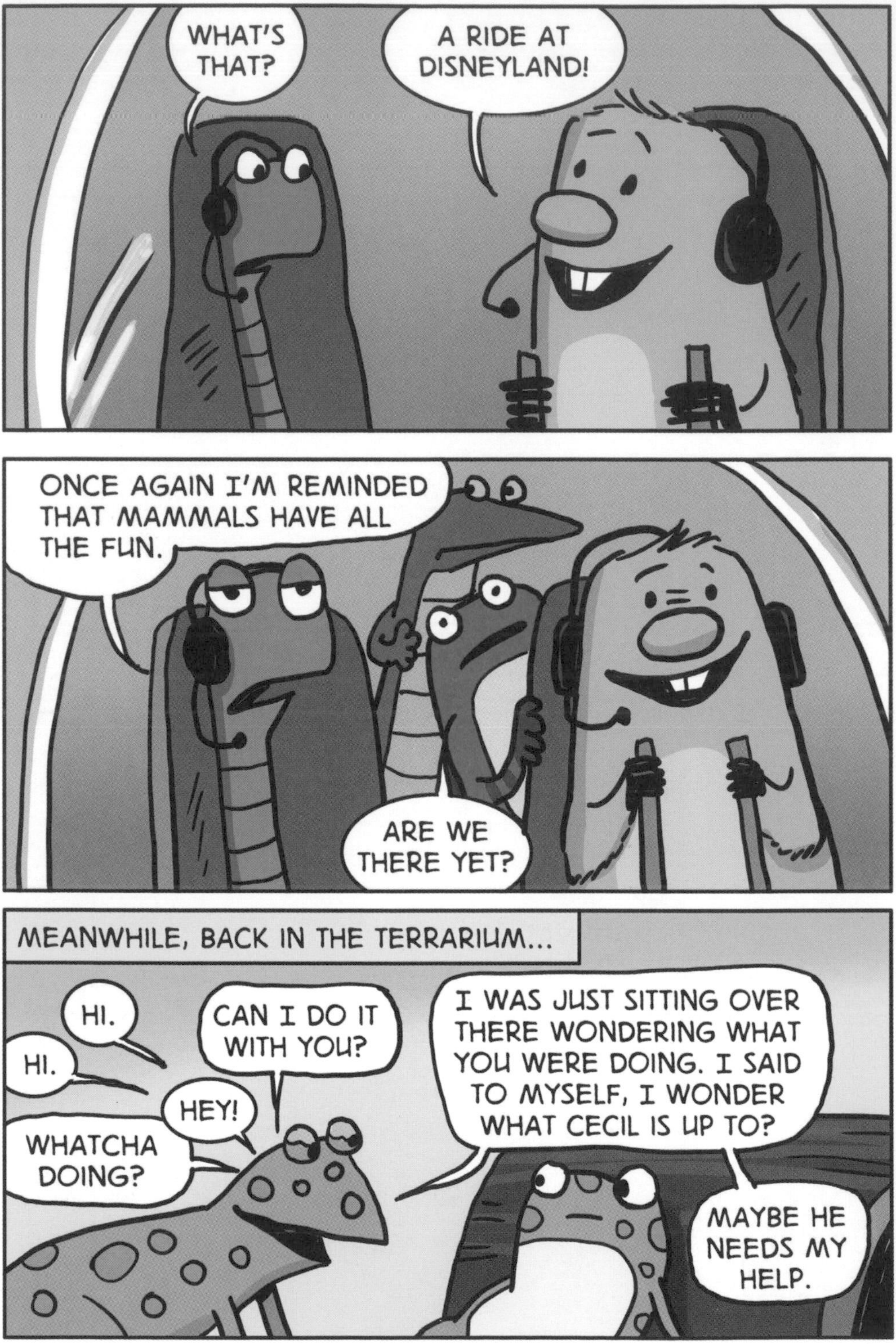
WHAT'S THAT?
A RIDE AT DISNEYLAND!
ONCE AGAIN I'M REMINDED THAT MAMMALS HAVE ALL THE FUN.
ARE WE THERE YET?
MEANWHILE, BACK IN THE TERRARIUM...
HI.
HI.
WHATCHA DOING?
HEY!
CAN I DO IT WITH YOU?
I WAS JUST SITTING OVER THERE WONDERING WHAT YOU WERE DOING. I SAID TO MYSELF, I WONDER WHAT CECIL IS UP TO?
MAYBE HE NEEDS MY HELP.

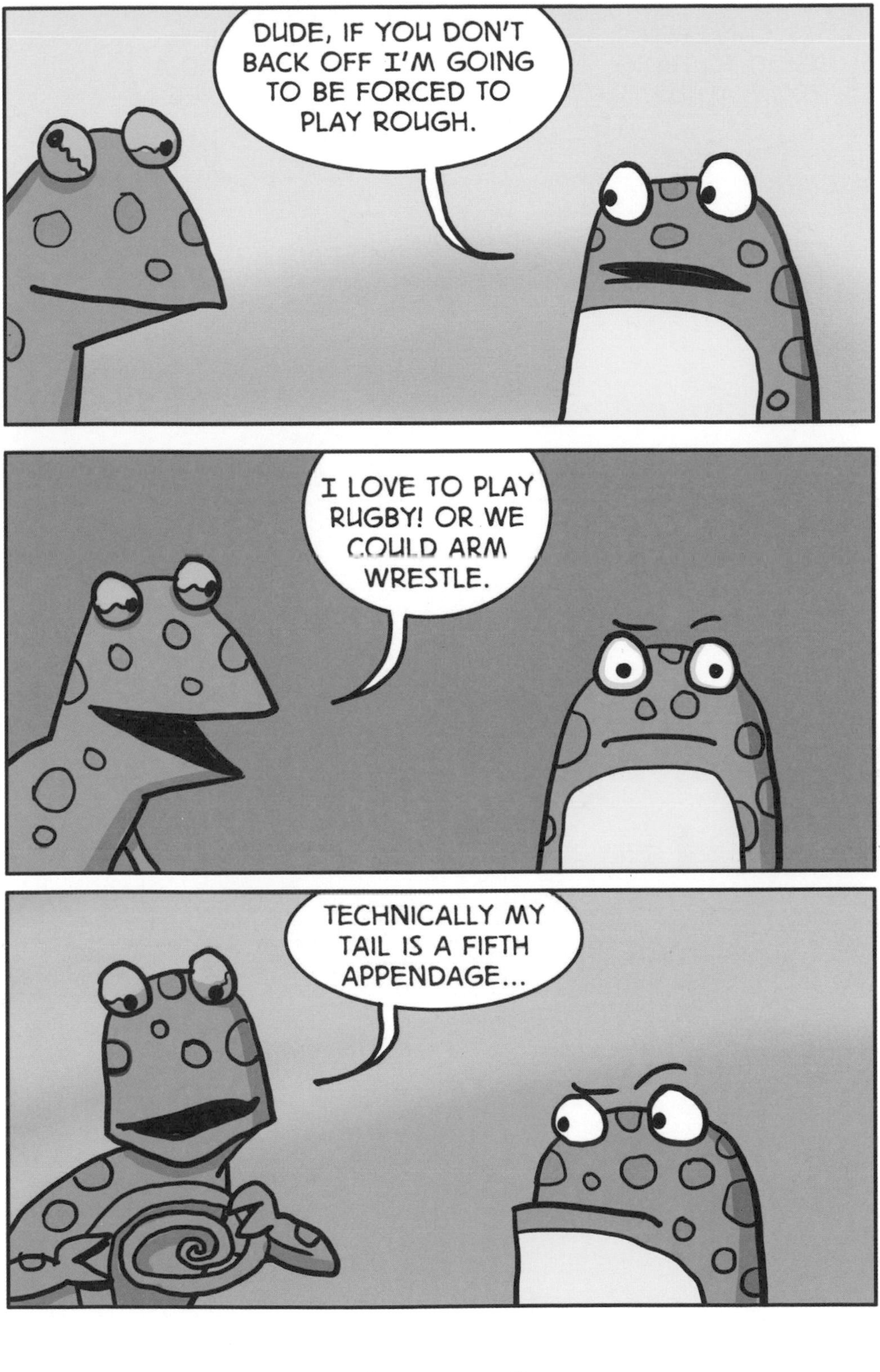
DUDE, IF YOU DON'T BACK OFF I'M GOING TO BE FORCED TO PLAY ROUGH.
I LOVE TO PLAY RUGBY! OR WE COULD ARM WRESTLE.
TECHNICALLY MY TAIL IS A FIFTH APPENDAGE...

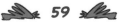

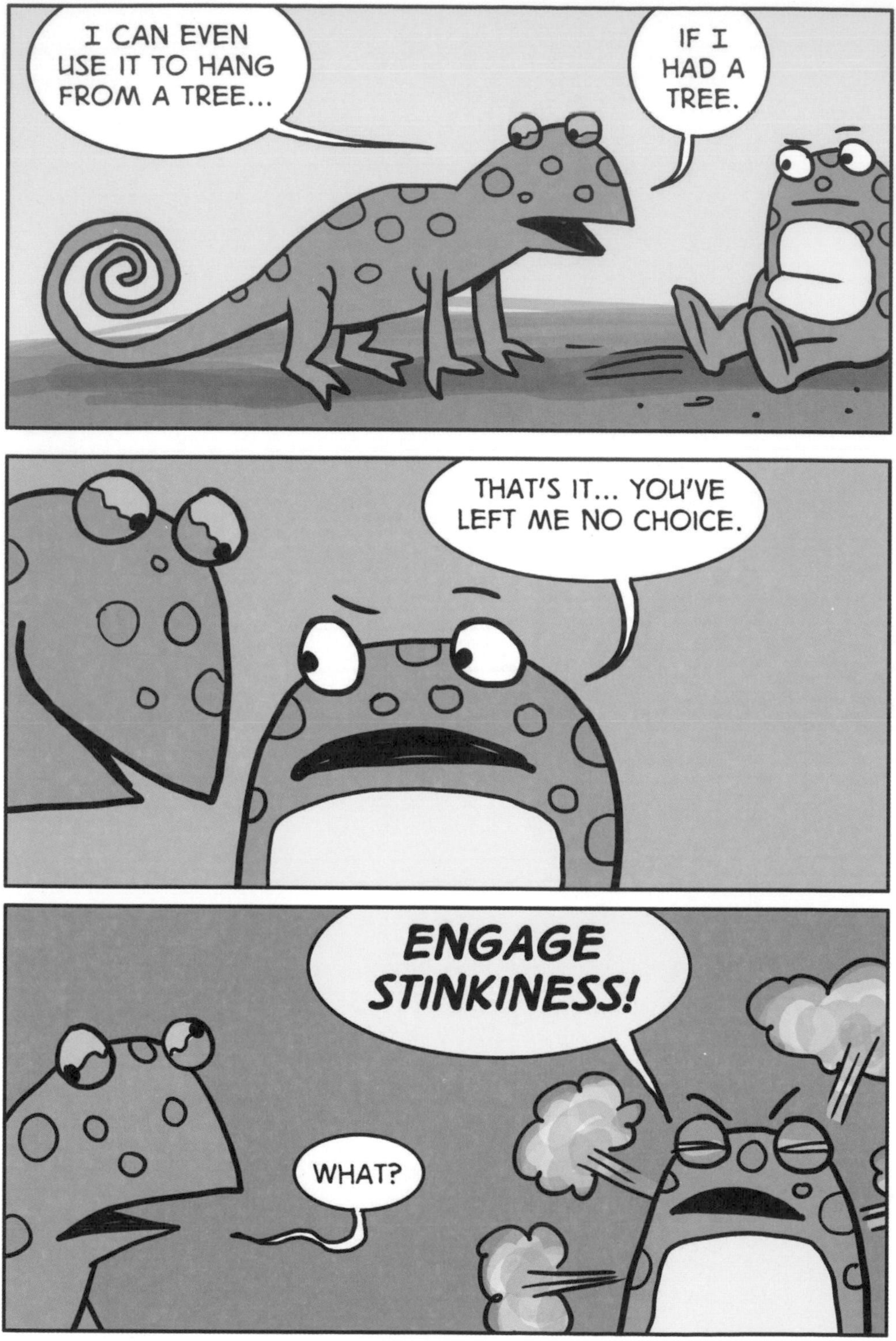
I CAN EVEN USE IT TO HANG FROM A TREE...
IF I HAD A TREE.
THAT'S IT... YOU'VE LEFT ME NO CHOICE.
ENGAGE STINKINESS!
WHAT?

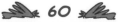

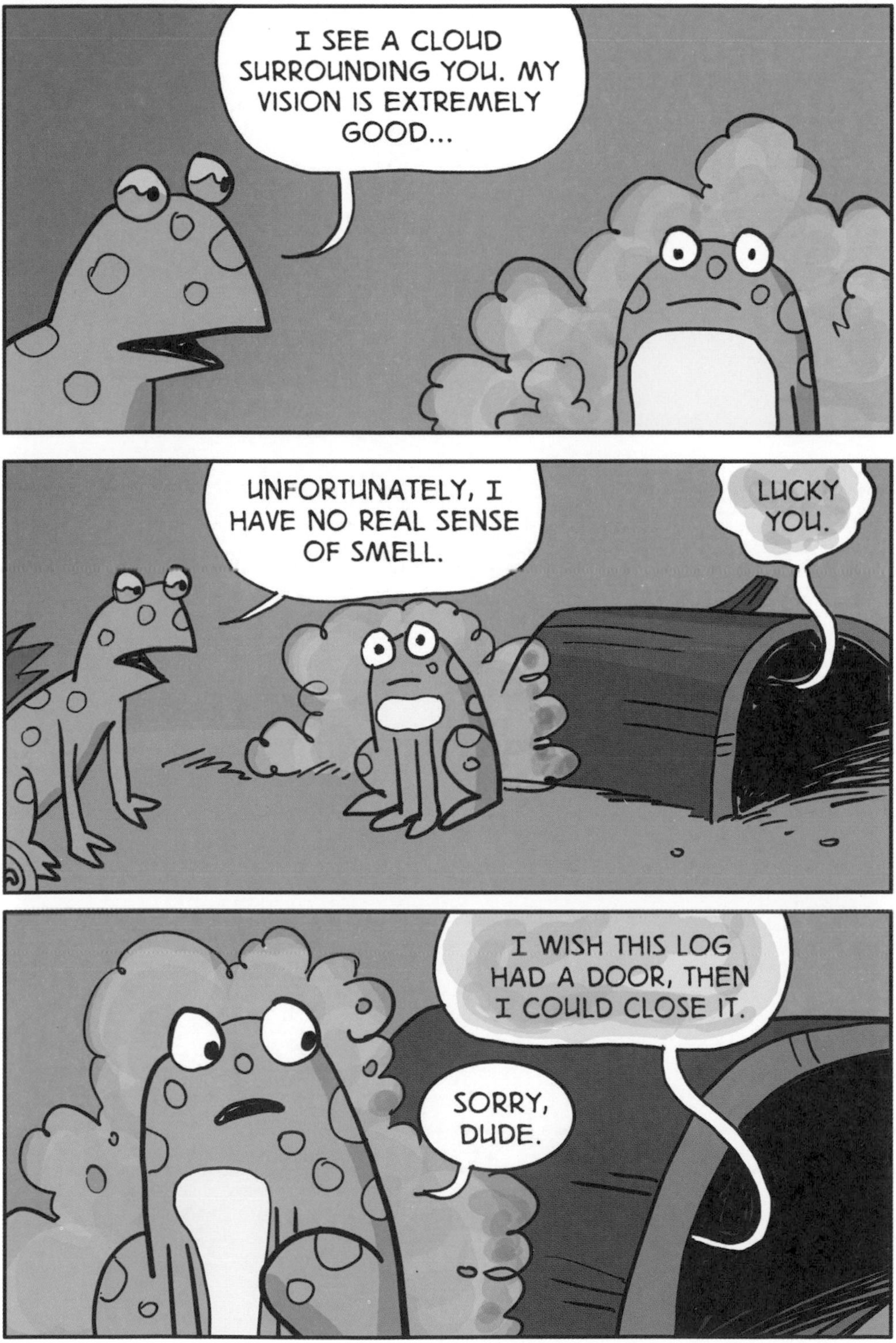
I SEE A CLOUD SURROUNDING YOU. MY VISION IS EXTREMELY GOOD...
UNFORTUNATELY, I HAVE NO REAL SENSE OF SMELL.
LUCKY YOU.
I WISH THIS LOG HAD A DOOR, THEN I COULD CLOSE IT.
SORRY, DUDE.

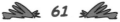

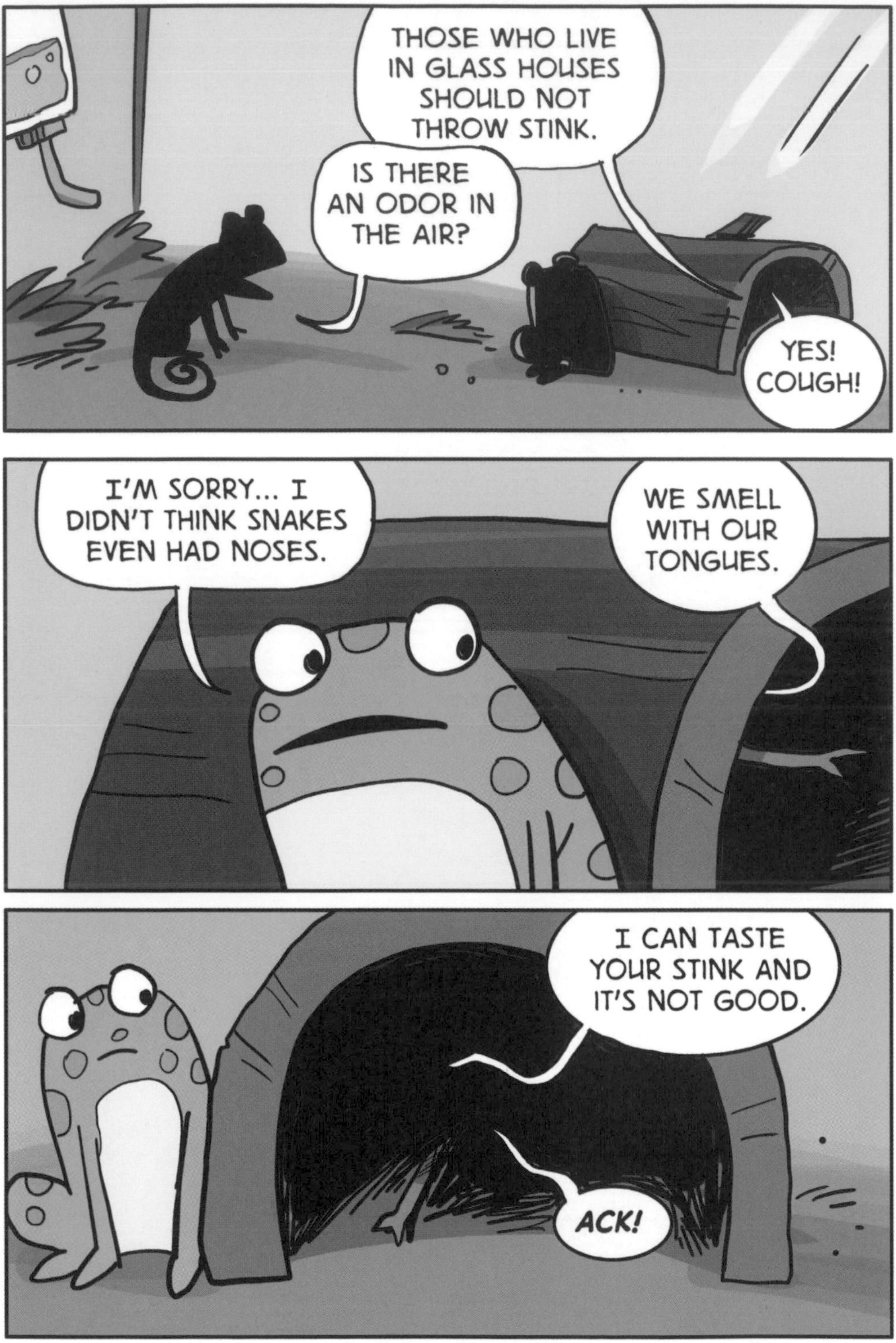

THOSE WHO LIVE IN GLASS HOUSES SHOULD NOT THROW STINK.
IS THERE AN ODOR IN THE AIR?
YES! COUGH!
I'M SORRY... I DIDN'T THINK SNAKES EVEN HAD NOSES.
WE SMELL WITH OUR TONGUES.
I CAN TASTE YOUR STINK AND IT'S NOT GOOD.
ACK!

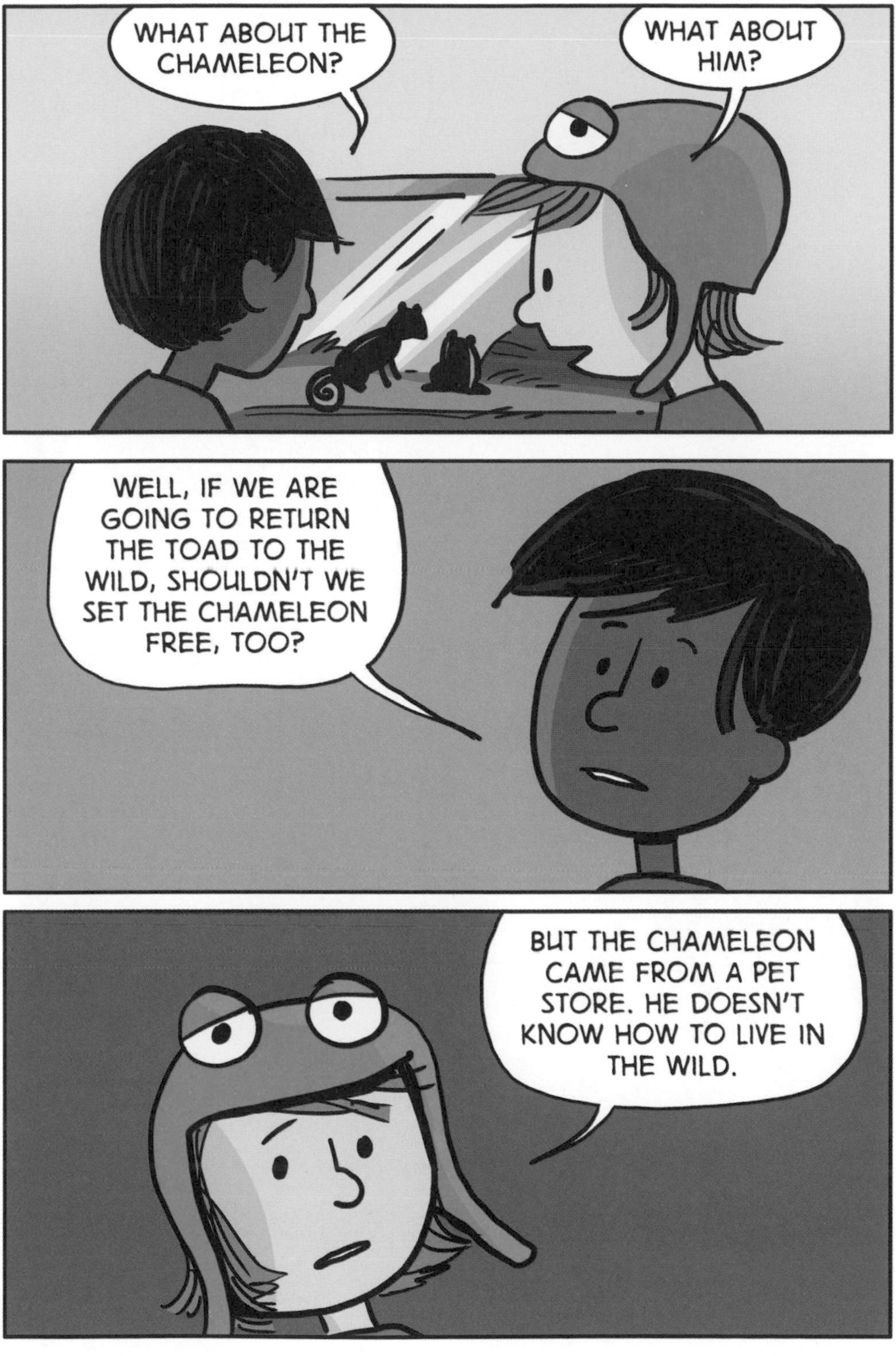
WHAT ABOUT THE CHAMELEON?
WHAT ABOUT HIM?
WELL, IF WE ARE GOING TO RETURN THE TOAD TO THE WILD, SHOULDN'T WE SET THE CHAMELEON FREE, TOO?
BUT THE CHAMELEON CAME FROM A PET STORE. HE DOESN'T KNOW HOW TO LIVE IN THE WILD.

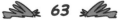

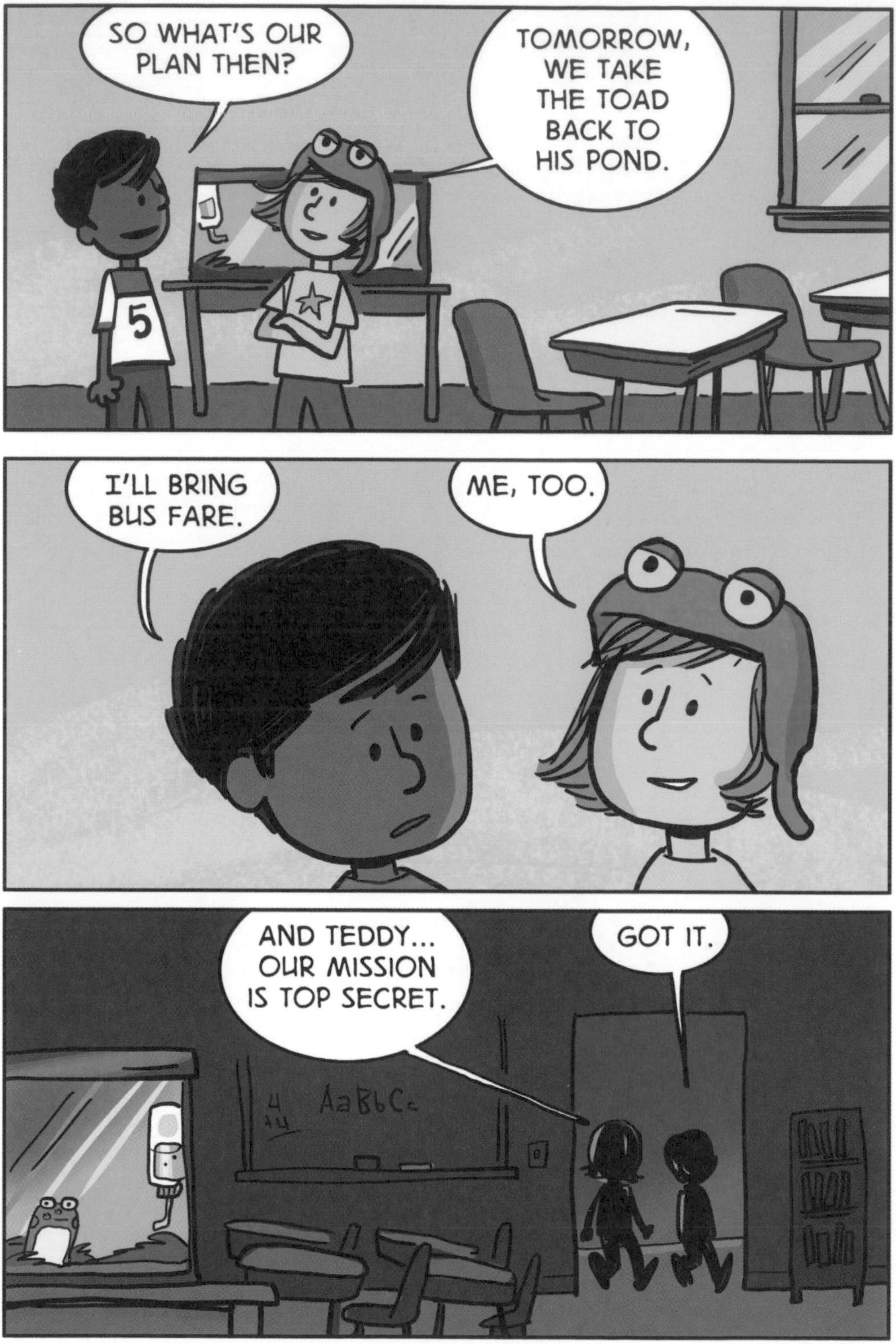
SO WHAT'S OUR PLAN THEN?
TOMORROW, WE TAKE THE TOAD BACK TO HIS POND.
I'LL BRING BUS FARE.
ME, TOO.
AND TEDDY... OUR MISSION IS TOP SECRET.
GOT IT.
AaBbCc

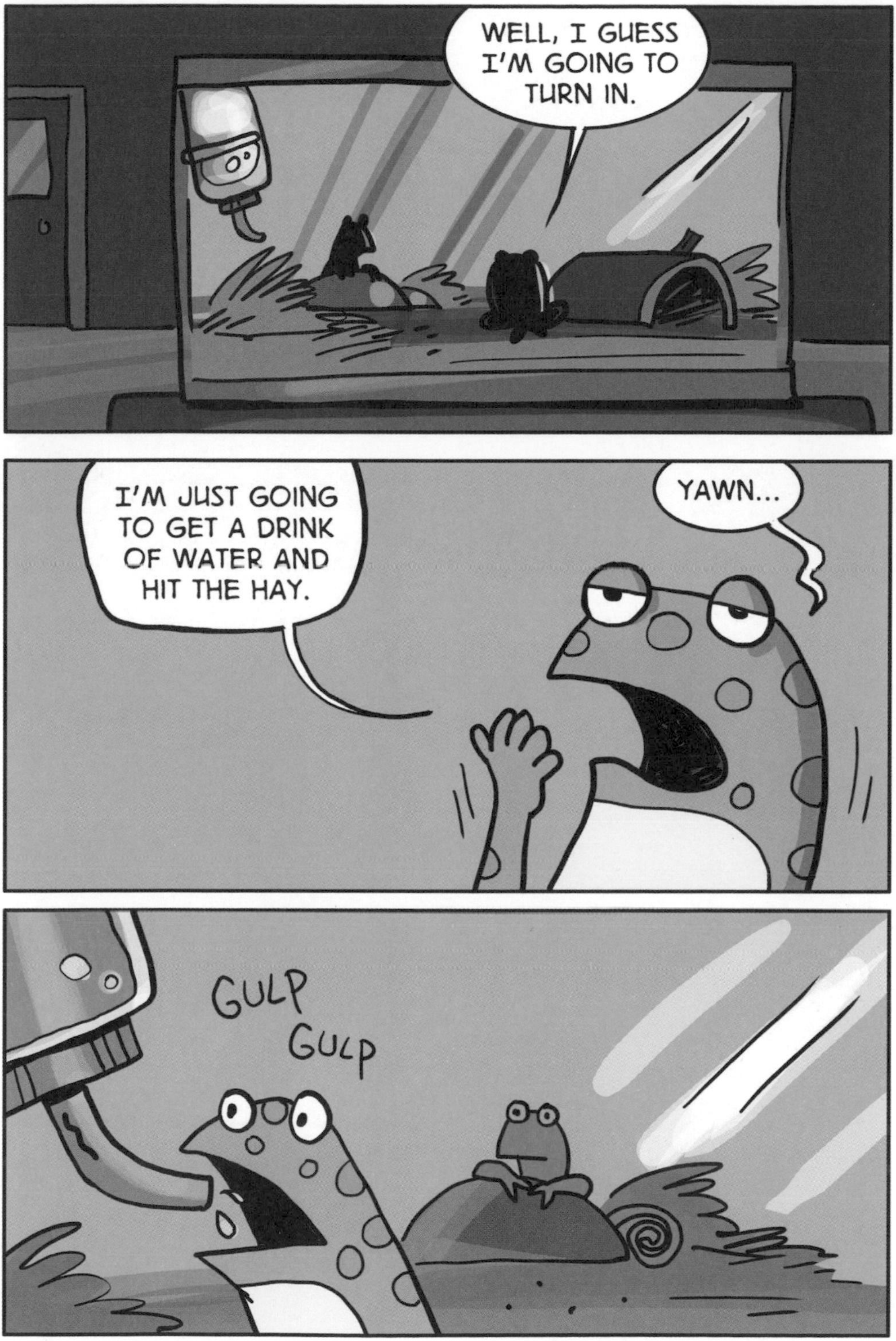
WELL, I GUESS I'M GOING TO TURN IN.
I'M JUST GOING TO GET A DRINK OF WATER AND HIT THE HAY.
YAWN...
GULP
GULP

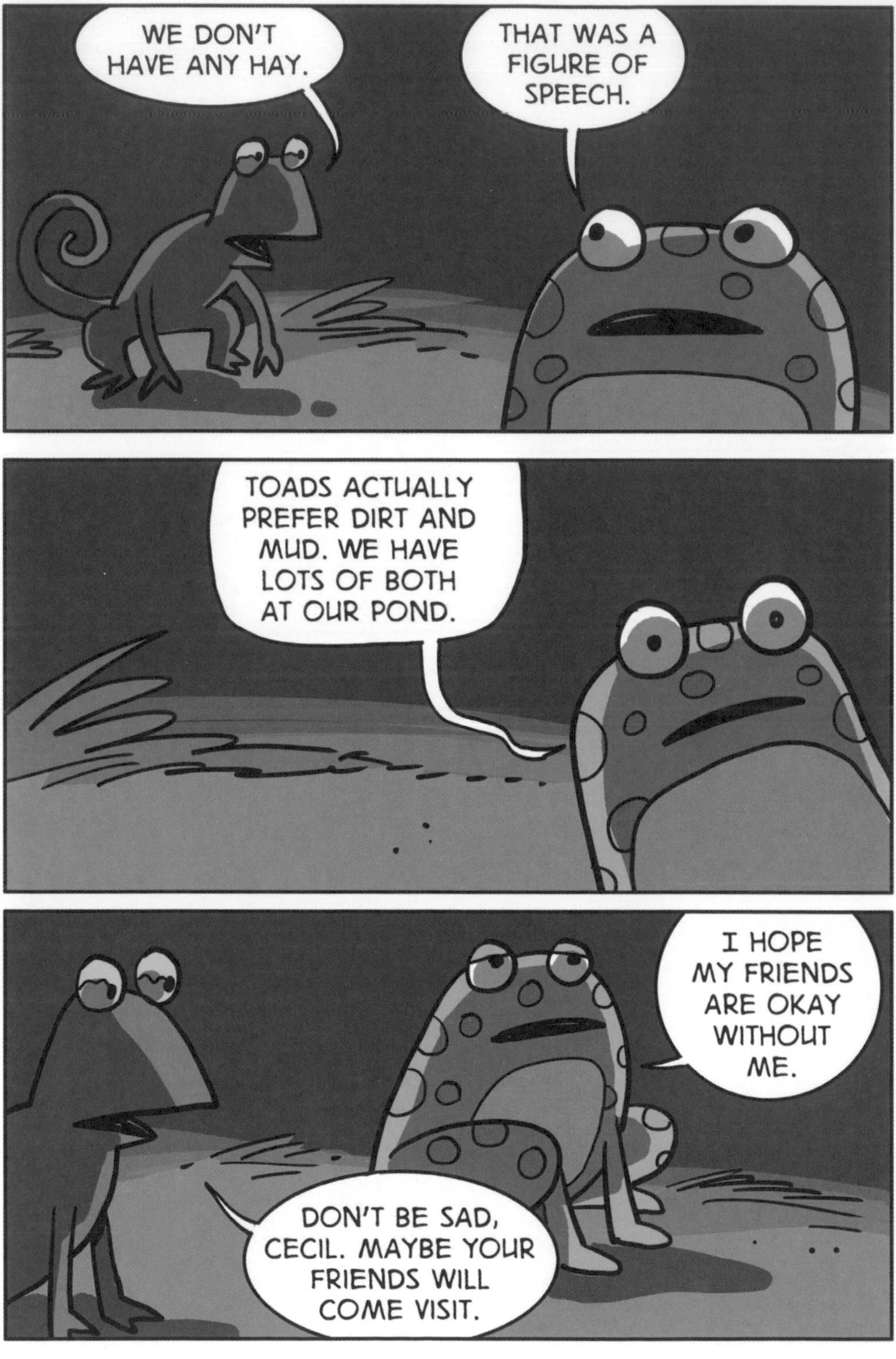
WE DON'T HAVE ANY HAY.
THAT WAS A FIGURE OF SPEECH.
TOADS ACTUALLY PREFER DIRT AND MUD. WE HAVE LOTS OF BOTH AT OUR POND.
I HOPE MY FRIENDS ARE OKAY WITHOUT ME.
DON'T BE SAD, CECIL. MAYBE YOUR FRIENDS WILL COME VISIT.

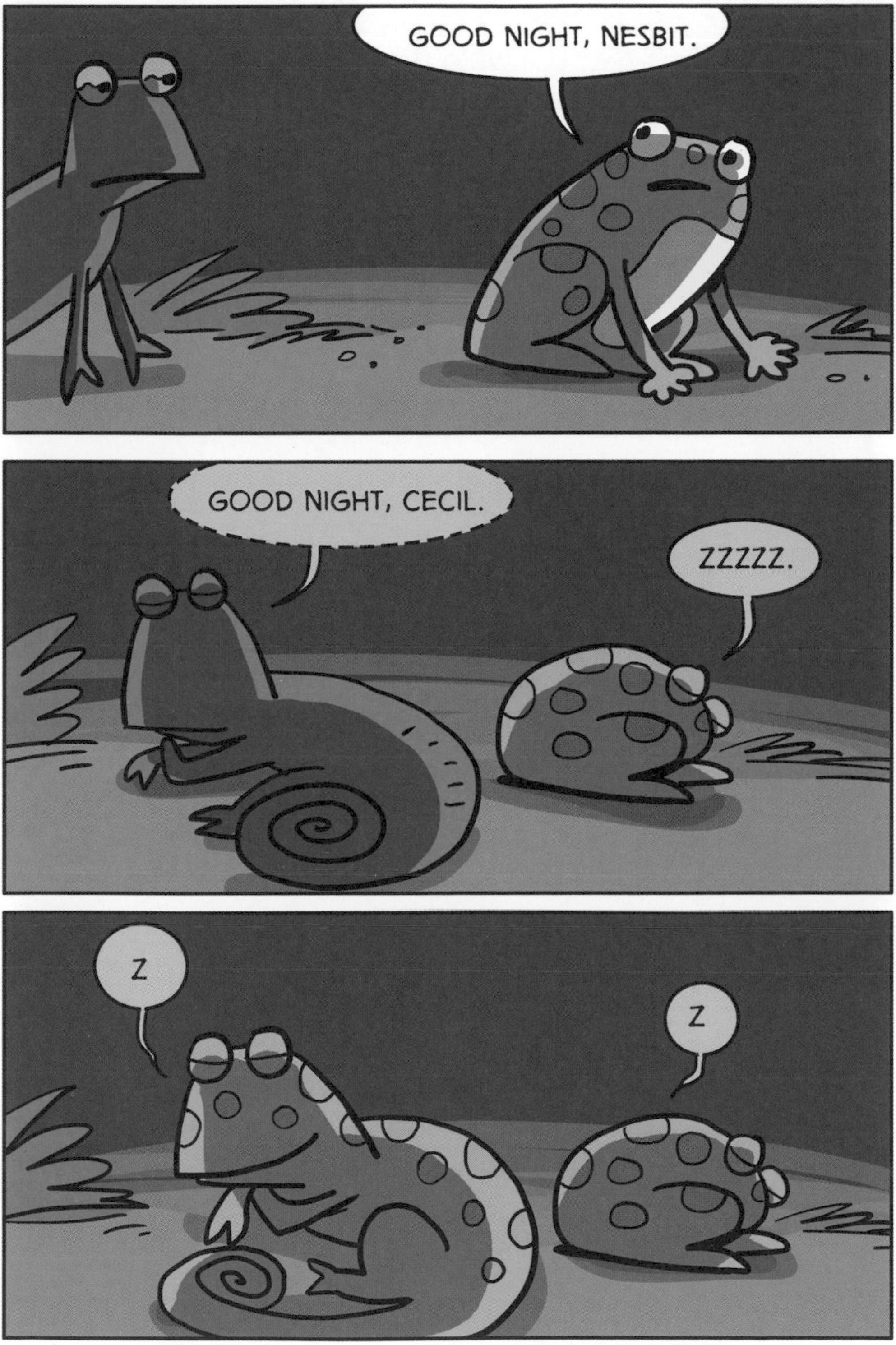
GOOD NIGHT, NESBIT.
GOOD NIGHT, CECIL.
ZZZZZ.
Z
Z

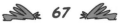

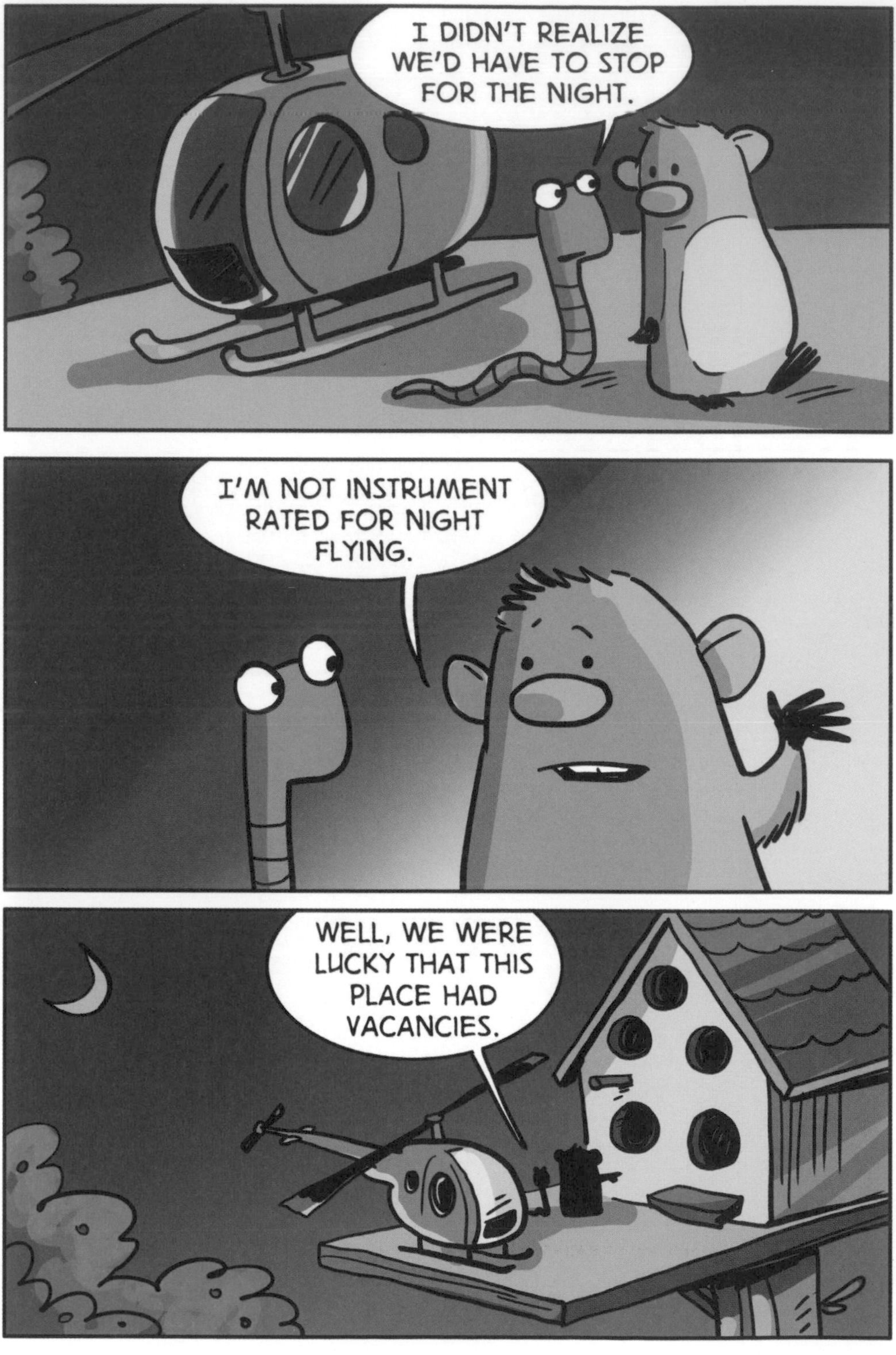
I DIDN'T REALIZE WE'D HAVE TO STOP FOR THE NIGHT.
I'M NOT INSTRUMENT RATED FOR NIGHT FLYING.
WELL, WE WERE LUCKY THAT THIS PLACE HAD VACANCIES.

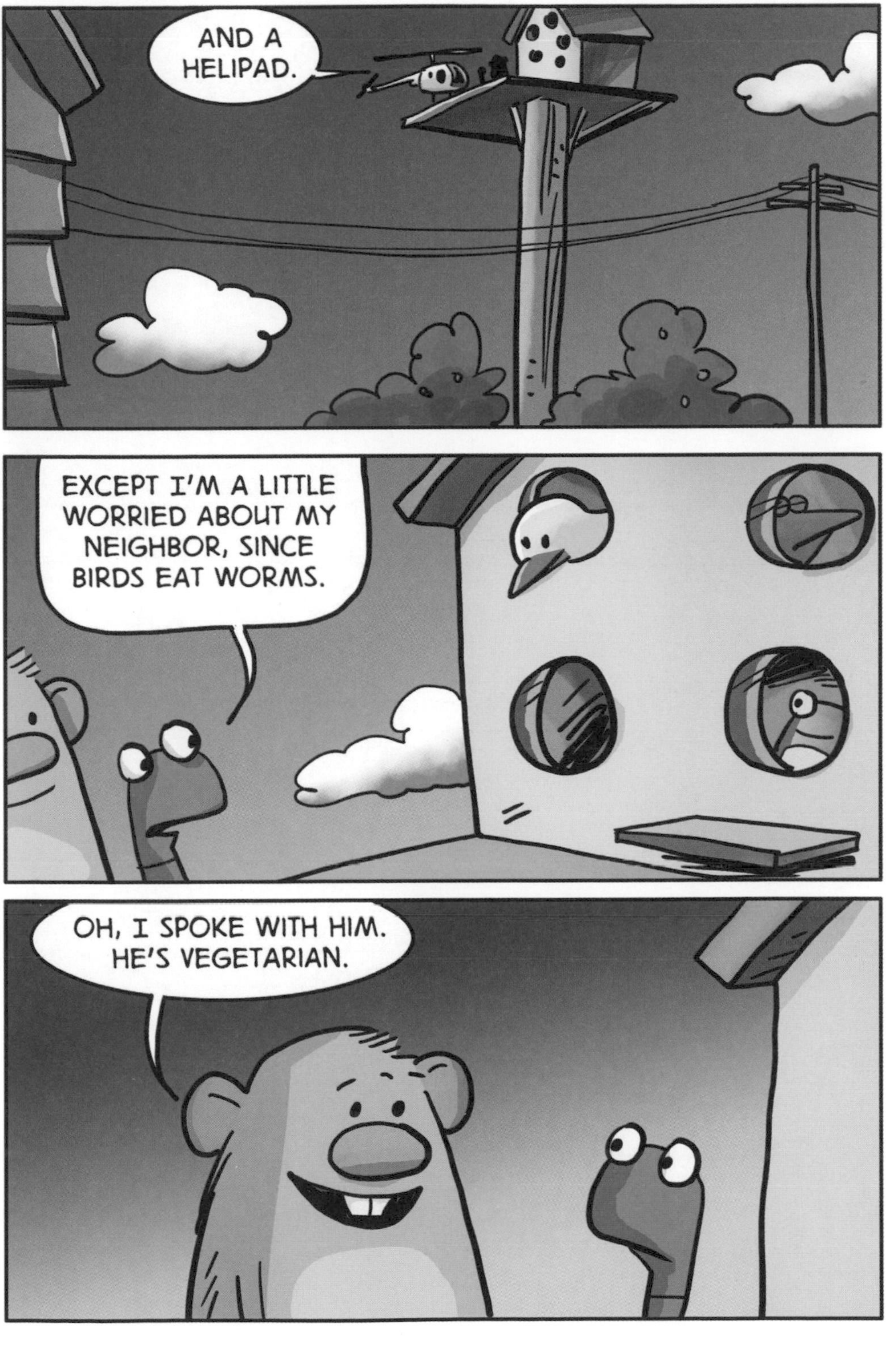
AND A HELIPAD.
EXCEPT I'M A LITTLE WORRIED ABOUT MY NEIGHBOR, SINCE BIRDS EAT WORMS.
OH, I SPOKE WITH HIM. HE'S VEGETARIAN.

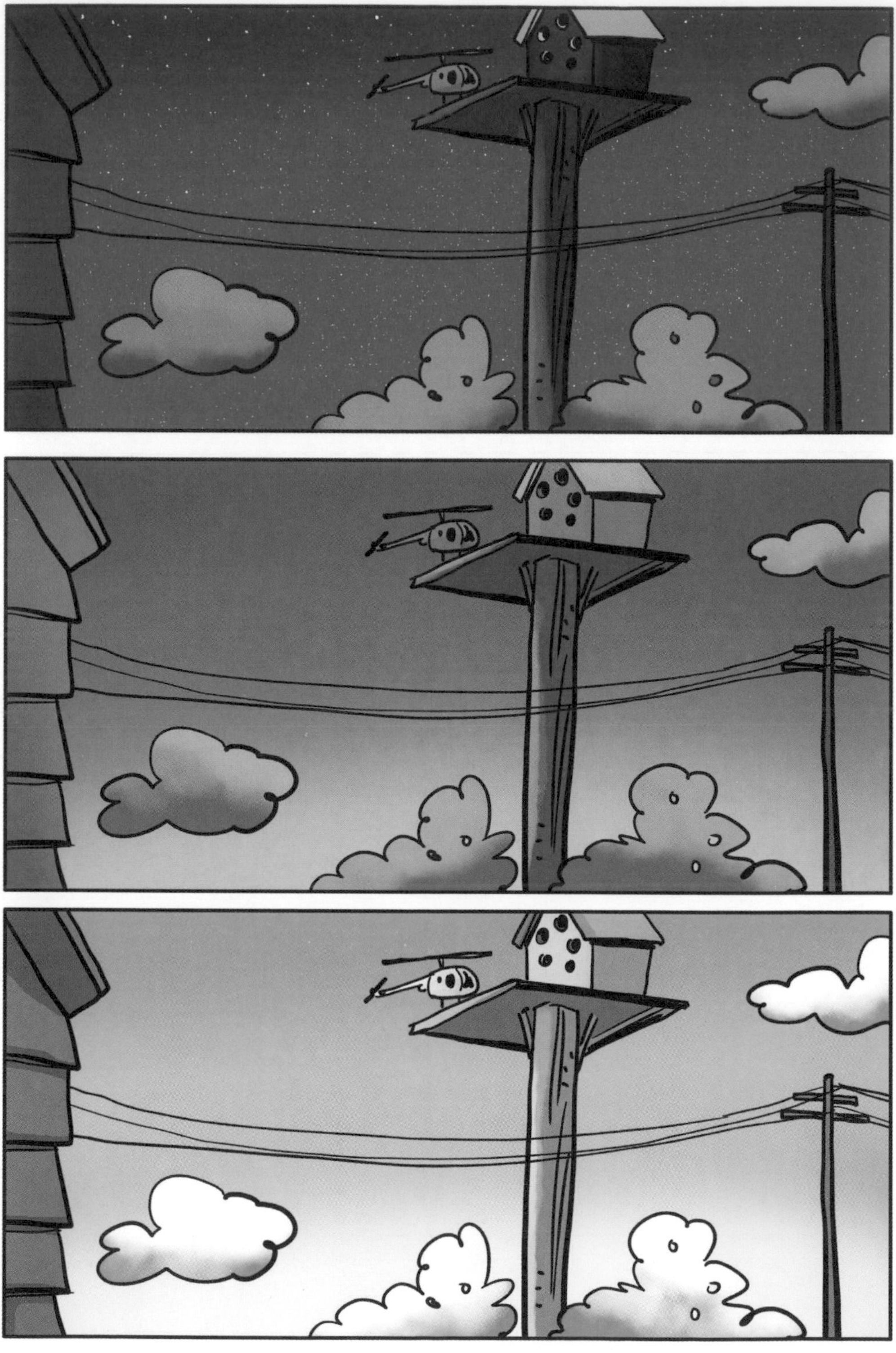

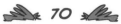

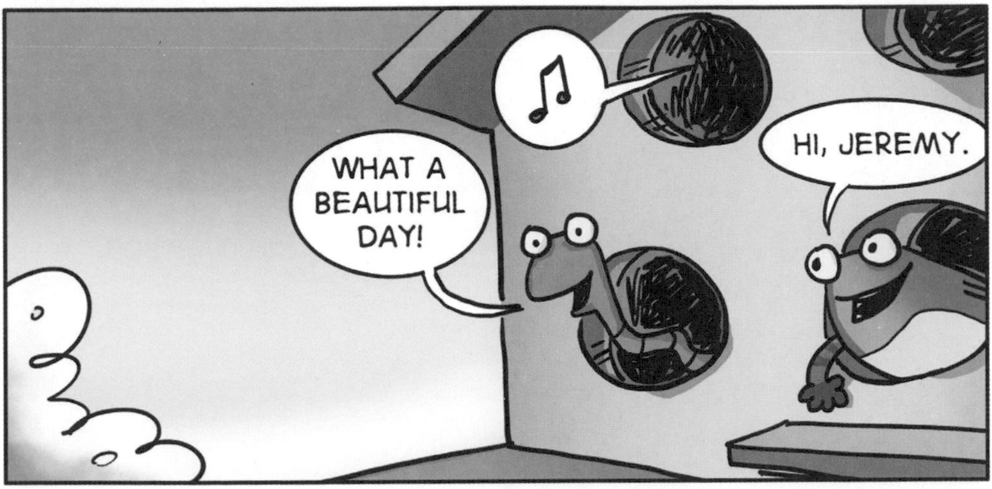
♪
WHAT A BEAUTIFUL DAY!
HI, JEREMY.

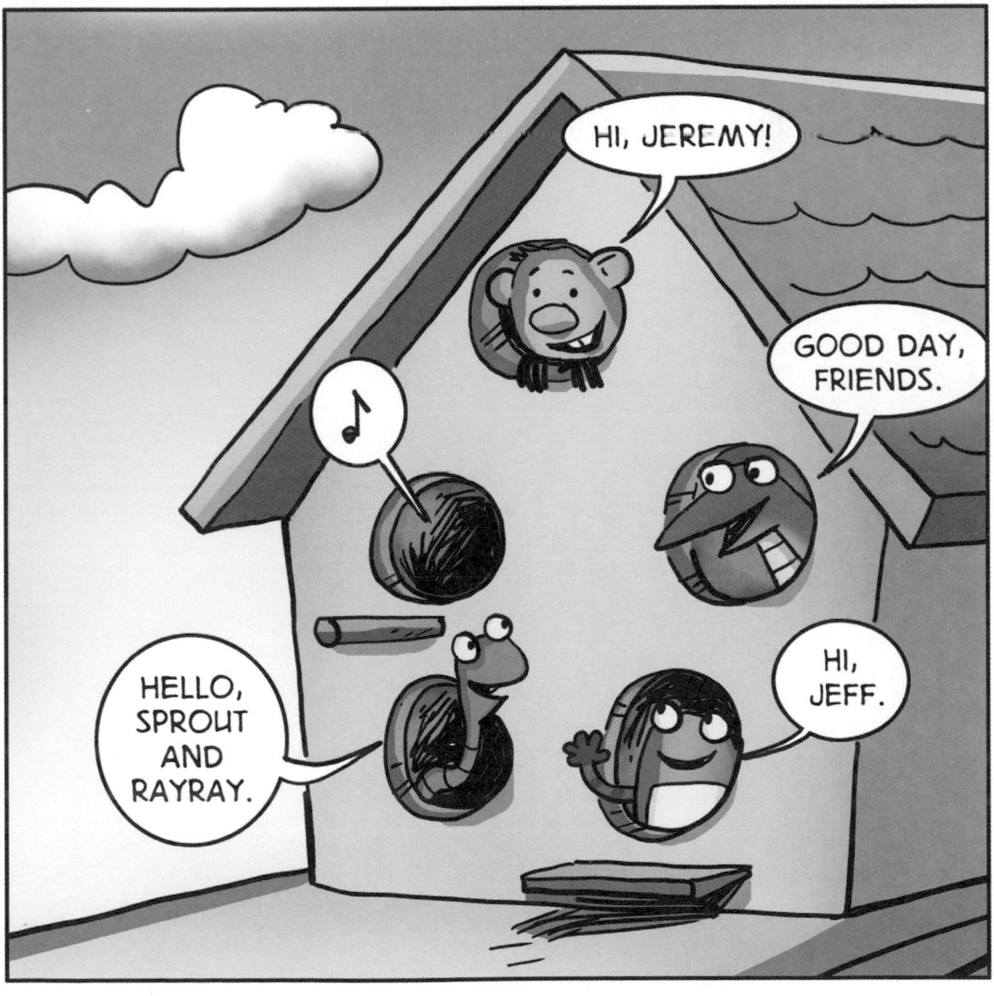
HI, JEREMY!
GOOD DAY, FRIENDS.
♪
HELLO, SPROUT AND RAYRAY.
HI, JEFF.

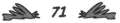

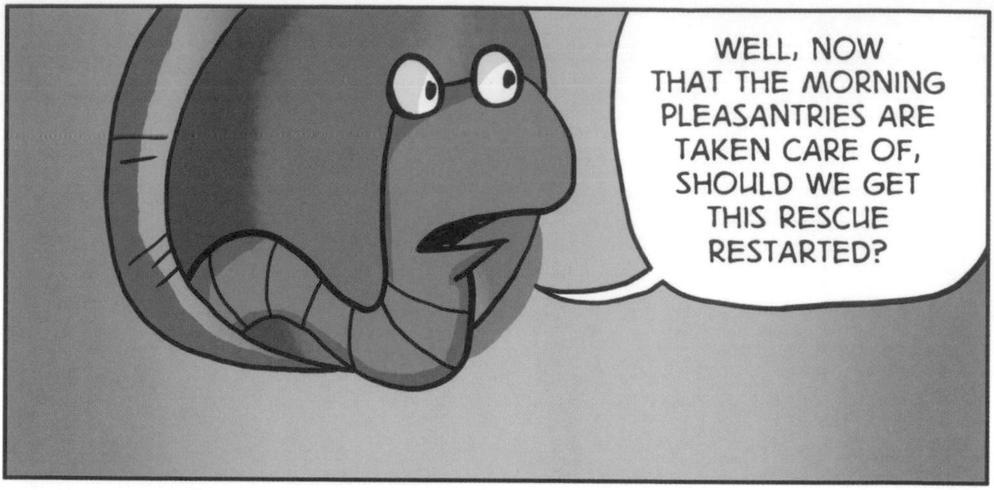
WELL, NOW THAT THE MORNING PLEASANTRIES ARE TAKEN CARE OF, SHOULD WE GET THIS RESCUE RESTARTED?

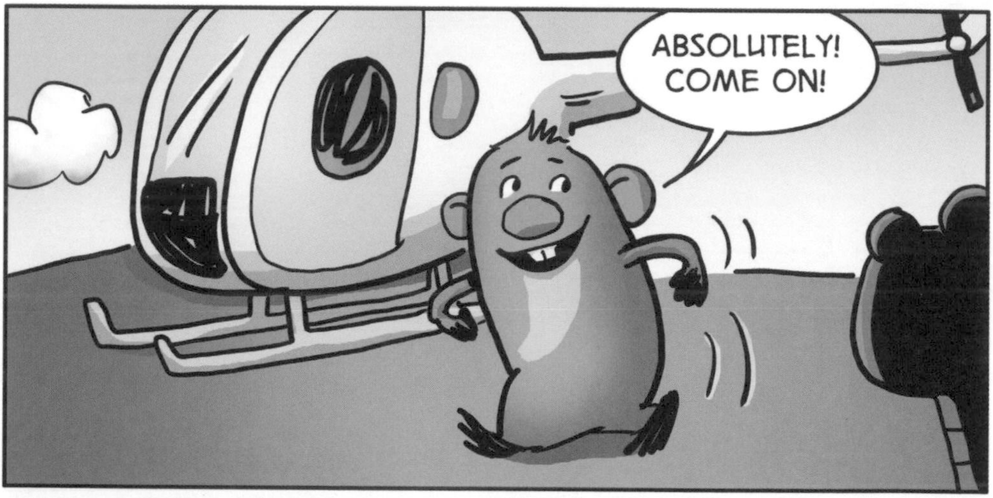
ABSOLUTELY! COME ON!

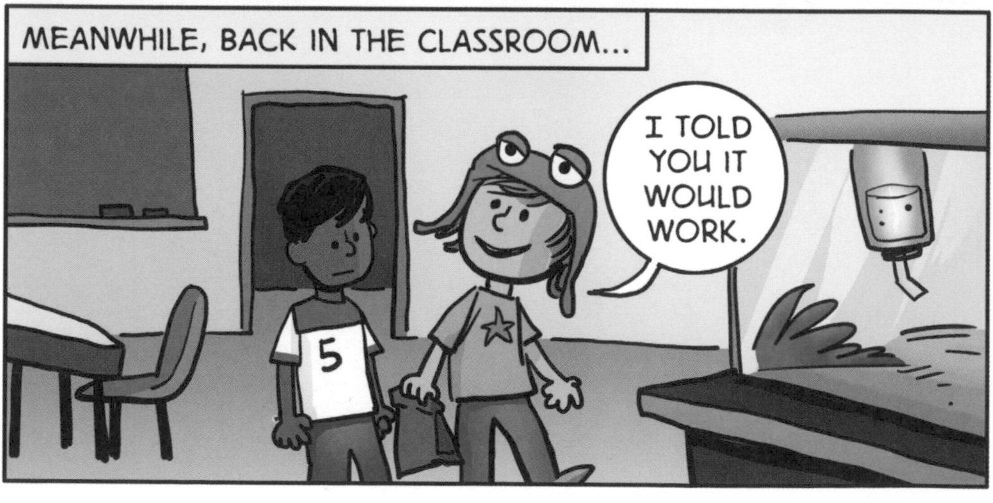
MEANWHILE, BACK IN THE CLASSROOM...
I TOLD YOU IT WOULD WORK.
5

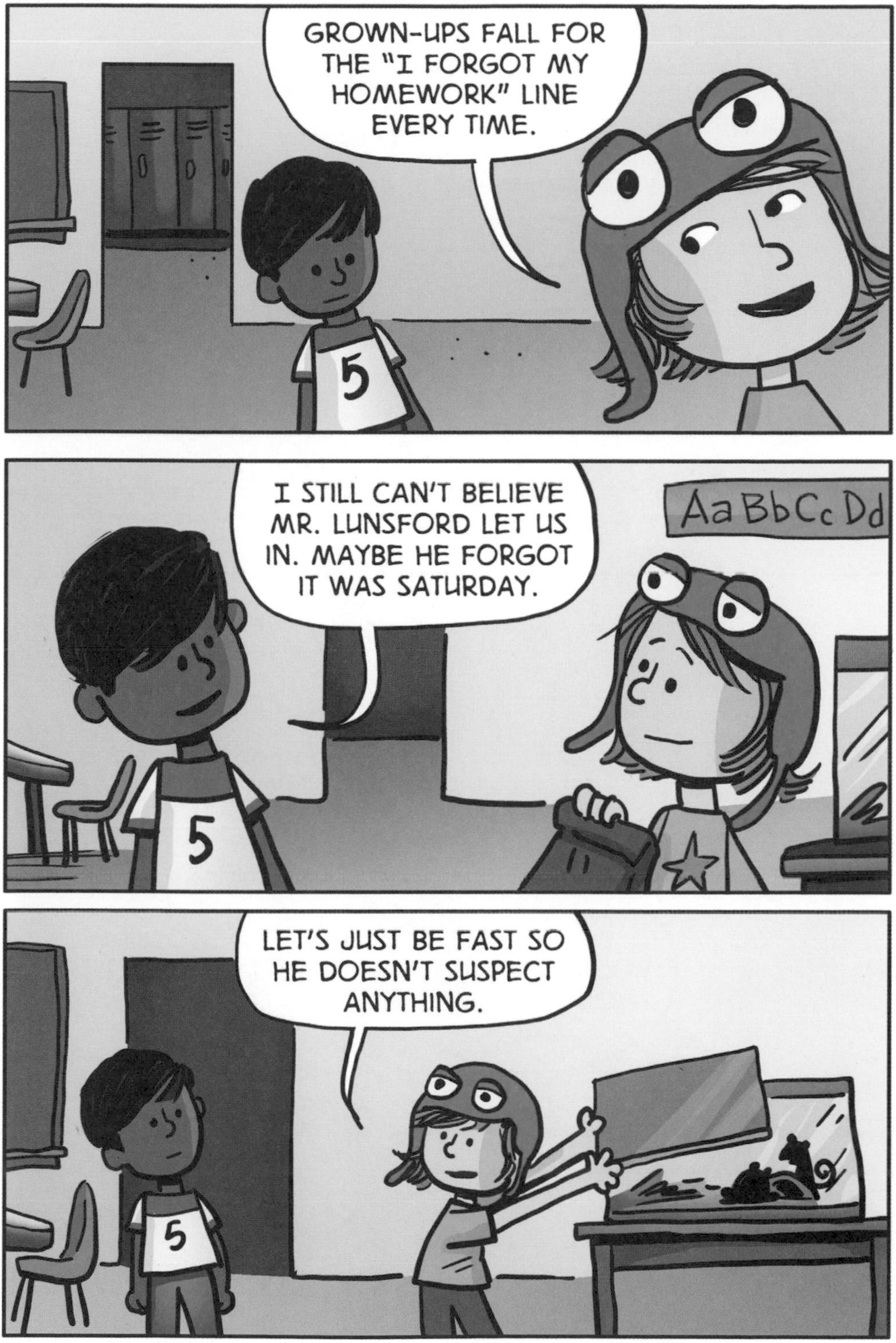
GROWN-UPS FALL FOR THE "I FORGOT MY HOMEWORK" LINE EVERY TIME.
I STILL CAN'T BELIEVE MR. LUNSFORD LET US IN. MAYBE HE FORGOT IT WAS SATURDAY.
Aa Bb Cc Dd
LET'S JUST BE FAST SO HE DOESN'T SUSPECT ANYTHING.

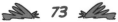

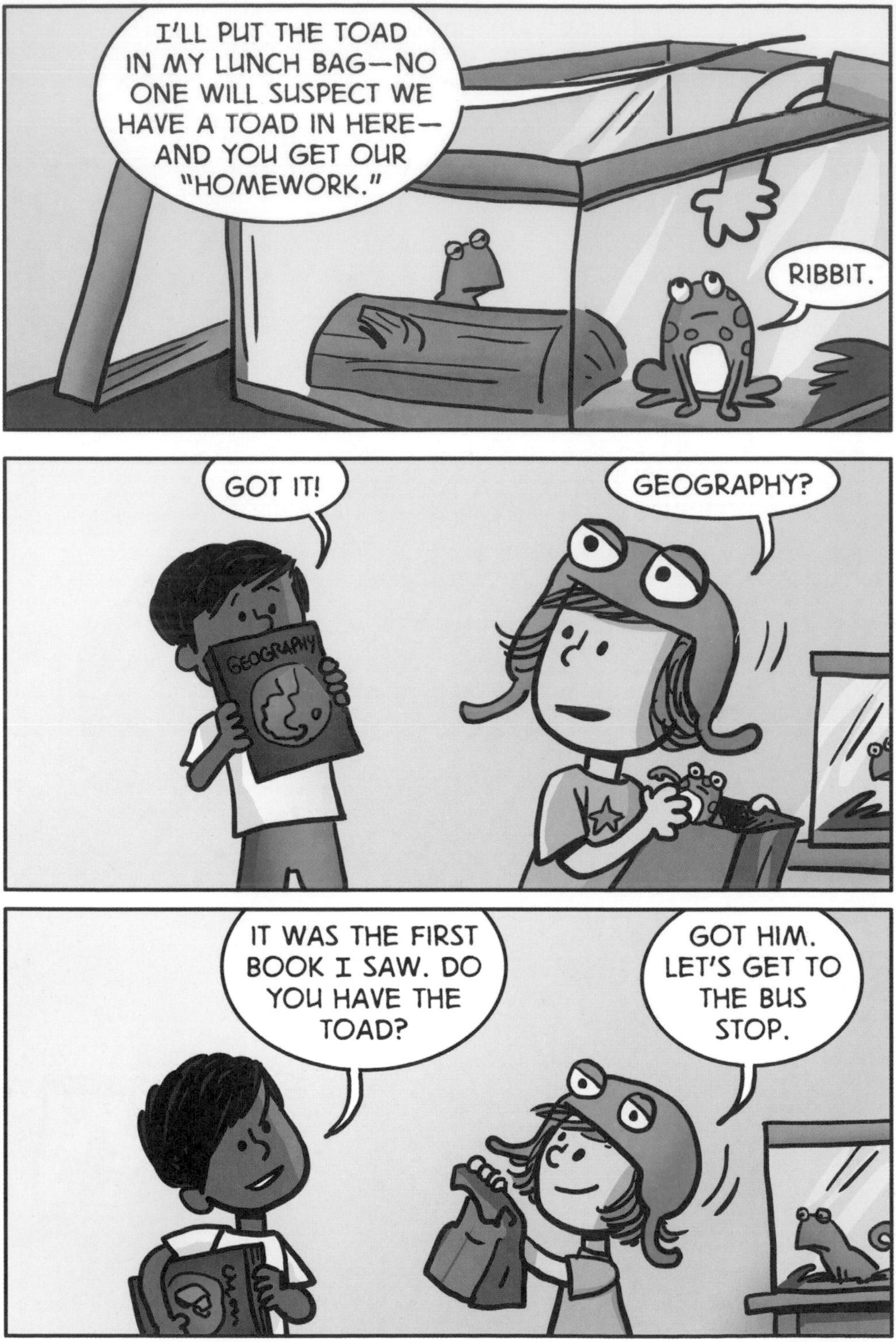
I'LL PUT THE TOAD IN MY LUNCH BAG—NO ONE WILL SUSPECT WE HAVE A TOAD IN HERE—AND YOU GET OUR "HOMEWORK."
RIBBIT.
GOT IT!
GEOGRAPHY?
GEOGRAPHY
IT WAS THE FIRST BOOK I SAW. DO YOU HAVE THE TOAD?
GOT HIM. LET'S GET TO THE BUS STOP.

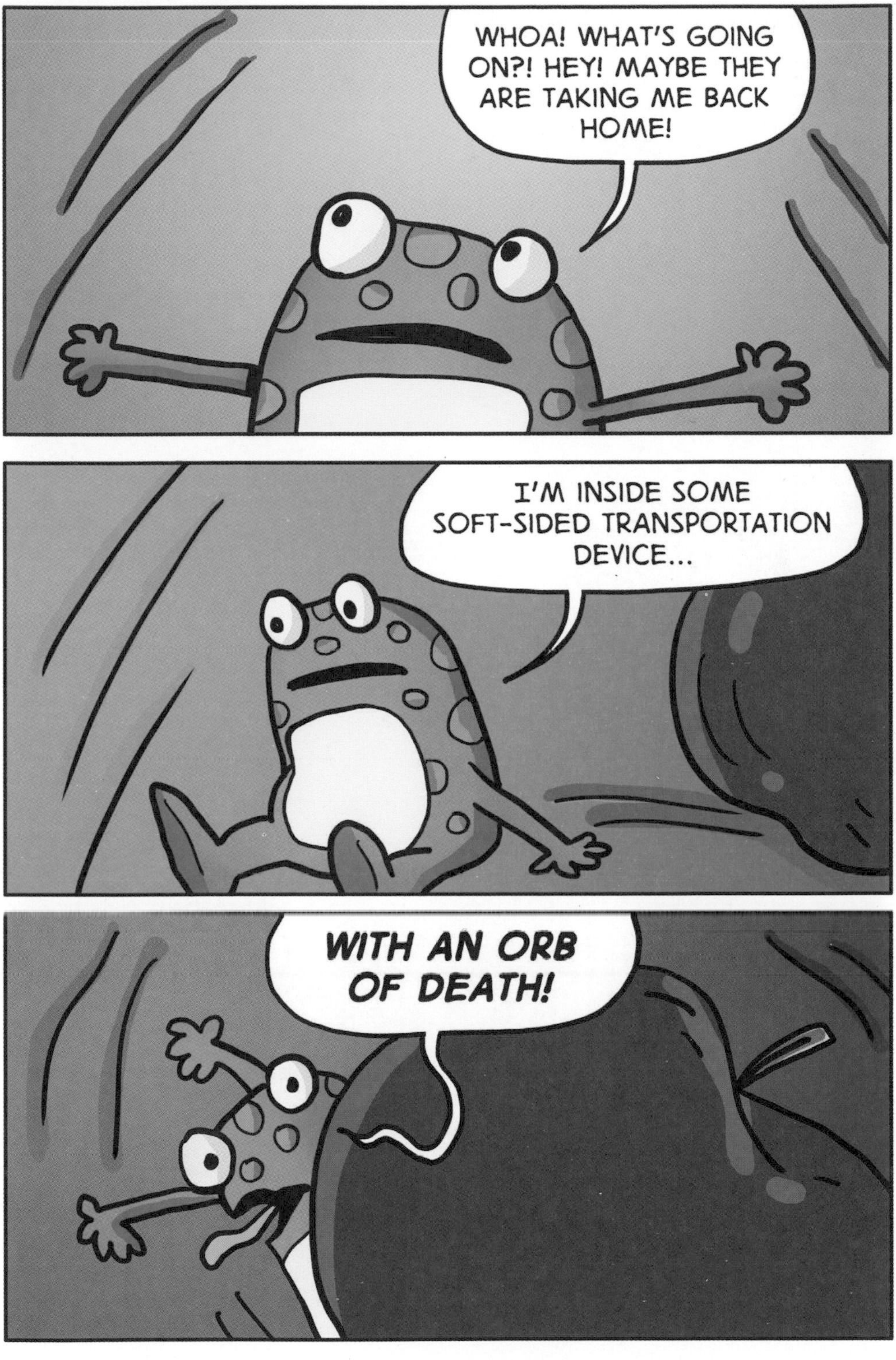
WHOA! WHAT'S GOING ON?! HEY! MAYBE THEY ARE TAKING ME BACK HOME!
I'M INSIDE SOME SOFT-SIDED TRANSPORTATION DEVICE...
WITH AN ORB OF DEATH!

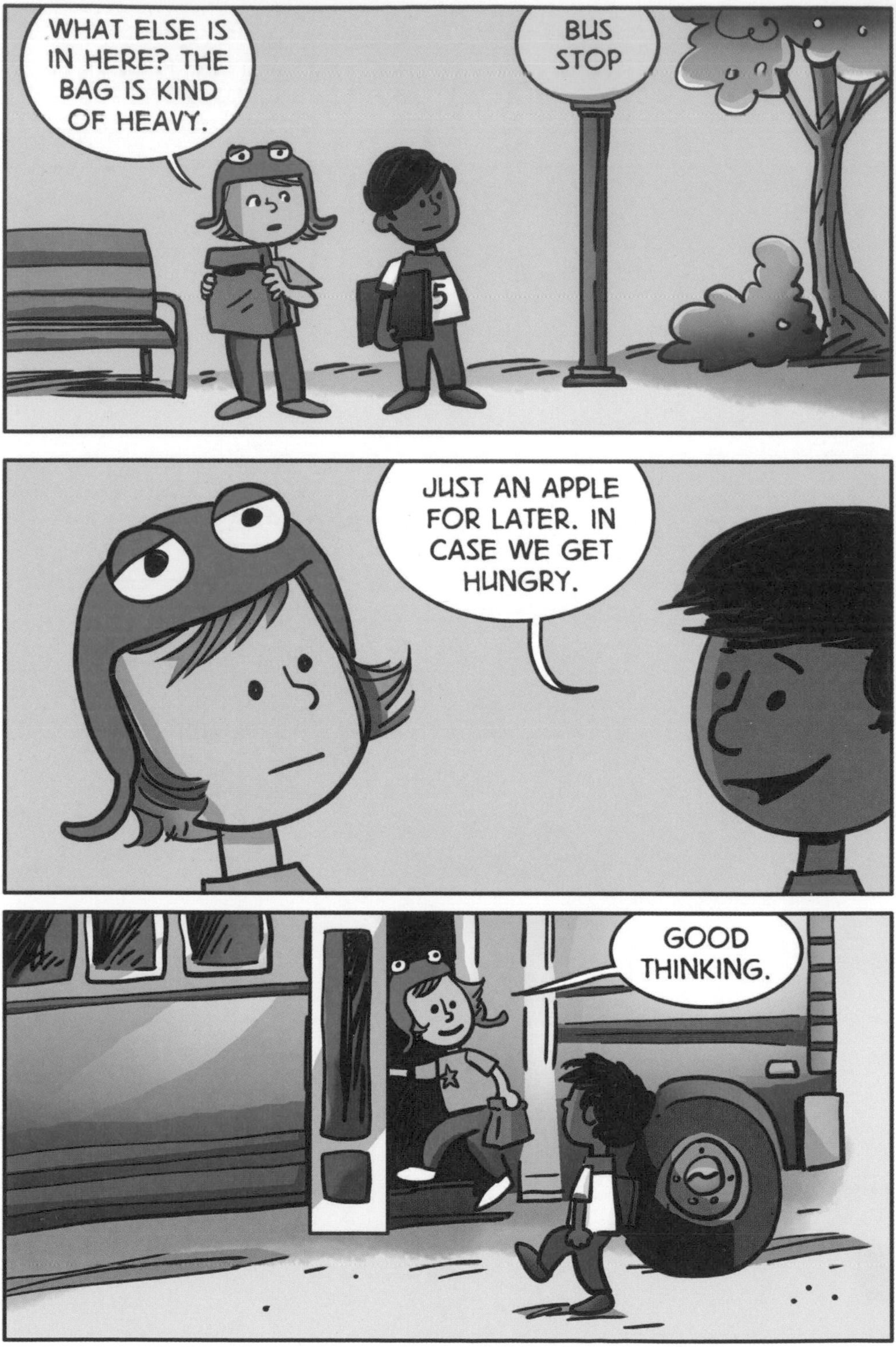
WHAT ELSE IS IN HERE? THE BAG IS KIND OF HEAVY.
BUS STOP
5
JUST AN APPLE FOR LATER. IN CASE WE GET HUNGRY.
GOOD THINKING.

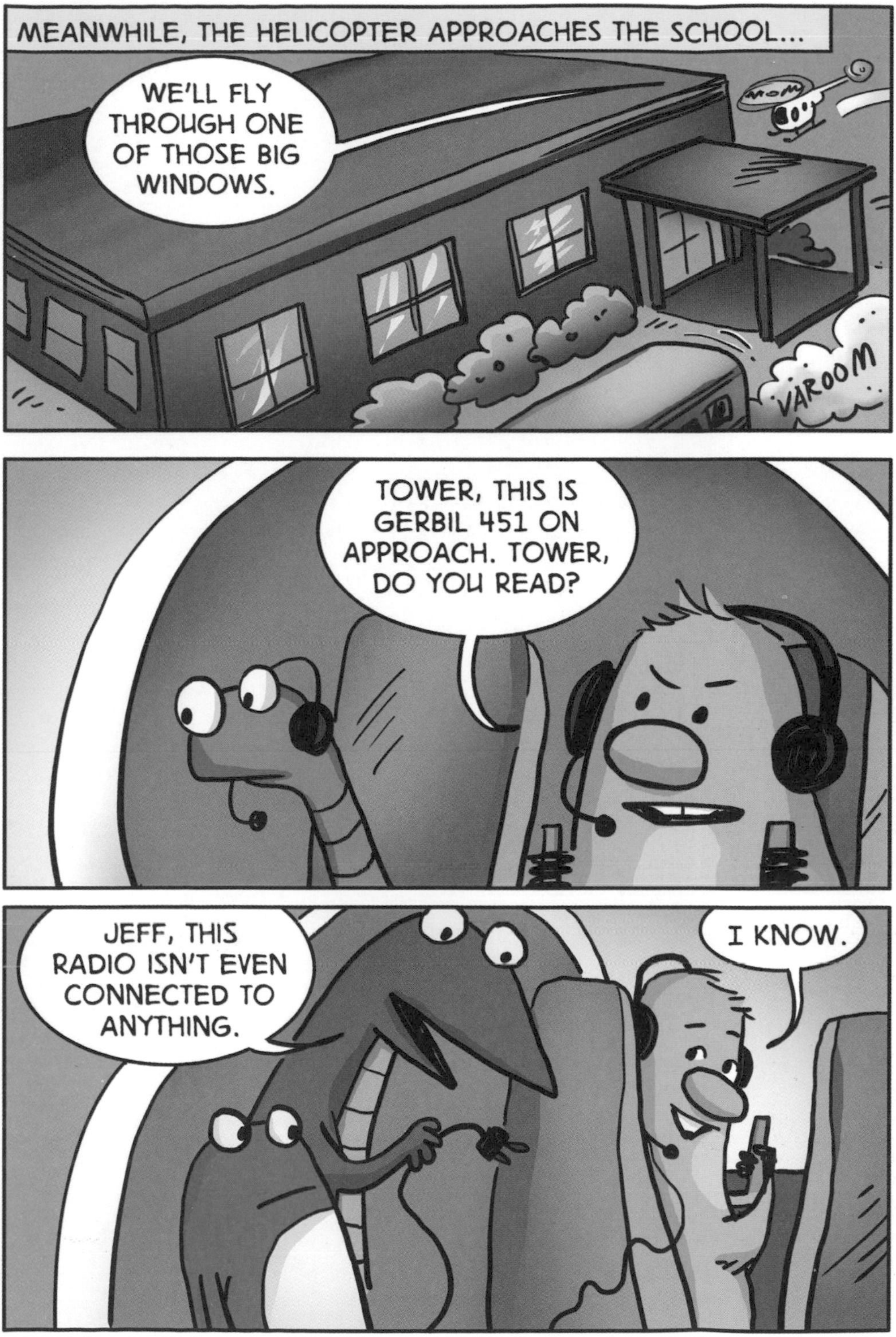
MEANWHILE, THE HELICOPTER APPROACHES THE SCHOOL...
WE'LL FLY THROUGH ONE OF THOSE BIG WINDOWS.
MOM
VAROOM
TOWER, THIS IS GERBIL 451 ON APPROACH. TOWER, DO YOU READ?
JEFF, THIS RADIO ISN'T EVEN CONNECTED TO ANYTHING.
I KNOW.

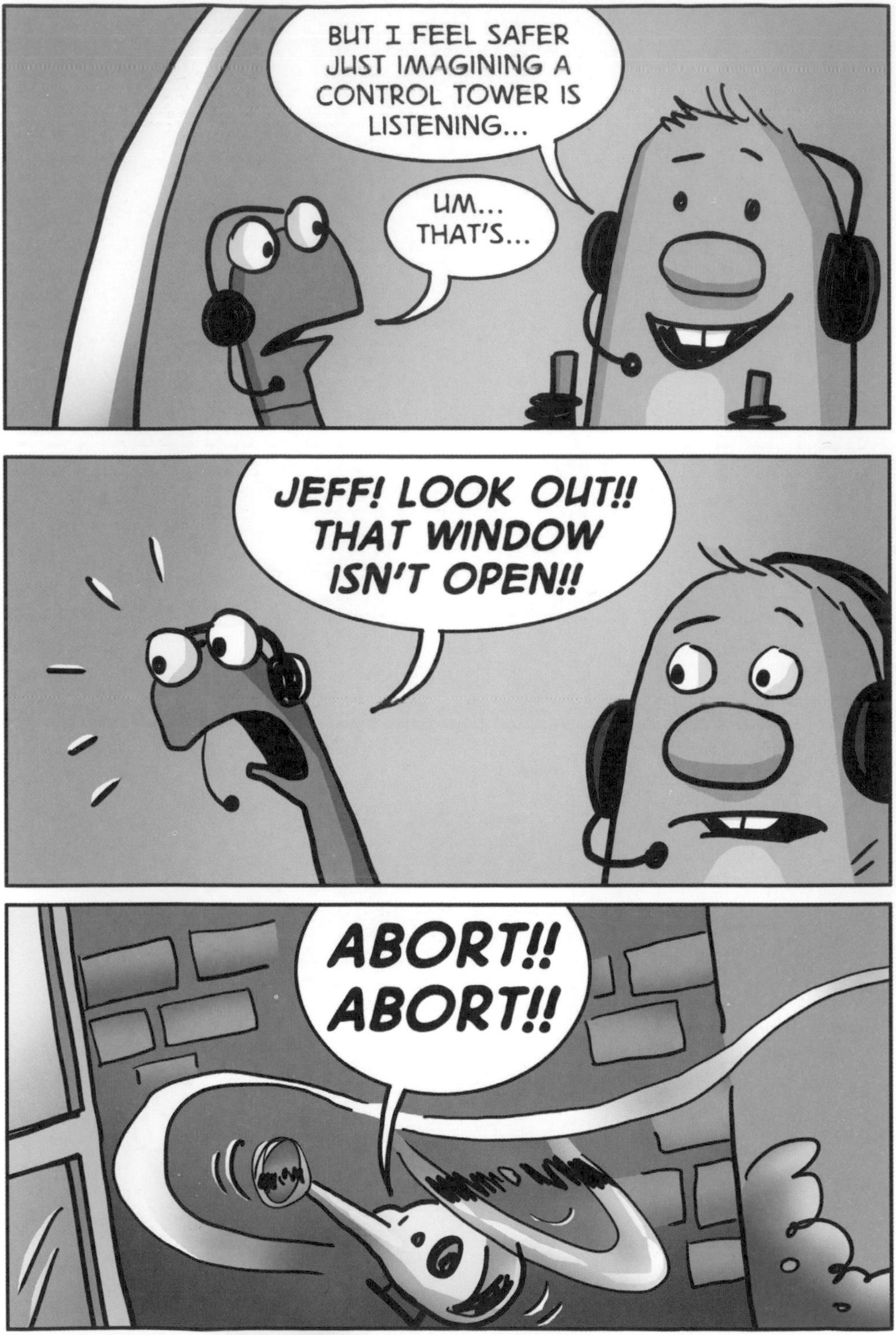
BUT I FEEL SAFER JUST IMAGINING A CONTROL TOWER IS LISTENING...
UM... THAT'S...
JEFF! LOOK OUT!! THAT WINDOW ISN'T OPEN!!
ABORT!! ABORT!!

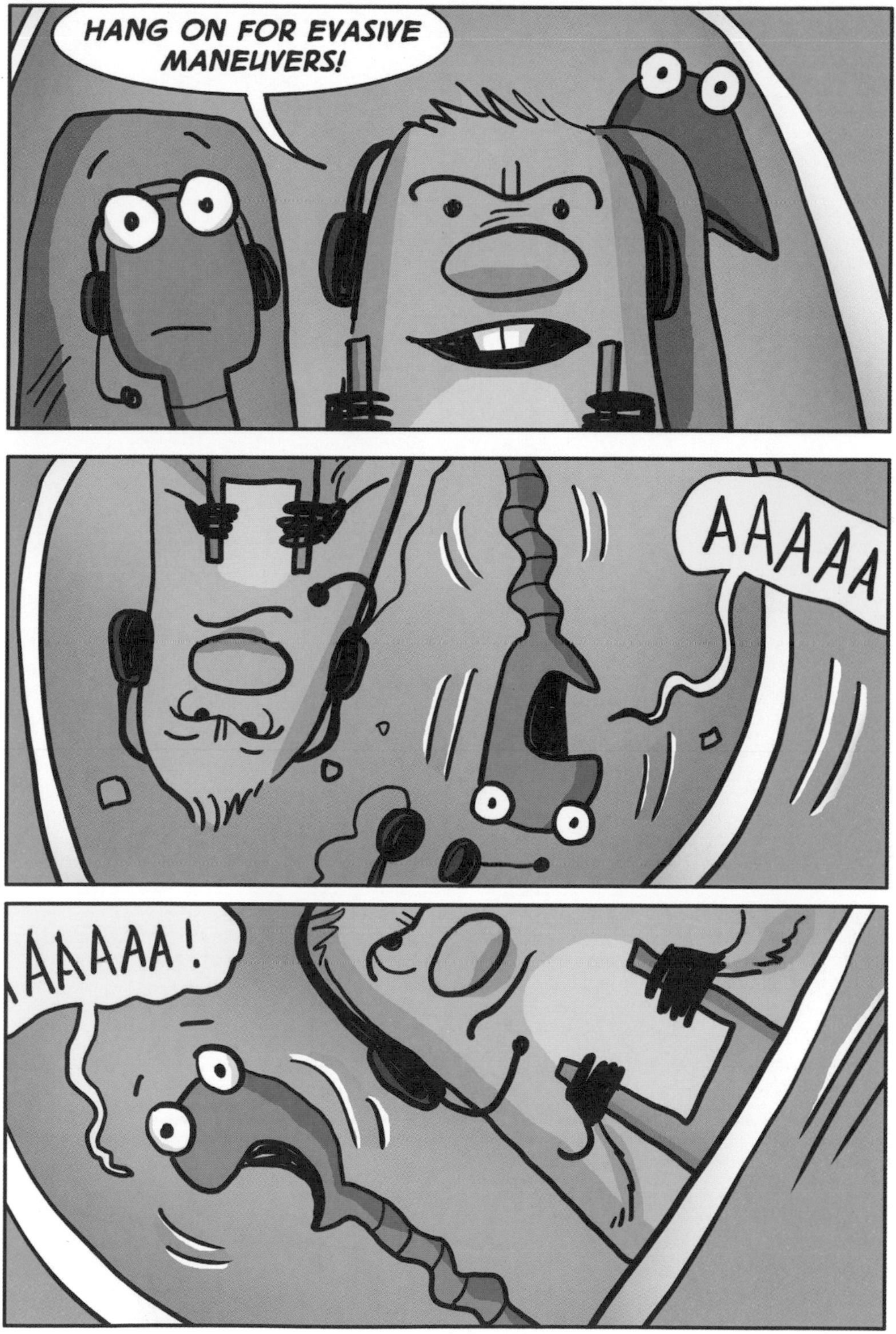
HANG ON FOR EVASIVE MANEUVERS!
AAAAA
AAAAA!

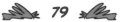

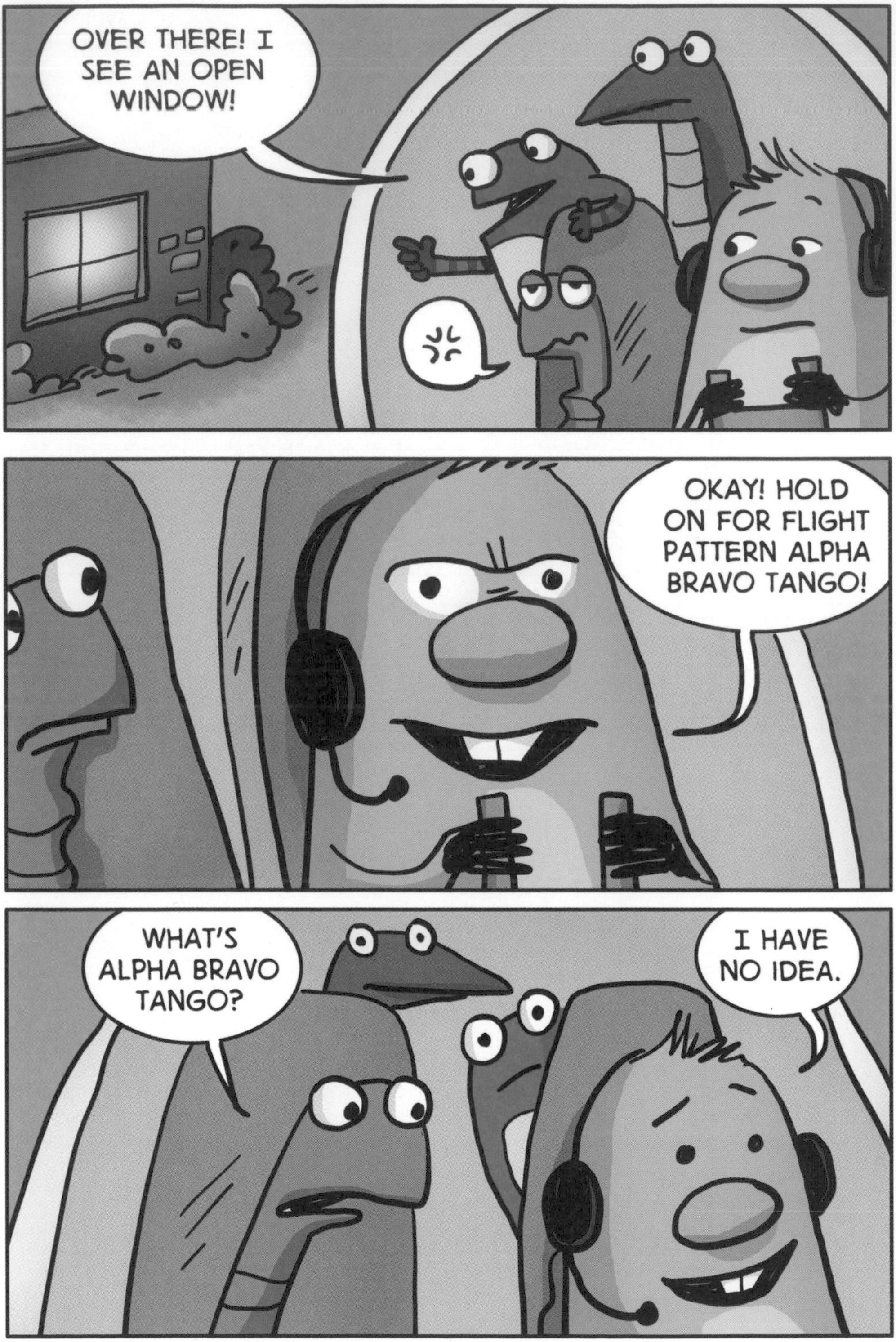
OVER THERE! I SEE AN OPEN WINDOW!
OKAY! HOLD ON FOR FLIGHT PATTERN ALPHA BRAVO TANGO!
WHAT'S ALPHA BRAVO TANGO?
I HAVE NO IDEA.

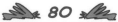

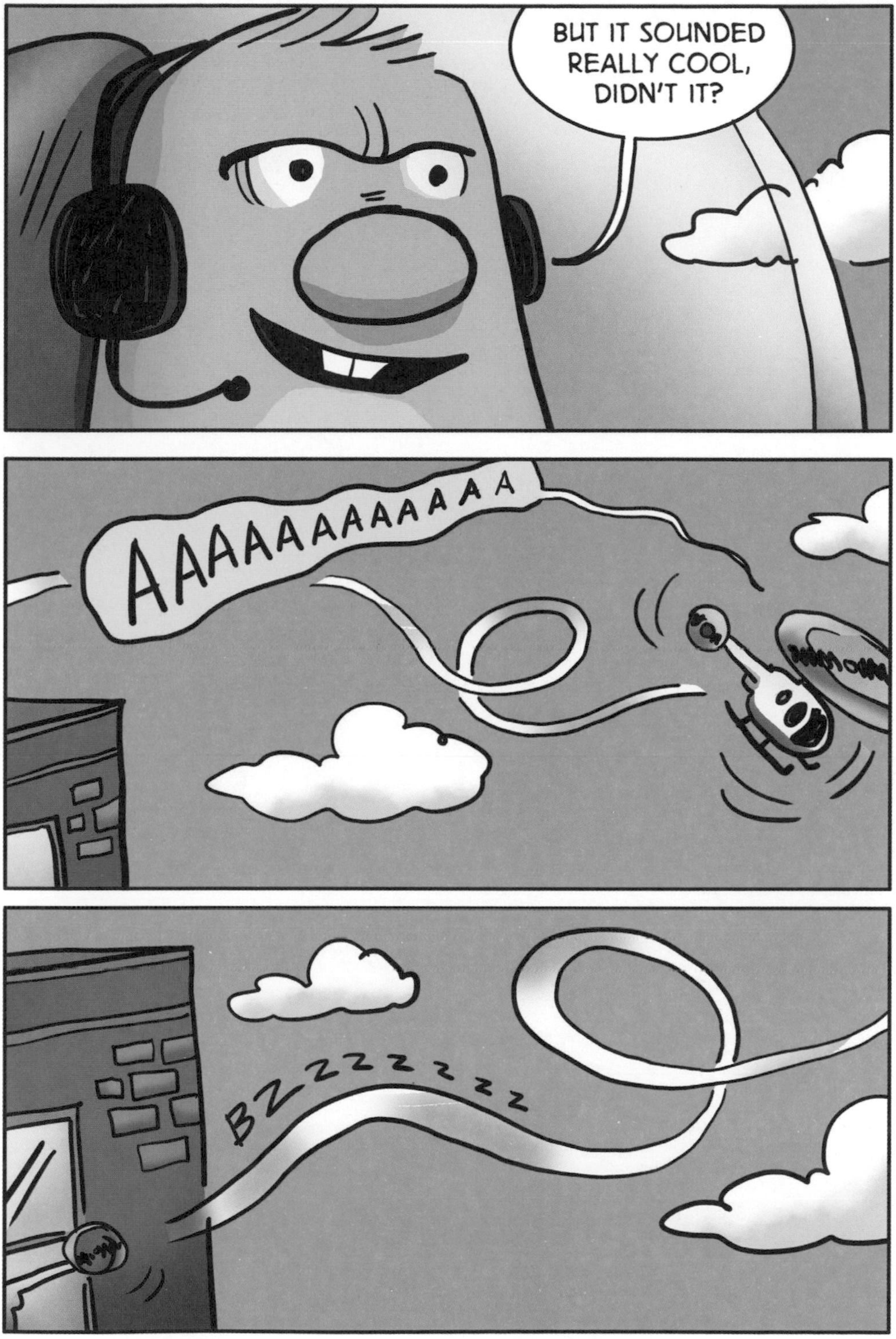
BUT IT SOUNDED REALLY COOL, DIDN'T IT?
AAAAAAAAAAAAA
BZZZZZZZZ

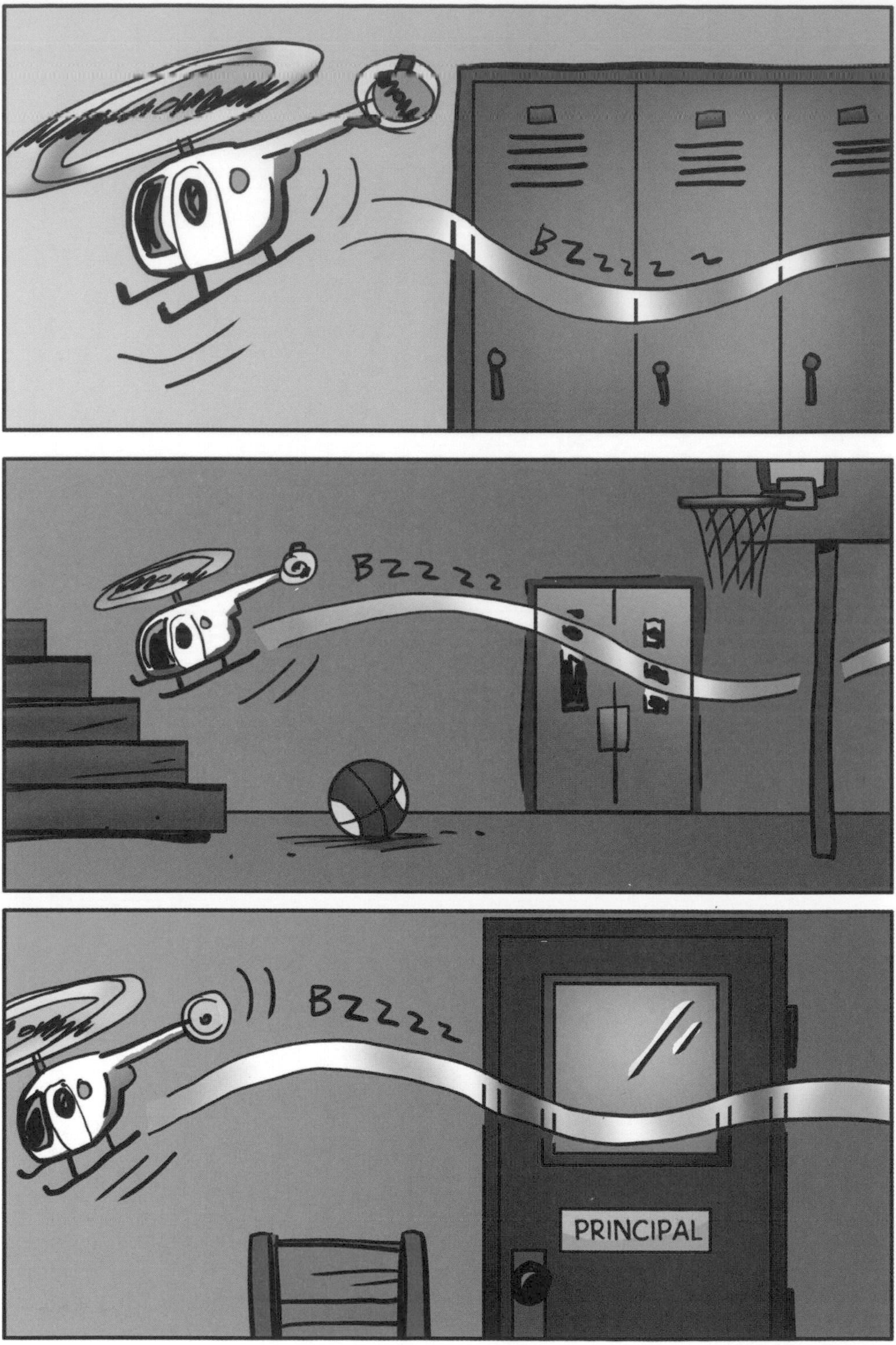
BZZZZZZ
BZZZZZ
BZZZZZ
PRINCIPAL

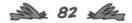

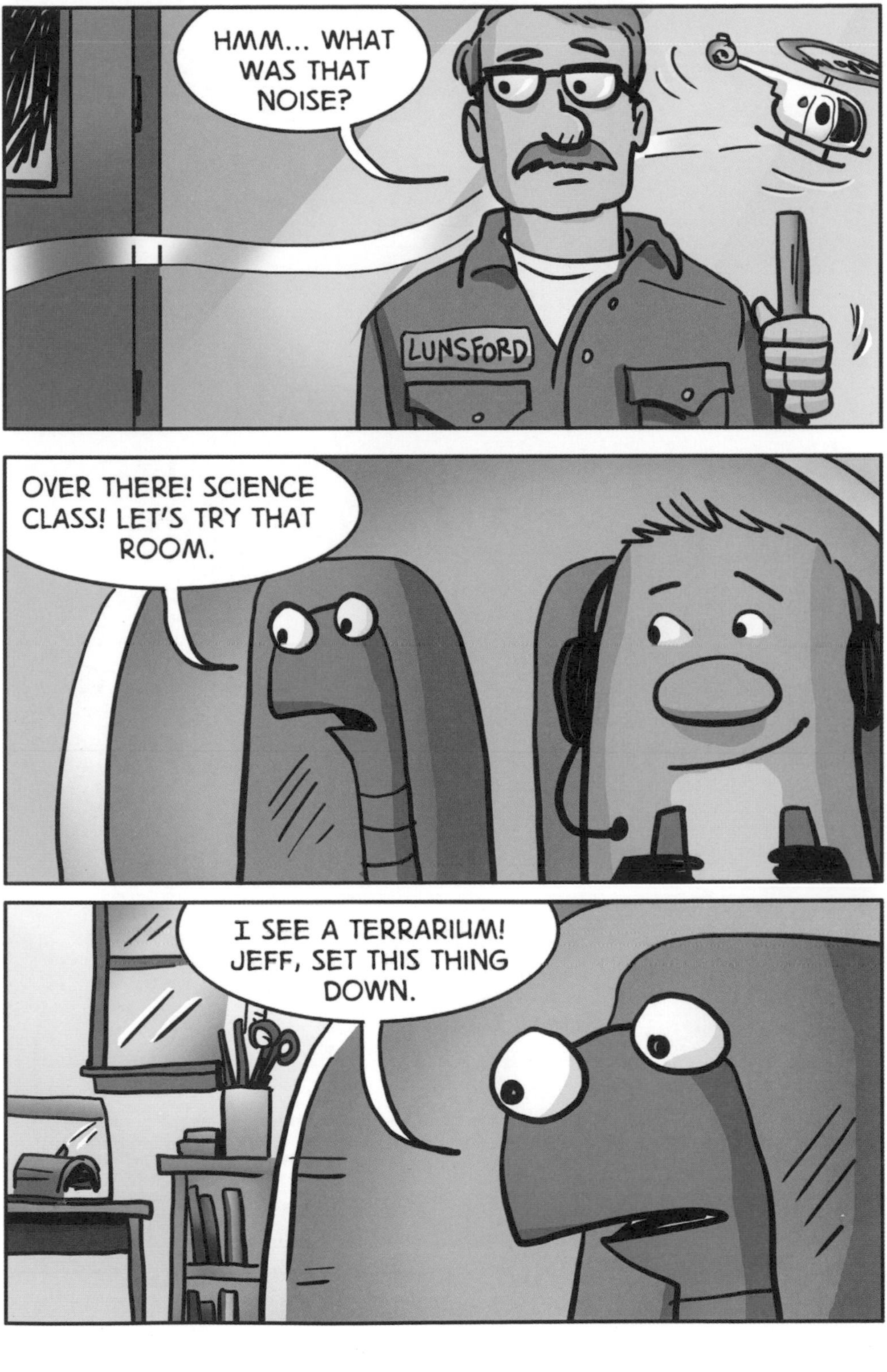
HMM... WHAT WAS THAT NOISE?
LUNSFORD
OVER THERE! SCIENCE CLASS! LET'S TRY THAT ROOM.
I SEE A TERRARIUM! JEFF, SET THIS THING DOWN.

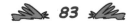

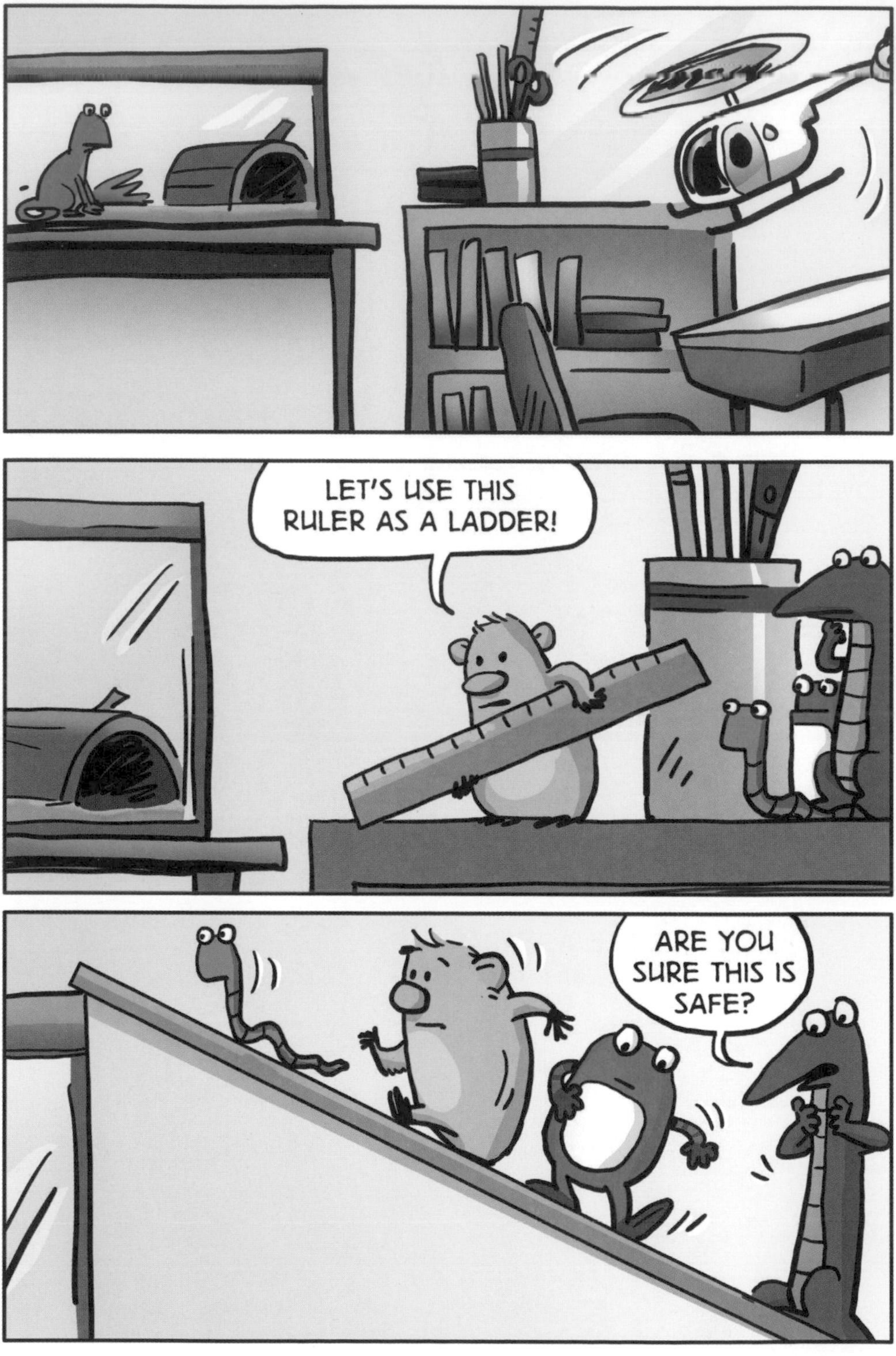
LET'S USE THIS RULER AS A LADDER!
ARE YOU SURE THIS IS SAFE?

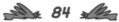

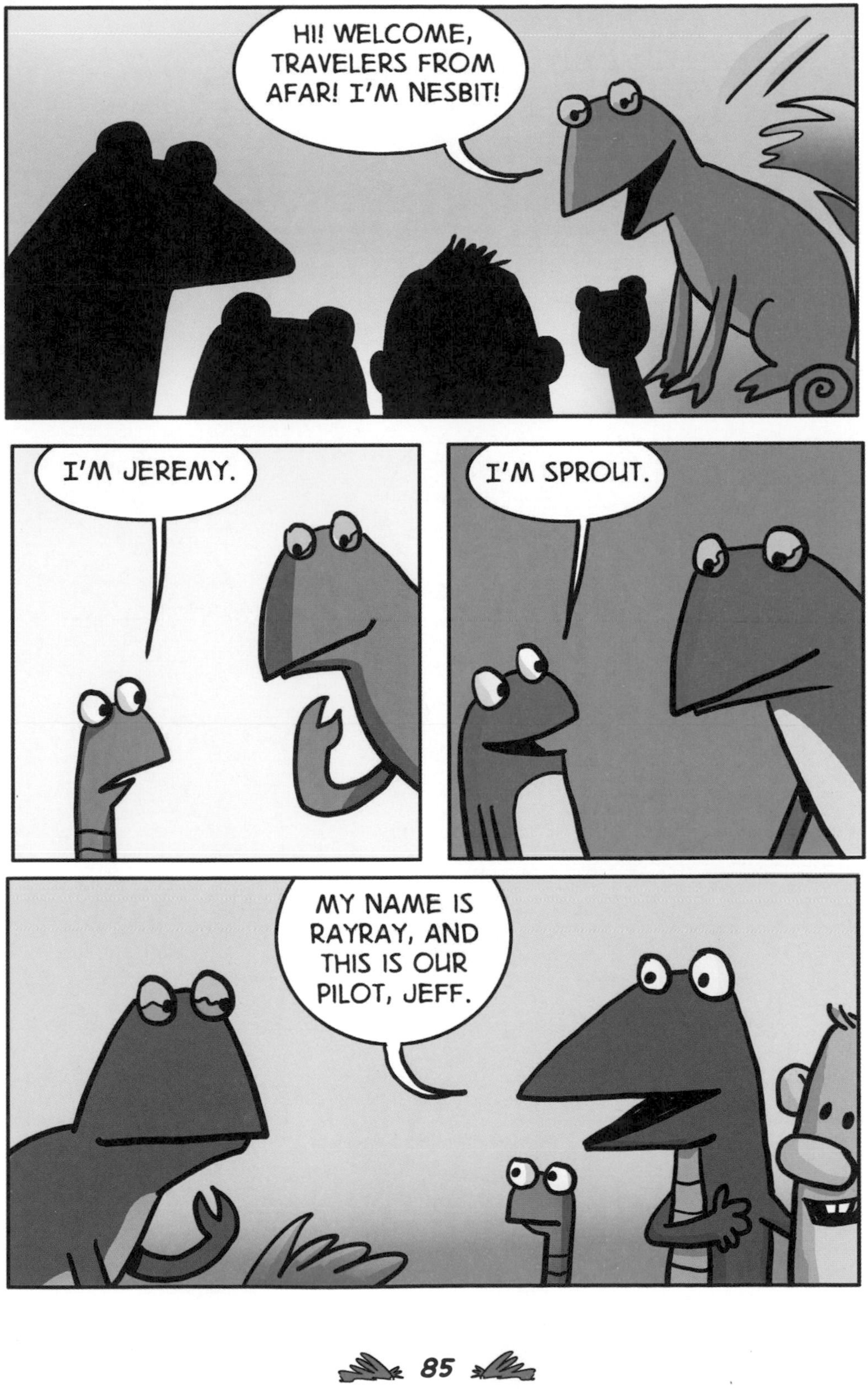
HI! WELCOME, TRAVELERS FROM AFAR! I'M NESBIT!
I'M JEREMY.
I'M SPROUT.
MY NAME IS RAYRAY, AND THIS IS OUR PILOT, JEFF.

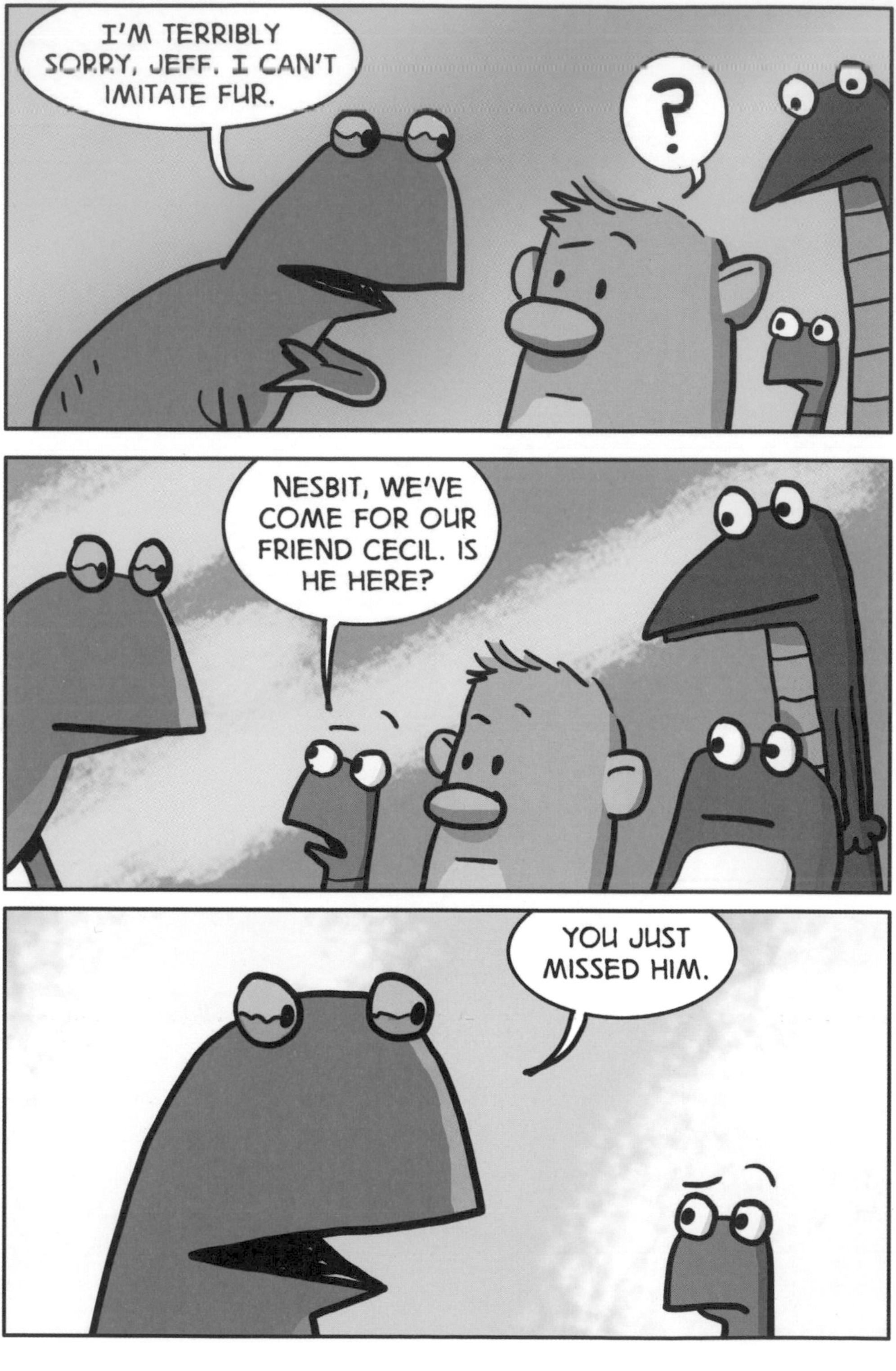
I'M TERRIBLY SORRY, JEFF. I CAN'T IMITATE FUR.
?
NESBIT, WE'VE COME FOR OUR FRIEND CECIL. IS HE HERE?
YOU JUST MISSED HIM.

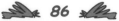

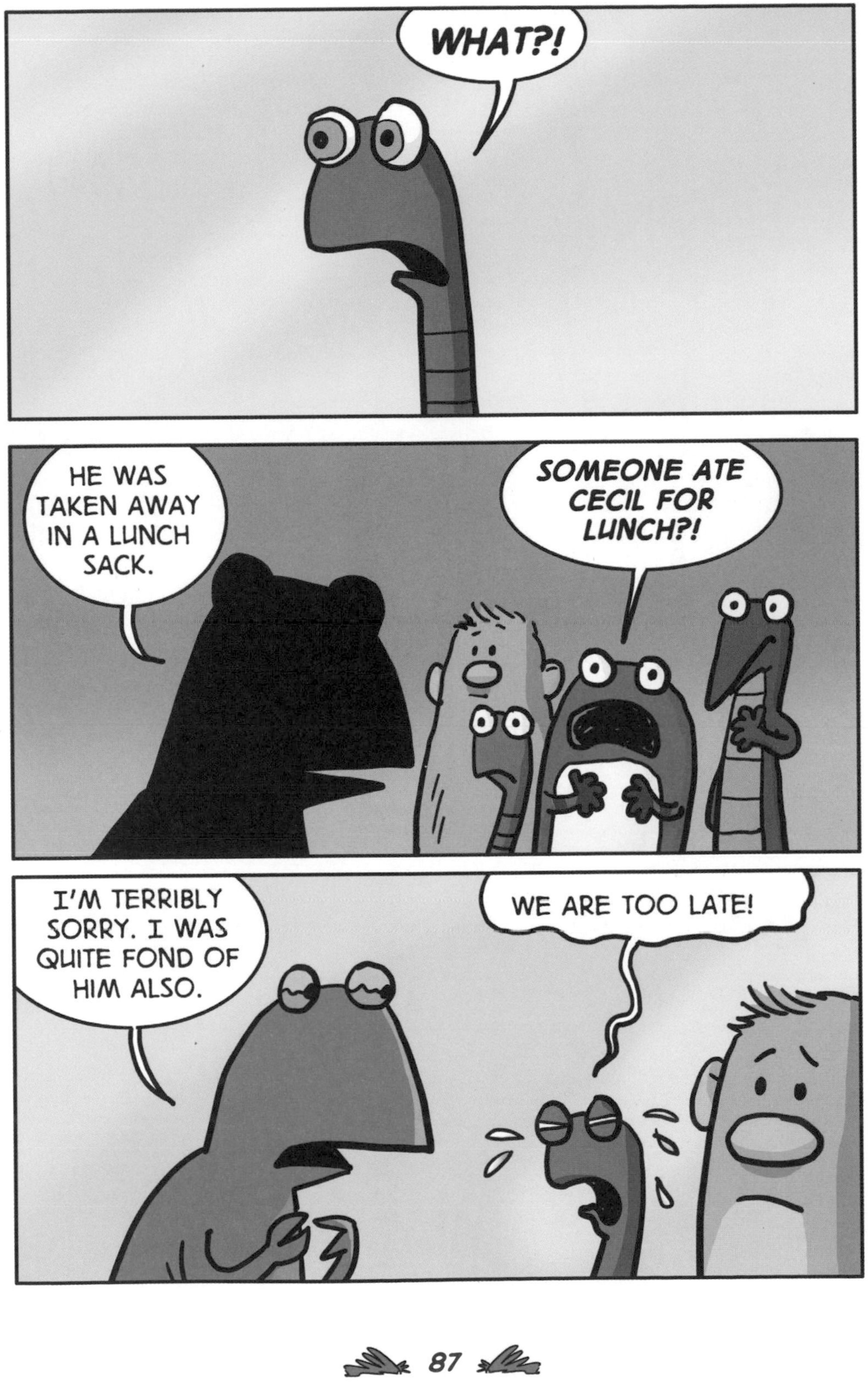
WHAT?!
HE WAS TAKEN AWAY IN A LUNCH SACK.
SOMEONE ATE CECIL FOR LUNCH?!
I'M TERRIBLY SORRY. I WAS QUITE FOND OF HIM ALSO.
WE ARE TOO LATE!

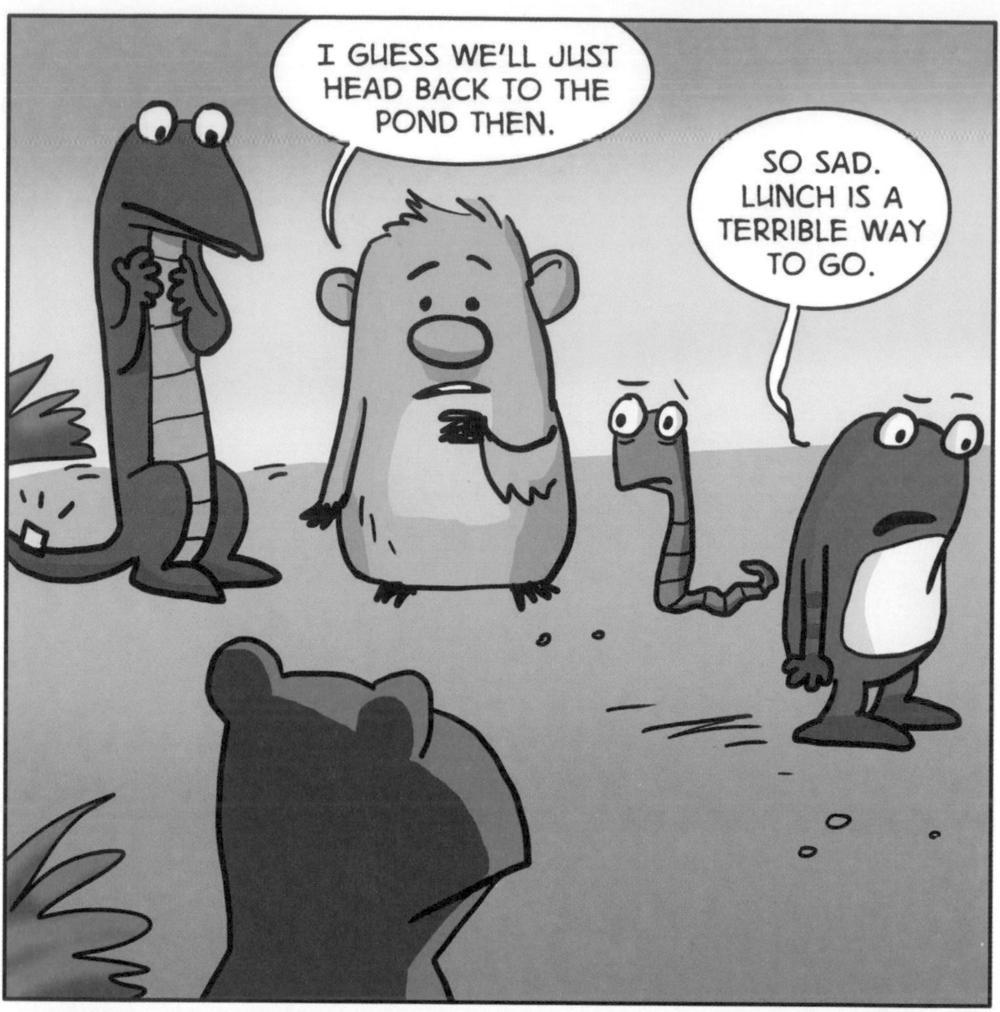
I GUESS WE'LL JUST HEAD BACK TO THE POND THEN.
SO SAD. LUNCH IS A TERRIBLE WAY TO GO.

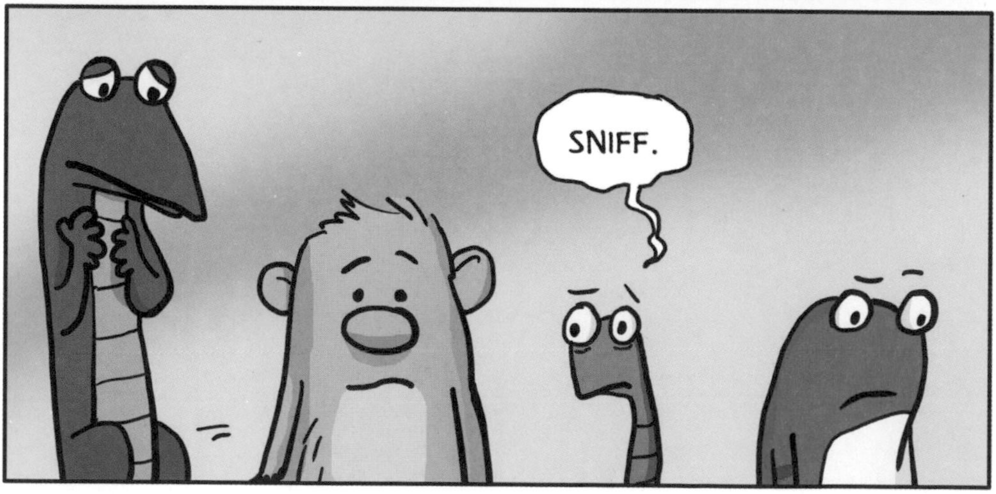
SNIFF.

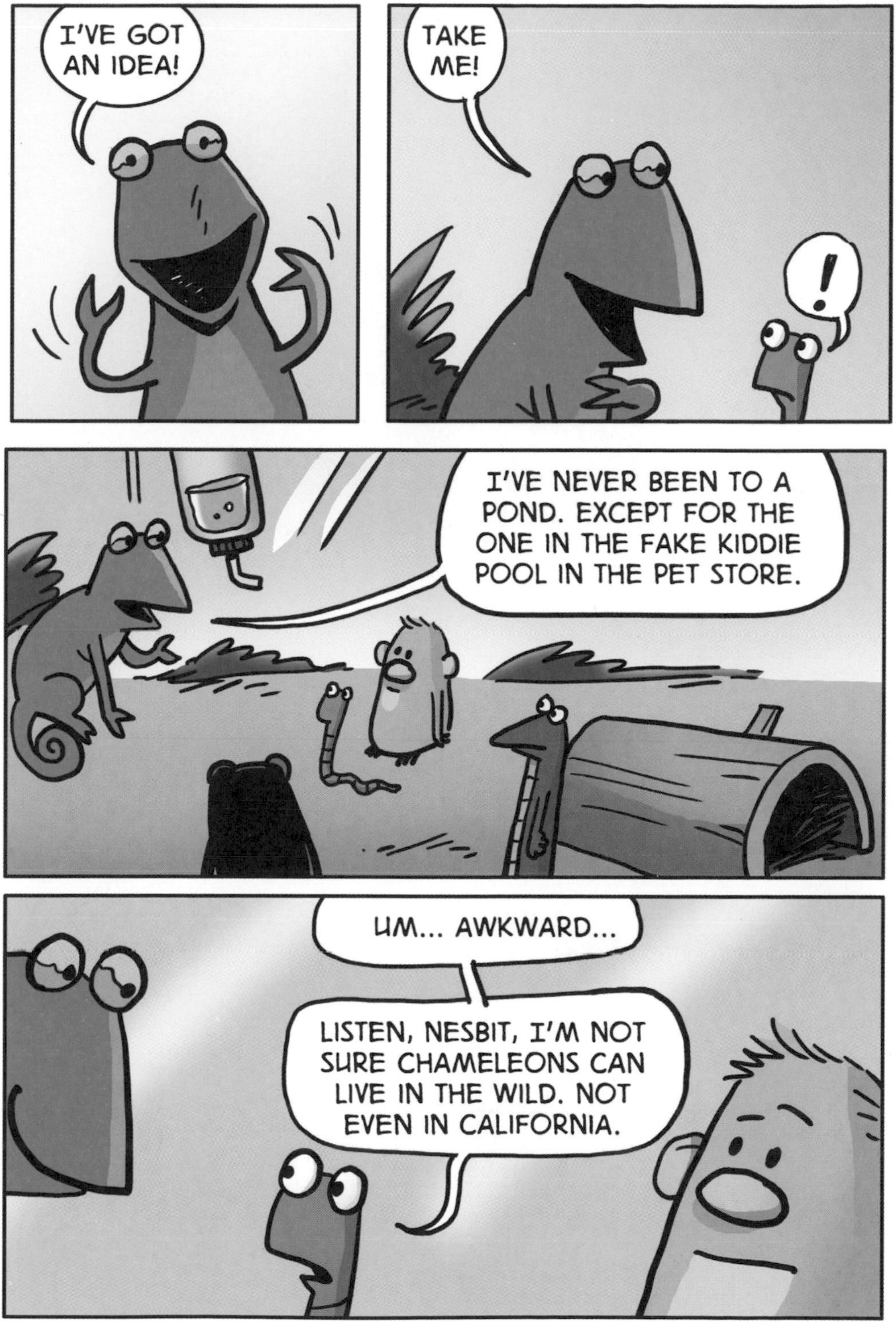
I'VE GOT AN IDEA!
TAKE ME!
!
I'VE NEVER BEEN TO A POND. EXCEPT FOR THE ONE IN THE FAKE KIDDIE POOL IN THE PET STORE.
UM... AWKWARD...
LISTEN, NESBIT, I'M NOT SURE CHAMELEONS CAN LIVE IN THE WILD. NOT EVEN IN CALIFORNIA.

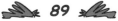

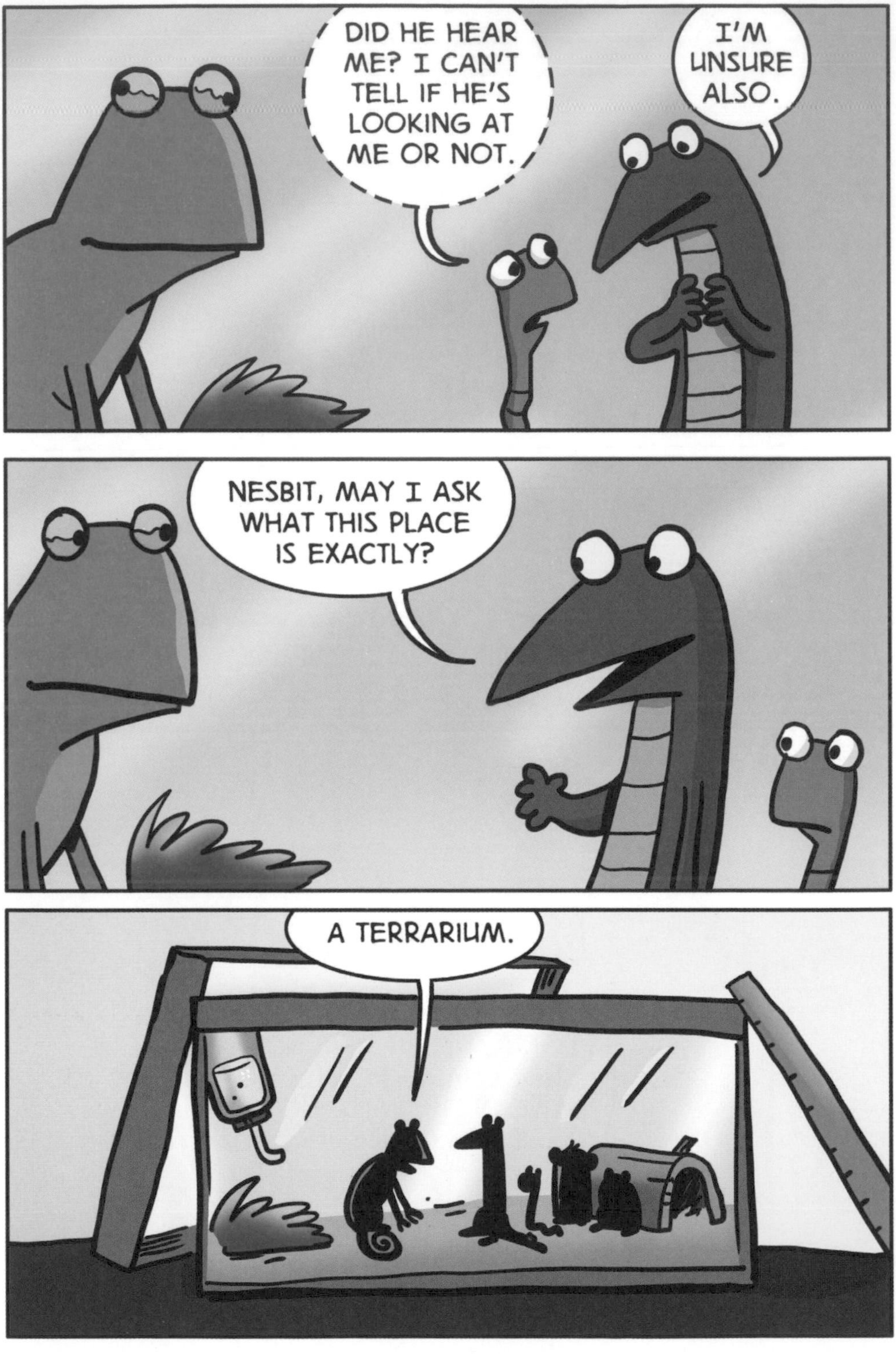
DID HE HEAR ME? I CAN'T TELL IF HE'S LOOKING AT ME OR NOT.
I'M UNSURE ALSO.
NESBIT, MAY I ASK WHAT THIS PLACE IS EXACTLY?
A TERRARIUM.

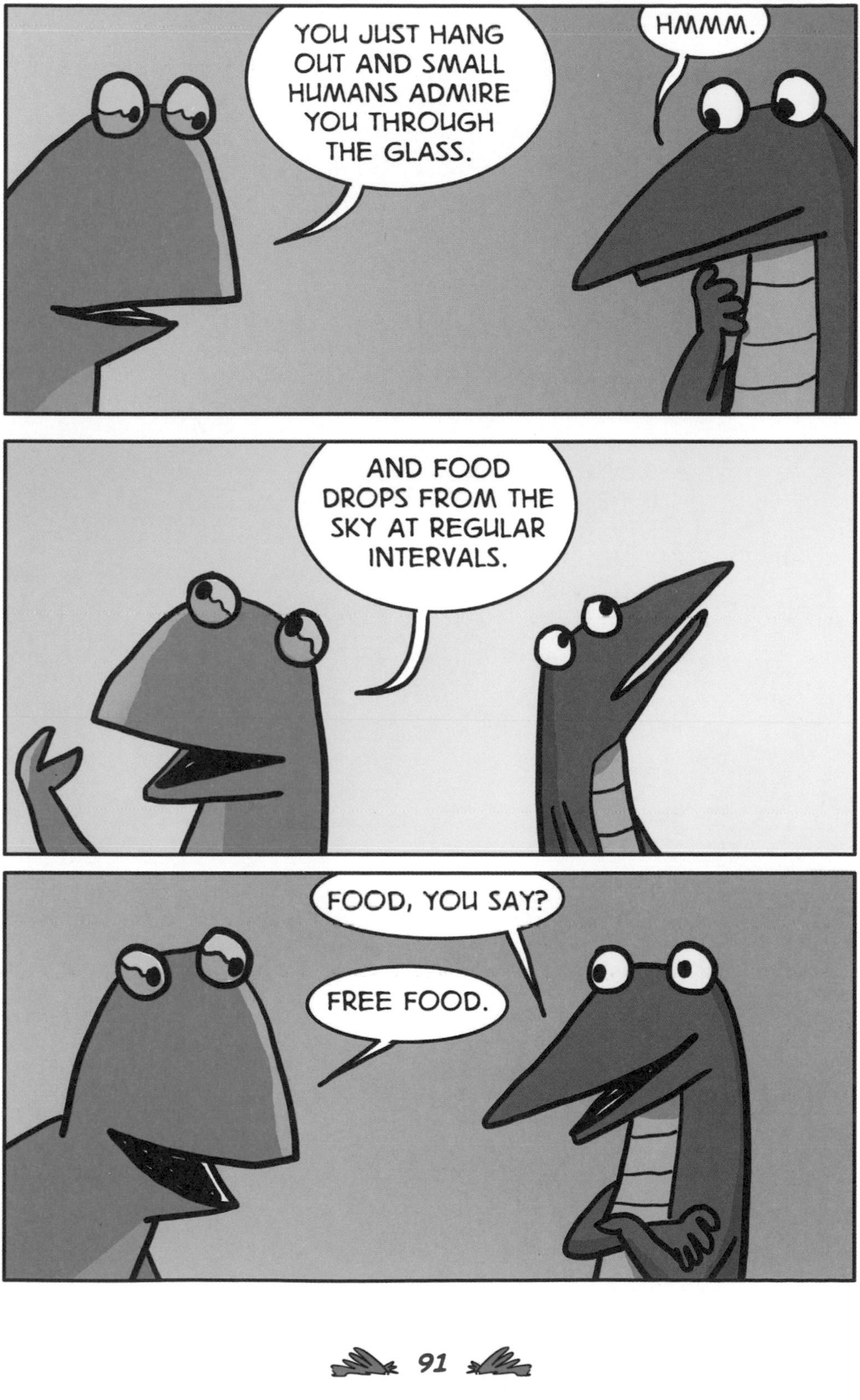
YOU JUST HANG OUT AND SMALL HUMANS ADMIRE YOU THROUGH THE GLASS.
HMMM.
AND FOOD DROPS FROM THE SKY AT REGULAR INTERVALS.
FOOD, YOU SAY?
FREE FOOD.

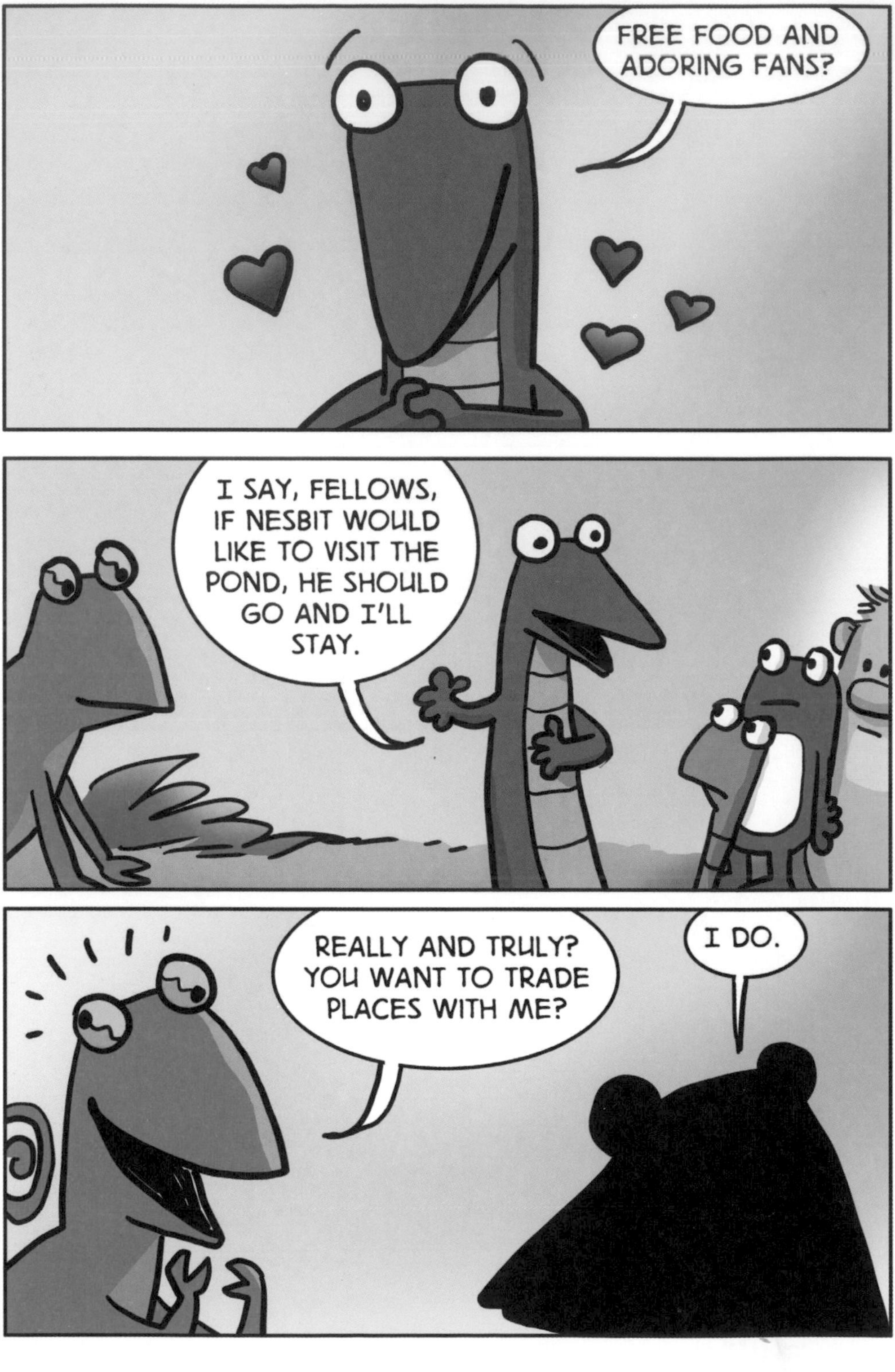
FREE FOOD AND ADORING FANS?
I SAY, FELLOWS, IF NESBIT WOULD LIKE TO VISIT THE POND, HE SHOULD GO AND I'LL STAY.
REALLY AND TRULY? YOU WANT TO TRADE PLACES WITH ME?
I DO.

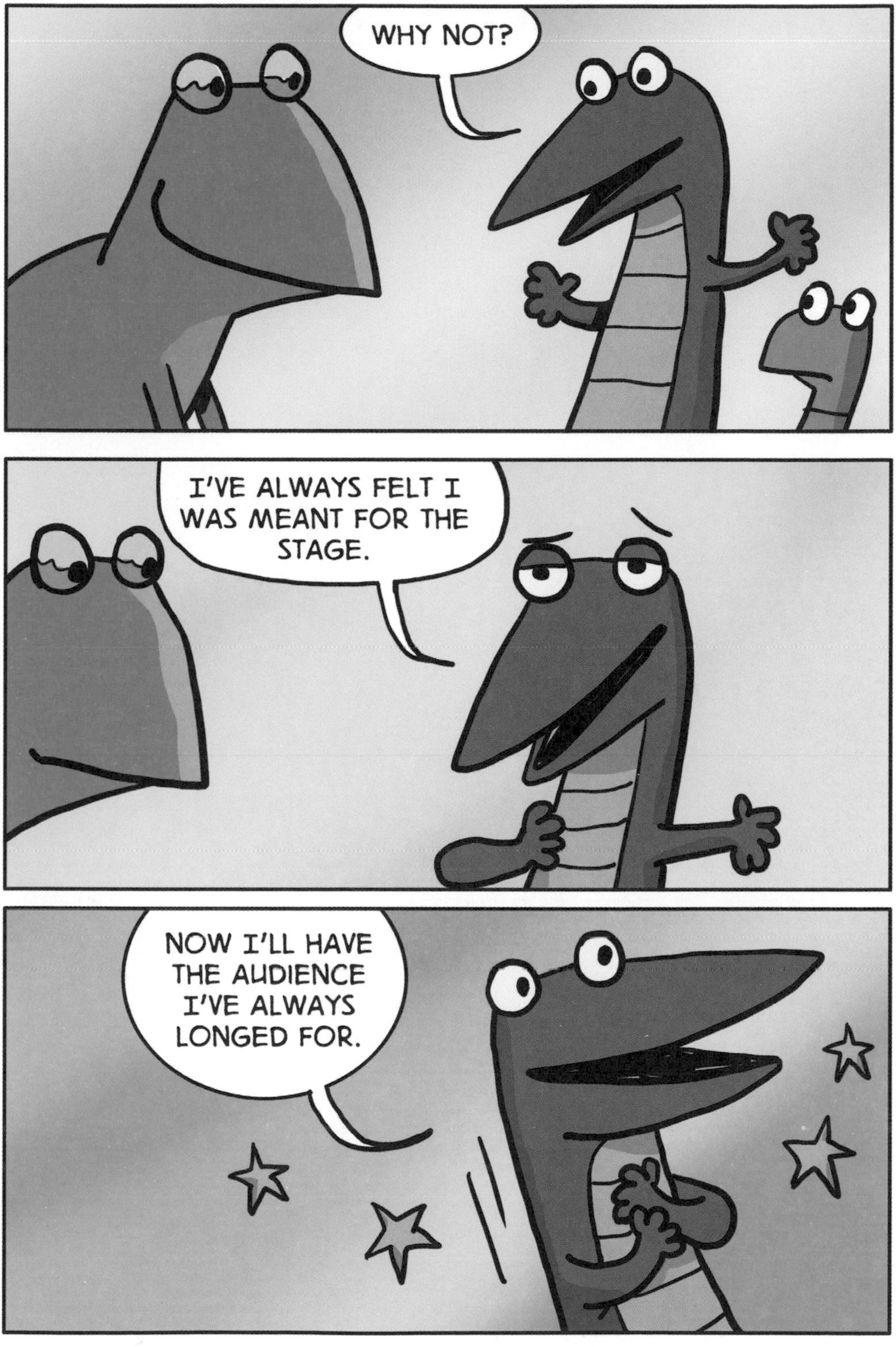
WHY NOT?
I'VE ALWAYS FELT I WAS MEANT FOR THE STAGE.
NOW I'LL HAVE THE AUDIENCE I'VE ALWAYS LONGED FOR.

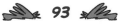

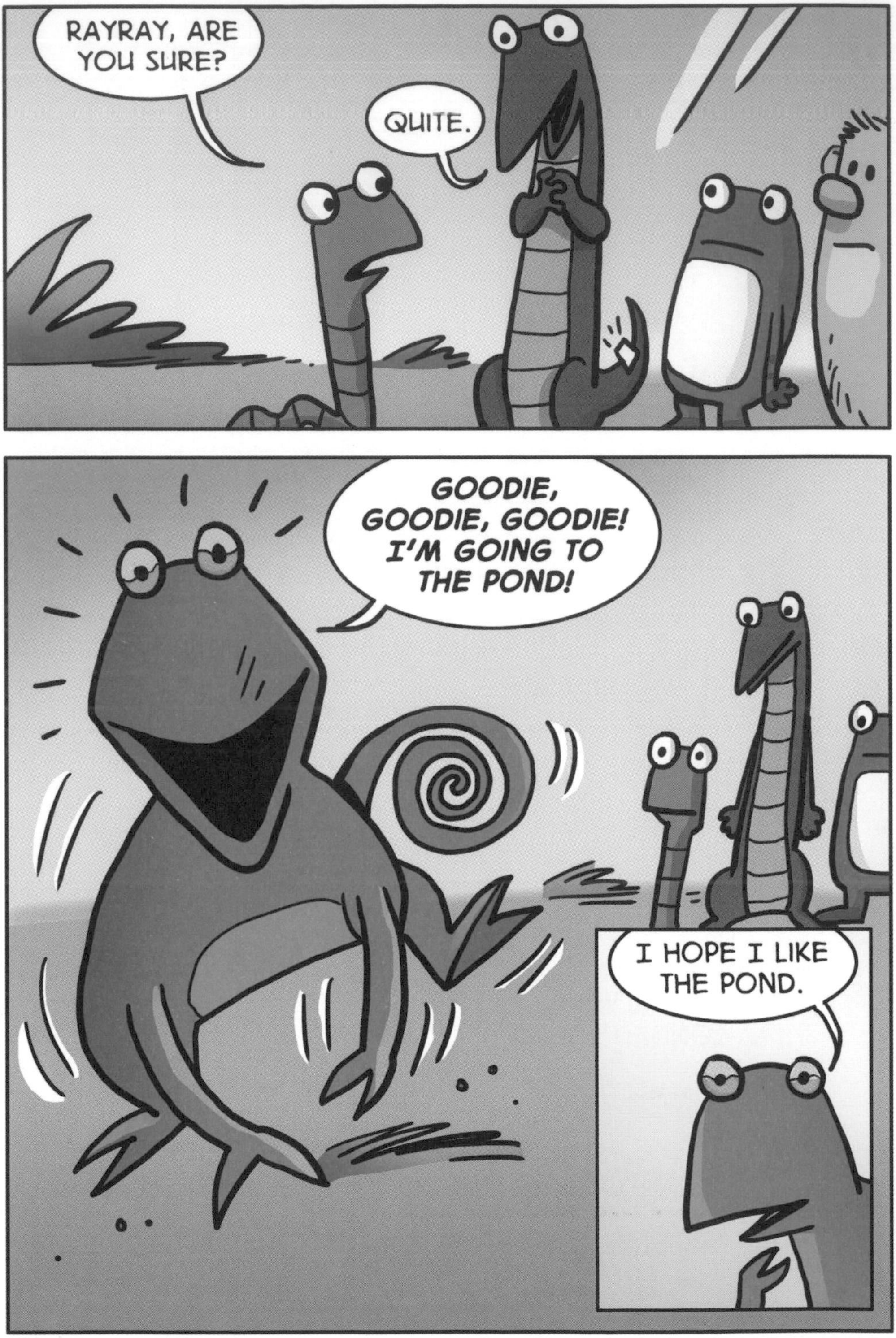
RAYRAY, ARE YOU SURE?
QUITE.
GOODIE, GOODIE, GOODIE! I'M GOING TO THE POND!
I HOPE I LIKE THE POND.

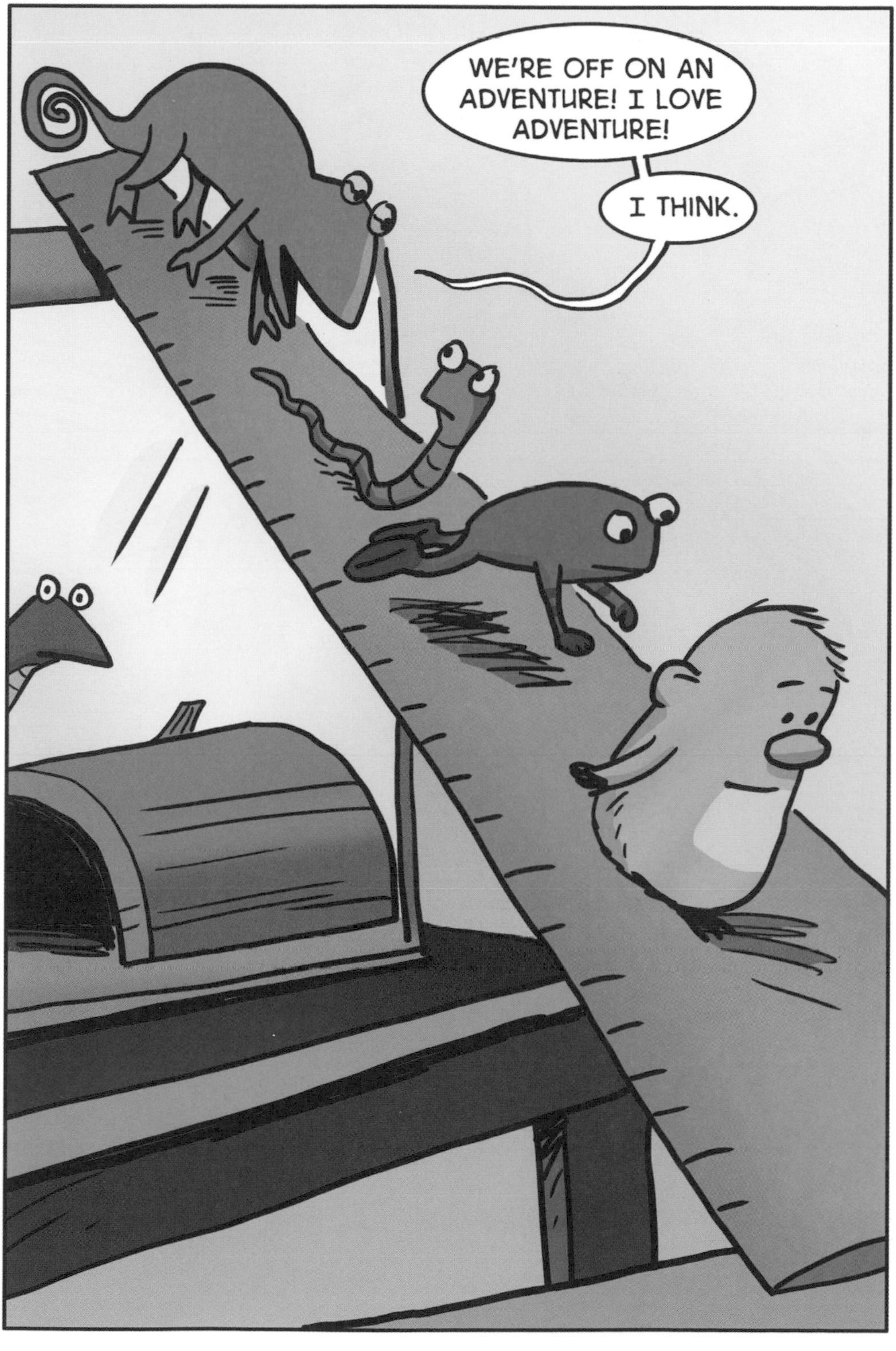
WE'RE OFF ON AN ADVENTURE! I LOVE ADVENTURE!
I THINK.

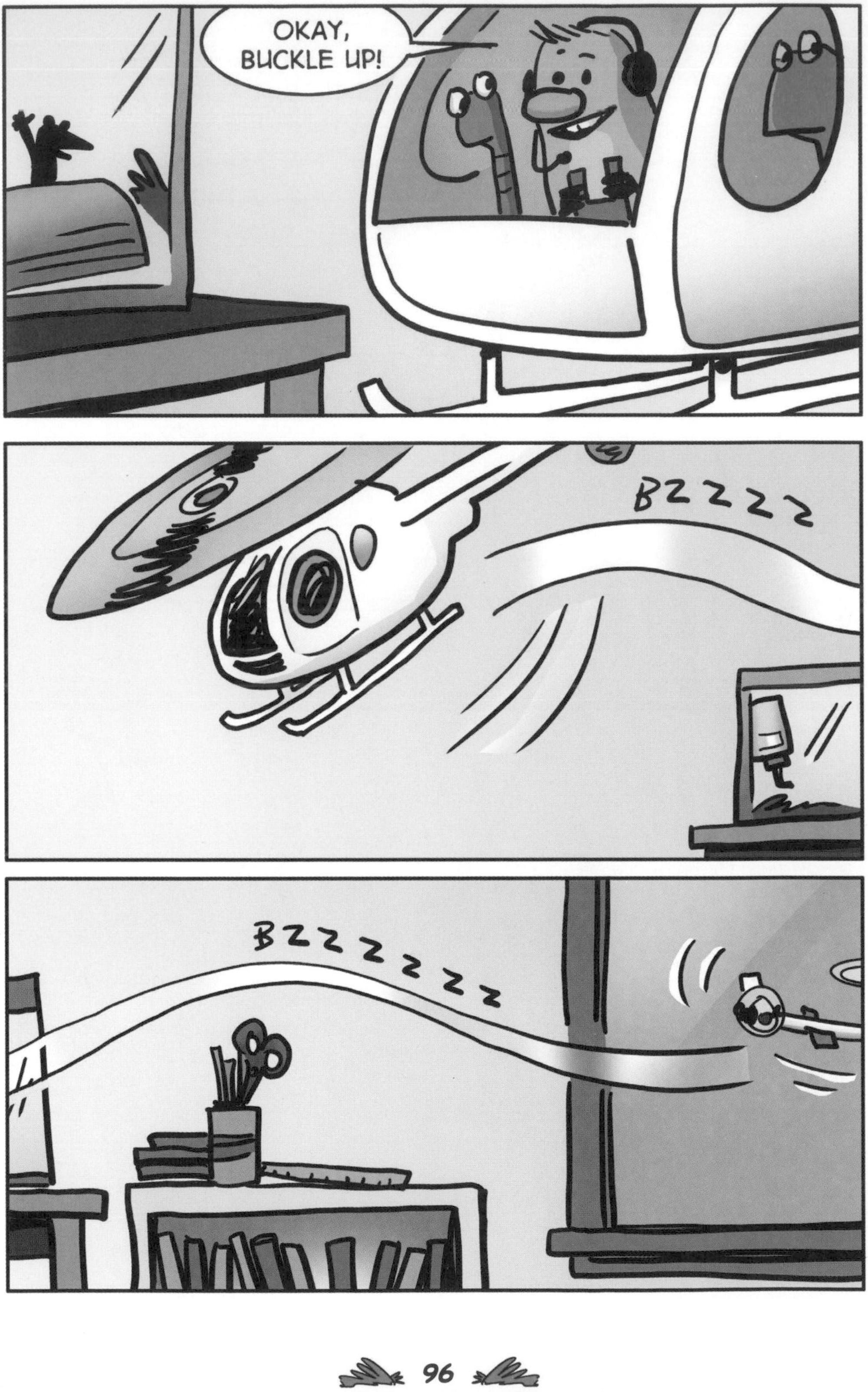
OKAY, BUCKLE UP!
BZZZZ
BZZZZZZZ

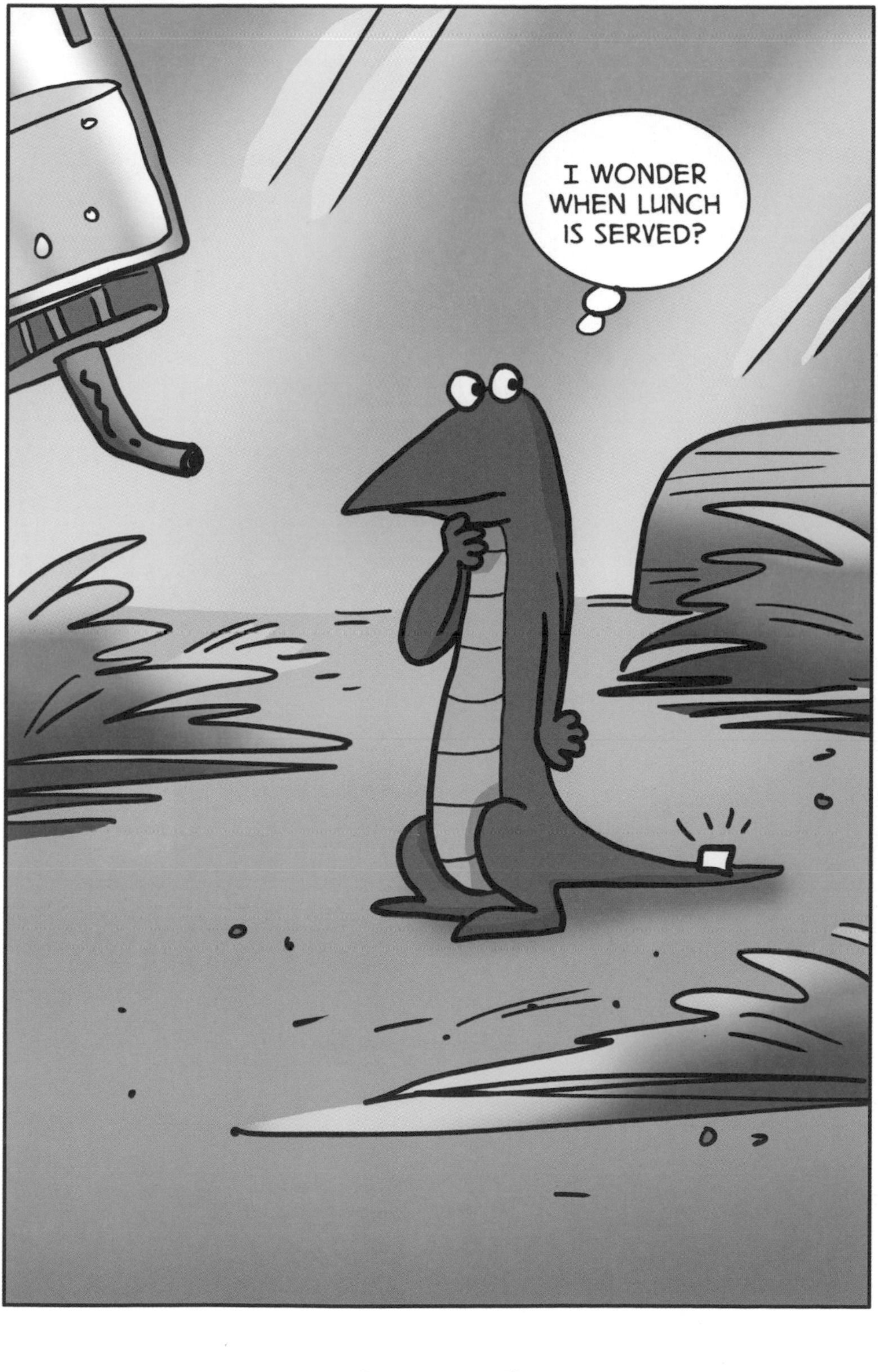
I WONDER WHEN LUNCH IS SERVED?

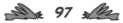

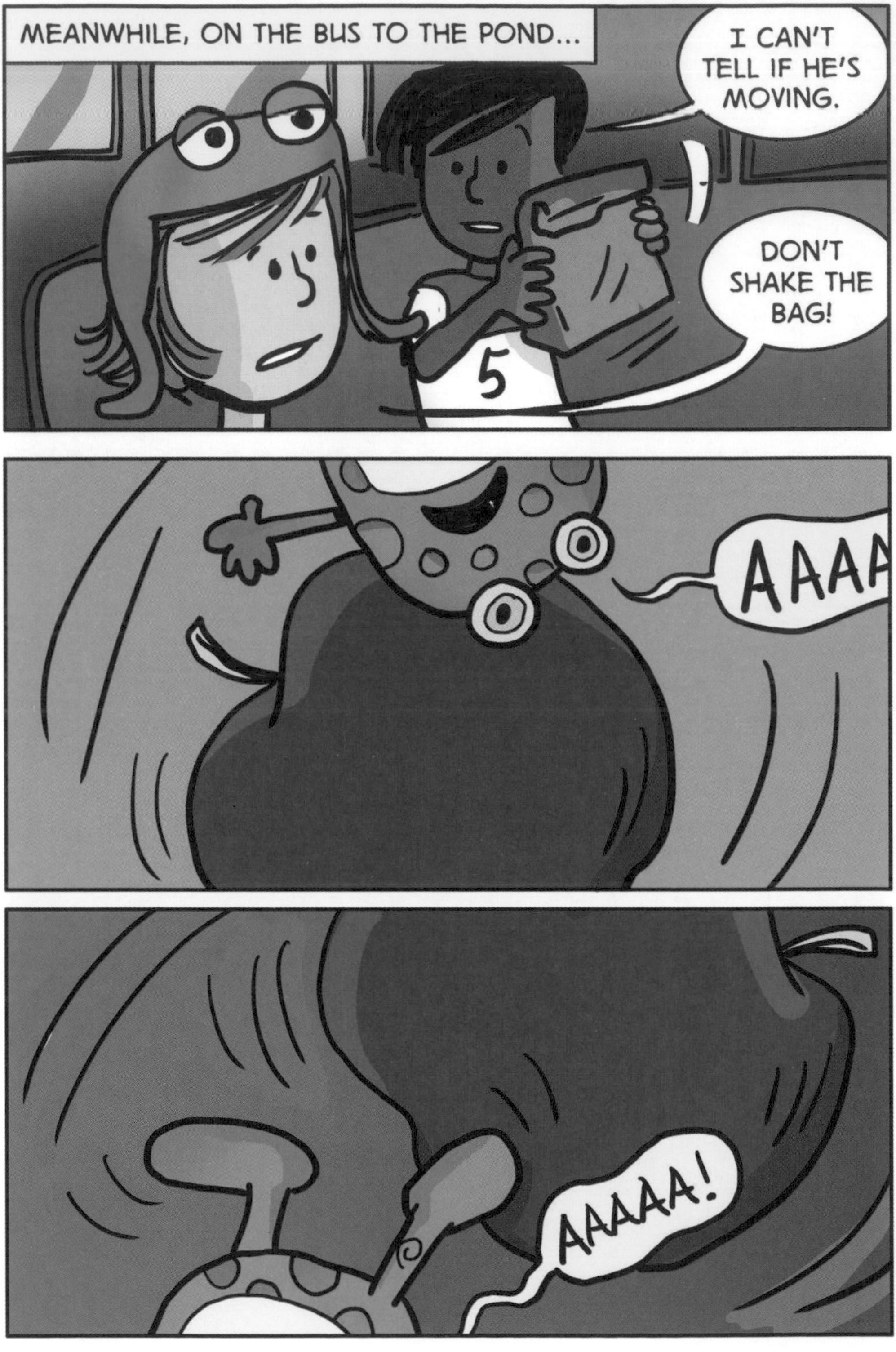
MEANWHILE, ON THE BUS TO THE POND...
I CAN'T TELL IF HE'S MOVING.
DON'T SHAKE THE BAG!
AAAA
AAAAA!

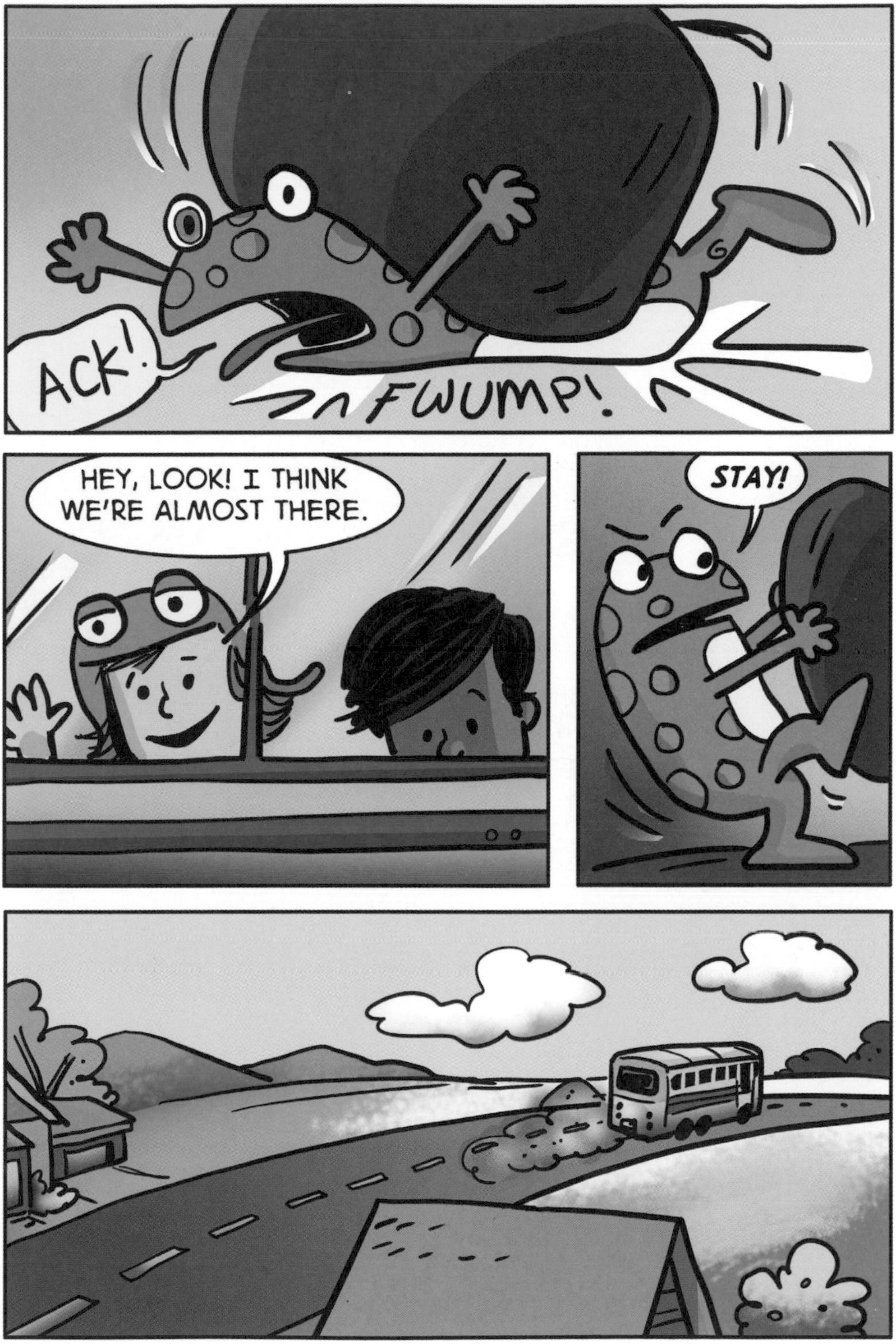
ACK!
FWUMP!
HEY, LOOK! I THINK WE'RE ALMOST THERE.
STAY!

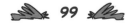

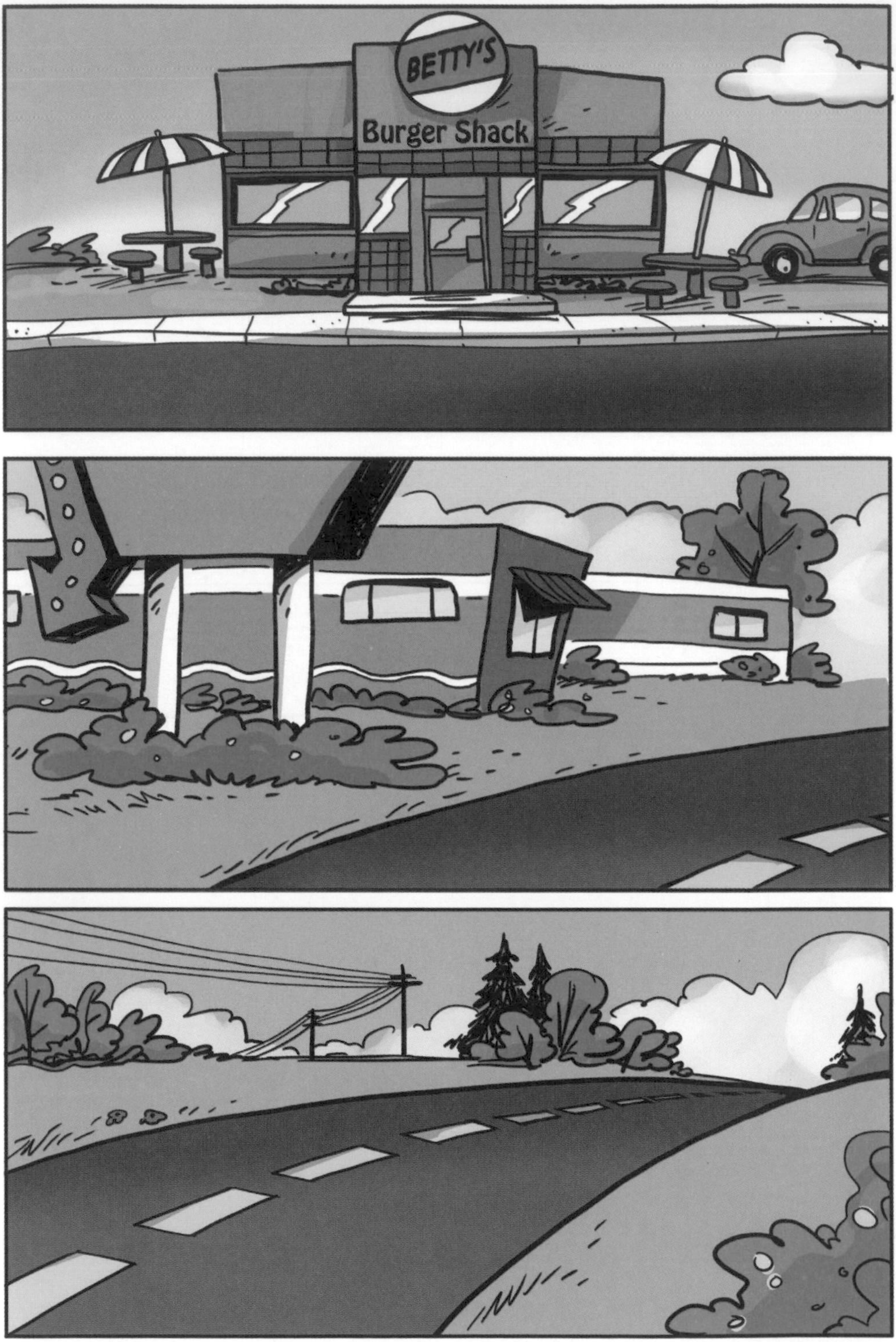
BETTY'S
Burger Shack

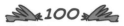

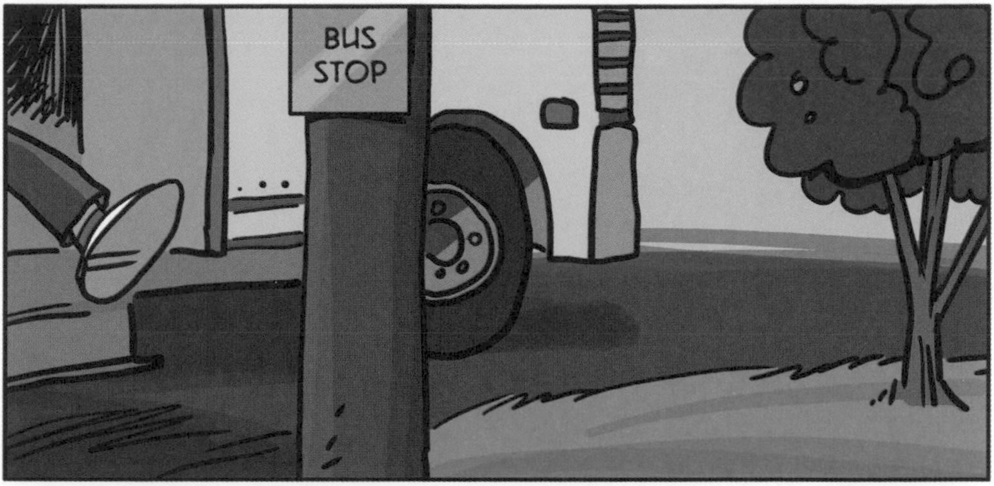
BUS
STOP

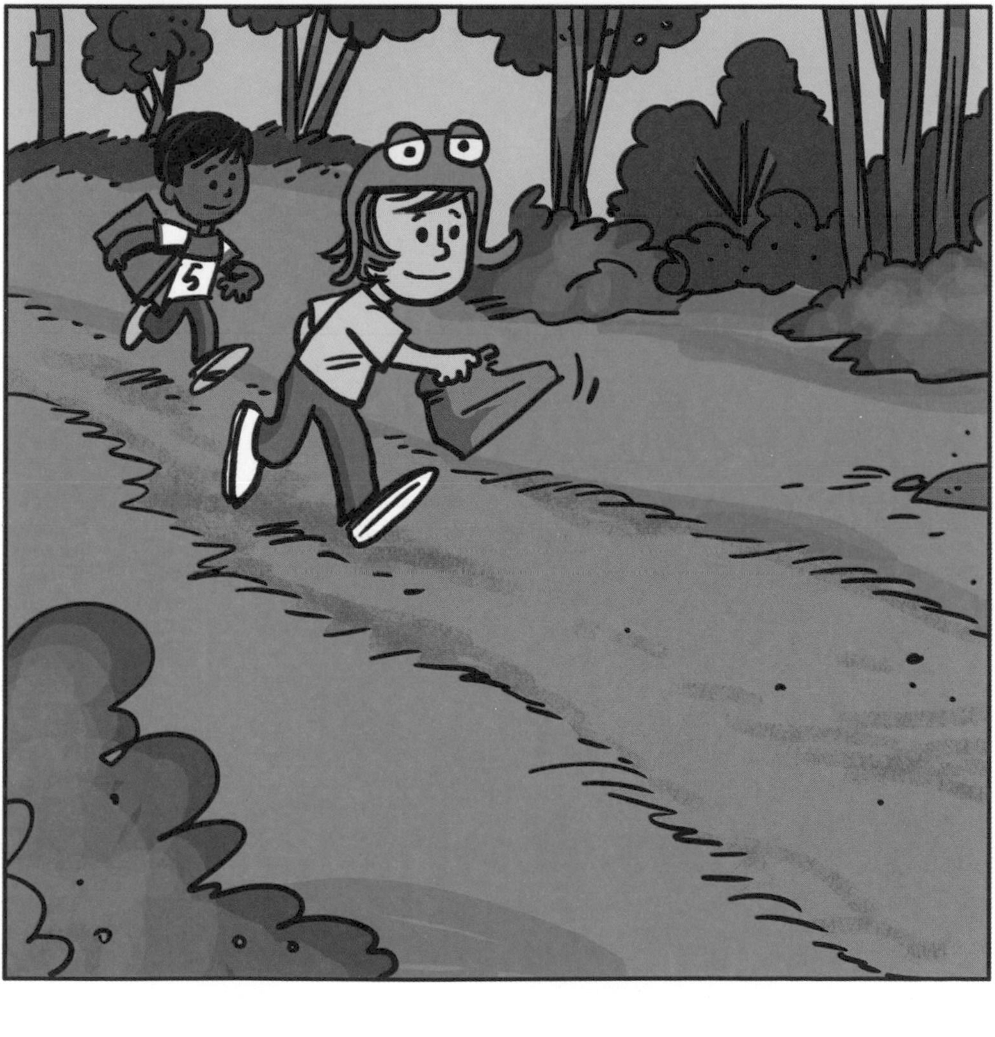
5

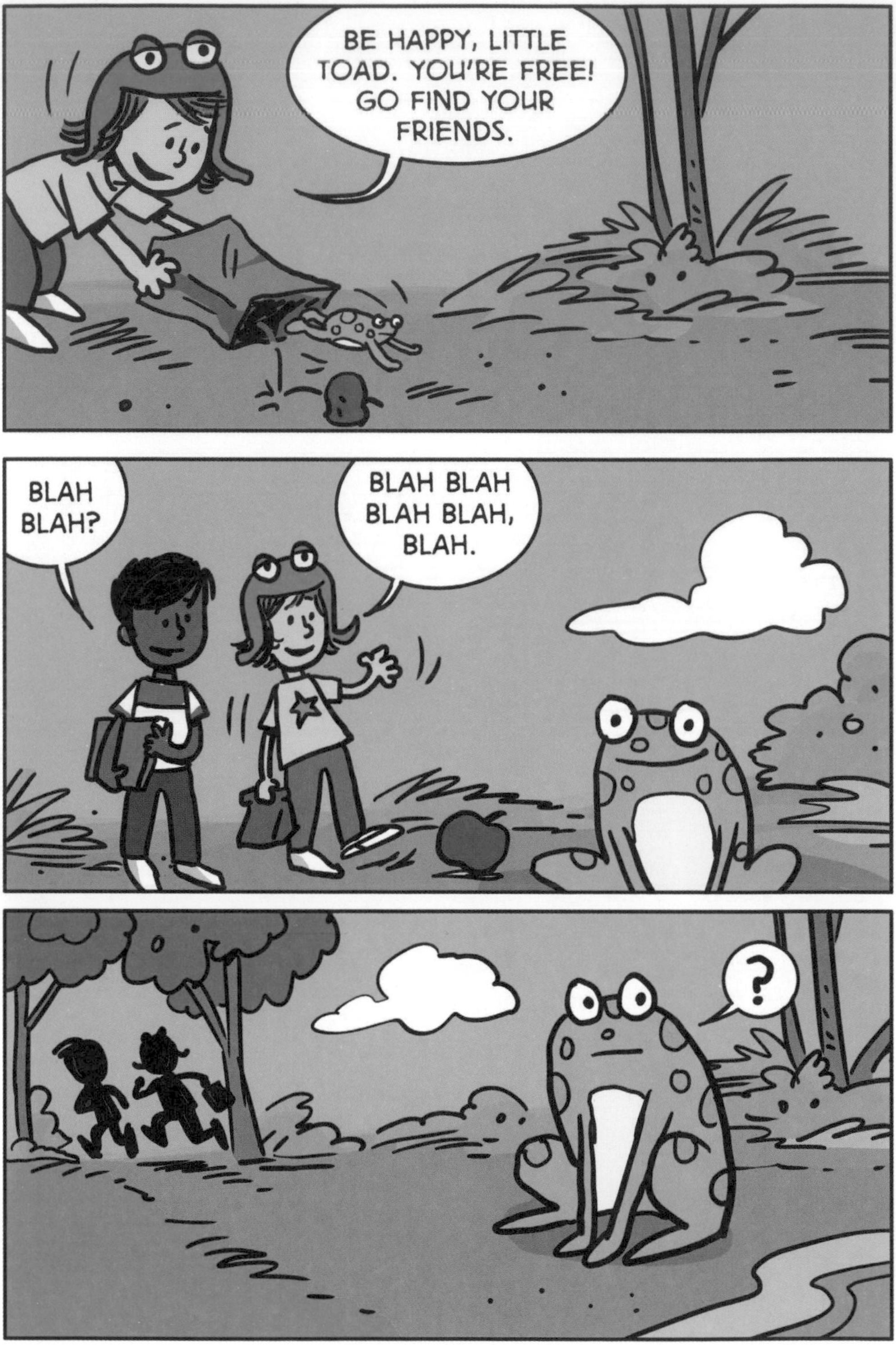
BE HAPPY, LITTLE TOAD. YOU'RE FREE! GO FIND YOUR FRIENDS.
BLAH BLAH?
BLAH BLAH BLAH BLAH, BLAH.
?

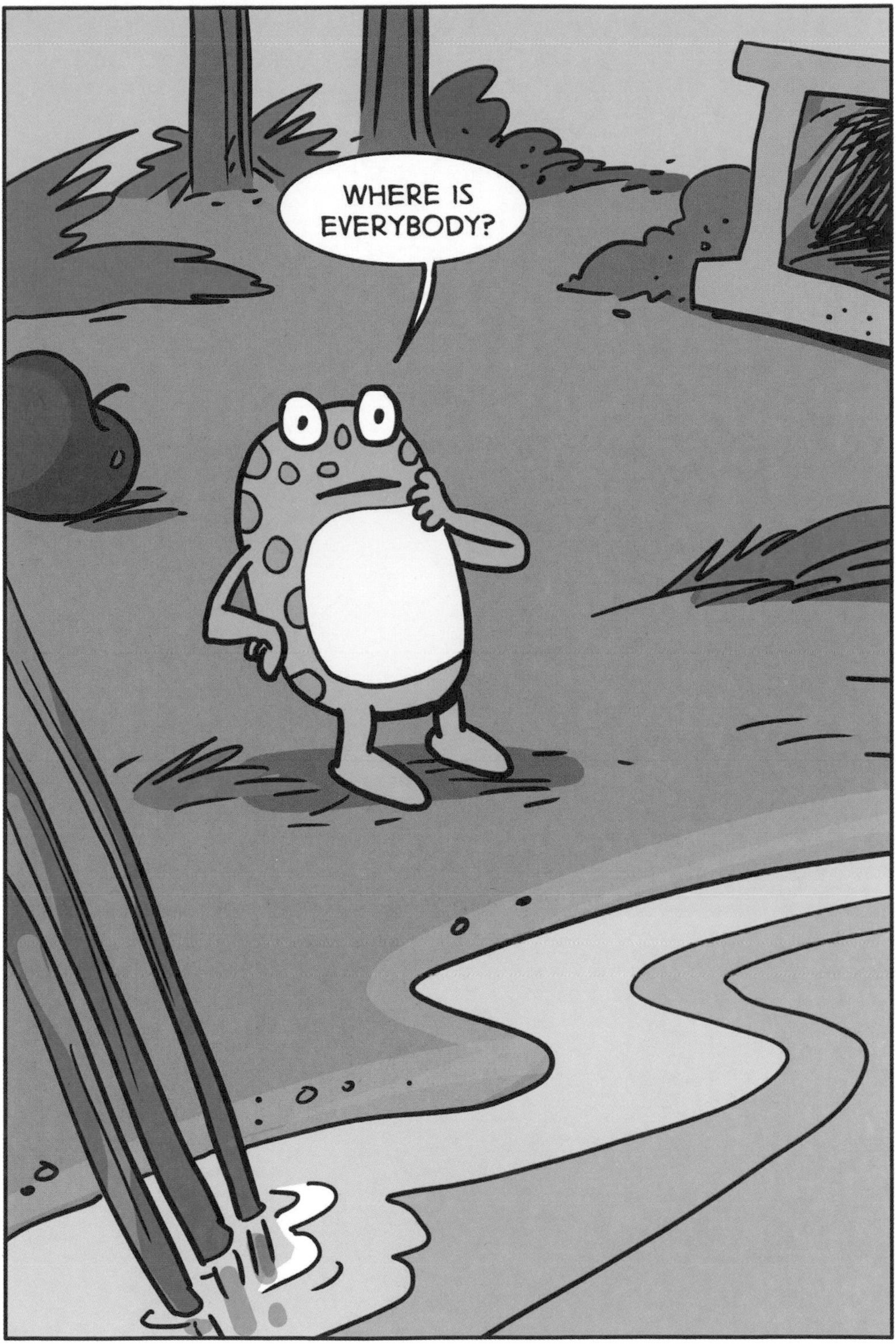
WHERE IS EVERYBODY?

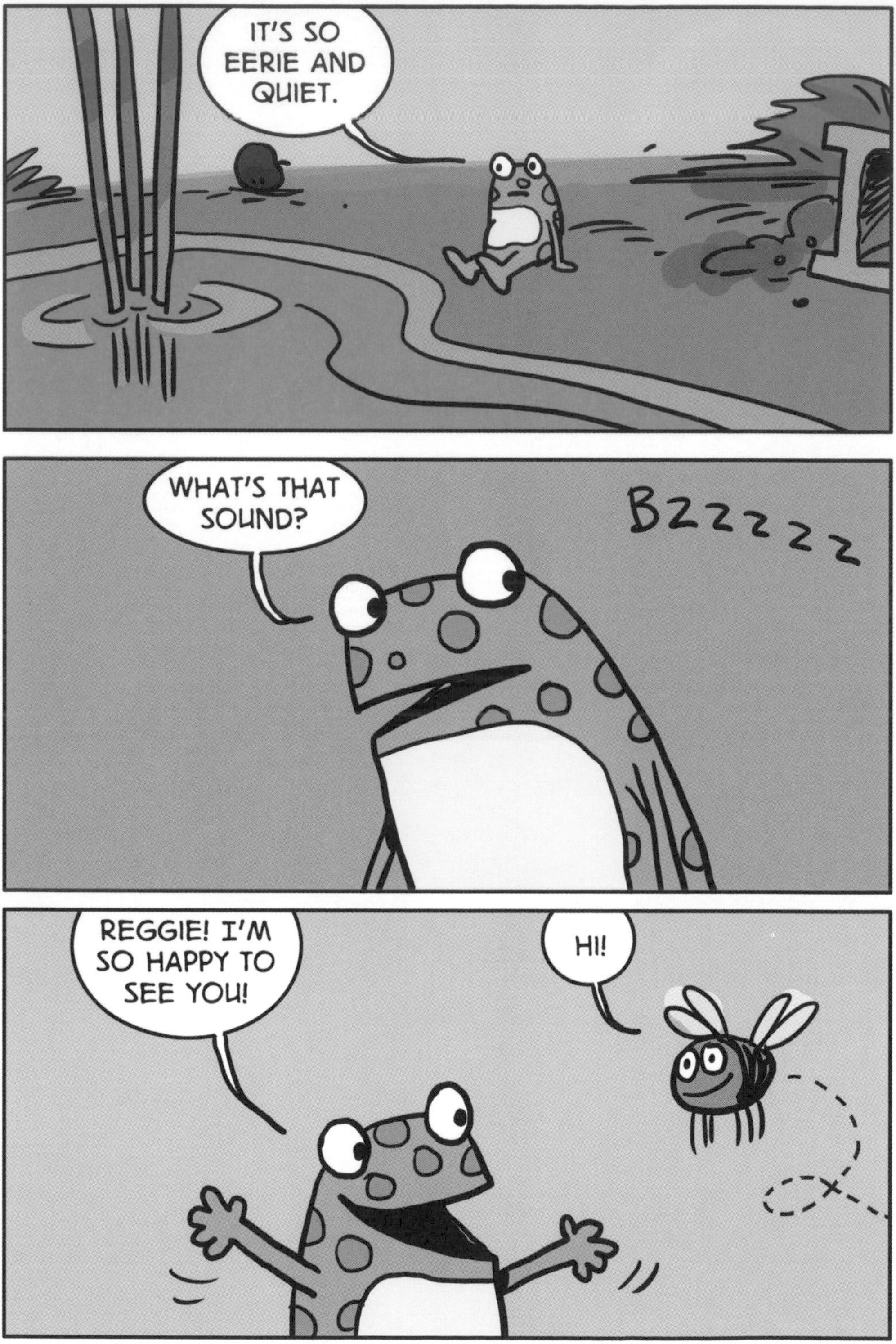
IT'S SO EERIE AND QUIET.
WHAT'S THAT SOUND?
BZZZZZZ
REGGIE! I'M SO HAPPY TO SEE YOU!
HI!

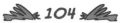

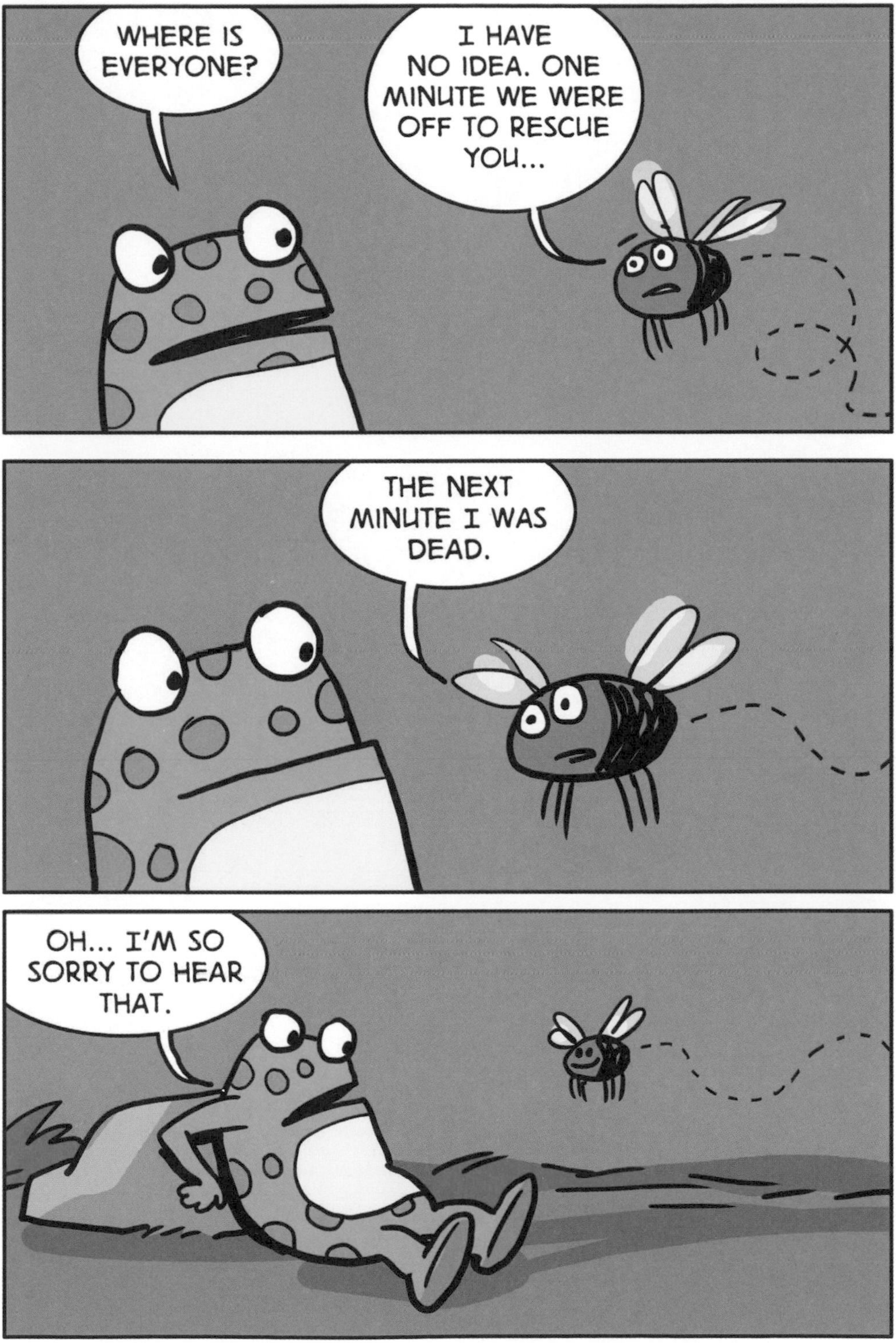
WHERE IS EVERYONE?
I HAVE NO IDEA. ONE MINUTE WE WERE OFF TO RESCUE YOU...
THE NEXT MINUTE I WAS DEAD.
OH... I'M SO SORRY TO HEAR THAT.

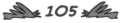

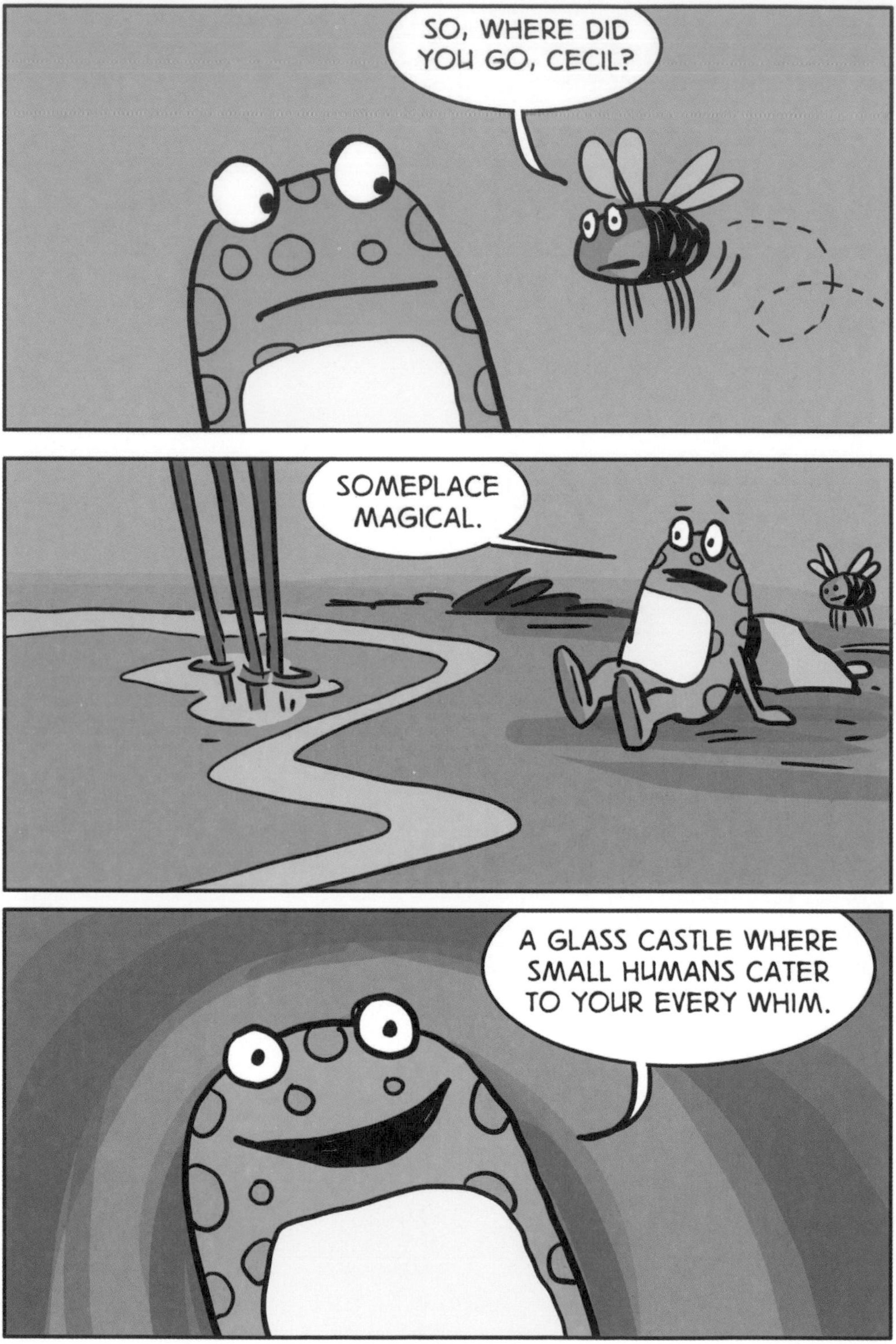
SO, WHERE DID YOU GO, CECIL?
SOMEPLACE MAGICAL.
A GLASS CASTLE WHERE SMALL HUMANS CATER TO YOUR EVERY WHIM.

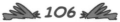

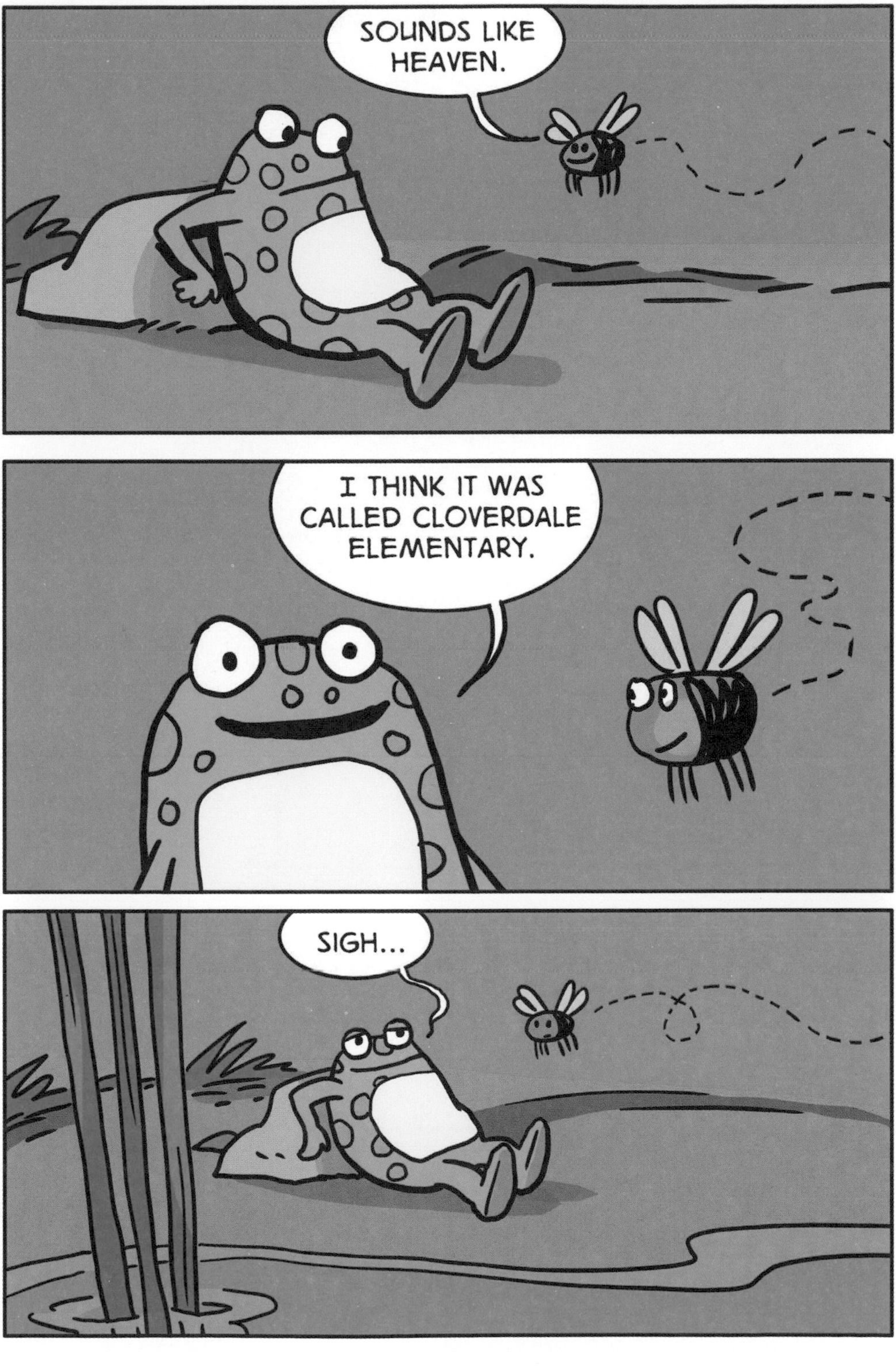
SOUNDS LIKE HEAVEN.
I THINK IT WAS CALLED CLOVERDALE ELEMENTARY.
SIGH...

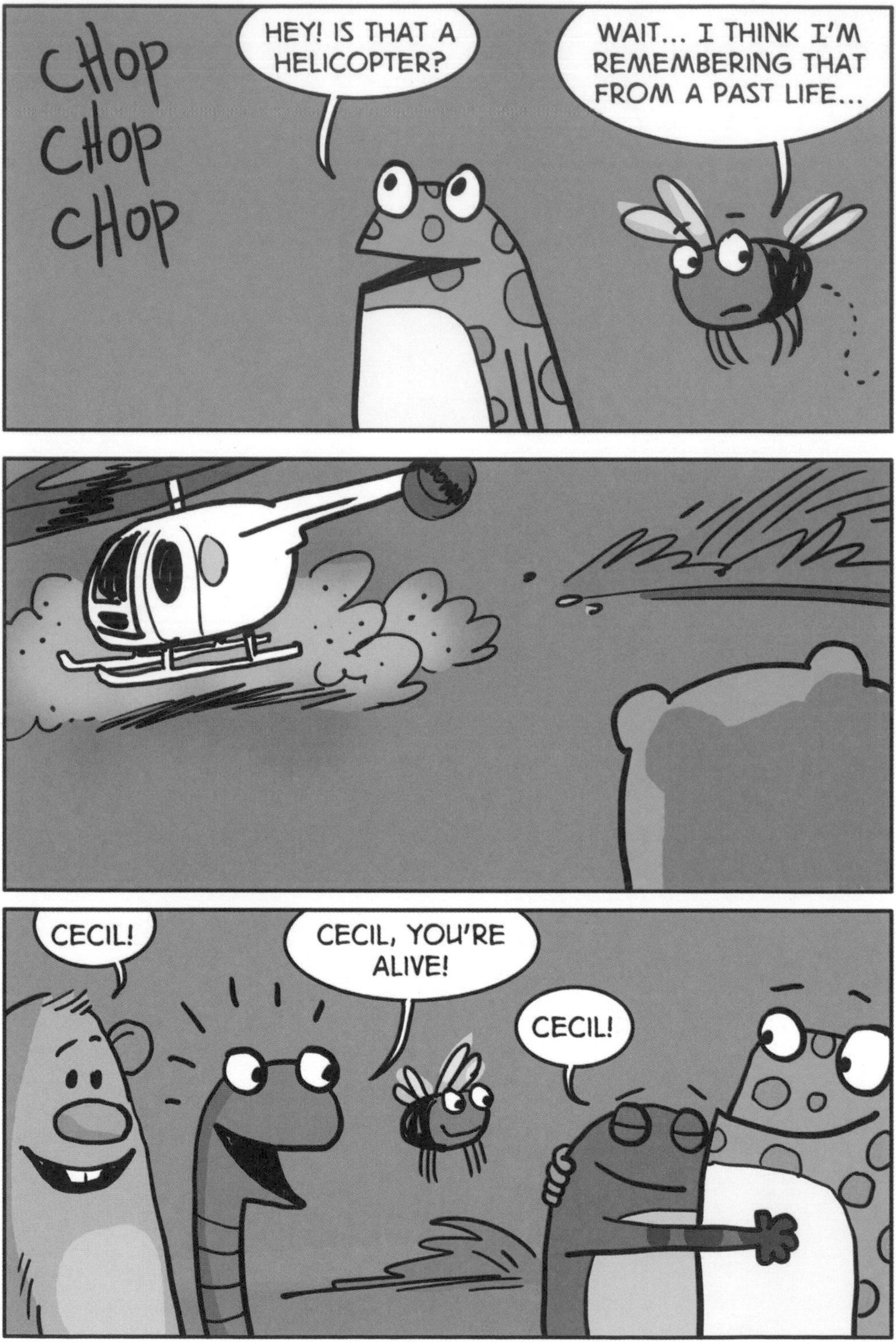
CHOP
CHOP
CHOP
HEY! IS THAT A HELICOPTER?
WAIT... I THINK I'M REMEMBERING THAT FROM A PAST LIFE...
CECIL!
CECIL, YOU'RE ALIVE!
CECIL!

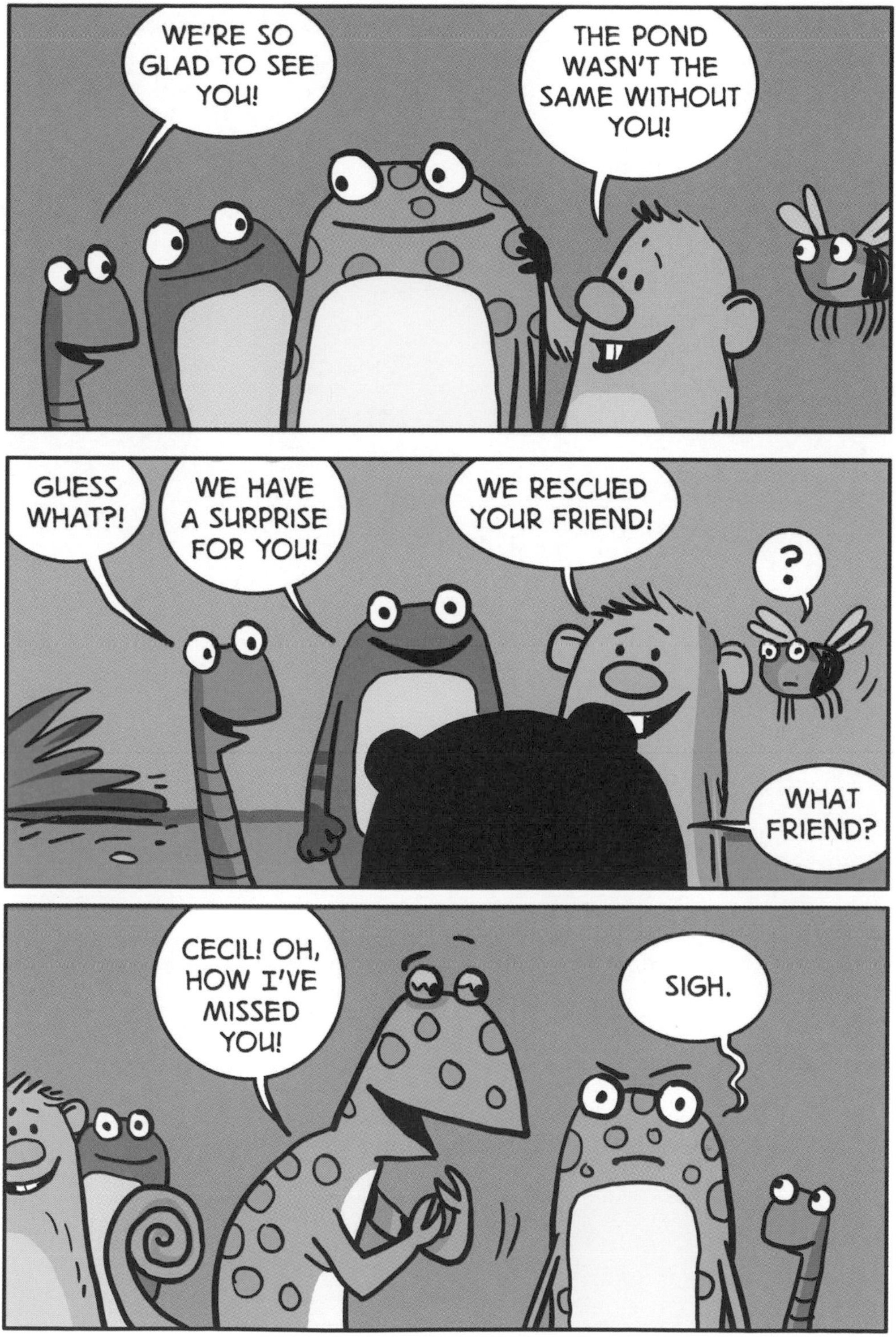
WE'RE SO GLAD TO SEE YOU!
THE POND WASN'T THE SAME WITHOUT YOU!
GUESS WHAT?!
WE HAVE A SURPRISE FOR YOU!
WE RESCUED YOUR FRIEND!
?
WHAT FRIEND?
CECIL! OH, HOW I'VE MISSED YOU!
SIGH.

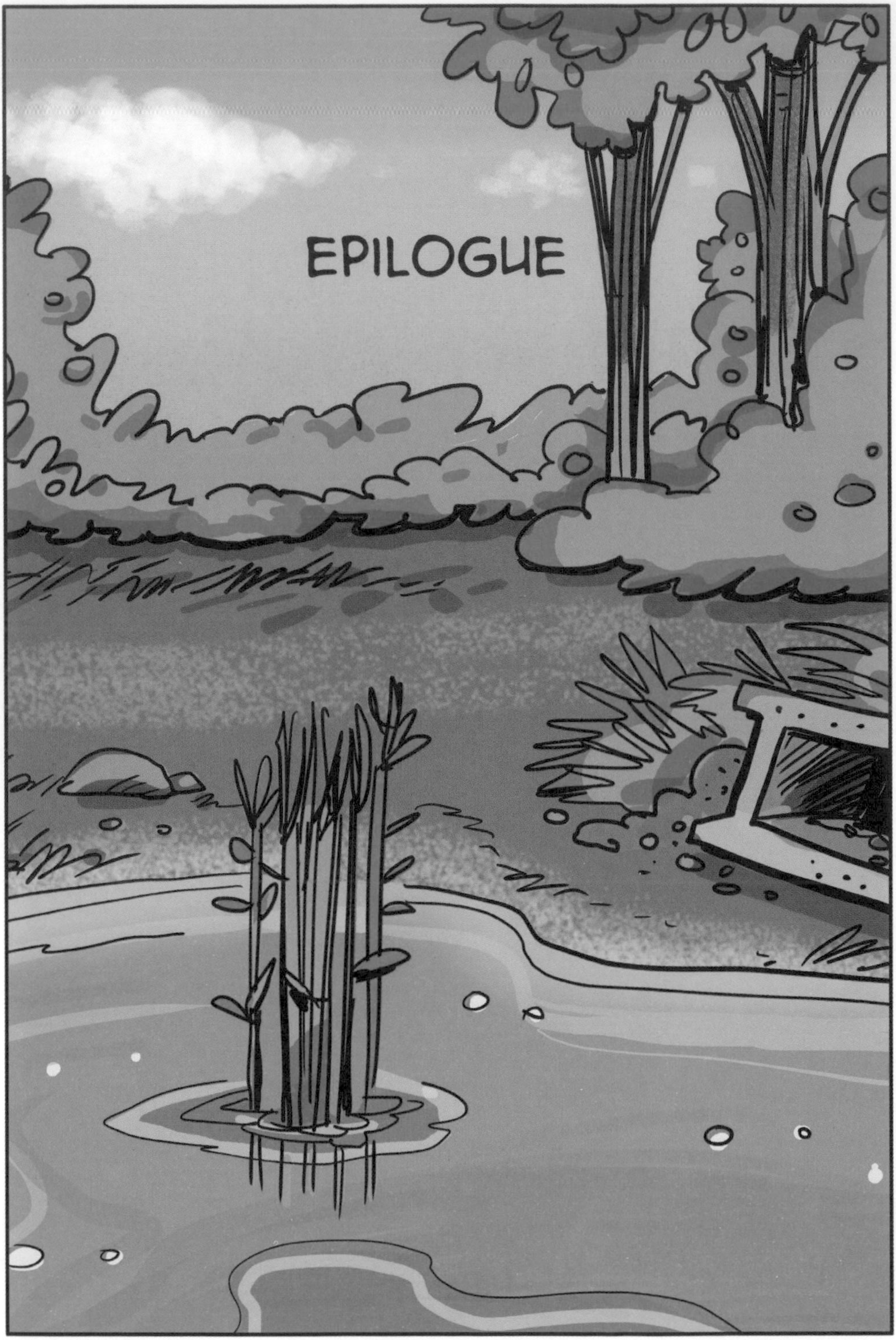
EPILOGUE

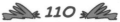

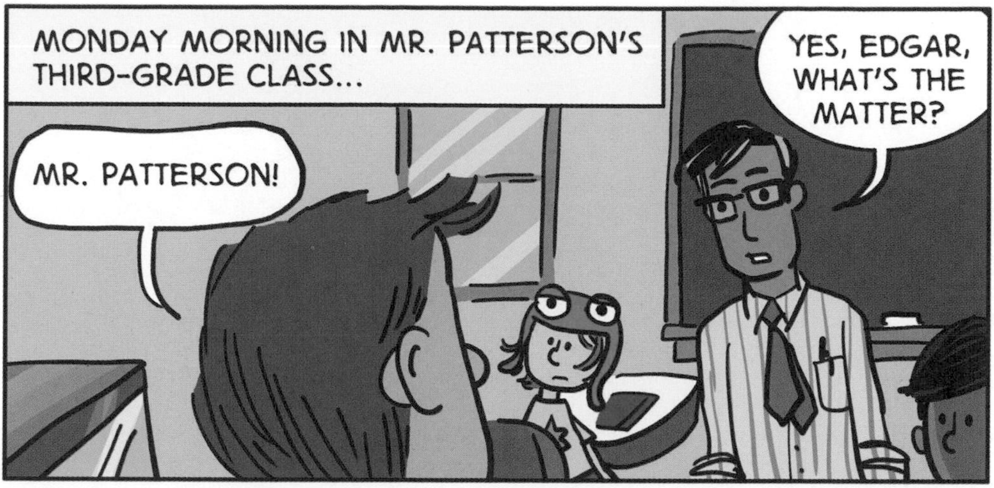
MONDAY MORNING IN MR. PATTERSON'S THIRD-GRADE CLASS...
MR. PATTERSON!
YES, EDGAR, WHAT'S THE MATTER?

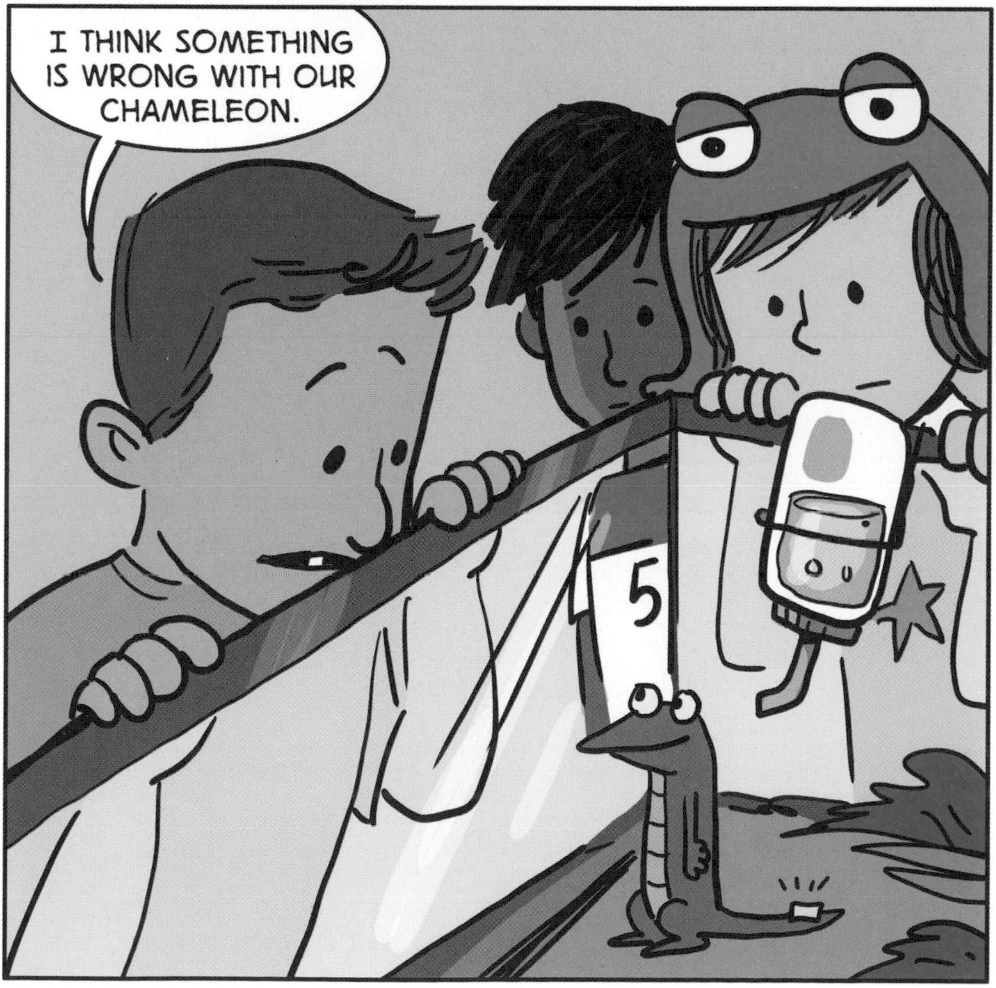
I THINK SOMETHING IS WRONG WITH OUR CHAMELEON.
5

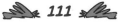

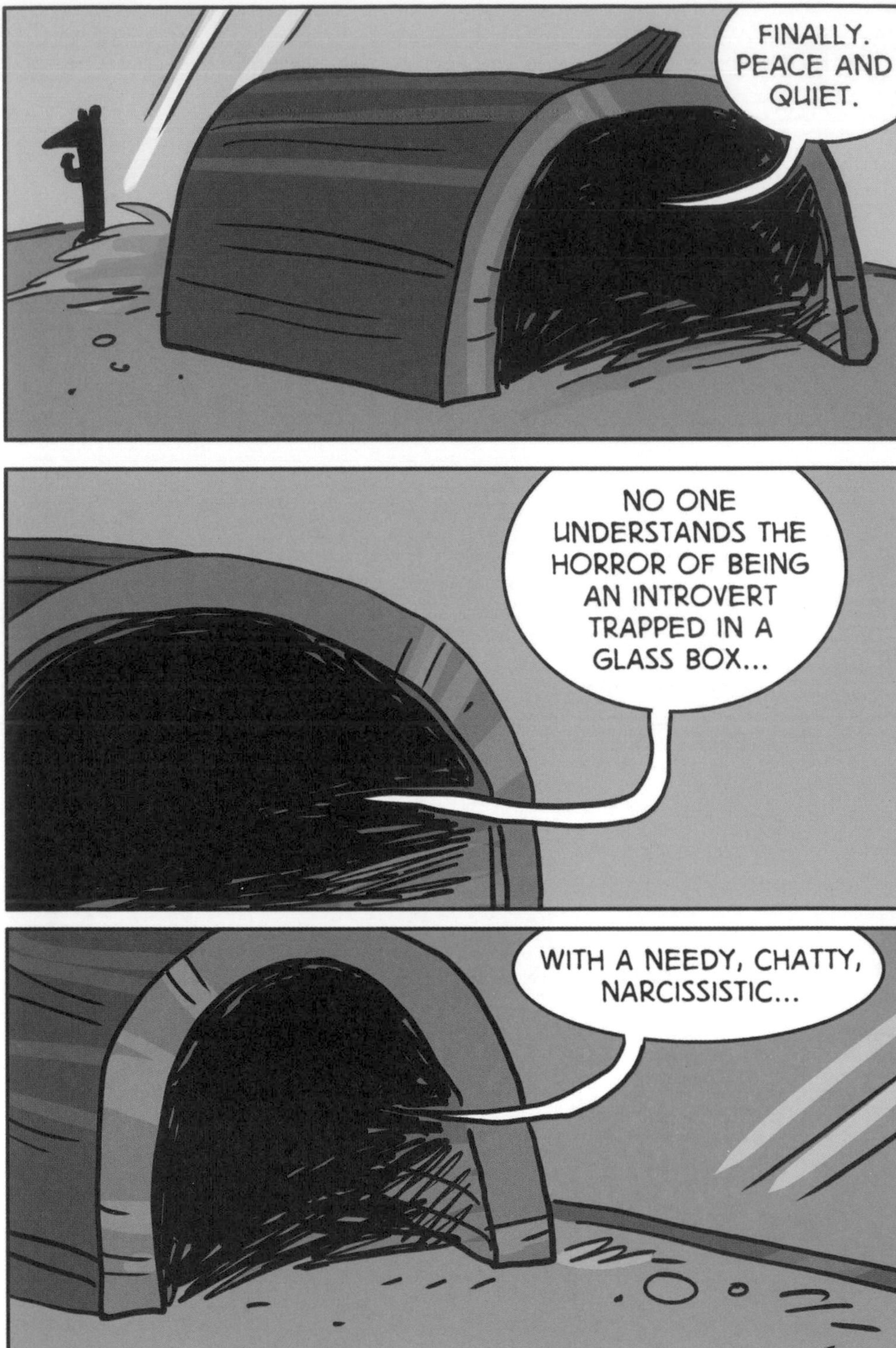
FINALLY. PEACE AND QUIET.
NO ONE UNDERSTANDS THE HORROR OF BEING AN INTROVERT TRAPPED IN A GLASS BOX...
WITH A NEEDY, CHATTY, NARCISSISTIC...

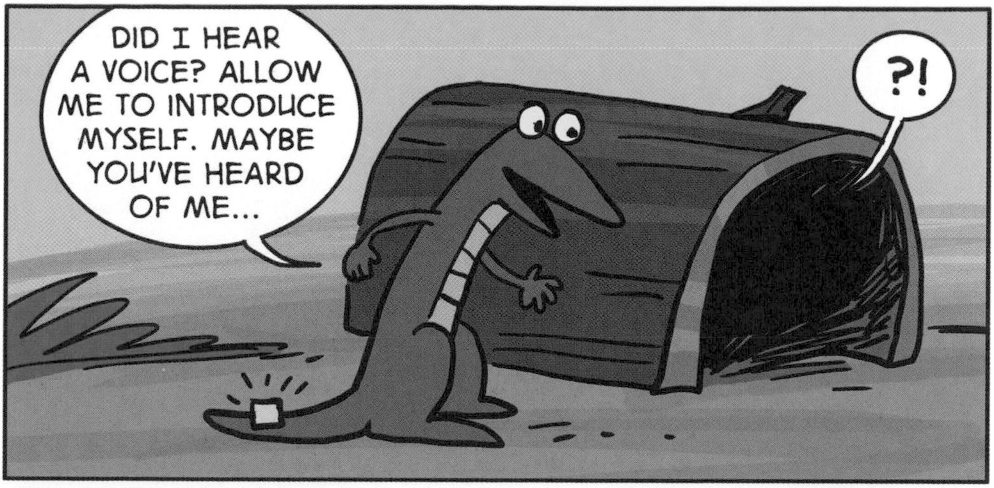
DID I HEAR A VOICE? ALLOW ME TO INTRODUCE MYSELF. MAYBE YOU'VE HEARD OF ME...
?!

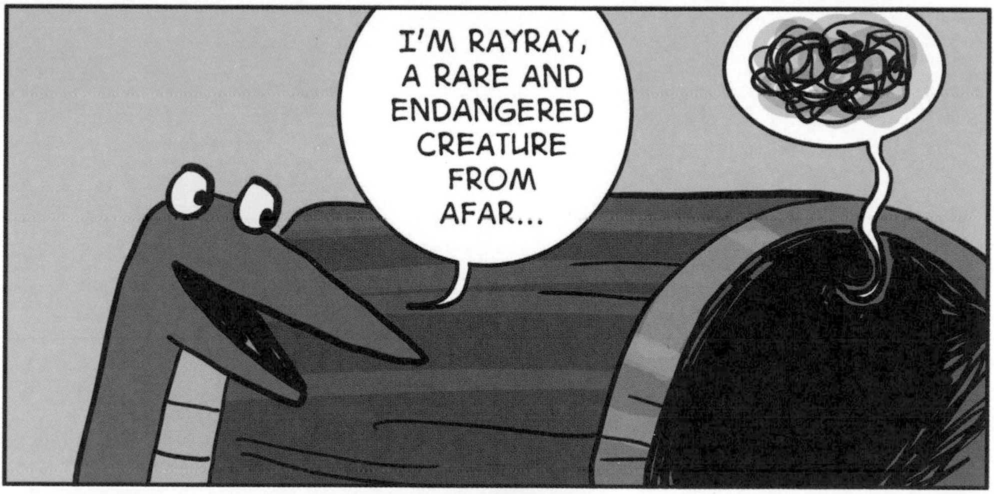
I'M RAYRAY, A RARE AND ENDANGERED CREATURE FROM AFAR...

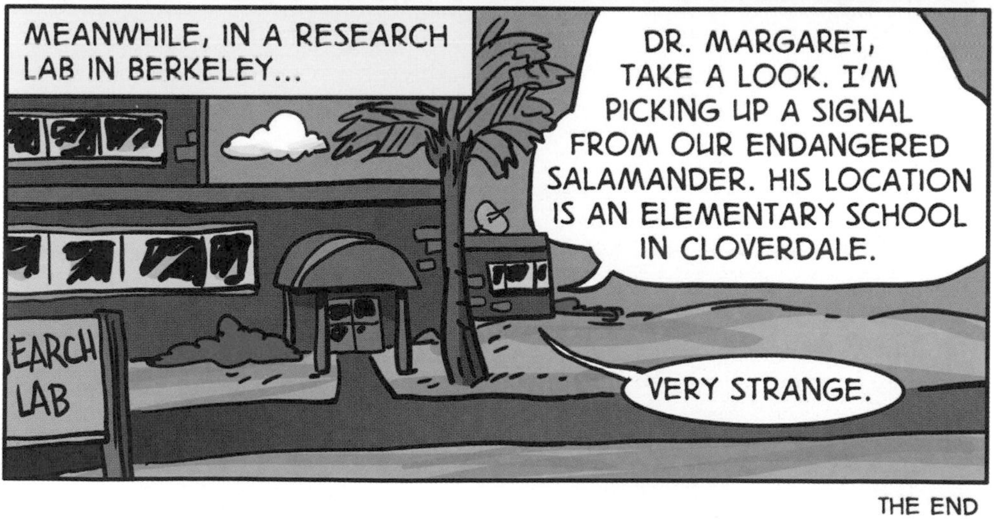
MEANWHILE, IN A RESEARCH LAB IN BERKELEY...
DR. MARGARET, TAKE A LOOK. I'M PICKING UP A SIGNAL FROM OUR ENDANGERED SALAMANDER. HIS LOCATION IS AN ELEMENTARY SCHOOL IN CLOVERDALE.
VERY STRANGE.
EARCH LAB

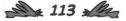

THE END

MORE TO EXPLORE!

FUN FACTS AND THINGS TO MAKE!

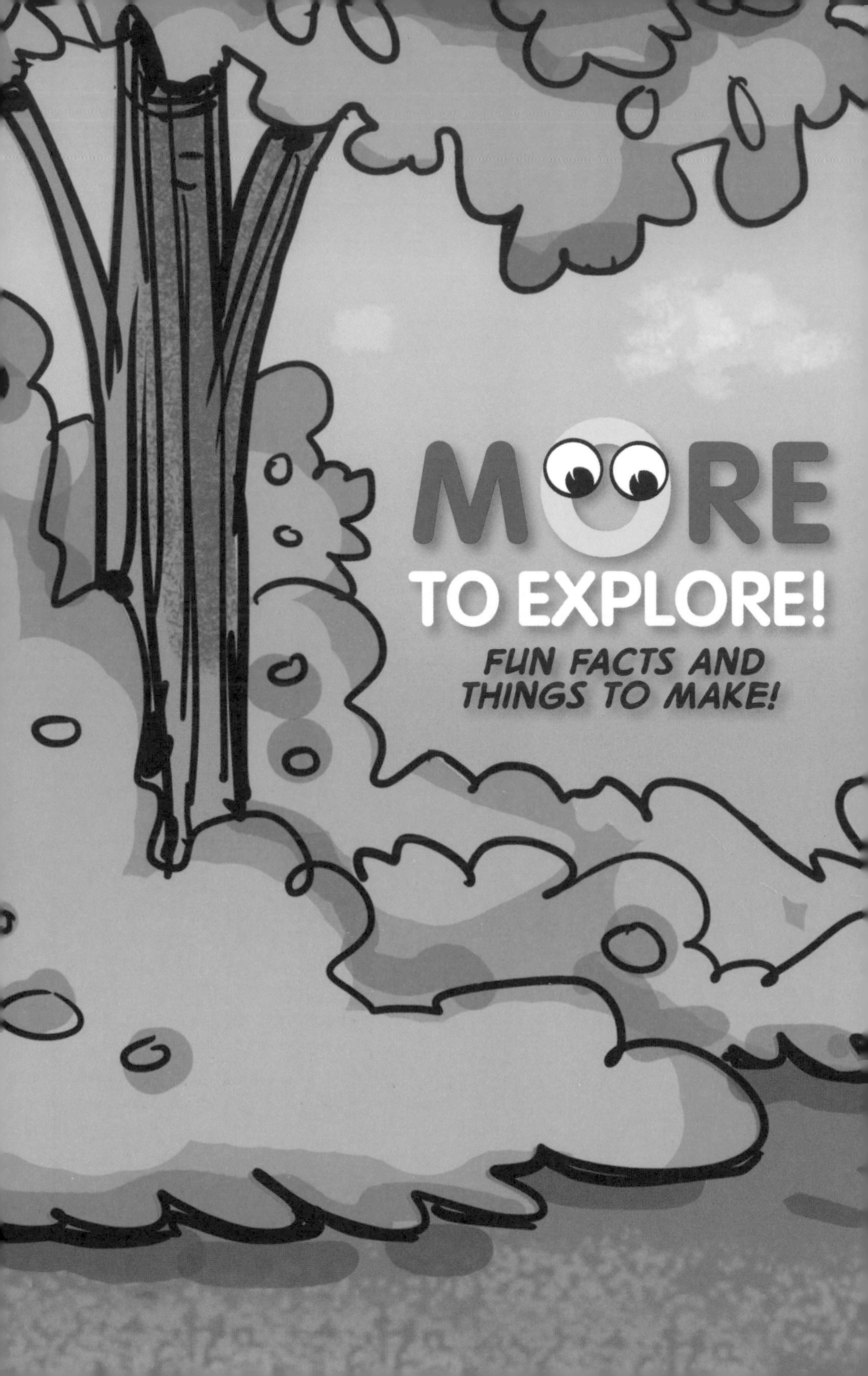

ABOUT THE CHAMELEON

THE *CHAMELEON* IS AMAZING. ITS EYES CAN LOOK IN OPPOSITE DIRECTIONS AT THE SAME TIME.

IT HAS TWO-TOED FEET THAT CAN GRIP LIKE POWERFUL TONGS.

A CHAMELEON CAN HANG FROM A TREE BRANCH USING ONLY ITS TAIL.

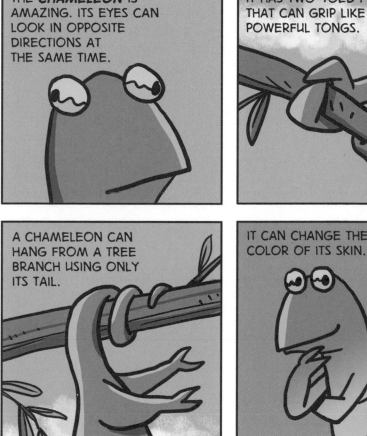

IT CAN CHANGE THE COLOR OF ITS SKIN.

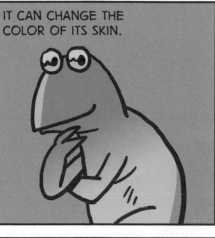

IN MINUTES, IT CAN CHANGE FROM GREEN TO BROWN OR EVEN CHANGE INTO STRIPES AND SPOTS.

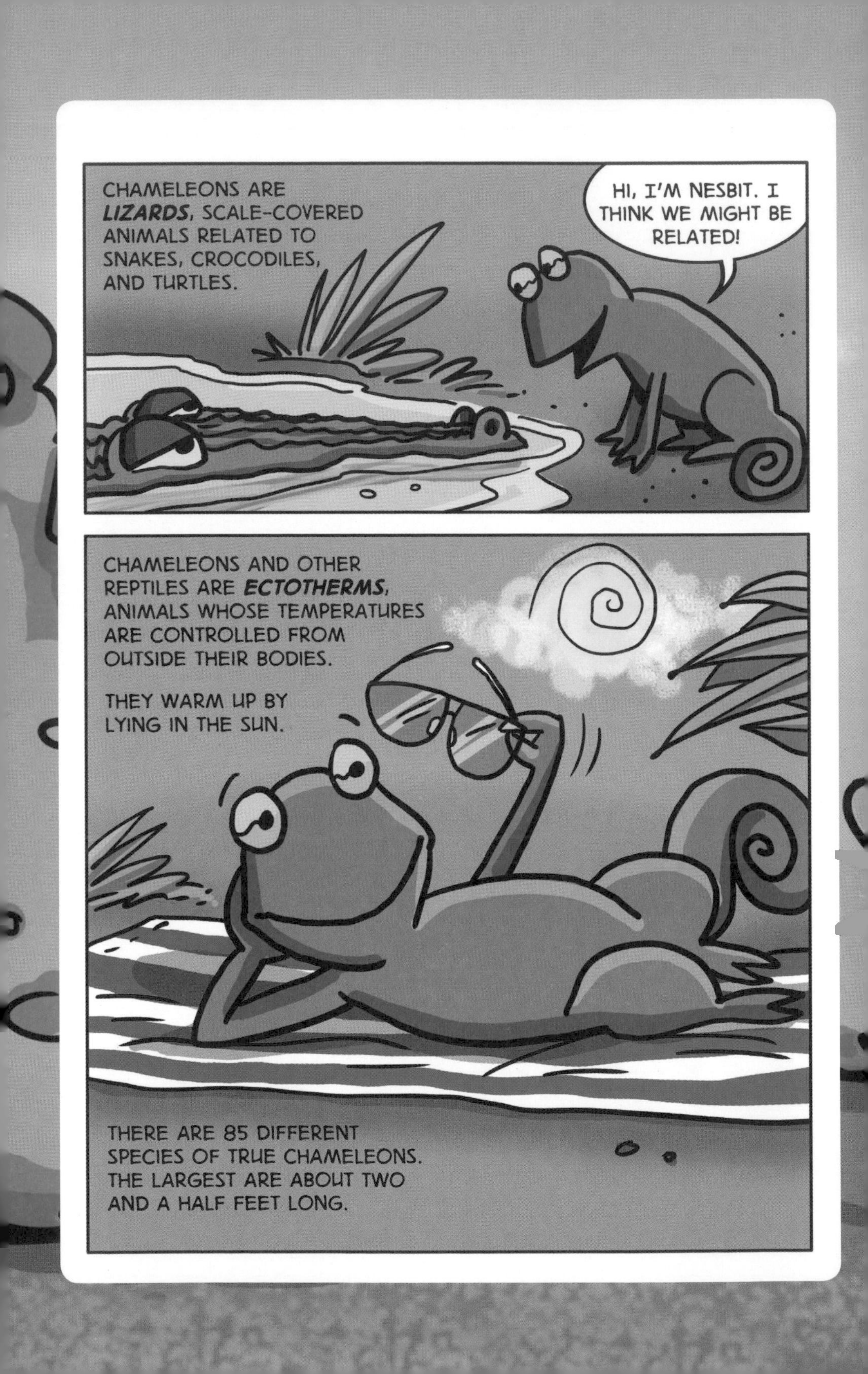
CHAMELEONS ARE ***LIZARDS***, SCALE-COVERED ANIMALS RELATED TO SNAKES, CROCODILES, AND TURTLES.
HI, I'M NESBIT. I THINK WE MIGHT BE RELATED!
CHAMELEONS AND OTHER REPTILES ARE ***ECTOTHERMS***, ANIMALS WHOSE TEMPERATURES ARE CONTROLLED FROM OUTSIDE THEIR BODIES.
THEY WARM UP BY LYING IN THE SUN.
THERE ARE 85 DIFFERENT SPECIES OF TRUE CHAMELEONS. THE LARGEST ARE ABOUT TWO AND A HALF FEET LONG.

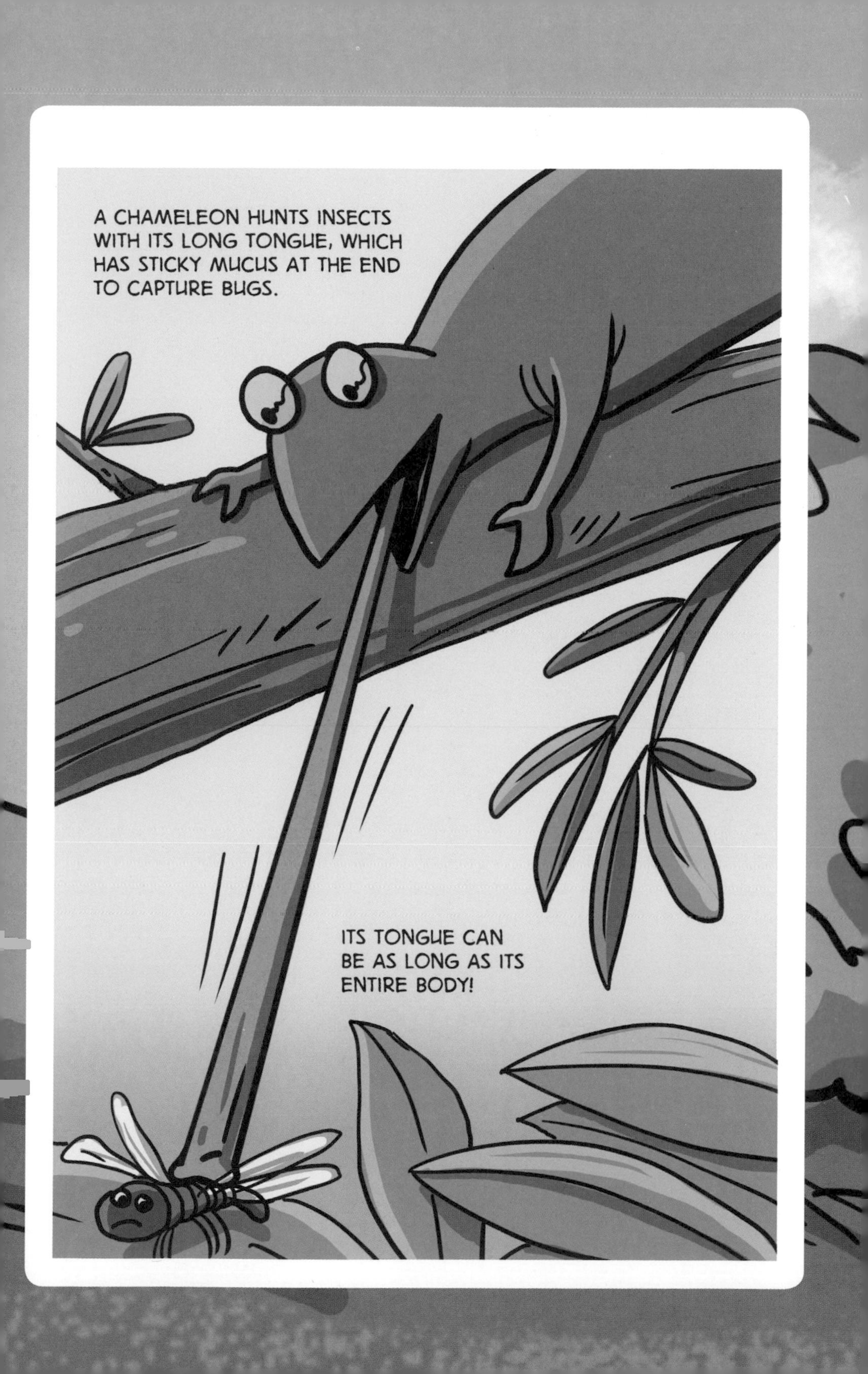
A CHAMELEON HUNTS INSECTS WITH ITS LONG TONGUE, WHICH HAS STICKY MUCUS AT THE END TO CAPTURE BUGS.
ITS TONGUE CAN BE AS LONG AS ITS ENTIRE BODY!

ABOUT THE GARTER SNAKE

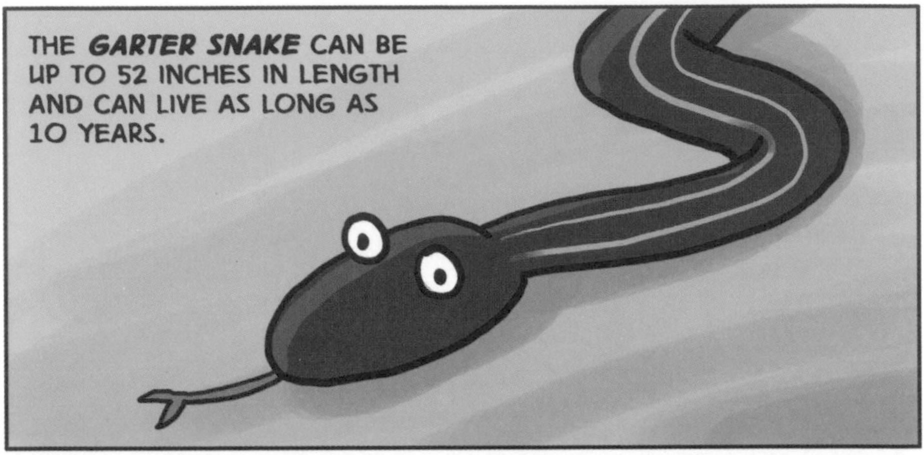
THE ***GARTER SNAKE*** CAN BE UP TO 52 INCHES IN LENGTH AND CAN LIVE AS LONG AS 10 YEARS.

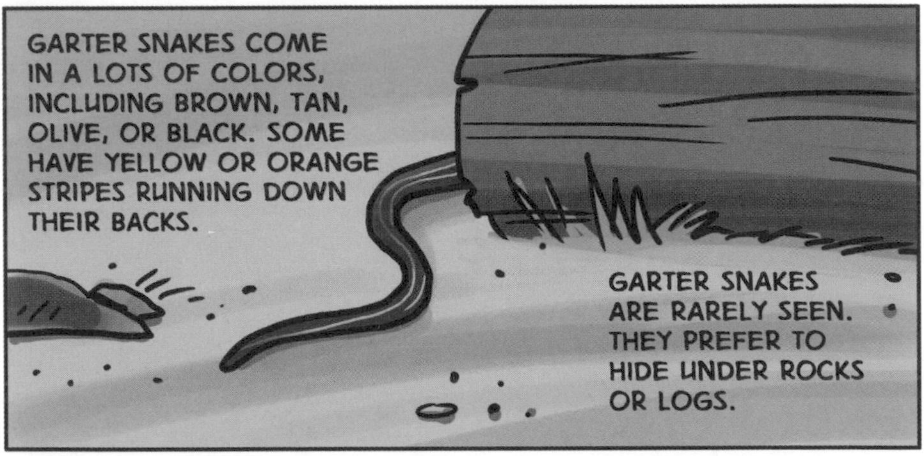
GARTER SNAKES COME IN A LOTS OF COLORS, INCLUDING BROWN, TAN, OLIVE, OR BLACK. SOME HAVE YELLOW OR ORANGE STRIPES RUNNING DOWN THEIR BACKS.
GARTER SNAKES ARE RARELY SEEN. THEY PREFER TO HIDE UNDER ROCKS OR LOGS.

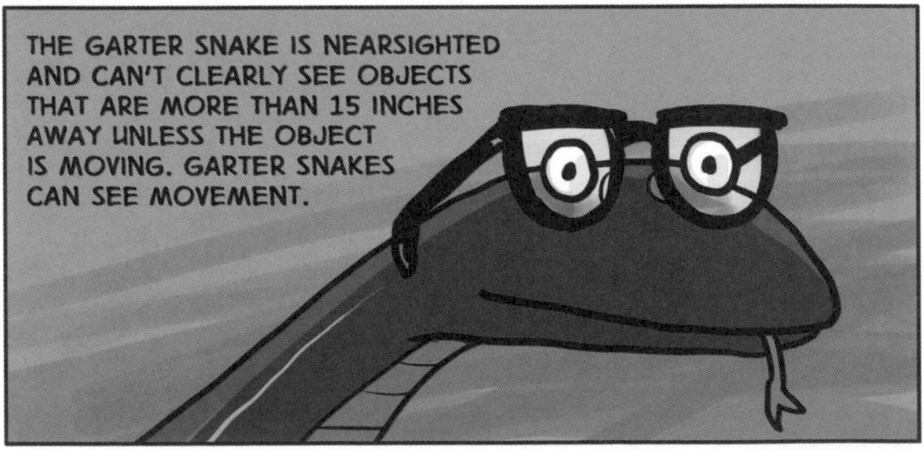
THE GARTER SNAKE IS NEARSIGHTED AND CAN'T CLEARLY SEE OBJECTS THAT ARE MORE THAN 15 INCHES AWAY UNLESS THE OBJECT IS MOVING. GARTER SNAKES CAN SEE MOVEMENT.

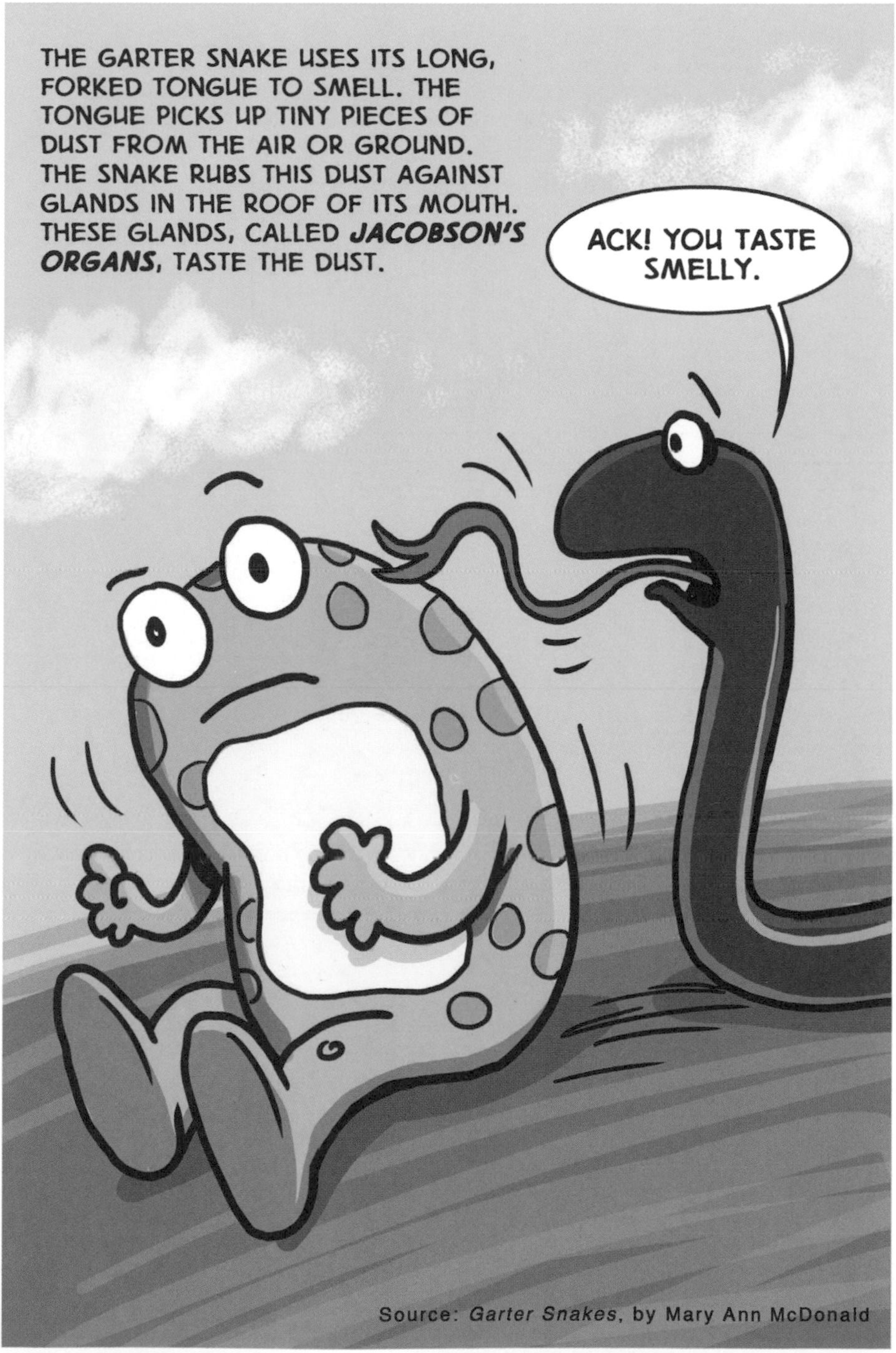
THE GARTER SNAKE USES ITS LONG, FORKED TONGUE TO SMELL. THE TONGUE PICKS UP TINY PIECES OF DUST FROM THE AIR OR GROUND. THE SNAKE RUBS THIS DUST AGAINST GLANDS IN THE ROOF OF ITS MOUTH. THESE GLANDS, CALLED ***JACOBSON'S ORGANS***, TASTE THE DUST.
ACK! YOU TASTE SMELLY.
Source: *Garter Snakes*, by Mary Ann McDonald

MAKE YOUR OWN TERRARIUM

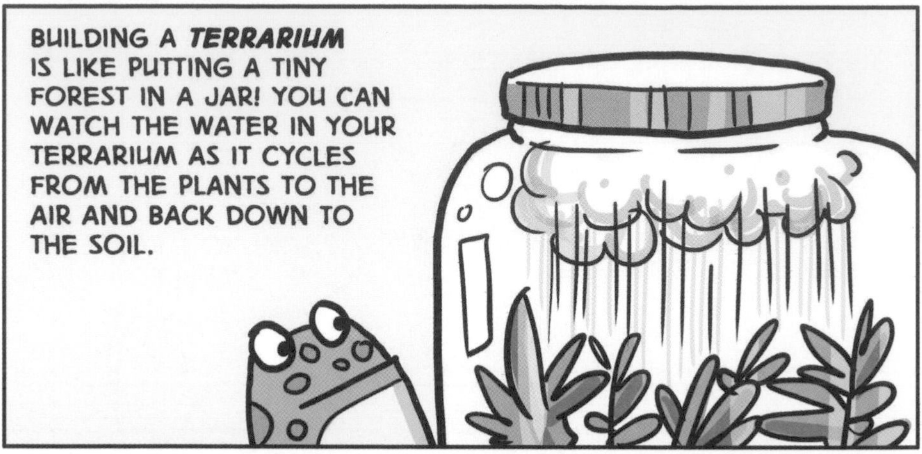
BUILDING A ***TERRARIUM*** IS LIKE PUTTING A TINY FOREST IN A JAR! YOU CAN WATCH THE WATER IN YOUR TERRARIUM AS IT CYCLES FROM THE PLANTS TO THE AIR AND BACK DOWN TO THE SOIL.

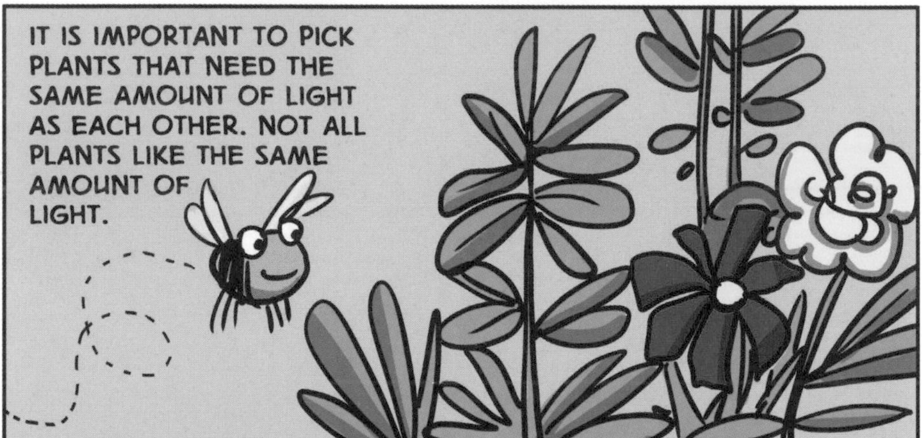
IT IS IMPORTANT TO PICK PLANTS THAT NEED THE SAME AMOUNT OF LIGHT AS EACH OTHER. NOT ALL PLANTS LIKE THE SAME AMOUNT OF LIGHT.

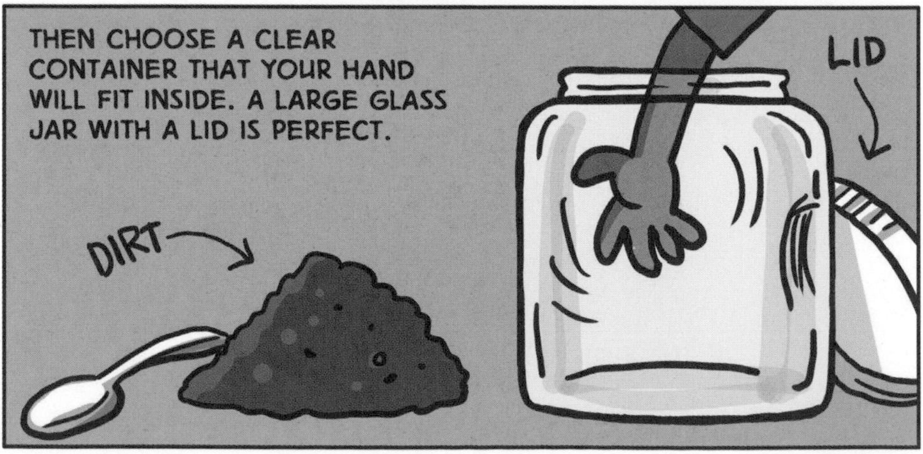
THEN CHOOSE A CLEAR CONTAINER THAT YOUR HAND WILL FIT INSIDE. A LARGE GLASS JAR WITH A LID IS PERFECT.
LID
DIRT

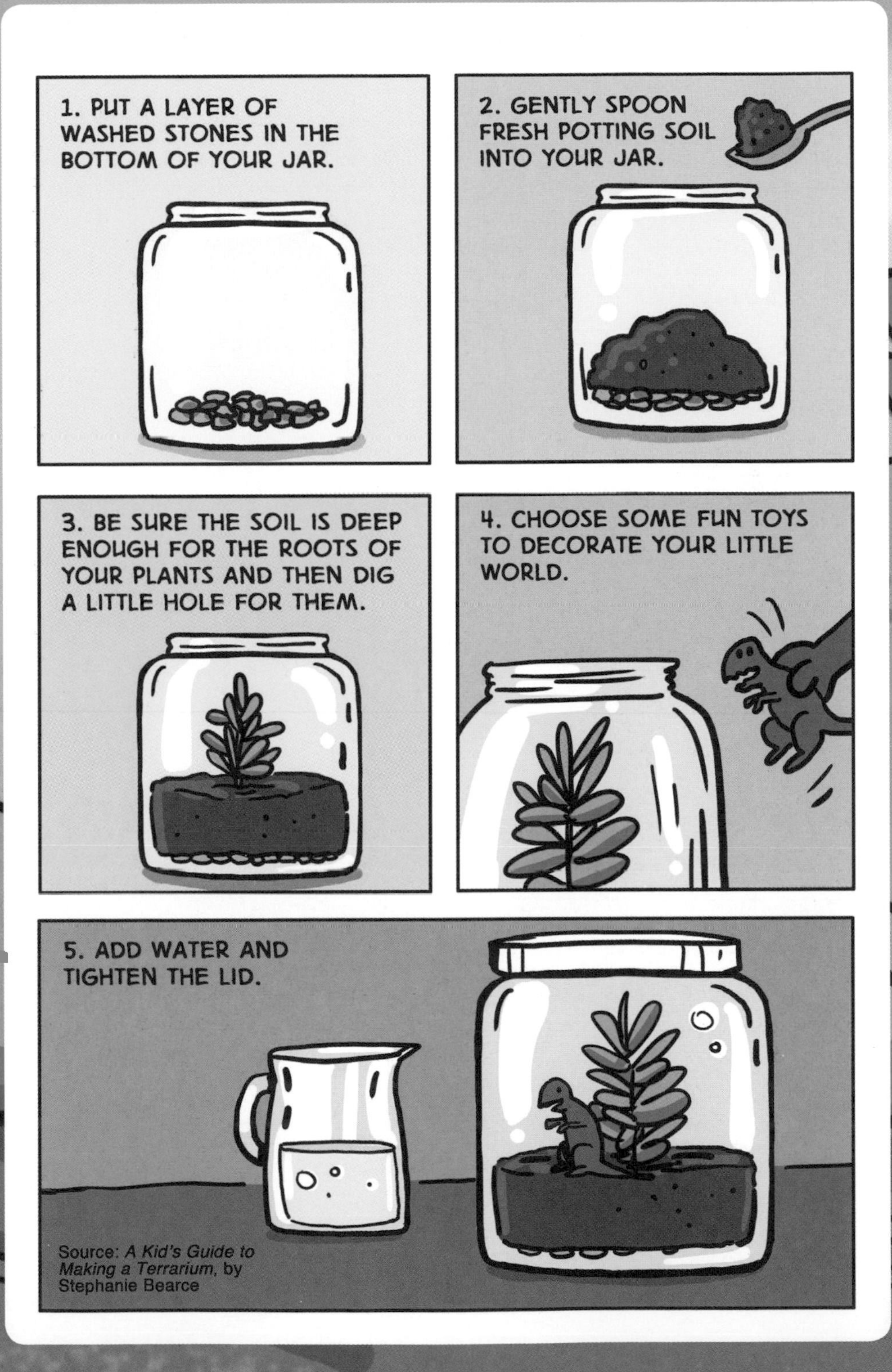
1. PUT A LAYER OF WASHED STONES IN THE BOTTOM OF YOUR JAR.
2. GENTLY SPOON FRESH POTTING SOIL INTO YOUR JAR.
3. BE SURE THE SOIL IS DEEP ENOUGH FOR THE ROOTS OF YOUR PLANTS AND THEN DIG A LITTLE HOLE FOR THEM.
4. CHOOSE SOME FUN TOYS TO DECORATE YOUR LITTLE WORLD.
5. ADD WATER AND TIGHTEN THE LID.
Source: A Kid's Guide to Making a Terrarium, by Stephanie Bearce

CHARACTER SKETCHES

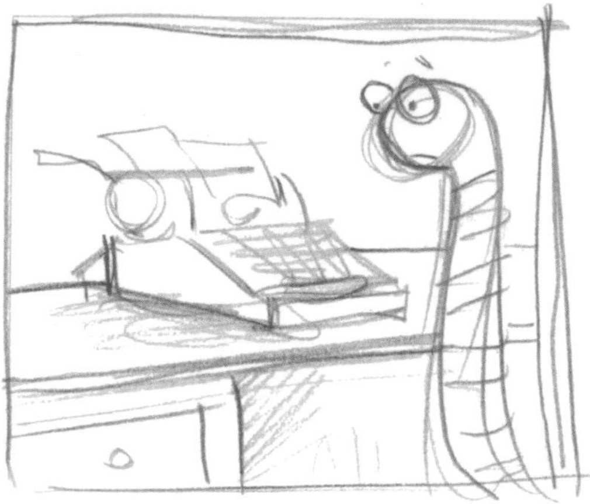

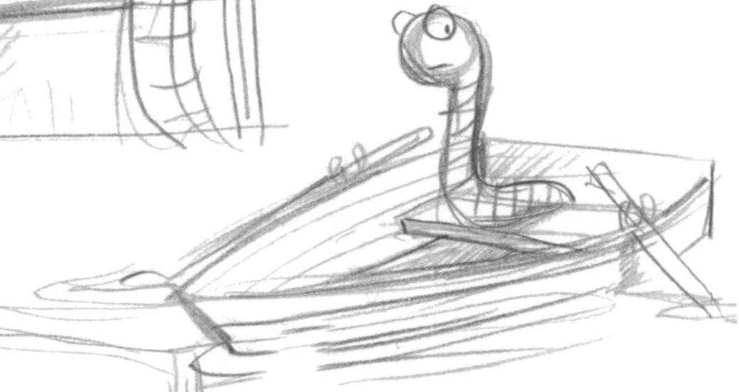

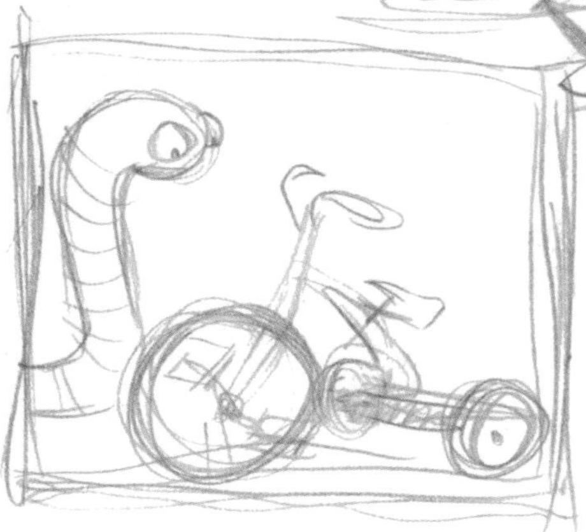

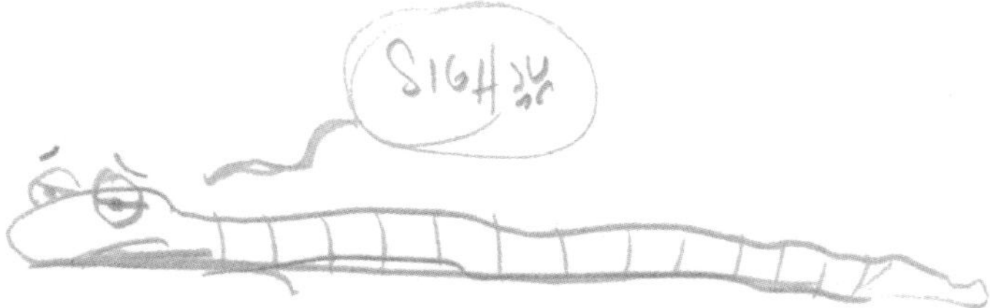
SIGH

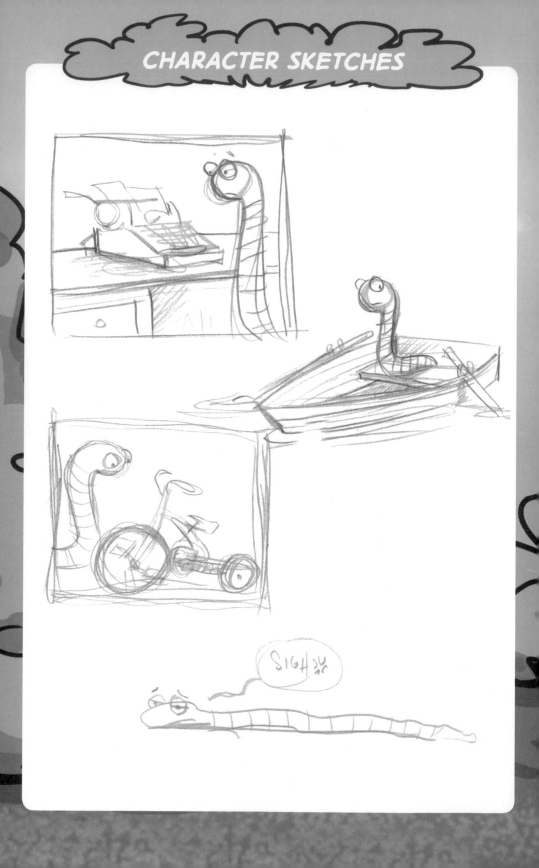

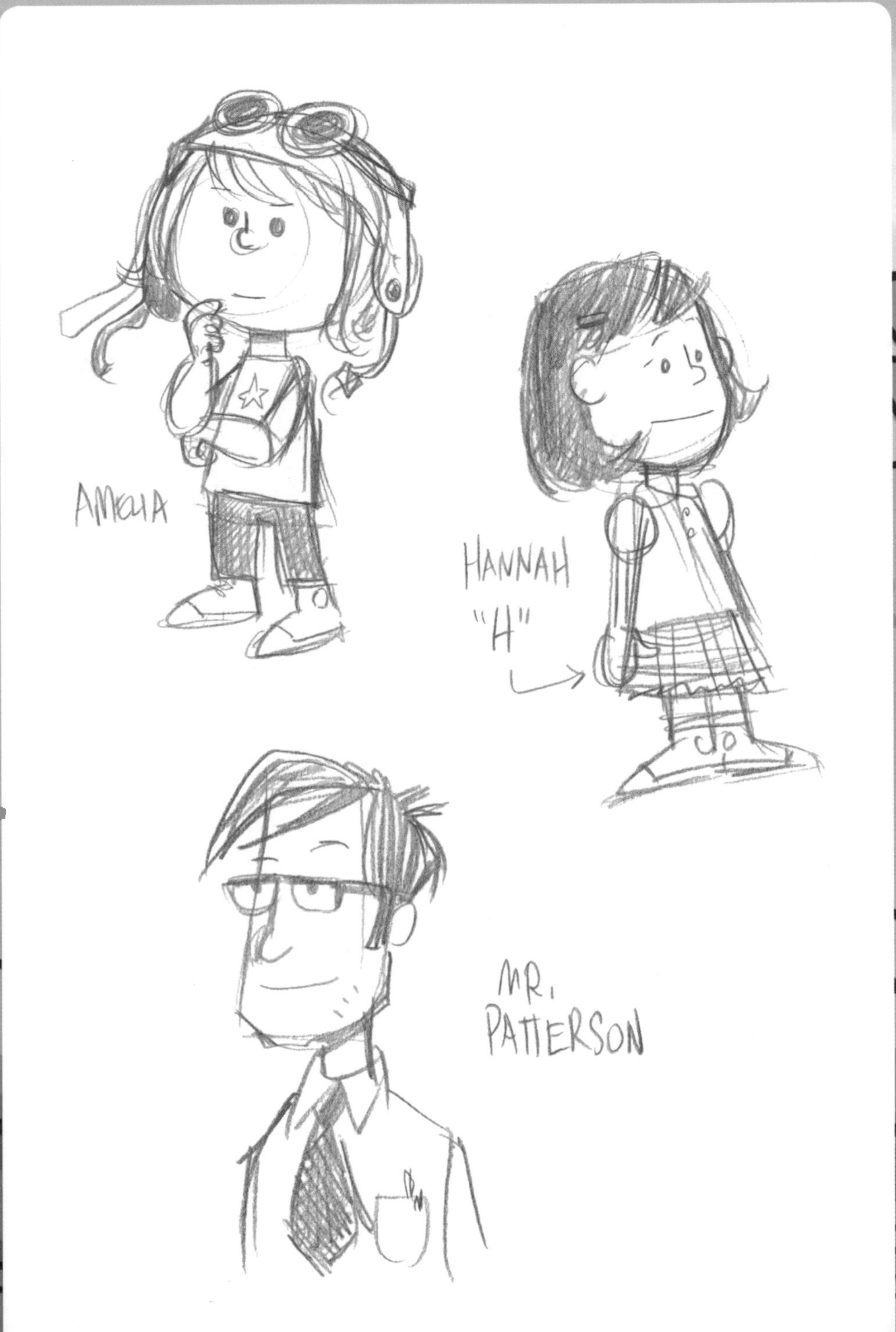
AMELIA
HANNAH
"H"
MR.
PATTERSON

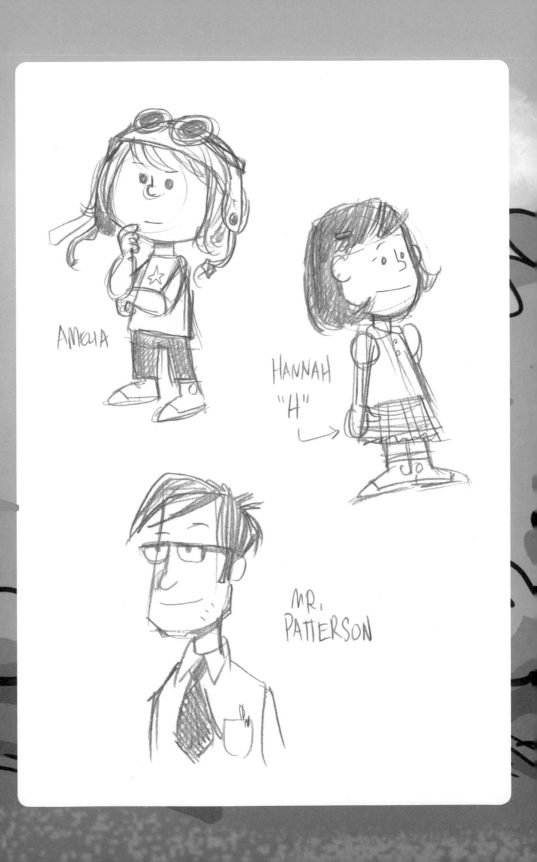

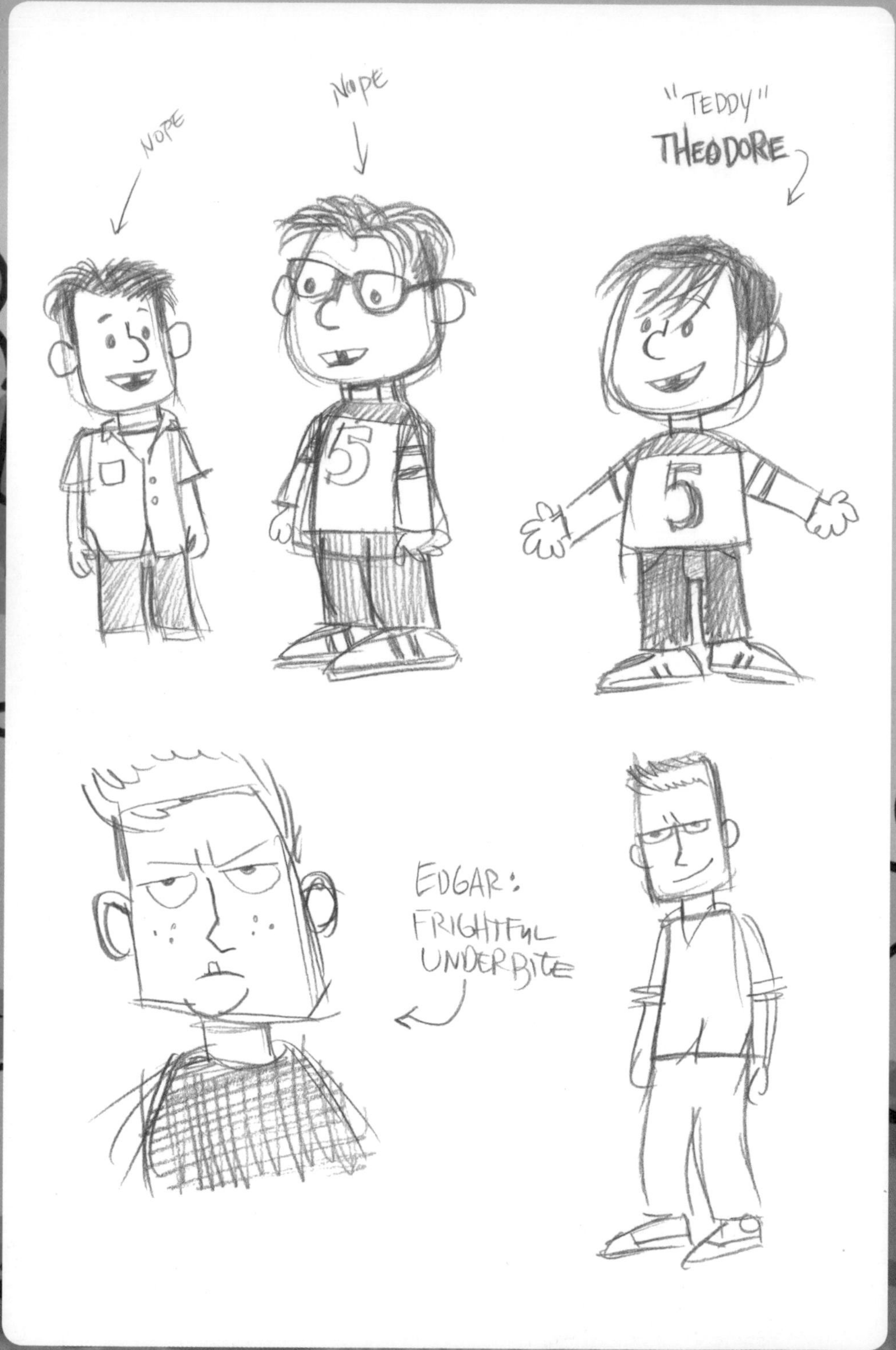
NOPE
NOPE
"TEDDY"
THEODORE
EDGAR:
FRIGHTFUL
UNDERBITE

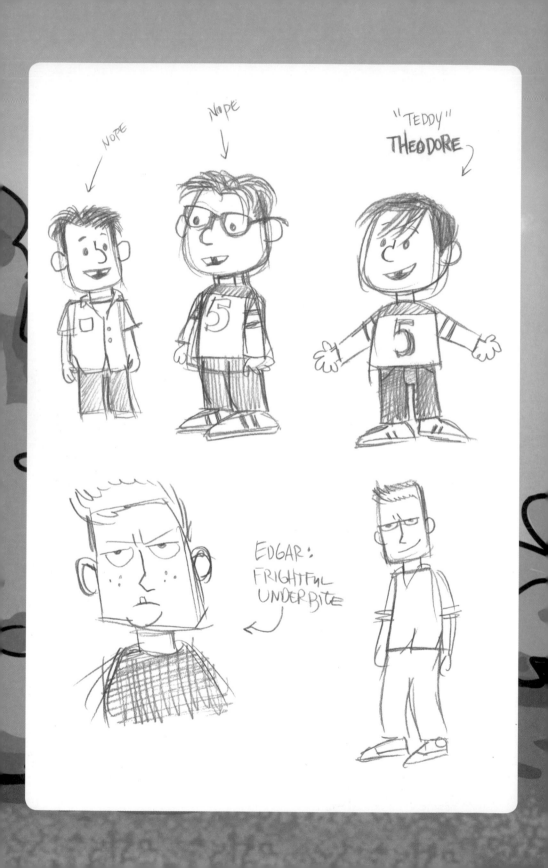

ACKNOWLEDGMENTS

To my editor, Andrea, thank you for taking a chance on Cecil and his pals. A big thank you to Jose Mari Flores for all his help on the coloring of this book. I'd also like to say thanks to my parents, Bud and Pat, for always supporting my dream to be a cartoonist. Thanks to my brother, Gueth, for being the best brother ever. And special thanks to Evelyn for coming up with the greatest title for a book series, Stinky Cecil.